The Reignbreaker

LELE BEUTEL

Published by Winnowing Words
Design by Publishing Hackers

Paperback: 979-8-9985227-1-0
Ebook: 979-8-9985227-3-4

Lele Beutel loves to meet and chat with fans! Reach out to her at apedersen6@comcast.net

Table of Contents

What would you do?

What would you do if the girl you hoped to marry one day was abducted? And this, after your parents had left for a land called Sur, beyond the treacherous Testus River, warning they might not return but not to come looking for them. You live in a sleepy hamlet called Gratville and have explored every inch of it, but never crossed the dilapidated, perilously unstable Testus River Bridge. And there are whispers about the land beyond the river being inhabited by the indescribable—evil giants and mysterious creatures. You, like the rest of Gratville's inhabitants, had been paralyzed by the dread of what lay beyond. But now you have no choice but to cross the bridge and face what you feared the most, because you must find her and perhaps uncover the reason your parents never returned.

"The Breaker will go up before them. They will break through, pass in through the gate and go out through it, and their King will pass on before them, the Lord at their head."

−Micah 2:13

To Charity and Phil—apples of His eye and mine—
and to all the children in search of a father...

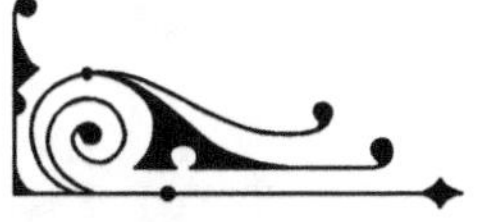

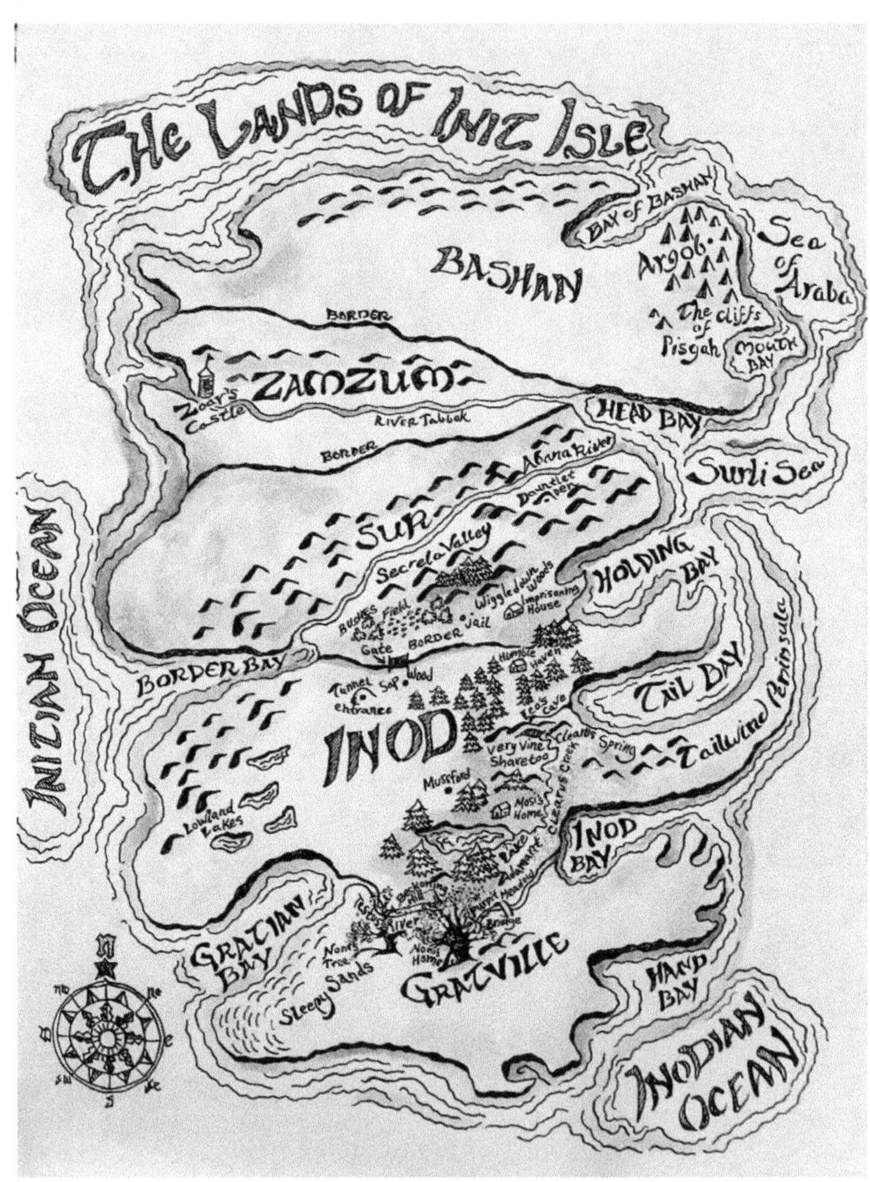

Drawing by Christina Machado.

chapter one
Dry Heaves and Screams

Noni gasped for air as he ran through the darkening woods. The twilight was cool, but sweat still poured down his brow. He stopped suddenly, startled by a death-boding sound that made him shake uncontrollably. The unearthly roar reverberated through the trees and triggered his legs to move of their own accord, this time even faster. But then his brain froze as he wondered, *Am I moving toward the roar or away from it?*

He heard it again and his heart raced. *What was making the sound?* He couldn't imagine, and he desperately wanted to head home. But he forced himself to plunge deeper into the woods. He could hear his friend Beehart's heavy breathing behind him. That pushed him on. They had to find Beehart's sister Ranni and Noni's brother Lelels. Especially since they'd found Ranni's blood-covered scarf and discarded basket thrown to the side of the road. They just knew something horrible had happened to the two of them.

Cobwebs clung to his face. He brushed them away as thorns snagged and ripped his fine leather tunic. He cursed but pressed on. Another sound caught his ear, and he stopped abruptly. A low groan. Bone-chilling but recognizable. Then a moan. He edged closer to the sound. There it was again…another groan. It was just beyond him. He peered ahead, trying to see between the shadowy tree branches that seemed to be waving him in one direction. Then he caught a glimpse of something sinister. He shuddered and started to shake. A body was propped up against a tree. *Was it alive or dead?*

Suddenly its head started to bob. *It was alive!* He trembled. *What was it? Was it one of the gruesome creatures he'd always heard about? The ones that lived in the lands beyond theirs. Was it what was making the unearthly sounds he kept hearing?* Cautiously, he drew closer. Then he heard more disturbing sounds coming from the creature. Not the fierce roars he'd heard, but more soulful and familiar. Whatever it was seemed completely undone.

He approached and looked down at the collapsed figure. Its face was covered with dirt and debris, but, suddenly, he recognized the brown-haired, bobbing head. Trying to control himself, his body shook, this time more fiercely. *It was his brother!* He dropped down beside him to grab and pull at one of his arms. Overwhelmed, he tried to shake his brother's large shoulders.

"Lelels, Lelels! What happened?" he spewed out the words in one breathless shriek.

"I don't know. I don't know!" His brother's head swung from side to side, unable to make eye contact, and Noni caught a glimpse of his swollen, dark-rimmed eyes.

Beehart scrambled through a thicket to join them and stopped abruptly at the sight of Lelels.

"What happened?" he gasped. *"Where's Ranni?'*

"A huge sort of monster took her before I could stop it. She was screaming and *I couldn't do anything!"* Lelels moaned and squeezed his eyes tightly shut, trying to block out the memory.

"What?" Beehart's face reddened and his ears turned a deep scarlet.

"Lelels, *tell us what you can!*" Noni pulled at the Lelels' arm again, but his much heftier brother pushed him away. Noni stood up and clenched his fists, not knowing what else to do.

"I only caught a glimpse," Lelels could barely rasp out the words as he pressed his eyes tighter and began to shake, "and I ran to help her." He took a stressed breath, trying to calm himself down. *"She was calling out to me!"* He looked up at Noni, his eyes watering and pleading as he squinted through puffy slits. "The monster-thing turned and stared at me as he threw her over his shoulder. And I froze. *I didn't know what to do!"* Lelels shuddered. "He was huge. And had stringy black hair. I could see it under his hood. His face was scarred and *horrible.* One eye was covered by a patch. The other was squinty and dark." His voice shook and he breathed heavily. "He pierced me with hate-rays!" He trembled. "And his hands and arms looked scaly *like snakeskin!*"

The creature Lelels described seemed unreal to Noni, and he wondered if his brother was exaggerating. Beehart had the same reaction.

"What are you *saying?*" Beehart's voice was overly shrill. "Are you telling us that a *monster* like a *snake* captured my sister?" He didn't want to believe what Lelels was describing.

"I don't know! *I don't know!*" Lelels rocked and banged his large head against the tree. *"All I know is what I saw!"*

Beehart suddenly bent over and started gagging. His dry heaves alarmed Noni and caused an unexpected reaction in him.

"Get up, Lelels! Get a hold of yourself, Beehart! Let's go! We have to find Ranni. Now!"

Beehart stood upright, wiped his mouth, and glared at Noni, his face bright red with anger, worry, and fear.

"It's all your fault, Noni! Why did you insist on us going to that bridge, leaving them alone! Why!!" He pushed Noni so hard that his friend toppled sideways, barely missing Lelels. Noni was so disturbed by Beehart's reaction that he had a hard time collecting himself. But he resisted

attacking back and tried to hold back his own feelings of overwhelming fear and regret.

As the sun descended, the three teens wandered through the darkening woods for hours. Trying to make their way through the creepy, shadowy brush over obscure paths in unfamiliar territory, they screamed Ranni's name over and over again. They inspected fading footprints and broken branches for any sign of her. As the sunlight dimmed, Noni climbed a tall tree and gazed out as far as he could see. But it was hopeless. Darkness soon shrouded the forest, with only the emerging new moon to light their way, and sinister sounds magnified their fearful feelings. Noni finally collapsed on the ground next to Lelels, who sat at the bottom of the same tree, rocking. Still in shock, he'd given up hours ago.

"Let's go home, bro'!" Noni reached over to touch his arm. This time, Lelels didn't push him away. "We can start early tomorrow. We'll find her. Don't worry, Lelels."

Beehart came up and plopped down wearily beside them.

"Why don't you stay with us tonight?" Noni half-smiled over at his friend, trying to forgive his friend's outbursts and thinking he may not want to be alone right now.

The three boys shuffled down the long road home. As they got closer to Noni and Lelels' underground tree home, they noticed something odd. The arched front door was wide open! Not as they'd left it. They approached cautiously. Once inside, they were alarmed to find all the furniture moved around. The kitchen table was turned over and the things Noni had placed on the counter were moved. A few things were even shoved to the floor and broken. He tried to act cool about what he saw, to keep the others calm, but he quickly bolted the door after they'd all entered. Beehart staggered over to the couch and fell on it, too overcome with fatigue and stress to notice much. Also oblivious, Lelels shuffled off to his bedroom, breathing heavily.

After right-siding the table and placing a few things back where they belonged, Noni boiled some water on the wood-fed stove and pinched some pungent spree needles into a teapot. He needed something to calm himself down. While the tea steeped, he sat at the kitchen table and breathed deeply, trying to regain his composure. But his heart sank lower as his thoughts drifted and guilt gnawed at him. As was his habit, he accepted accountability for most everything that happened, especially since his parents were gone and he was looked at by others as the most reasonably responsible one. But this came with a price.

What if Ranni is dead! he worried. *If she is, it's my own fault,* he sighed and laid his head down on the table, *for being so darned determined to reach a destination!*

chapter two

Ferocious Fantasies

That morning, Noni had rushed through his chores—getting the wood and water they needed that day. It was mid-summer—the best time to pick moggies. He was anxious to gather as many of the sweet blue berries as he could from the woods around them, maybe even going a bit farther away than usual. Since he'd spent so many hours that week chopping wood and exchanging some of it for food supplies in town, he had more time today to think about other things. So, after he lugged the water-buckets down the steps from the front door into his home beneath the tree, he called out to his brother.

"Hey, Lelels! I have a great idea!"

Loud snores greeted him, and he groaned to see his brother stretched out on their couch by the fireplace. Sweet smells drifted from a plate on the kitchen table, and he knew Groomhilda, who lived above them in the tree, had stopped by with treats. She watched out for the two boys and often brought them food, especially since their parents had mysteriously disappeared over a year ago. He walked over to the table and looked down at the empty plate with only a few crumbs left from some griffoons. He sighed to think how he'd missed tasting these scrumptiously-sweet biscuits baked lovingly by their neighbor. But this explained Lelels' early siesta. He muttered, knowing it would be hard to rouse his brother while his belly was full.

Noni set the buckets down and sat in a chair at the kitchen table. He made a cup of spree tea and, as he sipped it, he watched Lelels as his chest moved rhythmically up and down as he lay on his back. Feeling lulled himself, Noni began to daydream.

A distant northward hill, covered with colorful patches that glistened brightly in the sun, had beckoned to him early that morning from his favorite tree perch by his home that sat on a hill. He really wanted to walk at least that far today. He thought about his hometown—what he considered a sleepy hamlet of about a thousand people. His mind drifted to how Gratville was just one small town pretty far south in the land of Inod and how Inod was just one little piece of the greater Isle of Init, which was made up of other lands too—Sur, Zamzum, and Bashan. And, all of Init Isle was surrounded by the Initian Ocean on one side and the Inodian Ocean on the other. And who knew what lay beyond these? He didn't know anyone who'd ever ventured beyond the Isle, much less beyond Inod. And most people in town had never even left Gratville.

The more he thought about it, the more he wanted to explore these places! He'd never ventured across the bridge that spanned the Testus River—it was notoriously dangerous and unstable. It was the one thing that separated Gratville from the rest of Inod and the lands farther north. His parents had always forbidden it. But they were gone now. And a venturous lure pulled at him. From his perch that morning, the colorful hill beyond the river called to him, and he wondered how long it would take to get to the river and the beckoning hill. He wanted to find out…desperately.

He was really intrigued by Sur. His curiosity about the land was fueled by stories he'd heard about its inhabitants. People he knew in

Gratville were afraid to go there. He could understand why. They'd all heard the tales of the evil Surlies. They were supposedly larger than the Krochits who lived in Inod, but not quite as huge and warlike as the giants who lived farther north in Zamzum and Bashan.

Noni was close to a few of the Krochits who lived in Gratville, even though he was a Gomi. His neighbor, Groomhilda, was one. You could tell the difference between the two kinds of people. Krochits were taller with orangish skin, black straight hair, narrow dark eyes, and knobs on their temples. Gomies were shorter with pinkish skin and yellow, orange, or brown hair. Their eyes were more pronounced and colored blue, green, light brown, or a combination of blue and green. Noni, Lelels, Beeheart, and Ranni were all Gomies.

Noni's fascination with the Surlies, and the people of Zamzum and Bashan, made him less wary of them than others. He'd always considered Gratville a very dull place, and he shuddered with excitement just thinking about exploring a place where he might see a giant!

"Get out o' here, ya buggart!" Lelels yelled and flailed his arms as he fought an enemy in his dreams. His eyes suddenly popped wide open, and he stared at Noni as if he was a ghost. Noni ignored his odd behavior. He'd seen it all before at least a zillion times.

"Hey, Lelels!" he said, trying to sound upbeat, "how 'bout we go a bit farther today. I've heard there's better moggie pickin' down by the Testus River."

"No thanks," Lelels muttered and yawned as he sat up and stretched his arms.

Noni's face fell just as a loud *rat-a-tat-tat* sounded from the door. He darted up the few steps to peek through the peephole and jumped back when an eyeball peered back. He shook his head when high-pitched laughter came from the other side.

"Entrée!" He yanked the door open and swooped his arm to bow to Ranni and Beehart, like a knight showing deference to his queen and king.

Ranni sprang inside, her golden, pinned-up braids falling loose with each new bounce. A red-and-white-checked headscarf barely held them in check. She twirled to show off a new bright-red hooded cape. Under it, a white pinafore hemmed with purple flowers covered a red and white gingham dress that hung from her shoulders to the tops of her tall brown boots. A young teen, Ranni still displayed a childlike charm as she struggled to be more grown up.

"I made the cape myself!" She beamed, twirled again, and posed. She pulled the hood over her head and winked coyly at Noni from under it.

Noni blushed and escorted her to the couch. He frowned and gestured to Lelels to make room for her. Ranni's right cheek dimpled, and her blue-green eyes twinkled as she giggled and pushed Lelels over to plop down next to him.

"How 'bout some bruni'?" Noni offered politely. Not waiting for a response, he walked over to the stove to make the tasty, sweet, warm drink. He stirred together some bruni tree syrup and some sweet grat milk, then he heated these up on the stove. Bruni trees grew everywhere around Gratville, and Noni loved to collect and boil down the trees' sap into syrup and use it to make this drink or put it on top of flapcakes for breakfast. When he was small, his father had taught him how to tap the trees by drilling a small hole into the tree trunk and inserting a wooden spigot into the hole so the sap could run into a bucket beneath it.

The milk was easy to come by since gray-and- white-spotted, short-haired grats with wobbly ears and long legs roamed all over the hills nearby. Their town was named after the animals, whose big brown eyes made Noni feel peaceful and content. He hated it when people killed them to use their hide to make clothes, bags, and furnishings. He liked to help Lelels take care of Groomhilda's little herd of grats, and he sometimes milked them for her. She always shared the milk with them.

Noni handed mugs of the delicious drink to his guests.

"More please!" Ranni announced with a giggle, after guzzling it down.

As Noni poured the remainder into Ranni's mug, he glanced over to see Beehart sigh. His shoulders slumped as he gazed down at the bottom of his empty mug. Then he looked up at Noni sullenly. Noni was reminded how similar Beehart's and Ranni's eyes were—the same brilliant blue-green color that reminded him of a lake he once saw in a painting. But, unlike Ranni, Beehart's face was freckled and surrounded by wild clumps of curly orange hair. He also was moodier. Noni watched as Beehart reached for a thin chain that hung around his neck and fingered a key that was attached to it. He knew that, before Beehart's mother left with his parents, she'd given it to him along with a cryptic message that someday he'd need it. Now, it reminded him of her. Noni understood this.

Beehart stared back down into his mug as he held onto the key, like he was looking for something. Then his expression changed as his brows furrowed.

"Let's just get this moggie-picking business over with!" He glared at Noni. "Are we going *or not!*"

Noni quickly gathered all the empty mugs and set them on the kitchen table. He tried not to react to Beeheart's crankiness, because he understood what made him click. He knew, from all their years together growing up, that he preferred practicing thrusts with his carved dagger or making weapons to fight his imagined foes. But, mostly, he was just plain tired, since he worked nights as a bodyguard for Gratville's Mayor Dungtrap.

The round-bellied Krochit mayor was pompous, paranoid, and proud, and he insisted on having at least one Gomi bodyguard with him at all times. No one understood why, since Gratville was a sleepy little village. Although Gratians whispered strange tales about other lands and people, most of them had never seen anything strange or threatening…*ever!* Still, the townspeople obliged him and handpicked some young men, including Beehart.

Despite his small stature, Beehart had gained a reputation as a great marksman. He was handy with all sorts of weaponry and had perfected his ability while practicing with friends, mostly seeing who could hit a target using a slingshot or a bow and arrow. The contest was always futile and frustrating for others, since Beehart was so good with a sling or a bow. He could easily hit anything from a great distance and even send a stone shooting into a small hole in a tree from yards away. Sometimes he brought home animals he'd killed, to be skinned for dinner, despite Ranni's tearful objections.

Noni knew Beehart wasn't fond of the mayor but felt honored by his selection as a bodyguard. Even though the job required him to work the late shift several nights a week, he agreed to do it, because it paid so well. As the older brother, he needed to support himself and Ranni—a burden he assumed since their mother had disappeared, and their father had died some years before.

Impatient with the lulling silence in the room as Noni put a few things away, Beehart grimaced. His sensitive friend caught the keek.

"Let's go!" Noni said quickly, trying to sound cheerful. As Beehart and Lelels stood and stretched their achy muscles, Noni grabbed a stack of baskets that waited in a corner and handed them to each person as they passed through the door. While Ranni chatted and swung her basket outside, and the others impatiently waited, he glanced around the room. Though Noni was smaller and younger than his brother, he'd always been more conscientious and was the one put in charge of most things.

I don't think we're forgetting anything, he said to himself, wondering why he felt a little uneasy about going today. Then, he wondered whether he should lock the door. He hesitated, but decided there was no reason to. Nothing had ever threatened their life here in Gratville… before now. His emerald-green eyes darted around the room one last time before he exited.

Baskets in tow, everyone tried to keep up with Noni as he charged ahead down the road with Beehart right behind him. Lelels sauntered along at his own speed, and, trailing behind him, Ranni lingered to watch the brown furry smallets, who flicked their long bushy tails at her and ran up and down trees. She was also distracted by the black and red teesdalls that flew overhead and twittered from the branches. The smallets and teesdalls knew they were going to pick moggies and hoped they'd accidentally drop a few. Ranni laughed when a smallet came right up to her and sniffed at her bright cape with its moist muzzle. Its black beady eyes begged up at her from between two tiny, pointed ears.

"I'm sorry, little guy," she consoled. "We don't have any moggies yet. But I'll bring you some later!"

The smallet darted and scampered up a nearby tree.

"Ranni! If you promise *every* creature a moggie, you won't have any left for yourself *or for us!*" Lelels' belly growled.

"Don't worry. I *always* have enough!" Ranni flashed her contagious smile then began to hum a tune. The melody brightened even Beehart's moodiness, because it reminded him of their mother, who'd taught them many songs. The words poured out from her lips as she skipped along, swinging her basket.

Moggie picking is so much fun.
Filling our baskets one by one.
Twiddle dee and twiddle dum.
Twiddle dee and twiddle dum.

So much for work and tasks undone.
Our only plan is having fun.
Toodle dee and toodle dum.
Toodle dee and toodle dum.
Tra la lilly, hey found a good one!
The sweetest moggie under the sun!
Trickle dee and trickle dum.
Trickle dee and trickle dum.

Lelels hummed along at first but was distracted when he heard something rustling in the bushes by the side of the road. *It's gotta be a smallet,* he said to himself so he wouldn't feel so jumpy.

"Why don't we stop here and pick," he said, paying more attention to his grumbling stomach. It'd been a few hours since he downed Groomhilda's griffoons, and he was ready for another snack. Beehart stopped to wait for Lelels and Ranni to catch up with him. Noni, much farther ahead, sighed and trudged back toward the others, desperately wanting to reach the heralding hill.

"There's a much better spot ahead with *way* more moggies!" he yelled out, trying to entice them.

"This place looks good enough to me!" Lelels grumbled.

"Just a little farther! *Come on, guys!*" Noni insisted. "I'd like to see if we can get across the Testus River Bridge and look for moggies on the other side. I hear they are much larger over there. And there are more of them!"

"Noni, what the heck are you looking for? The *perfect* moggie?" Lelels grew grumpier.

"That idea scares me!" Ranni's cheerfulness faded suddenly, and her face showed concern. "If you two want to cross that bridge, go for it! There's no way I'm doing that! Lelels and I can pick moggies here. You two can go ahead!"

Beehart's curly redhead nodded numbly. He was always up for a challenge, and he feared very little. He really didn't care what they did, but he didn't want to be outdone by Noni. He really just wanted to get this moggie-picking over with. He could think of more exciting things to do, like finding ways to make an even more impressive weapon to fight the most challenging imagined foe. For now, he muttered as he stumbled tiredly after Noni down the road. Focused on his goal, Noni ignored him and pushed on, as the distance between them and their siblings grew wider and wider. And Ranni's laughter faded.

Noni watched the sun as it lowered gradually toward the horizon. It was now at about two o'clock. They still had time. He thought about his friendship with Beehart as he pressed ahead with his friend trailing behind him. It had changed over the last year. And this made him sad. Before, they'd play boyish games without a care in the world. Beehart had an unusual talent for mimicking the cries of wild animals. He'd hide behind a bush and wait for people to walk by, while Noni watched from a distance. As soon as travelers were within earshot, he'd growl like something fierce with the sounds growing more and more ferocious and loud. Invariably, passers-by would grow wide-eyed, drop whatever they held, and run as fast as they could toward the nearest road to town. Beehart would come out of hiding and laugh hysterically. Noni would shake his head. He didn't get what was so funny about scaring people half to death. But he still participated and, now, he missed the silly pranks and Beehart's jovial side.

After their parents disappeared, the stunts stopped. For a long time, Noni didn't feel like participating in these games anyway, because he was too worried about his mom and dad and obsessed with what might have happened to them. Beehart reacted differently. He became fixated on warlike games and grew more dangerous in the way he handled his weaponry. This bothered and alarmed Noni, and he worried about the change in his friend. It felt to him as if their childhood ties were coming unraveled. So, he tried to involve his friend in healthier activities, like moggie picking.

Now, Noni wanted to reach that hailing hill, but he knew Beehart's energy was lagging, and he had to be patient, even though he didn't feel like it. His destination was still a long way off, but he didn't want to give up yet. As he pressed on, his mind wandered, and his imagination took flight. He was a great, winged bird, flying far beyond Gratville, looking down on the Surli hills he'd seen from a distance. The sun was brighter and the clouds fluffier, the higher he flew. The flowers below him were so brilliant that they glowed fantastically, beyond imagination!

From his tree perch that morning he'd counted many different colors covering the distant hill with purple being the most prominent. They looked like they could be flower-patches sparkling in the sun and moving in waves, like bright bodies of water, as breezes blew across them. He'd never seen anything like this in Gratville.

His thoughts were interrupted by a loud grumbling.

"Grizzly grats!" Beehart's ears were bright red. *"How much farther do we have to go?"*

"Just a little farther," Noni said sheepishly. He could hear the roar of the Testus River not too far ahead. But, when he came closer, he stopped abruptly. He looked down a cliff at the wide, rushing river. Tree roots overgrew its sides, and a dangling wooden bridge swayed across it. Beside the bridge, a sign on a stake warned, *Cross at your own risk!*

He looked to the other side. The setting sunlight streamed through the trees and created lengthening dark shadows that stretched to the riverbank. The effect creeped him out, especially because it looked like the long fingers were reaching toward him.

"It's getting late," Noni finally admitted as his fears of the unknown overcame his adventurous curiosity. "We'd better head back."

He turned around and was stunned by the look on his friend's face.

"What is it, Beehart?"

His friend stared intently at some bushes beside him, and Noni's heart stopped when he saw beady eyes glowing back at him. Like shiny yellow stones with upright slits of black in the center, they pierced from behind the leaves.

"Let's go!" Noni's voice trembled.

"Yes-s-s," Beehart whispered back hoarsely, terror in his eyes.

They ran together down the road, retracing their steps. Then they heard loud rustling nearby, and their legs could not move fast enough. The dagger slammed against Beehart's leg as he raced after Noni. Then they heard the roars and moans and found Lelels collapsed under the tree.

chapter three

Dragons and Dreams

Back home, with nothing to show for their search and feeling totally despondent, Noni sat in the kitchen holding his warm cup of tea. He tried to distract himself from worries in the wee hours before dawn by moving one hand over the table his dad had made. *I miss him so much!* he thought, as he looked down at the little cracks and scars in the wood made by years of wear. They brought back so many memories of sitting here in the evenings with his dad and watching him sip his tea as he talked. He'd share about the people he saw when he went to town that day with a cartload of things he'd carved to sell or trade for things they needed. He was an expert woodworker and enjoyed carving most anything: furniture, artifacts, decorations, or tools.

As Noni shifted listlessly in his chair, he also thought of his mom, who'd designed the cushion he sat on. She would join him and his dad to listen and talk, sometimes late into the night. Lelels usually went to bed early, too tired to stay up after herding grats all day.

He remembered the day his parents left with Ranni and Beehart's mother. They said they were going to visit friends near Mussford and

Sapwood, two towns in northern Inod on the other side of the Testus River. Their parents had said they'd return in the next two weeks.

"But if we don't return," Noni's father had warned. "Don't come searching for us!"

These mysterious, cautionary words had scared Noni. And he wondered what they were really up to and why. But he knew they wouldn't tell him everything, so he resisted asking too many questions. When they didn't return, he remembered the warning and again wondered where they really went and what had happened to them.

Noni's parents trusted him and his brother to be able to handle things on their own. He knew that, but he still missed them terribly. Beehart's mom assumed the same about Beehart and Ranni. They knew they were responsible teens. They'd proven they could manage just fine, especially under Groomhilda's motherly supervision.

When the time for their return came and went, the people of Gratville sent out a search party, but to no avail. Since Surlies forbade Inodians from entering their land, they wondered if they were captured after illegally entering Sur. But there was no way to find out. The unexpected disappearance of their parents, and the possibility of them ending up somewhere in Sur, caused Noni to have an even more fearful regard for the mysterious land.

To never forget what they looked like, Noni drew their faces on paper he'd made from unrolled treebark. His pictures hung as reminders above the fireplace. He'd drawn his mother, Lona, with caramel-colored hair like his own in braids that wound around her head like a crown, decorated with shells and dried flowers. He colored her eyes soft brown, also like his own, and gave her a cheerful smile. He made her nose small and turned up at the end. Her pixyish face reminded him of Ranni.

When he drew his dad, Stade, he made him look gruffer, with bushy brown hair like Lelels'. He wore a wide-brimmed felt hat, and a thick beard covered his chin. He wasn't smiling, but his green eyes twinkled.

Noni sighed, wondering what'd happened to his parents and, now, Ranni. He considered the danger of going on a quest to find them, especially if he had to go into Sur or the other mysterious lands. *How can I do that?* he wondered, thinking there might be no alternative. He had to find them, especially vulnerable Ranni. And no one else would do whatever it took or go wherever was needed to get her back. Especially if it involved going farther north beyond the river. Too many had ventured there and never returned. *How long would it take?* he worried. *How long would I be gone, and who could help me along the way?* He felt quite alone at that moment and totally unable to handle all the possibilities. *If Mom and Dad were here, they'd know what to do.* His face sank.

As a trace of moonlight crept through the door's cracks, a soft knock interrupted his anxious thoughts. He got up and tiptoed stiffly across the room, so as not to wake Beehart, who slept soundly on the couch. He peeked through the peephole and was surprised to see Groomhilda. He quickly unlocked and opened the door.

Like most Krochits, she and her husband had built their home among the limbs of the huge housit tree where Noni and his brother lived. She lumbered up and down the winding stairway that circled the tree's massive trunk. Noni appreciated that she liked to check on him and Lelels, but he also understood that having this responsibility made her feel useful. Her husband had died long ago, her children had moved away, and she was sometimes lonely.

Noni motioned for her to come in. She bent down and squeezed through the small arched door, wobbled down the steps to the kitchen, and pushed her way into one of the wooden chairs at the table. After getting situated, she smoothed her mussed hair and rearranged the wrinkles in her long gray frock.

Noni imagined her sitting in her own padded den chair, surrounded by gold-framed family paintings. Though Groomhilda was not fancy herself, she kept many of her husband's things, to remember him. She enjoyed helping others, and Noni liked this about her. She often invited the brothers to join her in a meal, and it was then that they saw her larger, more elaborate rooms and were reminded of the differences between Gomies and Krochits.

Krochits enjoyed games like "See the Snees" and "Goley Holey." Groomhilda sat for hours with friends, counting snees, or clouds, and seeing how many goleys, or pegs, they could place in the holes of her wood-paneled walls. Most Gomies couldn't play these games since they lived below the trees and had no windows or paneled walls. Plus, they were far too busy working and doing chores. Gomies usually worked for Krochits and paid them rent to live under their trees. Noni used to complain that they had to live underground and do so much of the work, but he realized how bored he'd be if he had to sit around and play games. He loved doing things outdoors. Though he was grateful to be a Gomi, right now he wished he could stand with her on her porch with its breathtaking views. Even in the minimal new-moonlight, it might make him forget his worries.

Groomhilda's thick brows furrowed as she sat with him in his modest kitchen, and he wondered if she was offended by the surroundings, but then he thought, *No. How could she be?* He glanced around at the dirt walls, beautifully decorated with his mother's drawings of flowered hills, crystal lakes, seas of brightly-colored fish, and creature-filled forests. *Nice*, he thought. And as he looked around at the furniture his father had made, he was convinced that his little lair felt really homey. He glanced again at his guest and wondered why she'd come to visit at such a strange time.

"Would you like some tea?" he offered.

"Yes, please," Groomhilda smiled and nodded.

Noni picked out the best unchipped mug from their shelf and poured the last bit of spree tea from the teapot into it, then he handed it to her.

"I heard some commotion down here yesterday." She lifted the cup to her lips. "At first, I thought you were rearranging things, but then I remembered you were moggie picking. And I grew concerned. Whoever was here left by the time I climbed down the stairs, but the door was open. I peeked in and saw things scattered around, not neat or orderly like you usually keep things. I picked up a little, but I just don't have the energy that I used to." She glanced at Noni, who was looking down at his cup. "I heard you come back last night, and I heard your brother moaning. What happened? I just couldn't sleep. I needed to see if you were all right."

"Someone kidnapped Ranni," Noni answered hoarsely, trying not to get emotional. "When we went to pick moggies, Beehart and I left the other two alone. When we came back for them, Lelels told us a very creepy snake-like man had taken her. He said the person was like no one he'd ever seen. He was covered with dirty skins and had stringy black hair and a cruel-looking face partly hidden by a hood. He also had an eye patch." Noni drew a breath. "Lelels heard Ranni yelling. He ran to help her and saw this guy running away with her over his shoulder. She was screaming hysterically, but Lelels just stood there in shock. They disappeared into the woods. He's really upset and blames himself, of course." Noni's voice trailed off and he let out a weary sigh. "But it's really my fault, Groomhilda. I'm the one who suggested picking moggies. I'm the one who wanted to go farther. I left Ranni and Lelels alone, so I could go on. I never should have…." His voice trailed off. Groomhilda looked at Noni with compassion.

"I can only imagine how you must feel, but it's not your fault, Noni." She reached over to touch his arm. "There was no way you could've known this would happen," she spoke softly. "What will you do now?"

"We'll leave in the morning. We have to find her, and we may have to go pretty far." Noni let out a huge sigh.

"Maybe you and Beehart can go. Lelels can stay here in case she comes back or someone finds her. He could help me with the grats and watch your place. What do you think, Noni?"

"That's a good idea, Groomhilda. Could you keep an eye out for anything unusual?" Noni felt like he might melt as he looked over at her face that exuded the kind of peacefulness and understanding that he needed right now.

"Absolutely, and before you leave, I'll bring you some fresh griffoons and scaggons to take on the journey. Let me know if there's anything else I can do."

He watched the large woman rise and try to dislodge herself from the small chair. He walked behind her to the door and watched as she trudged back up the winding steps in the darkness. He appreciated her motherly care and the offer of griffoons and scaggons, a red juicy fruit that grew on the trees around Inod. He made his way down the hall to one of the three small bedrooms, just large enough for a bed, table, and chest of drawers, all made by his dad. He could hear Lelels snoring as he walked past his room. He crawled into his own bed, laid his head on a soft pillow, and covered himself with a wool blanket. He pulled it over his chin and thought about his mother. She'd lovingly woven it for him out of fur from the kinky-haired sapies that roamed the hills near Sapwood.

The blanket was soothing, but his sleep was not. A huge, warty black dragon clawed through his dreams with treacherous nails. It shook the sharp spikes along the ridge of its long neck and snorted through a foul mouth filled with jagged yellow teeth. It blew fire and steam from its nostrils and tried to create a blaze in the branches of a tree as it viciously scraped at its roots. The dragon's red eyes pierced fiercely upward, unwavering.

At the top of the tree, a little Gomi shivered and shook with fear as he clung to a quivering limb.

It was Noni.

chapter four

What Noni Didn't Know

The dragon's ferocious scraping and snorting grew louder until it sounded more like pounding and yelling.

"Noni, wake up! We need to go!"

Noni threw off his covers.

"All right! *All right!*" He flung open the bedroom door. Beehart stood there, red-faced, dressed, and ready to go. He wore his leather tunic, and his dagger was strapped at his side. Behind him on the floor was a bulging canvas bag. Noni was surprised to hear his usually moody friend so loud and energized.

"What time is it?" Noni croaked, rubbing his eyes.

"Early. But the sun's up, and *we need to go!* I saw Groomhilda outside, and she told me what she'd said to you last night. I agree with her. You and I can go, and Lelels can stay and watch out for Ranni in case she comes back. Geez, *you look terrible!*"

Noni's disheveled hair and dirt-streaked face made him look like he'd clawed his way through mud in a windstorm. Still wearing yesterday's clothes, he was rumpled and smelled musty.

"Just give me a minute. Get some tea and something to eat…whatever you want from the cupboard. Is Lelels up yet?"

"I saw him outside. He looks really bad." Beehart turned and headed toward the kitchen.

After throwing clothes and blankets into a bag, Noni dragged it down the hall to the kitchen, where he threw in a canteen, a mug, a plate, and some utensils. Tying the handles together, he dropped the bag next to Beehart, who sat munching on some stale griffoons he'd found in the cupboard. Not at all hungry, Noni wandered outside to find Lelels slumped under a tree. He put a hand on his brother's shoulder then wandered over to his lookout tree overlooking the hill at the edge of the woods. He climbed to a high sturdy branch and watched the sun rise over the faraway forests and hills. Even in his sleepy stupor, he grew fascinated by how the brightening, ascending orb spread its bloody fingers over the treetops until they were tinged with an ominous, reddish hue.

He glanced back to see Beehart, with neck veins bulging, stepping out of his home.

"We need to go, Noni!" His loud voice pierced through the morning stillness.

Just then, Groomhilda descended her stairway carrying two large bags full of fresh griffoons and scaggons. And a sweet smell wafted toward him.

"Oh dear." She sighed to see Lelels groaning under one tree, Noni at the top of another, and Beehart glowering at the door. She laid the bags down near Lelels, and Beehart stomped over to see what she had brought them as Noni silently climbed down from his tree. Looking at their stuffed bags by the door, he knew there wasn't space for her treats too, so he started pulling things out to make room. Also worried as to how they were going to carry these heavy bags on a long trip, he thrust some of his clothes and utensils aside.

Groomhilda, who'd placed a stool beside Lelels, interrupted Noni's intense exertions and motioned for him to come over. The boys sat at her feet and, feeling at the same time upset, angry, frightened, and ready to scream, they sheepishly gazed up at her face.

"Noni and Beehart, when you go, take Saron and Smithi." Her voice exuded serenity as she offered them her two favorite grats. "They can carry your bags."

"Thank you, Groomhilda. Thank you *so* much!" Noni muttered, feeling his emotions subside a little. He knew how much she valued her grats, and he silently vowed to bring them back safely to her.

"Yes. Thank you." Beehart's red face lessened in intensity.

"Please call me Grooma." Her lips stretched into a warm smile as she thought about how she'd always wanted to tell the boys to call her by her nickname. Then her face changed, and she pursed her lips. Noni was relieved when she finally spoke, but he wondered why she lowered her voice.

"There's something I must tell you, something you need to know. It may help you find Ranni."

They leaned in to hear her hushed words.

"Years ago, my mother told me a story. I've thought a lot about it over the years." She hesitated then continued. "When she was a child, a strange man showed up in Gratville. No one knew where he came from. He called himself Ameno. He was handsome with dark hair. His eyes sparkled like precious gems, Mother said. They were a beautiful blue-green like Ranni's. His skin was like bronze. And, when he smiled, his teeth looked like pearls. He wore a gray cape, and, wherever he went, people noticed him." Grooma's face and eyes shone as she described the unusual man. "When he spoke, you felt like you were being bathed in a clear mountain stream, refreshed and clean. His words were like poetry. He made you feel special, because, when he spoke to you, you felt as if you were the only one he saw or cared about.

"My grandmother, Mimi, was dying when he came to Gratville," she continued. "Mimi's heart was not beating right. Everyone thought she would die. My mother was a little girl, and she liked to watch Ameno. He fascinated her. One day, she saw him touch a baby grat who was stillborn, and the little guy got up and walked over to nurse from his mother. My mother couldn't believe it. She went over, took Ameno by the hand, and led him to Mimi's bedside. She asked him if he could heal her. Ameno kneeled down and touched Mimi's head, then her heart. Immediately her heart began to beat normally. He held her hand. She opened her eyes and smiled. She was healed.

"Mimi begged him to stay with them, but he had to leave. He said he'd return one day. Not long after that, a group of Surlies came to town. They walked into Mimi's house, looking for Ameno. They'd heard about how she was healed. But, by then, he was gone. No one knew where he went. Later, some Gratians said the Surlies had captured and killed him. No one knew if this was really true. Mother thought it was just a rumor.

"She described the Surlies as large men with long black hair, snake-like skin, and hideous faces. They were dressed in dirty skins, the way you described the one who took Ranni. That's the reason I needed to tell you this. I think a Surli has taken Ranni. Also, there are rumors that Ranni and Beeheart's mother, Ada, was visited by Ameno. I don't know. I'm just telling you these things because I think you should know."

"We may need to go to Sur to find Ranni." Noni's throat tightened. "I've never been there before. But we'll figure it out. We'll just have to take it one step at a time!" He looked down at his twitching fingers. "Thanks for telling us this, Grooma. There may be some connections."

"I had to, Noni. I don't know what it all means, but maybe knowing this will help you." Grooma's eyes drifted to Noni's nervous hands. "Now, how can I help you get ready?"

She watched as the boys strapped their bags onto the grats. Noni turned to say goodbye to Lelels, who stared at the ground.

"I feel guilty about staying behind," Lelels looked up slowly until his eyes met Noni's. "Especially since it was all my fault."

"*Your* fault?" Noni's eyes grew wide and his voice went up an octave. "What do you mean? If it was anyone's fault, it was mine! I pushed everyone to go in the first place. And I left you alone with Ranni! I should've been there to help you protect her. It's ridiculous for you to think that you caused this. And someone needs to stay here in case she comes back. If anything, you're doing us all a favor, Lelels! *Do you understand?*"

"No." Lelels looked down again. "But if that's what you want, I'll stay. I just feel bad that you and Beeheart have to take this on and face so much danger."

"It may be just as dangerous for you to stay here. *Did you think of that?*" Noni put his hand on Lelels' shoulder.

After saying goodbye several times, Noni and Beehart finally set out. Noni took Saron and Beehart led Smithi. They made their way down the same road they'd traveled the day before until they came to the river crossing. The water rushed and foamed furiously past them, too wide and deep and fast to attempt on foot. When they came to the bridge, they saw how risky it was to cross over on it. Rotting wood planks were held together loosely with frayed ropes. The bridge itself was connected by worn ropes to trees on either side. When the wind blew, the perilous structure swayed wildly. The boys looked at each other, trying to conceal their terror.

"There's no other way across." Noni gritted his teeth and looked over at Beehart, who was squinting his puffy eyes against the morning sun. He tightened his fist on Saron's rein and moved forward to the first plank. He stepped onto it and tried to steady his feet as the plank moved under him. He pulled at the rein, but Saron backed away and bleated loudly, showing the whites of her eyes. Noni gripped the rope railing and held out a juicy moggie to her. She stepped forward warily and stretched her neck out to nibble the treat. He encouraged her to move onto the plank and take it from his outstretched hand, then they moved to the next plank. When the bridge swayed too much, Noni would stop, grip the railing, and wait for Saron to steady her feet, not allowing her to back up. He held out another moggie, she reached for it, took another step, and they moved to the next plank. *One step at a time*, he thought again. So, step by step, they made their way across the unstable bridge. Once they reached the other side, Noni stood shaking on the sold ground.

"You can do it, Beehart!" he yelled to be heard above the swift-running river.

Unfortunately, his friend didn't have any moggies in his pocket, having consumed most of them before they left, and stubborn Smithi pulled hard against the rein, resisting every step. With enormous effort, Beehart managed to get halfway across. Then a sinking feeling came over him when he noticed that the ropes holding the planks were unraveling.

"Oh no!" he screamed. *"The bridge is breaking apart!"* Noni stood watching, wide-eyed, as Beeheart tried to push Smithi back across the bridge by using his hand against the animal's forehead. But the frightened grat dug his sharp hooves between the planks and caused the ropes to fray even faster. Beehart shrieked as the planks began to give way. He held onto the rope railing for a moment, but Smithi's weight pulled him down, and the two of them plunged, bleating and screaming, into the cold, roiling water. And they were carried away with the current.

Noni and Saron ran downstream, trying to outpace them. Reaching a bend in the river before his friend, Noni swooped up a long branch and held it out into the rushing water as far as he could reach. His face barely visible above the foam, Beehart grabbed the branch, as the river swept him along, near the bank. Smithi rushed past them, borne away by the current. With a sudden surge of adrenaline, Noni pulled his friend to shore, grabbed his tunic, and dragged him from the choppy water. Beehart crawled like a beaten bug onto the dirt and tried to catch his breath. He lay on his side for a while, wheezing, sputtering, and coughing.

Meanwhile, Smithi clawed his way onto some rocks at the edge of the river farther downstream. Sacks in tow, he was somehow strong enough to hoist himself onto the bank and make his way back to the boys. Exhausted and wobbly he stood by them shivering and shaking.

"R-r-remind me to s-s-save some m-moggies for Smithi tomorrow!" Beehart stuttered through chattering teeth. Noni watched him rub his arms and recalled another time when they were younger, and he had pulled his friend out of the river when he fell while they were teetering across a log that spanned the turbulent water. Noni had grabbed him just in time. This was another reason he and others were apprehensive about the treacherous Testus. He half-smiled now, thinking how Beehart owed him his life, not once but twice.

They sat for a while on the riverbank, feeling tested to exhaustion by the river's torrents. Noni threw aside Beehart's water-logged food and laid his things out to dry since both his bags were soaked. He worried a little that they might not have enough provisions for later. But, for now, he wrapped one of his blankets around his friend, since he was still wet and shaking with cold. He was glad he'd thrown an extra blanket into his bag. Then he opened his precious packet of Grooma's sweet griffoons and gave some to Beehart. After eating, they both stretched out on the sand to rest while Beehart and his bags dried out. The warming sun overhead felt good, even as it glared squarely into their flushed faces. After a while, they both sat up and blinked their eyes against the light. It felt like they'd been gone for days, but they realized they'd left home only a few hours ago.

"So, what's our plan and where're we headed?" Beehart asked groggily, still trembling.

Noni had meant to discuss a plan of action with Beehart that morning, but, with the worthwhile time spent with Grooma, then the rush to "get a move on," he didn't have a chance. Always the one with an idea or a dream, his answer wasn't what Beehart expected.

"I have no idea," Noni glanced over at his friend and half-smiled. "All I know is we're headed for Sur. And we'll have to take it one step at a time!"

chapter five
The Purpit Promise

Noni's bones creaked loudly as he repacked his blankets and remaining food. He turned to watch Beehart as he squeezed the remaining water from his blankets, repacked them, then tied his bags back onto Smithi. He seemed less shaky now.

They found a worn path into the woods and walked for a few miles. After emerging from a thicket of trees, Noni was captivated by a flowered meadow that blanketed the side of a hill. He cried out with joy when he realized that this was the color-patched mead he'd seen from his tree perch. As he approached, he gasped when the purple flowers leaned toward him with their flowered heads facing his direction, as if they'd been waiting for his arrival. He ran to look closer, forgetting to secure Saron. She trotted after him toward the entrancing space.

The peculiar plants were connected by vines that wound around a large area of the meadow. As he drew closer, he noticed that this unusual mound of flowers looked just like little people! The top petals resembled heads with faces, the side petals were like arms, and the bottom ones reminded him of legs. Thin yellow veins ran through each petal, and, in the center of each flower, a cluster of tiny red petals resembled a human heart. The small brown markings on each "face" looked just like eyes, a nose, and a mouth.

As he gazed down, dumb-founded, Noni was soon overwhelmed by the sweet smell of the plum-colored blossoms. Their fragrance was so overpowering that he lay down among them. He put his hands under his head like a pillow, looked up at the cloudless blue sky, then closed his eyes. His drowsiness was interrupted by shrill voices.

"*Ouch, ouch, ouch!*"

Saron had followed him into the mound and was stepping on the flowers.

"*What the heck?*" Noni sat up quickly and looked around. "*Who said that?*"

"*Purpits!* And your grat's crushing us! *Get her off!*"

He jumped up and stared in astonishment to see the flowers' eyes and mouths moving! He led Saron away to a grassy patch near the woods and tied her to a tree. Then he returned to the flowers.

"I had *no idea* flowers could talk!" He squatted down to take a closer look at their features. He wanted to touch them and make sure they were real.

"Well, *we can!* We're *Purpits!*"

Noni stood up and backed away as their chorus of voices pierced his ears.

"Can all flowers talk?" he wondered out loud.

"No. *Of course not!*" one answered, seemingly offended. "We can because we were once Gomies. Wicked Surlies turned us into flowers!"

"Why would they do that?" Noni bent closer.

"Because we know *too much!*" The talking flower squinted up at him.

"What do you mean?" He leaned in.

Walking more slowly to get his strength back, Beehart had taken his time to get to the meadow. Seeing his friend resting among the flowers, he'd also left Smithi tied up in the trees.

"*Who* are you talking to?" he asked. Alarmed when he heard weird voices, he reached for his dagger.

"*The flowers!*" Noni exclaimed.

"*Purpits!*" the flowers yelled in unison.

Beehart jerked around and scanned the landscape to find the source of the sound. He thought he was either dreaming or crazy. He rubbed his eyes, gazed at the meadow mound, then bent his head toward the ground, his eyes wide. He plopped down on a patch of dirt next to Noni and listened intently as one of the strange flowers introduced himself and started to tell a bizarre story.

"My name is Sir Hatwig," The one speaking drew himself up higher. "We were once Gomies living in Mussford, close to here, but we had a miserable life. That's because the Krochits looked down on us and called us 'little people,' and wouldn't allow our children to go to their schools. We were forced to live in the bad part of town. They had the nice homes. Nobody was satisfied. We Gomies never had enough, and the Krochits always had too much!"

Noni and Beehart glanced at each other. They'd experienced some of this same prejudice between Gomies and Krochits in Gratville.

"One day, a strange man came to town," Sir Hatwig continued. "At first, we rejected him, because he was so different from anyone we'd ever known. Some Gomies even threw things at him when he walked by. Their first reaction was to hate strangers, because they'd been mistreated for so long and didn't know how to be kind to outsiders.

"Then, our mayor, Lord Ludifus, grew ill. Many Mussians despised each other, but everyone loved Lord Ludifus. Even though he was a Krochit, the Gomies all respected him, because he was kind and had a good word for everyone. He even secretly dispersed food and supplies to the neediest Gomies and made sure they had a way to earn money. He knew there'd be retaliation from the Krochits if they found out, but he did it anyway. He was a good man. As the mayor's assistant, I was aware of the things he did." Sir Hatwig tossed his petal head and gazed up to make sure they'd heard him. "We were sad when Lord Ludifus got sick, and there was nothing anyone could do. The finest doctors came from throughout the land but couldn't cure him. Then this strange man called Ameno came…."

Beehart couldn't hold himself back.

"*We heard about him!*" He recalled Grooma's farewell story.

"Sure you did!" Hatwig rolled his eyes. "Anyway, Ameno came to see the mayor. He asked Lord Ludifus if he wanted to be healed. He said, 'Of course.' So, Ameno touched his heart with his hand and extended his other hand to the sky as if he was reaching up for something. All of a sudden, the mayor sat up and said, 'I feel fine now!'"

"That sounds like the story we heard about him from our neighbor," Beehart broke in.

"The whole town celebrated." Hatwig ignored Beehart's interruption. "We were all so happy! We wanted to know how he did it, so every day we went to hear him talk. There, on that hill." He swung his head toward the hill by the meadow. "He told us about kindness, forgiveness, and trust. He talked about his father. He called him Abba. And he showed us what he could do if we believed in his power.

"We were sad when he left, but we understood he had to go to different towns to help others. Before he went, he promised he'd come back." Hatwig sighed. "He made Mussford a different place. People changed. Krochits and Gomies ate together for the first time. Krochits let Gomies go to their schools and hired them for important positions. Together, they built sharetoos." He stopped for a moment. "Do you know what a sharetoo is?" He looked up at the boys, who swung their heads back and forth. "They're small buildings where people gather to share their belief in Ameno and pray to Abba." He paused then began again. "But, one day, after Ameno left, a group of Surlies showed up at the local tavern. They noticed that the townspeople seemed different.

They asked questions. The tavern keeper told them how a man had come and healed the mayor and changed everyone's lives. The Surlies got angry. You see, they wanted to take over the town, using the Krochits as their puppets. They created division between the Krochits and Gomies. This gave them a reason to oppress the Gomies and maintain greater control.

"They threatened the tavern keeper and everyone there. They told them to never speak of this man again. If they did, terrible things would happen to them and their children. They said this man was dead now. They caused a horrible commotion. Many began to worry and were really upset to hear that Ameno was dead. Attitudes began to change because they were afraid.

"Then the Surlies questioned the most fearful Mussians and found out how Lord Ludifus had helped the Gomies. They tormented the good mayor with harsh questioning and public ridicule. They burned his house down and kicked him out of office, replacing him with one of their own clones. He was tied to a post in the town square. Followers were forbidden to give him food or water. We were heartbroken to see him there but were helpless to do anything. It was all too much for him. He died soon after being released." Hatwig let out a loud sigh. "The Surlies boarded up the sharetoos and asked the townspeople which Mussians believed in Ameno. Fearful people betrayed us, pointing out where we lived and worked. Surlies forced us out to this field a few months ago, in early spring. They chose the very place that was most meaningful to us as the site where they'd bewitch us using sorcery. An especially evil Surli—a huge, horrible man with a hood and an eye patch—chanted over us and turned us into Purpits!"

The Purpits moaned in unison.

"The sorcerer sounds like the same monster who kidnapped my sister," Beehart blurted out. "That's why we're here. We're looking for her and trying to figure out where this evil guy took her. *It sounds like the same bad dude!*"

Hatwig squinted up at him.

"Well, all the more reason to help us! You can see we're trapped here! We need someone to release us from this curse. Summer will end soon. Then there's fall. And, when cold weather comes, we'll all *freeze to death!*"

Groans echoed across the meadow.

"How can we help?" Noni's eyebrows knit together.

"We need *you* to find someone called the Reignbreaker," Hatwig responded decisively.

"Who is this Reignbreaker?" Noni asked.

"We don't know exactly," Hatwig responded vaguely. "All we know is that when the hooded Surli changed us, we heard him say that the Reignbreaker must never find us, because only he could change us back."

"Why is this person called the Reignbreaker?" Beehart puzzled.

"We have *no idea!*" Hatwig snapped. "How could we? *We're stuck here!* It's up to you to find out and help us. You're our only chance. Everyone else is too afraid to get involved. *It's up to you!*"

"How do you expect us to find this Reignbreaker if we don't even know who he is?" Beehart's ears turned bright red.

"Go to Sur," Hatwig answered sharply, ignoring Beehart's outburst. "That's where you should start. But you'll have to disguise yourselves. If they recognize you as Gomies from another town and discover what you're after, *they'll kill you!*" His eyes squinted narrowly.

Noni looked up and noticed how the sun was now behind the trees on the hill. He bent toward the flowers.

"It's getting late in the day. Where should we go for the night? Do you know a safe place?"

"Yes—up the road in Mussford. If you hurry, you can reach it before sundown. Remember, it's not like it used to be," Hatwig warned.

"Mussians have gone back to their old ways. There's a lot of hatred and suspicion now. And Surli spies."

"So, how can we tell a trustworthy Mussian from a bad one?" Noni's brows were knit.

"There's one way you can identify the good ones. If you look closely, you can see them glowing." Hatwig smiled knowingly.

"What do you mean?"

"They're 'lit up' by their belief in Ameno, and a red glow comes from their hearts. If you can't see it, there's another way to know if they're a believer."

"What is it?" Noni was fascinated.

"Well, see if they can finish the 'Purpits' Puzzle.'"

"*What?*" Beehart looked at the flower like he was crazy.

"It goes like this," Hatwig explained.

"Once I heard tales of a wanderer,
Full of great wisdom and yen,
Marking a passage of distance,
Speaking of this time and then.

"A believer can finish the poem with:

"Relating a story of meaning,
Telling a tale of truth,
Revealing a new way resembling
A meadow of flowers forsooth."

"Is there anyone we should look for in Mussford? Someone you know to be friendly or helpful?" Noni persisted, not certain these methods would work.

"On the main street you'll find a place called the Treatise Tavern and Turret Inn. I know the owner's a man you can trust, if he's still there. Mention privately that you've seen the Purpits, and he'll take good care of you. He'll point you in the right direction to get to Sur."

"Thanks, Sir Hatwig. We'll do what we can for you," Noni said, but avoided looking at the flower.

When Noni and Beehart stood up, they were careful not to step on the Purpits. They tiptoed around the patch to the woods' edge to untie their grats then led them around the meadow that encompassed the lower part of the tall hill. They found a path that ascended into a wooded area that embraced the middle and upper part of the pike. As they walked away, they turned to look back at the flowers. When they were beyond earshot, Noni glanced over at his friend.

"I'd like to help them," he said solemnly.

"Yeah, me too," Beehart said. "But, you know, our main concern has to be finding Ranni."

"I know." Noni thought they'd probably never see the Purpits again, but he didn't want to voice this dismal thought. "We'll just have to take it one step at a time!"

"You always say that!" Beehart sneered. "What exactly does it mean, anyway?"

Noni didn't say anything, not being sure how to answer. But, behind them, across the meadow, the colorful heads bowed down as the sun set, and Noni swore he could hear a sad sigh. He wondered if it was the wind or the Purpits.

chapter six

The Mysterious Mussian

Dark clouds descended over them like a smothering blanket as they mounted the steep wooded hill. The light grew dimmer and the way more treacherous and difficult to maneuver as they climbed farther up. Closer to the top, they stumbled over loose rocks in the fading light, and they slowed down to test each unstable step with aching legs and feet.

Noni suddenly felt his rein jerk when Saron stepped on an unstable rock. It dislodged under her hoof, and she slid backward, causing an avalanche of rocks to cascade down over Beehart and Smithi, who were several yards below. Noni yelled to warn them and tried to stop Saron from sliding all the way down onto them. She dragged him a few feet with her, and he slid onto his knees to keep from falling headlong down the hill. The sharp rocks scraped his legs, until he finally let go of the rein.

With the first rain of rocks, Beehart acted quickly and jumped to the side of the path, dragging Smithi with him. They landed in a patch of prickly bushes right before the avalanche hit with Saron skidding past them partway down the hill. Noni heard her brawls as she fell, and he groaned, thinking about the shape she'd be in. He felt his way back down the path, trying not to slide, past Beehart and Smithi, and he found her lying in a pile of rubble on a plateaued area beside the path. She bleated plaintively, and he could see that she was in pain. She could barely stand with the load on her back, so he removed his bags from her shaking back, and, when she did get up, she held up a bleeding leg. Miraculously it wasn't broken.

Beehart crept down cautiously toward them, and he was relieved to see that they were all right, except for Saron's injured leg, which Noni wrapped in a rag to protect it from further harm. As they stood there, surveying the situation, Noni looked up at the dark canopied sky and knew it was getting too dark for them to make their way back up the slippery path.

"I hate to say it, but there's no way we can get over that hill tonight, especially with Saron's hurt leg and not being able to see our way very well over those loose sharp rocks," Noni grimaced. Beehart nodded in agreement and they both started looking around for a place to settle down for the night.

Next to the plateaued area, they found a somewhat flat, cleared area by a sturdy tree behind some bushes, Noni tied a rope to Saron's halter and wrapped the other end around the tree. He laid his bags under a bush, and Beehart followed suit. They took blankets and spread them out for themselves and the grats. Then they took out some food and the canteens, set out bowls of water and food for the grats, and sat down to eat and drink.

Propping his head on a rolled-up blanket, Noni gazed up at the sky, barely visible through the scraggly trees and bushes. The dark clouds were gone now, replaced by a few twinkling stars and the growing light of a newly waxing crescent moon. It felt eerie here in this strange place on the side of a mountain. And he listened for any mysterious sounds. In the distance he could hear howling sounds, and he wondered what unearthly creature was making them. They gave him the creeps and make him shiver. But, he was so exhausted from the events of this first travel day that he drifted into a sound sleep. Beside him, Beehart dozed with one hand on his dagger, and Noni could tell he was feeling uneasy too.

The next morning, they were a little refreshed as the sun peeked through the trees. Noni unwound the rag around Saron's leg, decided it looked better, then rewrapped it. *At least she can stand and walk without too much pain,* he thought. So, they packed up to leave.

Thankfully, they found an easier, more-worn path nearby. It was zig-zaggy going uphill, and it took them longer, since it didn't go straight up. But it was less treacherous. The climb was still stressful and hard. Noni sighed as Saron stopped often to rest her leg, and his own scratched-up knees throbbed with each step he took. When they reached the top, they could see evidence of a town on the other side. The houses were hidden among the trees, but they could see smoke curling up from the chimneys,

They slowly made their way down on a rougher path, groping the large rocks along the sides and trying not to slip and slide on the small ones. At the bottom, they stepped onto a dirt road that seemed to lead to a town, and, in front of them, an alluring path meandered off the road and through some trees to a small log cabin. Morning sunlight reflected from a lake on the far side of it, causing the water to sparkle like a field of diamonds. A lamp glimmered from one cabin window in the dim early morning light, and they could see a large shape moving inside.

"We'll have to take our chances here." Noni gritted his teeth from the pain in his scraped legs. "It'll take a while to reach the inn, and we need to rest." He pointed to his legs and to Saron, limping badly from having to walk on her still-sore leg.

Beehart nodded, and they took the narrow path. The cabin looked inviting, set amid tall, fragrant spree trees, but Noni wondered if the person inside would be friendly. As they approached, something strange burst out from under the porch and yapped fiercely at them. It was small and furry with floppy ears, short legs, a wriggling nose, and beady eyes. They'd never seen anything like it before. It growled viciously and Noni kicked at it with his boot, trying to keep it from biting his sore legs. Beehart drew his dagger and held it out. The creature growled, and another one came running up, snapping its jaws at them. Before Noni could defend himself, the second one set its teeth into his leg, and he shrieked.

Beehart swung his knife at its head. And a big man came running out of the front door, holding up a shovel.

"What's going on here?" he yelled. *"Who are you* and *what do you want?"*

Noni was bent over in agony. He squinted in pain, terrified by the man, but too hurt to react. He cowered, and Beehart's hand shook as he held out the dagger.

"We're G-G-Gomies from G-r-r-ratville, sir," Noni finally eked out, then took a breath to stop from stuttering. "We're on our way to Sur. We just need a place to rest." He pointed to Saron's bandage and his own hurt legs. We couldn't make it all the way to Mussford. Can you help us?"

"Why did you come *here*?" the man asked gruffly, pointing the shovel at them as if it was a weapon. When he got no response, and realized how upset and scared they were, he lowered the shovel and shushed the two animals. Their yappy howls subsided, and they panted with their tongues hanging out. They sidled up to the man and squinted up at him.

"Now what's this all about?" His voice was still stern. "You say you're Gomies? I've not heard of Gomies traveling this far from Gratville." He eyed them suspiciously. "What are you after?"

Noni could see that the man had a bushy dark beard and hair that stuck out from under a wide-brimmed black hat. He was tall and wore a green plaid shirt, a leather vest, and long pants. His face looked gruff, but his twinkling eyes reminded him of his father's. He looked at the man's chest to see if he could see any sign of a glow, as Sir Hatwig had suggested, but he was unable to detect it. He shifted from one foot to the other, trying to relieve the pain in his bleeding legs and throbbing knees. When he wondered what to say, all he could think of was Sir Hatwig's poem. At first, he felt silly saying it, and wondered how the man would react. But thinking he had nothing to lose, he repeated the words slowly in a raspy whisper:

> *"Once I heard tales of a wanderer,*
> *Full of great wisdom and yen..."*

Suddenly the man dropped his shovel, and it thudded to the ground. Noni jumped back, afraid. Then he heard the man speak to the animals in a much gentler voice.

"That's enough now, Berles and Marples," he said to get them to stop their low rumblings. "Calm down. Everything's all right. These are our friends," his voice soothed. The creatures slipped behind him. Then, to Noni's surprise, the man continued the poem, speaking with a soft sort of cadence:

> *"Marking a passage of distance,*
> *Speaking of this time and then.*
> *Relating a story of meaning,*
> *Telling a tale of truth,*
> *Revealing a new way resembling*
> *A meadow of flowers forsooth."*

He walked over to them, took the reins from their hands, and led the grats toward a small barn a few yards from the cabin, motioning for them to follow. Stunned, Noni and Beeheart staggered after him into the open entrance. They watched as he tied their leads to a post, took off the bags, laid them aside, then reached for a jar of ointment. After unwinding Saron's bandage, he applied some of the cream to the wound. Then he led each grat into a separate stall and made sure they had hay and water inside. After taking care of the animals, he pulled Noni over, made him sit on a bale of hay, and slavered the ointment on his legs. It felt good and Noni sighed as it quickly eased his pain.

As they stood there, they noticed another tall four-footed animal in the stalls. Beehart's face lit up. He had always been fascinated by graynights and wanted to ride one. A Krochit in Gratville owned one, and, whenever he rode by on it, Beehart would beg him to stroke its short gray fur and touch its black swishy tail and bushy black mane. The man noticed his eager look and smiled. Motioning again, he led them back to the cabin. And, after they entered, he shut the door and turned to face them. Eyes wide, they peered up at his face, and they wondered nervously what he might say or do.

"*Who* exactly are you?" he asked.

"I'm Noni. This is Beehart. We're looking for Beehart's sister, Ranni, who might've been taken by a Surli."

"That's dangerous business." His face changed, and his eyebrows knit into a frown. He pursed his lips under his thick moustache. "Surlies are treacherous to deal with. They're evil." He paused. "And what would they want with your sister?" He set his eyes on Beehart.

"We don't know. That's what we're trying to find out. But right now, we just need a place to stay for the night." Beehart's voice wavered under the man's intense stare. He raised himself a little taller, shook his red hair away from his face, and asked boldly, "*Who* are *you?*"

"My name's Mosi. I've lived here all my life. My father, Leopol, was a carpenter. He made furniture, houses, wagons, and anything else he could make out of wood. I followed in his footsteps, and I, too, am a craftsman."

"Like my dad," Noni interrupted. Mose continued.

"Here are pictures of Leopol, his father, and other relatives." He swung his arm toward one wall. Noni's eyes followed his arm to a skillfully carved log wall covered with pictures of bearded men wearing wide-brimmed hats and standing near piles of logs.

"This one's my father." Mosi pointed to one of the men. "You won't see my mother. She died when I was a baby." He motioned for them to sit down, and a cozy couch under a large window beckoned to them. They sank into its thick cushions and sighed as they eased their throbbing legs and feet onto some footstools. The small creatures that had yapped and bit at them now jumped up beside them on the couch and made themselves comfortable.

"These are my pet shoonums, Berles and Marples," Mosi explained. "They've decided we're all friends now!" He laughed.

As he looked around the room, Noni noticed one picture sitting alone on the mantel above the stone fireplace that took up one side of the room, to the right of the couch. A bearded man in a decorated uniform stared down at him sternly, holding a sword. Noni squinted at the man curiously. *Why did he look so familiar?*

Beneath the soldier's fierce gaze, a fire crackled in the fireplace and warmed the room. On the other side, a cushioned chair faced the fire, a small table beside it. And a colorful round rug cheered them from the center of the room. Across the room, an arched opening led to a dining room, where a large knotty-wood table with four chairs on one side, and a cushioned bench on the other, filled the space. Above the bench, a large, half-curtained window hid the view outside, and Noni thought about the unusual sparkling lake.

He was also mystified by the cleanliness of the place. All his life, he'd heard that Mussians were not very tidy, because they raised musses.

He'd never seen a muss, but he'd heard they were ugly pinkish animals that snorted through snouts and wobbled on short legs that could barely support their large bellies. They wallowed in mud and ate just about anything. But this Mussian's cabin was spotless, and he felt unusually at home here.

Mosi plopped with a grunt into the cushioned chair by the fireplace and picked up a pipe and a pouch of fragrant tobacco from the small table next to him. He lit the pipe, drew on it with his eyes half-shut, sighed, and cleared his throat. As he spoke, Noni glimpsed a glow from between his shirt buttons. He poked Beehart with his elbow, and the two smiled at each other.

"A couple of years ago, my father disappeared mysteriously, and I was never able to find out what happened to him. This made me very sad, since he was the only parent I ever knew and we were very close."

Noni glanced at Beehart, thinking of their own parents' disappearance.

"When I was small, he taught me the poem you recited," Mosi continued. "He told me that if I ever wondered whether a person was true-hearted, I should ask if he or she knew the riddle, as my father called it. If the person did know the words and the meaning, then I was assured of a good heart. I thought about him when you recited the poem. Only a few Mussians know it, and most wouldn't understand what it means. Parents used to teach it to their children. It was how we could tell a true Mussian from one who was not. It's been a long time since I heard it recited. How did you know it?" Mosi drew on his pipe, leaned his head back, and looked over at Noni and Beehart, his eyes twinkling.

Noni wondered what Mosi knew, if he could be trusted, and, more importantly, whether he'd be willing to help them. Leaning on his feeling to trust the man, and the fact that he'd seen his heart glowing, he recounted their adventure so far.

"We left Gratville to find Ranni, with just a vague description of her captor. We heard he's large and hideous, with black stringy hair, a patch over one eye, snakelike skin, and a cloak with a hood over his face. A neighbor told us he sounded like a Surli. That's all we know. We crossed the Testus River with our grats...."

Mosi put his pipe down.

"You made it *across* the Testus River!" His voice boomed across the room. "I don't know anyone who's done that. Those are treacherous waters—quite a feat!"

Beehart folded his arms across his chest.

"We *did* cross it, but I almost drowned, thanks to a poor excuse for a bridge. Then we found some weird talking flowers called Purpits."

"I'm sorry. Did you say *Purpits?*" Mosi leaned forward.

"Purpits are flowers that used to be people," Noni explained and looked over at Mosi to assess his reaction, wondering if he believed them or thought they were crazy. Mosi just sat quietly, so Noni continued. "They were once Gomies. The Surlies hated them, so they took them to a meadow near Mussford and changed them into flowers using sorcery—a spell or a curse or something. We think one of the Surlies who did this might be the same one who grabbed Ranni."

"I heard rumors about that," Mosi mused. "But the people who whispered them seemed a bit touched in the head, and the story seemed far-fetched. I wondered about it, but I've kept to myself since my father left. It's possible. I just never saw any proof of it. Maybe I should've investigated it for myself. Why do you think the Surlies did it?"

"Sir Hatwig, one of the Purpits, said the Surlies were targeting anyone who believes in Ameno," Noni offered. "It seems that people who follow the man's teachings don't exactly comply with the Surlies' agenda to control the land."

"I remember Sir Hatwig. Kind of a pompous guy who worked for the mayor. You know, My father used to talk about Ameno," Mosi picked up his pipe to repack it with tobacco. "He'd often discuss the man's teachings with others here at the cabin. When I was a little kid, he taught me a special prayer to make be brave. We'd recite it together every night before bed. It went like this:

"In the night, when the dragon roars,
Protect me, Ameno, with your sword.
Help me trust in you alone,
Here within my humble home.
On this side of Adamant's shore,
Visit often, we implore.
Remind us of your presence sure.
Give us your strength to endure.

"It brings back memories." Mosi's eyes met the floor. "I tried to forget so many things after my dad disappeared...." His voice trailed off, and he looked up at them with a painful look in his eyes. "I'm sorry. I'm forgetting my manners. You must be hungry."

Noni and Beehart looked at each other, not wanting to appear rude and reveal how starved they were. Mosi got up and walked into the dining room. He pushed through a swinging door on the right side that led into the kitchen. They could hear loud clanking sounds, and they figured he was making something for them. Despite their growling stomachs, they waited patiently. After a while, he called out to them.

"Seat yourselves at the dining room table! It's been a long time since I had anyone here to cook for, so I prepared a feast!"

They sat down on the cushioned bench as he pushed through the swinging door, gripping the two handles of a pot. He set it carefully in the center of the table.

"This is muss-meat stew with chopped bettas and tatas."

They'd never tasted this kind of stew since muss meat was expensive and rarely served in Gratville. They were familiar with bettas—round red roots—and tatas—oblong brown roots—and had often eaten them with meals. Noni's mouth watered when Mosi removed the lid with a flourish, and a pungent aroma escaped from the pot. He watched him ladle the stew into two bowls.

"Thank you for your hospitality," Noni said as Mosi handed him a bowl.

Mosi didn't stop with the stew. He brought out baskets of warm griffoons, bowls of grat butter, moggie jam, mashed tatas, and pickled bettas, a pot of sweet spree tea, and frosted cakes. Noni couldn't believe it. He'd never feasted like this before! At least, not since his mother and father had gone. As they sat sipping tea, their bellies full at last, Noni was soothed by a soft rain that pattered on the roof. He was thankful, when he heard it, that they weren't traipsing through it now. Also grateful for the warmth from the fire, he realized how tired he was from not having slept much on the cold, hard ground the night before. Added to this was discomfort from the chilly night air, the eerie night sounds, and his throbbing knees. Now, he sleepily glanced at shelves of books between the windows.

"You noticed my collection." Mosi nodded his head toward the shelves. "My father loved to read. On cold winter nights, when the wind blew and snow piled up, and we were holed up in here, he'd pull one out and read to me. I have fond memories of stories read by the light of a crackling fire." He smiled and puffed on his pipe.

"What's your favorite book?" Noni asked.

"I have many." He got up and walked over to the closest shelf and scrutinized a few moth-eaten covers and fading titles. He pulled out one book after another, savoring the musty smell of each one before replacing it on the bookshelf. Suddenly, he turned and looked at them as though an idea had just come to him. "Get up for a minute." He motioned for them to move from the bench.

As they stood watching him, he pulled the cushion off the bench then lifted the hidden lid. He reached inside and drew out a book. He set the lid back down carefully and replaced the cushion. Noni and Beehart repositioned themselves, and Mosi returned to his seat at the head of the long table, dusting off the small black book he held in his hands. Its cover hung precariously from the binding. He opened it slowly then carefully turned the yellowed pages, his watery eyes gazing fondly down at the words written there.

"My father used to read this book to me. It's called *Ameno's Manna*. He told me, *'Manna is a kind of food that everyone needs, but not everyone knows it's available or how it can help them.'* He emphasized that it sometimes appears unexpectedly and always comes whether we deserve it or not." He looked at the book as though he held a rare gem. "My father underlined his favorite passages. Here's one: *'The Breaker… will go up before them. They will break through, pass in through the gate and go out through it, and their King will pass on before them, the Lord at their head.'*"[1]

"What does it mean?" Noni asked.

"I'm not sure. But here's another one: *'Out of him…shall come forth the Cornerstone, out of him the tent peg, out of him the battle bow; every ruler shall proceed from him.'*"[2]

"I wish I knew what they meant," he said, after several long moments of silence, as he puffed on his pipe.

"The Purpits spoke of someone they called the Reign*breaker*," Noni recalled. "They heard the Surlies say it was important that he never find them. I guess this person was the only one who could free the Purpits from their spell."

Mosi's puffs grew more intense. Suddenly he closed the book.

"This is dangerous stuff," he said. "If the Surlies catch us with this book, they'll…." He drew a flat hand across his throat. "My father kept it hidden in the bench. He told me what happened to anyone who was caught with it. Sometimes the Surlies killed them on the spot. Others were hauled off to a prison in Sur and never heard from again. I never wanted to find out what they'd do to me, so I've kept it concealed."

Noni and Beehart looked down into their empty cups. Finally, Mosi spoke up again.

"Well, we won't figure it all out tonight, and it's getting late." He rose from the table then snuffed out his pipe, tapped the ashes into a tray, and placed it with care in a bowl-shaped holder.

Looking at the large window behind them, they realized that the sun's light no longer seeped in. Noni glanced up at the gap between the half-curtained part and the top of the window and saw how, through the darkness, the waxing crescent moon was thicker now—a little brighter than last night. They watched as Mosi walked into the living room and opened a narrow door to a cupboard next to the fireplace. From inside, he pulled out two down-filled comforters. He placed one on the couch; the other he draped over the stuffed, fire-facing chair.

"You'll have to draw straws to decide who sleeps on the couch and who sleeps in the chair. We'll talk some more in the morning." He walked through an open doorway that led from the left side of the living room down a hall to his bedroom. Noni curled up in the chair, letting Beehart take the couch. He was too tired to care where he slept. Berles and Marple lay on the floor at his feet as if they were guarding him.

The calming rain grew angry during the night as a strong wind whipped it into a frenzy. And it began to pound against the doors and windows. Noni again dreamed about the dragon. It was pacing restlessly outside back and forth, clawing against the windowpanes and snorting viciously, like it was waiting for him to come outside and fight.

Noni shuddered, pulled the comforter over his head, and finally drifted off into a restless sleep.

53

Phantoms and Flashbacks

Sunlight flitted in through the living room window and warmed Noni's face. He threw off his comforter and realized his knees and legs were no longer throbbing. He wondered if Mosi's ointment had some kind of miraculous healing power. *Hmmm,* he wondered. But he was too distracted by the sights and sounds around him now to think much about it. Despite the interrupted sleep, he felt stronger and ready for anything. He listened as spree needles brushed gently against the window, and he could smell their sweet fragrance even through the panes. He bounded out of the chair and darted into the dining room. Pushing the half-curtains back, he peered through the picture window above the bench.

"Incredible!" he yelled out, trying to wake Beehart, who was still curled up on the couch with his comforter over his head.

"Wha-a-at?" Beehart sleepily pulled the cover down, stretched his arms, and rubbed his eyes. "Can't a fellow get any rest around here? *Geez!*"

"You *have* to see this!" Noni ignored his friend's crankiness, still peering out the window.

"Ok. Ok. I'm coming." Beehart swung his legs slowly over the side of the couch and felt around for his boots. Reaching underneath, he dragged out one, then the other.

"You take forever! By the time you get here, it'll be *sunset!*" Noni taunted.

Beehart shuffled across the room, squinting at the light.

"*Look!*" Noni exclaimed.

They both stood and stared, their mouths open. A small boat bobbed from a buoy on a sparkling turquoise body of water. It was surrounded by white-capped waves that lapped toward the shore. Beyond the boat, they spied an island covered with trees tinted orange and gold by the emerging sunlight. Directly below them, a yard covered with dainty yellow flowers sloped down to the water.

Suddenly, a loud voice interrupted their intrigue.

"Did you fellows sleep well?" Mosi boomed cheerfully. Their heads nodded absently. "Well, then, I guess you're ready for breakfast!" He chortled at the intentness of their gaze. "Haven't you two ever seen a lake before?"

"*Nothing* like this!" Noni said. "The water is so...."

"So blue, so green, so *beautiful?*" Mosi ventured.

"The color reminds me of an amazing stone my mom once showed me," Beehart reflected. "It was a combination of blue and green...kind of like that."

"I remember a painting your mom had of a scene like this," Noni recalled. "What do you call this lake?"

"Lake Adamant," Mosi said with a sigh as he sat down on the bench. He reached across the table for his pipe, packed down some tobacco in the bowl, and lit it with a match. He sighed again as he puffed.

"How did it get the name?" Beehart turned toward him.

"My father once explained it with a tale about a woman caught between two kinds of people," Mosi didn't miss a beat. "He loved the story, because it really suited him, since he was a Gomi married to a Krochit. He appreciated all people and refused to look down on anyone just because they weren't like him."

Noni and Beehart glanced at each other. The night before they'd quietly argued about whether Mosi was a Krochit or a Gomi. His bronze complexion and dark eyes made him look a little like a Krochit, but they couldn't see the telltale knobs on his temples under his hat. He was hatless this morning. They saw no sign of knobs, and his bushy, reddish-brown hair resembled that of a Gomi.

"The woman, named Ailis, lived on that little island with her husband Ret." Mosi gestured toward the wooded isle in the middle of the lake. "She was a headstrong Gomi, not much liked by other Gomies, especially after she married a Krochit. Even her own family rejected her. So, she came to live here with Ret.

"Back then, the lake was filled with slithery creatures and covered with slime. The color—a yellowish green—was very different from how it looks now. No one ever ventured here, since it was so wild and hard to maneuver through safely. It even smelled funny, I've heard, like dead fish. But Ailis believed it could be beautiful. Every day, she and Ret pulled weeds along the banks, trimmed the trees and bushes, cleaned debris and dead fish from the water, and trapped the harmful creatures. They'd row their boat back and forth from the island for tools and food.

"Then they discovered a spring—now called Clearus Spring—that trickles out from the rocks in some cliffs near Mussford. Ailis and Ret spent months redirecting the spring's clear, clean water into a creek that flowed into the lake. The now-fresh creek water eventually purified the putrid lake water, and its color began to change as the slime disappeared. It was Ailis's persistence that made the lake beautiful."

"Why didn't they name it Lake Ailis, after her?" Beehart gazed out the window.

"Well, there's more to the story." Mosi blew a few rings of smoke. "Even more than creating a pleasant place to live, Ailis wanted a child. Over the years, the lake changed for the better, but poor Ailis did not. She got older and feared that she'd never have a baby.

"One day, Ameno came to visit her, and he told her she'd have a daughter, and she'd name her Adamantine, because the child would be strong and persevering, like her mother. He told her that the 'Adamant' was a legendary stone, so hard it couldn't be broken, and that Adamantine must be courageous for her own sake and that of her descendant. So, the lake's name stood for Ailis' perseverance and the strength of her child later. Some say she and Ret discovered the symbolic Adamant stone when they located the spring."

"Did she ever have this child?" Noni asked, fascinated by the story.

"Yes, two years later she surprised everyone and had a baby girl. Of course, she named her Adamantine. Sadly, something happened a few years after that, and they went into hiding. Another mystery. See the boat there?"

They both nodded as they watched it bob gracefully. Suddenly Beehart's eyes lit up.

"I just noticed the name on her side. It says *Adamantine!*"

"Right, my boy! My father told me that Ailis and Ret gave the boat to him when they moved away."

"Whatever happened to Adamantine? Did she grow up and have her own children?" Noni asked.

"I heard that she did. It was rumored that, when she grew up, she got married and had children."

"Where'd she go?" Beehart wondered.

"No one knows. She just disappeared, like so many folks." Mosi's face darkened and his eyes wandered to the window.

Noni gazed out at the island. There was no sign of life there now. He could see the glistening trees along the shore, and he thought he spotted a small structure close to the water. Could that be where Ailis and Ret lived? He thought he saw something moving and rubbed his eyes.

"No one's lived there since they left." Mosi noticed Noni's intent gaze. "It's gone back to the wild, I'm afraid—overgrown with weeds again. I'm the only Mussian who dares to remain here. Most people stay in town. They've heard too many scary stories." Mosi took one last puff before tamping his pipe down and setting it in its holder. "Well, that's enough of folktales. I'd best be making something to eat before we all faint from hunger."

Noni noticed some unusual carvings on the pipe holder. When Mosi left the room, he picked it up and inspected it closely. On one side, a young woman in a long dress was pulling weeds. Turning it clockwise, the same woman and a man sat together in a boat. Next, the woman held a baby. The last scene showed an older woman handing a stone to a little girl with braids. Noni quickly put it down when Mosi leaned through the door.

"So, you noticed my pipe holder!" he laughed. "Yes, it also tells Ailis' story. Let me interrupt your musings for a moment. Do you want flapcakes or floodle?"

Noni and Beehart looked at each other.

"Since we don't know what floodle is, we'll let you choose," Noni offered.

"Sounds like you've had flapcakes before. The way I make them, with griffa flour, they're really good. I put jam and butter on them. Floodle is hot cereal made from crushed griffa grain. I put grat milk on it."

"Flapcakes sound great!" Noni didn't hesitate.

"Sounds good to me," Beehart nodded.

"Then, flapcakes it is." Mosi closed the door.

"Can we help?" Noni yelled.

"No, indeed! You've helped enough already!" Mosi yelled back. They weren't sure what he meant, but they sat and gazed contentedly out the window. Soon they heard Mosi humming. Then they heard him burst into song:

"Catch a bit of sunlight.
Hold it in your toes.
Let it guide and take you
To wherever sunlight goes.
Never fret or worry
When manna is nearby.
It'll feed you with its goodness.
It'll lighten any eye.
Spread a bit of sunshine
Wherever you may go.
Let the manna lead you—
Smiling down the road."

Suddenly Noni caught a glimpse of something swaying between two trees outside.

"Look! A hammock!"

He'd seen one in Gratville, where Krochits had hung it between some trees. This one was large, swinging back and forth and beckoning to them.

"Do you mind if we swing in your hammock?" he yelled to Mosi.

"Go ahead!"

The boys pulled open the large log door that led outside from the dining room and darted down flagstone steps to leap across the flowered yard toward the hammock. Noni dove in first. It immediately flipped over, and he landed hard on the ground. Beehart burst out laughing. Another try, and they were both swinging successfully. Lying sideways with their legs dangling over the side and their arms behind their heads, they gazed up into the branches at the chirping birds.

Noni was mesmerized by the rhythmic swinging and the lapping waves against the shore. He stared out across the lake and sleepily squinted toward the boat and the island beyond. He imagined himself sitting in the small vessel, bobbing on the water. Then he gazed up and saw a huge, blue-tinted eye staring down at him from between the clouds that hid the sun. Startled, he opened his eyes wide and sat straight up in the hammock, waking Beehart beside him.

"Wha-a-at! *What!*" Beehart blurted out.

"Dunno," Noni whispered, trying to figure out if it was a figment of his imagination. "Thought I saw something strange, but I mighta just imagined it."

Then they heard Mosi calling.

"*Come in, boys!* Food's ready!" He stood at the top of the steps in his food-splattered apron. Scrambling, they got tangled up in the hammock and flipped over onto the dirt. Laughing, they brushed themselves off and bounded into the cabin to be greeted by sweet, savory smells. It didn't take them long to wolf down a platter of flapcakes smeared with butter and jam, washed down with scaggon juice.

After helping their host clear the table, they joined him in the den by the fireplace. Mosi lit a fire, then his pipe.

"So where are you off to today?"

"We need to get to Mussford to a place the Purpits told us about called the Treatise Tavern and Turret Inn," Noni replied.

"Well, before you go, I think someone here might want to take a ride on my graynight." Mosi winked at Beehart, whose ears perked up. "That is, after we check up on your grats."

"*Could I? That'd be amazing!*" Beehart's eyes grew wide.

Mosi put his pipe down, got up, and walked toward the door. Beehart jumped up and followed him to the barn.

Noni volunteered to stay at the house and finish washing the dishes. He was also eager to peruse *Ameno's Manna*. But he got a little nervous when he finally had a chance to sit down, and Mosi and Beehart still hadn't returned. He started toward the barn to see what was taking them so long. Through the trees, he could see Beehart in the barn, talking excitedly to Mosi, who was showing him how to groom the graynight. Noni had never seen him so animated.

"Well, we're almost ready!" Mosi yelled when he saw Noni. "Make yourself at home while we're gone. Guard the nest, as they say. Help yourself to the food, and, if it gets too cold, stoke the fire!" Mosi placed his foot into a stirrup and heaved himself up onto the saddle. Reaching down, he pulled Beehart up behind him onto the graynight. Noni chuckled when he saw how small Beehart looked behind Mosi. His friend heard his laugh and shot him a dirty look.

"Hold onto my belt, Beehart!" Mosi yelled and flicked the graynight's neck with his reins. He steered the animal up the path then turned to wave and call to Noni before disappearing down the road.

"We'll be back soon!"

Beehart grinned as they rode away. And Noni faced the cabin alone, his senses heightened as he ascended the porch steps. He smelled the pungent spree trees nearby and let the freshness fill his lungs. Then he was startled by a loud snort and remembered his dragon dream the night before. He looked around nervously. Something darted out from under the porch, and he screamed. But it was just Berles, aroused from a nap! Noni sank down on the steps and the fluffy shoonum snuggled up in his lap. Noni looked down and sighed, his anxious feeling gone for now.

chapter eight

The Thrusts of a Sword

Noni stroked Berles's soft fur until the shoonum spied a smallet and sprang from his lap. Marples followed from under the porch and barked after Berles. After a while, they came back to huddle with him, until the smallets crept closer to tempt them into another chase. When the shoonums took off after them, the smallets raced up a tree. They hung from the branches and taunted as if to say, "*Na-na-na-na-na!* You can't catch us!" And the shoonums yapped up at them. This game of "Catch me if you can" went on until Noni grew bored and went inside.

The fireplace beckoned warmly, as orange, yellow, and red flames licked at the wood. The fire reminded him of the fall colors in Gratville, when the white-barked towser tree leaves turned into glistening yellow ornaments, and the brown bruni trees' leaves were highlighted with orange and red. Housit leaves glowed golden, and the color contrasted nicely with their black bark.

Noni recalled fall's "Happy Housit Days," when everyone in Gratville celebrated with parades, picnics, plays, and games. It was the only time when the Gomies and Krochits forgot their differences and worked together to plan an event that everyone remembered fondly throughout the year. This "Festival of Booths" also allowed people throughout Inod to set up tents and sell what they grew: scaggons and tatas, bettas and honey, grat butter and moggie jam. Some people, especially those from out of town, camped in the nearby woods for days during the festival, and Noni's family would join them for the camaraderie.

He sighed and plopped down on Mosi's cushioned chair. He tried to shake a feeling of sadness as he thought about how he might miss those special days this year. His mind drifted to his tree home and Lelels. He thought about Ranni's kidnapping and felt growing anxiety for her and his brother at home. Restless, he stood up and walked into the dining room. He lifted the bench cover and reached inside. His fingers identified the worn cover, and he drew out *Ameno's Manna*. Settling back down in the chair, he thumbed through it, until he found an underlined passage that read, *"He has sent me to bind up and heal the brokenhearted, to proclaim liberty to the…captives and the opening of the prison and of the eyes to those who are bound."*[3]

A strange feeling came over him. Somehow, he knew this verse was meant for him.

"Does it have something to do with Ranni?" he asked aloud. "Is she in prison? Am I supposed to free her?"

Before this trip, Noni hadn't spent much time thinking about anything but moggie-picking, meals, chores, and Ranni. Except for his parents' disappearance, his life had stumbled along without much interruption. But, since the incident with Ranni, he felt fear unlike any he'd ever experienced, and he struggled with increasing anxiety. His dad had always encouraged him to push through his fears. "Do it afraid!" he'd said whenever Noni brought him a challenge he felt fearful about or uncertain in his ability to prevail over it. This would help him overcome feelings of helplessness. But, since his dad was gone, along with his support, he wondered how to calm his nerves, and he wanted to think that someone was watching out for him and could help him.

He was especially puzzled by the coincidence of meeting the Purpits, and now Mosi, who'd been a tremendous help to them. *What other mysterious things might happen to us on this journey?* he wondered. *And who will show up next on our path?*

His mind was in a whirl as he tried to connect all the dots. He read passages and reflected on them until he fell asleep, then he twitched uncontrollably as dragon dreams tormented him again. He imagined it was nighttime, and the gnarly dragon blew its hot breath toward the cabin and set it on fire. Noni watched as huge flames licked at the logs that held up the porch, and he saw a man appear from behind the trees. With piercing blue-green eyes, the man gazed over at him from under the hood of a cape, then he pulled a shining sword out to fight the dragon. The sword's thrusts caused the beast to rear up and screech loudly. Finally, it retreated, wounded and bleeding, into the forest. A trail of steam followed as it snorted angrily away.

Noni sat up, alert now. As he stared into the dwindling fire, and wondered about the dream's meaning, he thought he saw a girl's face in the embers. Hooded by a red cape, she cried out to him. Hearing her voice made him question his sanity. Shaking, he quickly got out of the chair and went to the window. His heart slowed down when he saw Mosi and Beehart riding up the path. He ran outside, still shaken by the dream and the vision, and helped Beehart down from the graynight. He noticed his friend's shining face and enlivened smile, and Mosi nodded his head toward the Beehart as he led the grayknights to the barn.

"That boy really takes to graynights. I've never seen anything like it. And they seem to like him."

When Beehart returned from the barn, still grinning, they all sat down to a meal of leftover stew and griffoons. Noni told them about his dream and vision.

"The dragon is your adversary," Mosi speculated. "Sounds like he's been after you for a while, but you also have a protector—the one who came out of the woods. Your vision's obvious. Ranni's crying for help. At least you know she's still alive."

Noni gazed down at the little bits of floating tatas in his stew.

"She was so desperate. It made me feel the same way I did when I met the Purpits. They really need help, but how can I help them? I don't even know where she is." The corners of his mouth drooped.

Mosi sank down in his seat.

"I don't know how to find Ranni, and I can't go with you. I need to stay here and take care of my animals. I'm sorry I can't be of more help to you. But I *can* give you some things for your journey. And I do believe you have a hidden guide." He gazed down at his hand, poised with a spoon above the bowl. "This gives me some relief, and I'll be here when you come back. You can always depend on me for food and shelter." He looked at them. "Your true guide will reveal himself to you. Be assured of it!"

"What do you mean? Who do you think it is?" Beehart looked intently at Mosi.

"It's just a feeling I have. I think you'll find out soon enough." Mosi smiled. And Noni considered again this man's unearthly insight into so many things.

After the meal, the boys repacked their bags with supplies Mosi provided, including more griffoons, some flapcakes, and a small jar of the magical healing ointment. It was early afternoon, and they could still make it to the inn in Mussford by evening. Mosi knew the owner's father and spoke highly of him.

"Oni used to know about a secret way into Sur. And he was the only one who could safely guide people there. His son's name is Bleamer. I don't know him very well, but maybe he can help you."

While the boys waited in the cabin, Mosi went to the barn for the grats and tied them to a post near the porch.

"Saron's cut is healed," he announced when he came inside, and the boys were amazed. Noni looked down at his scrapes and saw how they were almost invisible now.

"My dad made that special salve," Mosi explained when he saw how they marveled at the results of the miraculous cream. "He told me he got the ingredients from Ailis, who understood their healing properties. Sadly, I don't have the recipe. What I gave you and this is all I have left." He held up his own large jar. Then he changed the subject. "I have something else I need to get for you before you leave." He excused himself and went back to the barn. When he returned, he was holding a silver sword with a gilt handle.

"This was my grandfather's," he said proudly as he drew the sword out of its sheath to show them. Now, he turned the blade in his hand. "He used it in the Surli War. Years ago, the Inodians decided to fight against the Surlies, after they gained control of Inod's resources. For years, they took our best food and animals. They also seized our waterways—the lakes, rivers, and springs—and we had to pay them for our water! We got tired of it and organized a rebellion. Mussians joined with Gratians and Sapians, and we all formed an army. We were strong because we were united.

"My grandfather, Sagius, led vigils late into the night. He strengthened the Inodians and gave them courage to fight. You may have seen his picture on my mantel."

"I wondered who that was in the uniform," Beehart said.

"So did I." Noni remembered how the picture had caught his attention.

"He was a great man." Mosi held out the sword. "This was his. If you look closely, you'll see an inscription on it."

They bent closer to read what was engraved on the blade: *"The right hand of the Lord does valiantly and achieves strength!"*[4]

"I want to give this to you, Beehart," Mosi handed it to him. "If you want it, it's yours."

Beehart's eyes grew wide as he stared at the beautiful blade. He glanced at his own primitive wooden instrument, and his hand brushed over its rough surface. Trying to hide his eagerness, he slowly extended his hand to accept the precious prize.

"Thank you," he whispered.

Noni was happy for his friend, but wondered, *What about me?* And his heart felt a sharp stab.

"It will be useful to you later." Mosi motioned to the sword and smiled. "Just remember that it alone doesn't win battles. It must be used together with the strength you can get from *Ameno's Manna*."

"I'll call it *Truelight*," Beehart announced, smiling proudly.

Mosi nodded his approval.

Beehart walked outside to practice thrusts with this prized possession, and Mosi moved toward the fireplace. He picked up the picture of his grandfather.

"Because of the courage he got from his belief in Ameno, we won the war against Sur," he reflected.

"When I was younger, I heard about a war, but I didn't know what it was all about." Noni tried to stifle his feelings as he sat on the couch with a lump in his throat.

"The Inodians fought bravely," Mosi recalled. "The Surlies retreated and didn't dare to rear their ugly heads until a few years ago. After Ameno left, and people forgot the things he taught them, the Surlies started raiding their towns again. Recently they've gained more control, and things have gotten worse. But most don't have the courage to stand up to them. I'm not as brave as Sagius, and I'm definitely not up to doing anything alone. We desperately need a new leader."

Noni's brows were furrowed in thought.

"Mosi, you know how you said your father disappeared a couple of years ago?" He looked up as the man nodded. "Well, our parents went missing too about a year ago. And we don't know what happened to them. We were hoping we might find out on this trip."

Mosi walked over to his chair and picked up *Ameno's Manna*, which was lying on the seat where Noni had left it.

"I want to give this to you, Noni. It'll remind you of your father, as it's reminded me of mine. I can see how you're drawn to reading it. It will give you needed courage. But you must read it every day. You both have given me renewed hope, and I believe you'll need this more than me." He placed it in Noni's hands and put a hand on the cover. "You must be careful with it. Remember to keep it well hidden. If the Surlies catch you with it…. Well, I hate to think what they might do to you, and there are many spies out there."

As Noni held the book, he felt energized by it, and he pondered its power. Its yellow pages glowed like gold as light streamed in from the window behind him, and he wondered how he could ever really conceal it.

"Thank you," he breathed.

Mosi watched the boys strap their bags securely onto the grats. Noni carefully placed *Ameno's Manna* inside a small canvas backpack with shoulder straps that Mosi had given him to carry the book. He hung it in front, under his tunic.

"Ok, then," Mosi said. "Guess you fellows better be off."

Berles sidled up to Noni and rubbed against his leg. Noni reached down to pet him and suddenly felt sad about leaving. Beehart fiddled with his bags until he finally turned to say good-bye. His eyes couldn't conceal his sadness, and Mosi came over to hug him. Noni felt left out until Mosi motioned for him to come over and complete the embrace.

The three of them hugged for a few minutes. Then Beehart extended his carved dagger to Mosi.

"Please keep this until I come back some day," he said, and Mosi accepted it gladly.

When the boys reached the main road, they turned to see Mosi still standing on the path to the cabin, watching them and leaning against a post.

chapter nine

Secrets in a Secretary

It was late afternoon when the boys reached Mussford. On the main street, Mussians wandered along boardwalks and peered into shop windows. The women wore mostly gray dresses, and the men wore black hats and boots and long gray coats. Some rode graynights. Others bounced along in wagons. As they approached, Noni and Beehart noticed a sign that read "Well-to-Do Way." Beehart tried to hide Truelight under his tunic, but the sword was so long that its pointy end stuck out beneath the tunic's frayed edges. He pulled his hood over his face, and it pushed his red curls down over his eyes, making him look sneaky and suspicious. Noni laughed at the sight of him, until a passing Mussian snickered at his own torn tunic and scuffed boots. Beehart sneered.

They walked quickly to the end of the street, where they spotted the tavern Sir Hatwig mentioned. A board hanging above the entrance read: "The Treatise Tavern and Turret Inn." Noni guessed the word "turret" referred to the tower on one side of the building. Its cone-shaped, red-tiled roof hovered over whitewashed walls like a huge, fancy hat.

The medieval-looking inn seemed interesting, almost alluring, despite its odd addition, and the boys tied their grats to a post in front and trudged up the steps to the imposing front door. They pounded several times on the double wooden entrance using a large, round wrought-iron knocker on one side, but no one responded. So, together they pushed until one door opened enough for them to slip through and step onto the frayed carpets of an empty lobby.

On all three sides were open archways. They'd left the front door open by a crack, and a draft blew past them through a large room in front of them, filled with tables and chairs. Across the room, a stone fireplace sucked the draft up its chimney with a whoosh, and Noni heard a tiny creature scamper into a hole in the wall. The door to the left led to a dark room with a bar and some smaller tables and chairs. The arched entrance to the right led into a small room that held only a tall desk and two stuffed chairs.

Pictures hung around the yellowing walls of the entryway captured faded images of people. Noni and Beehart walked closer to peer at one intriguing photo, but their attention was interrupted by the sudden appearance of a plump young man.

"Hello! Hello! What can I do for yous?" Round-faced with short blond hair, he propped his spectacles on the end of his nose and walked past them into the small room to the tall desk. Wrapped in a soiled apron, he resembled the man in the picture they were viewing.

"Hello," Noni said, returning the greeting. "We need a place to stay tonight. We also want to meet the owner."

"That would be me!" His lips stretched into a smile. "My name's Bleamer." He held out a hand to shake theirs.

They followed him to the desk in the small room and watched as he pulled some papers from a drawer. Turning his back to them, he pulled off his apron then turned back to face them, assuming a more dignified pose. Standing taller than the boys, he pushed a form toward them.

"Just sign here." He pointed to the bottom of the sheet. "Be sure to write where you're from." He watched as Noni stood on his tiptoes to write his name and the name of their town. "Gratville, eh. We haven't had anyone from there in quite a while! What brings you two to Mussford?"

Noni wondered how to answer his question, not knowing whether the man might prove to be a friend or a foe. Beehart sensed his friend's wariness and gazed at Bleamer's chest for any sign of a glow. He jumped when he noticed the innkeeper's eyes behind his spectacles. They reminded him of his mother's.

"We're searching for my friend's sister," Noni finally blurted out.

"Searching for a sister, eh." Bleamer looked down. "And you've no idea where she went?"

"No idea yet." Noni stared at Bleamer. "We were hoping you could help us."

"*Me?* Help you? What would give you that idea?"

Noni glanced around the room then leaned into the desk and whispered, "*The Purpits.*"

Bleamer sputtered. Choking and grasping his throat with one hand and the paper with the other, he motioned for them to follow him. The boys grabbed their bags and followed him past the chairs and tables in the larger room. Through a window, they saw a garden full of flowers, a fountain, benches, and a gazebo. On the far side of the room, Bleamer held a door open. A sweet fragrance overwhelmed them as they walked down a few steps and along a flowered path to a tool shed.

Bleamer opened a creaky wooden door to the shed, and they immediately smelled musty dirt, rusty cans, and mold. Mud-crusted tools and pot-filled shelves lined the walls. Another door led to an attached glass-walled greenhouse, stocked with unusual plants and flowers.

In the darkness of the shed, Noni was struck by a single glimmer of light that streamed in. He walked closer and saw that it came from a window painted black so no one could see in. But a crack in the pane let in enough light so they could see their way around the shed.

Bleamer set three cobweb-covered stools in a circle and brushed off the seats. Noni almost fell backward as he wobbled on his stool's three uneven legs. Now that Bleamer felt safe enough to talk with no one overhearing, he whispered.

"How do you know about the Purpits?"

"We just stumbled onto them," Noni spoke softly.

"I've never seen them, but I heard about them. Did they tell you the sad story about our mayor, Lord Ludifus?"

"Yes. Sir Hatwig told us how the Surlies killed him." Noni looked over at the innkeeper's face to detect any reaction. Bleamer just looked puzzled.

"It's amazing to me that two Gomies from Gratville—I'm assuming you're Gomies—would happen to find the Purpits! Most people in these parts have never seen them and avoid talking about them. Oh, they used to tell the story, up until recently. But now they're too afraid. Everyone acts like none of it ever happened. I've searched for the Purpits, but I could never locate them. I wondered if what I heard really took place."

"How did *you* avoid being changed into a Purpit?" Beehart questioned warily.

"When the Surlies were on their way to round up Ameno's followers, I was warned by a secret friend." Bleamer nodded.

"What do you mean, a *secret* friend?" Noni wondered.

"I'm not sure how to answer that." Bleamer scratched his head. "All I can say is that he shows up now and then to help me. I never know when he's coming. He just appears. He stays for a while, then he leaves. He reminds me of the wind—he blows this way and that. Kind of unpredictable. He rarely says a word. And I don't know where he comes from. But the day the Surlies came, he showed up and told me to hide. I listened to him and hid here in the tool shed. I stayed here all day and night. I could hear people screaming as they were gathered and taken away. It was terrible. The Surlies got the names of those disloyal to their cause by terrorizing citizens with threats of death to their families. They even raided my tavern. They turned over tables and chairs, ripped pictures from the walls, and smashed glasses and plates. It was a mess. I was just thankful I was spared. They never thought to look in here." Bleamer sighed and sat silently on the stool. After a while, he looked up at them. "How can I help you find your sister?"

"Someone told us you might know how we can get into Sur without being caught. We believe Surlies captured my friend and took her there. We think she's still alive." Noni's voice strained. "Obviously, we can't just prance through the Surli gate. We need to find a way in."

"There *is* a way. My father found it. It's not through the wall between Inod and Sur. That's too well-guarded, and Inodians aren't allowed through the gate. But my father discovered a secret passageway."

"Where is it?" The boys asked simultaneously.

"I wish I could tell you." Bleamer looked down at his folded hands. "He never told me where it is. All I know is it's somewhere near Sapwood. He was trying to protect me. He didn't want me to go through it and get caught. And I don't know anyone who has. I did hear of a man in Sapwood who knows the way. Before you leave, I'll give you his name, but you need to know the danger you might be walking into." He took a deep breath. "Sur is ruled by a king in Zamzum, the land north of Sur. See, the Zamzummim are wicked giants who are even larger than the Surlies. They treat people like slaves and control them with torture. I've never seen King Zoar or the Zamzummim here, but we will. I'm sure of it. We've already seen the results of his reign in Sur by the way the Surlies do things. They're filled with the same kind of hate as the Zamzummim, and, in some Inodian towns—the ones closest to Sur—we see how they're gaining control through fear.

"Here in Mussford, we're thankful that we've only had to deal with the Surlies so far. The Zamzummim are worse, and there's the threat that one day Zoar will invade our land. Up until now, he uses the Surlies to rule over us. They take what they want and give part of it to him. The Zamzummim are horrible, cruel people." Beads of sweat formed on Bleamer's forehead and upper lip, and he wiped them away with the back of his sleeve. "We need to go back to the inn." Bleamer stood up. "I may have customers waiting, and I'm the only one working right now. Since the Surlies took so many good people away, there are only a few I can trust to help me anymore. Now, I'm the greeter, bartender, cleaner, and cook. A few young Mussians help me wait tables and clean up after meals. Otherwise, it's just me." He walked to the door. It creaked again loudly as he pulled it open. "Did you bring any animals with you?"

"Two grats," Noni replied. "They're tied up out front."

"I'll have someone take them to the stable." Bleamer led the way back. "It's next to the inn."

Back inside, he took them upstairs to a room in the turret that overlooked the garden.

"Just so you know, I'm putting you in the best room we have, because you're special guests. Plus, there's no one else staying here tonight!" Bleamer chuckled as he opened the door to a beautiful room bathed in light from the setting sun.

When they walked into the room, Noni noticed two things right away. First, a large bed with four posters and a canopy of white lace filled most of the space. The mattress was so high up that he wondered how they could climb onto it. A fluffy, white comforter made it look even taller. He was glad to see a stepping stool underneath the bed. He also saw a small wooden chest at the foot of the bed and wondered what treasures lay inside.

As he looked around at the walls, his attention was also drawn to more black and white framed photos.

"Who are the people in the pictures?" he asked.

"Just some of my parents' relatives. They're all gone now," Bleamer spoke matter-of-factly. "These two are my parents." He pointed out a photo of two somber-looking people. The man wore a stiff black suit, and the woman half-smiled, looking uncomfortable in a long white dress with a high collar. They both wore spectacles. Noni looked closely at their faces, trying to find some resemblance to Bleamer.

"There's no similarity." Bleamer read his mind. "I was adopted. These are my stepparents, Oni and Milli. And they never told me who my real parents were. They said telling me would put us all in danger. Some say I look like a Gomi. Who knows?" He smiled and stroked the top of his short blond hair with one hand. "I just know that my adopted parents were Krochits." He noticed Noni now eyeing the chest. "You're probably wondering what's in it. Well, sadly, I can't tell you. It's always been locked, and I've never been able to find the key. After my mother died, and my father got sick, I took over running the inn. Before Dad died a few years ago, he told me it held precious cargo and asked me to wait to open it. He said it might be dangerous to unlock it while the Surlies are around. He told me that the key was hidden and gave me some clues for finding it. He was a funny man! He loved mysteries, riddles, treasures-hunts, and maps. I've been trying to unravel the chest's mystery and decipher his clues, but, so far, I've been unsuccessful."

"Why's it in the guest room?" Beehart wondered.

"Actually, this room was my parents' room. I only let special guests stay in it." Bleamer walked over to a wooden secretary against one wall and pushed back the rolling cover to reveal a desk with six small drawers above it. He took out jangling keys from his pocket and fingered them to find the smallest one. He used it to open one drawer. Reaching in, he pulled out a small, folded piece of paper. He unfolded it carefully and gazed at it through his spectacles.

"This note holds clues my father left. I've looked at it before, but it never made much sense to me. It reads, 'Someday, you will have unexpected visitors, and one of them will bring you a needed key.'" He turned his eyes toward the boys, who shrugged their shoulders. Then he read, "'They will help you understand who you are.' How odd is that?" Bleamer gazed at Noni and Beehart again through his spectacles, his eyes appearing larger through the glasses. They shuddered under his glare. Amused by their nervousness, Bleamer rubbed his chin and chuckled. Then, noticing the dimming light outside, he pulled down the windows' shades along one side of the room.

"I'm hungry. I'm sure you are too. I'll go rustle up something to eat. You make yourselves at home. The bathroom is through that door. Freshen up a bit, then come downstairs when you're ready." He hesitated before leaving. "Just so you're aware, most Mussians who come to my place are not the uppity-ups. What I mean is, I have a bad reputation for being sympathetic to Gomies, so I'm snubbed by some Krochits and the Surlies in town. But that's ok with me."

He carefully placed the note back in the drawer, locked it, then walked out the door and down the stairs. His footsteps echoed through the hall below. Noni and Beehart looked around to see what other mysterious things they could find in this room. They saw nothing else unusual, so they washed up and went downstairs.

In the bar area, they chowed down on another version of Mussian stew and ate plenty of biscuity griffoons with grat butter. They sat at a table near Bleamer, who stood behind the counter, and they watched him wait on townspeople, who came to drink ale and express their views about the current mayor.

"The Surlies gave him power and there's nothing we can do about it!" one man shouted. "He controls our pay and our jobs. The mine where I worked 'as been shut down for months. There's still plenty of coal, but me boss says he hasn't got any money from the gov'ment for the batch o' coal we delivered a while back. Meantime, the mayor lives a life o' lux'ry! He gets what he needs from the Surlies." The man's face was darkened from years of mine-work, and his clothes were tattered and covered with soot.

Other Mussians swore angrily in agreement. Lifting their glasses, they yelled *"Huzzah!"*

Noni and Beehart sat silently savoring their food. Gradually, the grumbling died down as the Mussians departed one by one to drench another tavern with despair before heading home. The boys' eyelids grew heavy, and Bleamer suggested they head to bed.

"Tomorrow will be a big day for you. We'll talk more then." He winked.

They trudged up the stairs, unlocked their door with a key Bleamer gave them, removed their tunics, and ascended the footstool to the huge, fluffy bed. It felt like they were climbing onto a cloud. Cool air drifted in from the open window with the growing crescent moon thrusting its almost-half-moonlight boldly through the shade, and they snuggled under the thick comforter, appreciating its warmth.

But struggling beneath the cover, Beehart tossed and turned, wondering what hidden treasures lay inside the mysterious chest.

chapter ten

The Turret's Treasure

Noni woke up suddenly. He lay in bed listening to something rustling. At first, he thought it might be another upsetting dragon dream. But this was different. He knew he was awake, and he wondered if some strange creature was moving around the room in the dark. The noise grew louder. And, he sat bolt upright and looked around, feeling next to him. Beehart was gone. He scooted to the edge of the bed and looked over to see his friend sitting on the floor near the window in a pool of moonlight that seeped in through the shades. The chest was beside him, and the lid was open. Around him on the floor were papers and objects.

"What in the world? How did you get it open?" Extending his foot over the edge, Noni felt around for the stool. Not finding it, he plunged to the hard floor with a thud. Feeling a cold morning draft, he wrapped a blanket around him and darted toward his friend, who held up a small gold key.

"Where did *that* come from?" Noni asked, incredulous.

"I had it all along!" Beehart shook his head.

"What do you mean?" Noni stared at his friend and the key.

"Last night, I couldn't sleep. I kept thinking about Bleamer's father's message that 'one of them will bring you the needed key.'" Beehart looked down at the key in his hand. "As I lay in bed, I reached up and felt the key around my neck—the one Mom gave me. And I had this crazy thought that it might unlock Bleamer's chest. So, I climbed down and tried it. *And it worked!* I couldn't believe it! The chest opened right up! Since it was dark, I thought I'd wait until the sun came up to see what was inside. But I couldn't go back to sleep. I was so anxious to look inside!"

"What did you find?" Noni raised all the window shades to let in more moonlight then sat down next to him. Together, they inspected the papers and objects, holding each one up to the soft, silvery light that streamed in. They were so intrigued by what they found that they didn't notice as tawny sunlight glistened through the panes and replaced the gray-tinged moonlight. When loud footsteps pounded up the stairs, and a voice bellowed outside their room, they were jostled from their captivation.

"Are you up and at 'em, fellows? Breakfast is ready! Rise and shine!" Bleamer burst into the room and was stunned to find the boys on the floor, surrounded by the contents of his treasured chest. "What the…?" His jaw dropped as he stood frozen for a moment then pulled a chair up from the corner of the room. "How did you get it open?"

"Easy!" Beehart held up his key.

Brows knit thoughtfully, Bleamer took the key from him and turned it over and over.

"Where did you get it?" He looked over at Beehart.

"My mother gave it to me."

"How did she come by it?" Bleamer asked in measured tones.

"I have no idea." Beehart stared at the treasured object in Bleamer's hand. "When she gave it to me, she just said I'd need it someday. I didn't know what she meant. I just figured one day I'd find out."

"Tell me about your parents." Bleamer knew the boy's blue-green eyes hid something deeper.

"All I know is that she wasn't from Gratville. She never talked about her parents, so I never knew anything about them. I always suspected she had a deep, dark secret—something she couldn't tell us.

"My sister, Ranni, and I talked a lot about this," Beehart continued, "especially after our mom disappeared. We always wondered where she came from and what brought her to Gratville. My father was from the area. My mother met him in his parents' pasture, where he tended their grats. She worked for a Krochit family nearby and cared for their animals. When he saw her, he thought she was pretty and had beautiful eyes. I remember him telling me that." Beehart glanced at Bleamer's eyes, magnified through his spectacles. "There was something else special about her. She had a dimple on her right cheek, just like my sister, Ranni. I never felt like I could ask her about her background. I didn't think she'd tell me." His voice trailed off as Bleamer redirected his gaze to the key in his open palm.

"What was your mother's name?" Bleamer asked.

"Everyone called her Ada," Beehart sighed.

"Hmmm." Bleamer handed the key back to Beehart then picked up a small photo from among the things on the floor. He gazed at a beautiful woman holding two babies with a small chest at her feet. "I'm not sure who they are, but I do recognize this." Bleamer pointed at the chest. He turned the picture over and read a name that was written on the back: "'Adamantine.' That's interesting." He scratched his head and handed the picture to Beehart.

"Mosi told us about Adamantine," Beehart reflected after seeing the name. His heart pounded as he handed the photo to Noni. "He said she was Ret and Ailis's daughter."

"I heard the stories about Ailis," Bleamer said. "I heard how she changed a lake and the land around it and how she wanted a child and finally had one." He looked over Noni's shoulder at the picture and then squinted. "I wonder if your mother, Ada, was actually Adamantine. Could it be the same person?"

"I don't know." Beehart's hand shook as he took the photo from Noni. "It does look a little like a younger version of her. I see the same dimple on her right cheek. The babies she's holding don't look like Ranni or me, though. I've seen our baby pictures."

Seeing the boy's emotional response to the picture, Bleamer changed the subject by picking up a small figurine of a man in a robe that lay nearby.

"This reminds me of my secret friend," he said, holding it up to the light that drifted in from the windows. He then lifted an embroidered cloth and noticed the flowered pattern along its edges. "Purpit flowers," he said. Then he picked up a coin. On one side was the face of a bearded man. Under his head was the inscription, "Ameno Amends." On the other side was a purpit flower with the inscription, "Purpits Prevail."

"I remember seeing coins like this a few years ago. But when the Surlies came, they confiscated most of them." He closed his fingers over the precious coin.

Beehart reached inside the chest, pulled out a book, and recognized its title.

"Here's a copy of *Ameno's Manna!*"

"I haven't seen one of those in years." Bleamer smiled. "I remember my parents reading passages from it. When I was little, they'd read it to me every night before bed. I remember this verse." He pointed to some underlined words and read aloud, *"The wind…blows where it wills; and though you hear its sound, yet you neither know where it comes from nor where it is going. So it is with everyone who is born of the Spirit.*[5]" His eyes glistened with unshed emotion, and he wiped at them with his apron. "So many memories."

He stood up and walked over to one of the windows. Looking down toward the garden, his face became animated. Silently, he motioned to the boys to come over. They jumped up and peered down his pointing finger.

"There! *There!*" he whispered. "*Do you see him?*"

A caped figure moved mysteriously near the fountain. A gray hood hid his face as he raked dead leaves into a pile. As they watched, he leaned his rake against the fence, bent to gather the leaves into a canvas bag, then carried it to a small furnace beside the shed. He emptied the dead leaves into the furnace opening, and fire crackled and shot out flames.

"It's *him*," Bleamer breathed. "It's *my secret friend!*"

Just then, the man looked up, and his visage shone from under the hood like the bronzed face on the coin. Two glowing orbs shot flames at them, and Noni shuddered. He recalled the eye in the sky at Lake Adamant.

chapter eleven

Mysterious Maps

The man's gaze was too intense. Noni turned and searched Bleamer's face for answers. The innkeeper's eyes were still fixed on the man, so Noni looked down again but was surprised to see he had suddenly disappeared.

"How'd he do that?" Beehart was alarmed.

Noni stared, hoping the man would reappear.

"He does that sometimes," Bleamer spoke matter-of-factly. "He'll come and look at me like that when he wants to warn me about something. Then he'll just disappear. He knows you're here. He wants us to be wary of something."

Feeling lightheaded, the boys followed Bleamer from the window and watched as his eyes darted around the room until they landed on the chest.

"Let's see what else is in there," he said. "Beehart, reach in and see if there's more treasure."

Beehart sat down and dug his hand inside the chest again and pulled out some papers.

"Now, what do we have here?" Bleamer asked.

Beehart held up three detailed, brown-edged, paper maps with special landmarks and paths marked with small eye symbols. He read out loud the title of one, "Crossing Clearus Creek."

"Clearus Spring pours into Clearus Creek," Bleamer explained. "Right now, the Surlies are trying to direct the creek's flow away from Lake Adamant into Sur since most of their water is polluted. Surlies often hang around the creek, but you might have to cross it on your way into Sur. This map may show a safe way to get there. But it's still through Sapwood. Hmmm."

"Are you concerned about Sapwood?" Noni asked.

"It's close to Sur, and the Surlies' controlling mindset has rubbed off on the Sapians. I do see a house marked in Sapwood." Bleamer pointed to a tiny note on the map that read, "Humbert's Home—a friendly fellow." "But, from there, I don't see how to get through the dangerous forest areas." He frowned.

"This one called 'Friendly Forest Paths' might help us!" Beehart held up another map.

"Yes, I see. And what's the name of the third map?"

"It's called 'Secret Passage to Sur.'" Noni handed it to Bleamer.

"The first two seem to give details, like which paths to take through Inod and where to stay along the way. Once you reach the mountains closer to Sur, the third map shows some secret cave-ways to avoid danger," Bleamer reflected.

"I wonder how whoever drew these found the caves and passageways without getting caught," Noni wondered.

"I don't know for sure, but I believe my stepfather drew them," Bleamer surmised. "He was a good artist, and he traveled a lot. During his day, it was easier to get from Inod into Sur. He'd be gone for days, when business at the inn was slow. He'd go from town to town, meeting people and promoting the inn. Sometimes he went pretty far into

Sur. We had people from all over the place staying here, at least until the last couple of years."

"Doesn't it seem odd that he made a special effort to make and preserve these maps?" Beehart interrupted. "It's like he knew someone would need them someday."

"It does seem strange." Bleamer pressed his lips together. "It couldn't have been just chance that you came here, either, and you happened to have that key! There's way more to it, I'm sure. Maybe more than we'll ever know!"

Clattering sounds drifted up from downstairs, and Bleamer glanced at a clock on the secretary. It was eight o'clock.

"I need to serve this morning. And I have new helpers in the kitchen. I'd better get down there before they break something!" He laughed and headed out the door.

Noni and Beehart both had similar thoughts as Bleamer's running through their heads. They'd ended up on a journey far more mysterious and dangerous than they could have imagined. But, somehow, at every turn, someone was ready to help them. They gazed at the maps and the other treasures of someone's memories. And then they stared at each other, dumbfounded.

Bleamer interrupted their thoughts when he yelled for them to come down for breakfast. In the dining room, they were surprised by the number of people. Bleamer seated them at a small table in a corner by the fireplace, where a roaring fire warmed them.

"On Saturday mornings, many Mussians come for breakfast, since it's their day off," he explained. "I have extra staff here to help. We have specials every weekend, and today we're serving turntoo eggs with muss bacon and fresh griffoons with moggie jam."

"What are turntoos?" Beehart asked.

"They're brown and white birds that run around the yard turning this way and that, thus the name 'turntoo.' They lay eggs that are delicious scrambled. Try some!" Bleamer brought filled plates over, and Beehart dug in hungrily, while Noni picked at the eggs with his fork.

"Mmmm," Noni smacked his lips after finally tasting them. He was surprised at how delicious they were.

While they ate, a bearded man at the next table raised his voice so everyone could hear him. Others tried not to stare but couldn't help glancing at him.

"It really bothers me!" he yelled. "An' I still can't believe they has the right to jus' take people away for no reason!"

"You're right 'bout that!" another Mussian heartily agreed.

"I heard the Gomies jus' happened to be there, visitin' the sharetoo 'n' not harmin' no one or nothin'," someone else spoke up.

"I heard they were on their way to visit a relative!" another chimed in.

"Whatever the case, they were 'rested 'cause they were s'posedly prayin'!" the first man exclaimed.

"Well, tha's wha' people used to do in sharetoos, ya know!" The conversation heated up.

"I know. But how do they know they were actu'lly prayin'? Maybe they were jus' restin' for a spell!"

"No one knows," the first man concluded. "We'll never know. The Surlies will always say what they want to cover up their evil."

A deadly silence fell over the room when a sinister-looking man wearing a black hooded cape appeared in the entryway and stood at the dining room door staring in. Nervous whispers spread throughout the room. Noni and Beehart turned around to get a good look at him. When they did, their eyes grew wide. They'd never seen anyone like him! He was huge and hunched over, as if he was hiding something. And a horrible smell drifted from him. The people closest to him started coughing.

They couldn't see his face, but when he pushed back his hood, they recoiled at the unusual snake-like orange skin on his arms and his disfigured face and black stringy hair. Two prominent knobs protruded from either side of his forehead. Noni gasped when he spotted a black patch over one eye, and Beehart choked on his food. *It must be him*, they both thought. *Ranni's kidnapper—the one Lelels saw in the woods.*

When Bleamer emerged from the kitchen, he saw the man and almost dropped a pot of tea. Pale-faced, he approached him as everyone in the room stopped eating to watch.

"How-w-w can I he-e-e-lp you, sir?" Bleamer stuttered.

"*I wanna table!*" the man demanded. He pierced through Bleamer with his serpent-like eye then shot a hateful beam at Beehart. The boy shuddered.

"There are no tab-b-b-les available right now sir," Bleamer said with a nervous half smile, "but one should be ready soon."

"Well *make it quick!*" The man's blue lips parted to reveal jagged yellow teeth. He smashed his orange fist against the wall next to him and left a large dent in the plaster.

"I'll do my best." Bleamer's eye twitched as he pointed behind the man to the entryway. "There're benches there if you'd l-l-like to wait."

The man turned and threw himself onto a bench. Bleamer winced and rolled his eyes as he brought the teapot over to refill the boys' cups.

"A Surli," he whispered. "In case you couldn't tell. But this one is really hated by folks here. About a year ago, some visitors were accosted in a sharetoo and dragged away. It was rumored that he was responsible. I wouldn't doubt it. He's so-o-o evil. I've heard about the things he's done to Gomies."

Noni and Beehart glanced at each other.

"He may be *the one*," Noni said under his breath. "I mean *the one—the guy who took Ranni!*"

"You think it's *him?*" Bleamer's eyes grew wide. "Hmmm. So, what are you gonna do?"

"Not sure." Noni gazed down at his half-eaten plate of eggs. "I guess we could follow him."

"Not a good idea," Bleamer murmured and leaned closer. "He'll notice. Then you're done for."

"So, what do you suggest?" Beehart looked up from his cleaned plate.

"Let's talk about it…later. I have to go now. Other people to serve." Bleamer started to walk away.

"We're done," Non said quickly. "Let him sit here so you don't get *killed* for not having a table available! We need to pack anyway."

"After things settle down here, I'll come up to say good-bye and see you off." Bleamer turned to go.

The boys walked stealthily through the crowded dining room and tiptoed past the Surli, trying to avoid eye contact with him. Arms crossed, he glowered and muttered a curse as they passed by. Beehart could feel hate directed at him and it made his muscles stiffen and his heart pound. His face and ears burned, and he clenched his fists. Then something inside his brain burst. He stopped abruptly and faced the man. Through narrowed eyes, he glared at the monster, trying to show him that *he was not afraid of him*. After shooting him a power stare, Beehart purposely directed his eyes away from the evil man's face. As he glanced up toward a picture on the wall, he did a double take and forgot the Surli for a split-second. Then he stomped defiantly up the stairs, shaking off any lingering feelings of hate, anger, and fear.

As he climbed, he wondered what had shocked him the most—his brain-bursting response to the evil Surli, or the portrait on the wall, because *he was certain the people in the photo were his parents.*

chapter twelve

No Place to Hide

After the last customer left, Bleamer lumbered up the steps to the boys' room. He found them sitting on the floor next to their packed bags, inspecting the maps.

"He's gone," Bleamer sighed, wiping sweat from his brow. "I'm thankful he left without starting a fight or assaulting someone. *Whew!* And don't even think about following him! He stormed out before I could seat him. I watched him ride right out of town. *Fast!* He must've gotten wind of something."

"The guy was shooting me with hate beams the whole time he was here!" Beehart let out a pent-up breath. "I finally shot one back at him when I just couldn't stand it anymore. By the way, do you know the couple in the picture above the bench downstairs? They look a lot like my parents!"

"Old friends of my parents," Bleamer answered. "They introduced me to them once when I was a boy, but I don't remember their names. I just kept the picture, because it meant something to them."

Bleamer pointed out the best route to the spring on the "Crossing Clearus Creek" map. They'd use the "Friendly Forest Paths" map to get into Sapwood. The "Secret Passage to Sur" map would help them the rest of the way.

Warnings on the maps alerted them to possible danger, but also stirred up new anxieties. Noni wondered, *Were the drawings still accurate? What if these places no longer existed or the people were gone now? What if wild animals or evil people inhabited the tunnels and caves on the maps? What if the passages weren't secret anymore and the maps led them into a trap?*

"I wish I could help you more." Bleamer detected Noni's uneasiness. As he watched them scrutinize the papers, he had questions of his own. "I never knew the maps existed. If I'd known about them, I would've asked a few questions myself. Of course, I think your finding them was no coincidence."

"Well, I guess we'll never have all the answers," Noni sighed, releasing some of his pent-up emotions.

Bleamer glanced at the clock and saw that it was noon.

"You really need to go before the day's spent," he said. He helped them carry their bags downstairs and out to the stable. Outside, he stopped suddenly.

"I didn't see it on the maps, but there's an inn in Sapwood called Prior Place. A guy named Fendem runs it. I never met him myself. I just knew some people who stayed there once. They said he seemed friendly."

In the stable, Noni looked over Saron's leg. He was pleased to see that the scrapes were about healed, since he'd need to reload his bags onto her and now they contained more food from Bleamer's kitchen. Before taking the reins, he hugged and thanked Bleamer then set out with Beehart following. Before rounding a bend in the road, they both waved good-bye to their new friend, who was wrapped in a soiled apron. He swung his arm, and his whole body waved back enthusiastically.

"Take care, my friends!" he called out, and the boys hoped they would see him again one day.

As they walked, they were struck by the number of deserted homes along the road, and they wondered what Mussford was like in its heyday.

"When Lord Ludifus reigned as mayor, business boomed. Kindness prevailed, and greed was 'buried under blankets of blessings,'" Bleamer had told them. "But everything changed when the Surlies took over."

The boys quickly realized that the maps weren't exactly to scale. What looked like a short distance was actually farther than what the map indicated. At least the landmarks were still there. A marked housit tree, with a knothole in its trunk, still stood outside a wooden fence on the outskirts of town. The home at the base of the tree's huge trunk reminded Noni of his home in Gratville. He waved at the tree-dwellers, who sat comfortably in wooden chairs by the open front door. A man smoked a pipe like Mosi, a woman sewed a quilt like his mom, and two little Gomies played nearby. They could've been him and Lelels when they were small. He sighed as he thought about his brother at home and wondered how he was doing.

Farther down the road, they saw a sharetoo. Beehart spotted it first. He recognized it from the descriptions he'd heard from Mosi and Bleamer. There were no sharetoos in Gratville, so he was really curious to see this one.

"We need to be really careful about being seen around it." Noni worried, recalling the conversation in Bleamer's dining room about the people abducted from a sharetoo. Beehart ignored his concern and proceeded boldly toward it. Noni followed cautiously.

Partly hidden by trees and bushes, the sharetoo seemed forlorn and neglected. Though its white body paint peeled off in strips down each side, a tall spire ascended proudly from a shingled roof and pointed up to the sky, while purple-flowered vines worked their way up the walls and tried to reach the spire. The blossoms purposely faced the late afternoon light that filtered through the trees. These purpit flowers couldn't talk, they realized. But they still reminded them of their friends in the field.

Noni was fascinated by the stained-glass windows that decorated the sharetoo's sides and drew attention away from the peeling paint. He had never seen such fancy windows, and he wanted to look closer at them. But he was even more curious about what was inside the building. So, he climbed the broken steps that led to the arched, purple double doors. He looked up to see faded words under the eaves. They read, "I am the Very Vine."

He turned the handle of one door and was surprised when it swung open. He looked behind him to make sure no one was watching and jumped when something rustled in the bushes. A black smallet peeked out from under a pile of leaves, and he sighed with relief. Beehart, behind him at the bottom of the steps, had also balked at the sound. Seeing Noni's apprehensions and realizing he had some of his own, he kept one hand on the hilt of Truelight.

On the other side of the door, they were greeted by a stale, musty smell. A threadbare red runner summoned sadly up an aisle, and cob-web-covered pews on either side slumped forward, solemnly bearing dusty white candles in wooden holders at each end. Noni tiptoed past the pews up the aisle and spotted a forgotten copy of *Ameno's Manna* in a rack on the back of one bench. He walked over to it, pulled it out carefully, and opened it. Thumbing through the worn, neglected pages, he turned to the page that had caught his eye at Mosi's house, and he read, *"He has sent me to bind up and heal the brokenhearted, to proclaim liberty to the…captives and the opening of the prison and of the eyes to those who are bound."*[3] He was reminded again of his mission and relieved to see that the words were the same as in his copy.

At the front of the sharetoo sat a wooden platform with a table in the center that was covered with a white cloth. He noticed that the cloth's edges were embroidered with lavender flowers. A silver cup and a bowl sat in the middle of the table. Tucked under the cup was a mysterious piece of paper. Spying it from a distance, Noni bounded up the steps onto the platform and pulled it out to read its message: *"Blessed are you who hunger and seek with eager desire now, for you shall be filled and completely satisfied!"*[6] And he wondered at that moment, *Was this message just for him? Was it left there so he would find it?*

On the right side of the platform stood a wooden podium with words carved into its front that said, "The Purpits' Pulpit." On the left side sat an old organ, waiting patiently to be played. But his attention was drawn upward to a large window above the platform, where the remaining rays of sunlight sifted through stained glass and revealed a face peering down at him. He thought immediately of the face on the coin in Bleamer's chest. What caught his attention most were the eyes. They were almost off-putting because they were so brilliant, like deep pools of clear-blue, crystalline water. They pierced right through him. And he shuddered when he remembered the eyes he'd seen along the way—those of Bleamer's secret friend, the caped man in his dream at Mosi's, and the huge eye in the sky at the Lake Adamant. But instead of feeling afraid, he experienced something altogether different—a calming sense of warmth and peacefulness.

The face suddenly disappeared as clouds blocked the setting sunlight, and the room grew dark. Adjusting his eyes, Noni walked slowly back down the aisle toward the open front door. Beehart, who was sitting in a back pew, listened to the sounds outside for any sign of danger. He got up and followed Noni out the door.

They'd hidden the grats in a wooded area behind the sharetoo. Now, as they watched the daylight grow dim, they decided that this place might be as safe as any to spend the night, as long as they stayed out of sight. So, they removed their bags, fed the grats some grain, and made sure they had access to a rain barrel. Bringing their bags inside for the night, they found some matches and lit two pew candles. Then they settled down in a corner near the front, beside the organ, and made makeshift beds with their blankets. Bellies filled and warmed by

Bleamer's hearty snacks and containers of spree tea, they listened to the wind stirring outside. As rain began to beat against the windows and tap-tap-tap on the roof, they snuggled under their blankets.

Noni woke first. An unusual, diffused light disturbed his sleep. Out of the corner of his eye, he spied a ghostly form sitting at the bottom of the platform steps. Half-moonlight filtered through the eyes of the window above them and seemed to follow the figure as it moved. Startled, Noni, feeling creeped out, poked Beehart, who grumbled and opened his eyes. Barely able to see in the semi-darkness, he detected a look of horror on Noni's face. He sat up, instinctively knowing to be quiet. His eyes followed Noni's finger to the thing lurking on the steps. They both stared, their mouths open, trying to discern who or *what* it was.

Suddenly it stood up. Frightened out of their minds, they huddled together and stared in horror as it slowly moved toward them. With one hand, Beehart gripped Noni's arm. With the other hand, he reached beside his blanket for Truelight.

"I've been waiting for you," it breathed eerily as it drew closer.

"*Who-o-o* are you?" Noni's voice trembled as he felt like screaming but didn't. He tried to sound brave but couldn't manage it.

"You'll know when you see me," it answered mysteriously.

"*How* do we know you?" Beehart used his toughest voice as he got ready to jump up and thrust his sword toward its caped body.

It didn't answer, but continued to move up the steps, its face darkened beneath a hood. *Was it the Surli from the inn?* Noni was paralyzed with fear and scooted backward toward the wall, looking frantically for a way of escape but realizing, *There's no place to hide!*

When the figure was within a few feet, Beehart sprang to his feet.

"*Stop!*" he screamed and thrust Truelight forward. But, just as he lunged, a mysterious wind blew down the aisle, whipped around the platform, and swept the figure's hood back. Beeheart froze mid-stream and couldn't inch another step. As he stood there like a statue, with Noni sitting behind him, eyes wide and mouth gaping, he began to shout.

"*You! You!*" His voice rasped as he gazed at the face.

"*You* were in Bleamer's garden!" Noni jumped up and started when Beehart stopped abruptly. "You're *the secret friend!*"

The man's revealed eyes shone brightly as words came out of his mouth.

"That's a perfect gift for you, Beehart!" He stepped forward and touched the tip of the sword with his palm. "But soon you'll hold an even greater gift."

Startled, Beehart dropped Truelight, and the sword clattered onto the platform.

"How did you know my name?" He looked from the fallen sword to the man.

"I've known you since you were a child."

Beehart's eyes grew wide.

"*How?*" Beehart wheezed.

"Your mother is a friend of mine," he said. "I visited her before you were born. When you were a baby, I saw how much she loves you."

Beehart's eyes moistened as he thought about his mother.

"Do you know where she is?" he ventured.

"*Yes.* I do."

"How do you know? *Where is she?*"

The man didn't answer, and he turned to face Noni.

"I've known you too, Noni, since you were a babe, laughing in your father's lap." His aqua eyes sparkled.

Speechless, the boys wondered what he would say or do next. After a few seconds, they relaxed as he stooped to draw a pattern in the floor's dust with his finger. It was a picture of a family. He looked up at them, his eyes smiling.

"Where are you from?" Noni ventured.

"From my father."

"Who's your father?" He was genuinely curious.

"I call him Abba."

"Where does he live?" Beeheart asked this time.

"Most people have never seen him. That's because he lives in a world you can't see. But a few people have peered into his world, and they've described him as flying on '*the wings of the wind.*'"[7]

"If hardly anyone's ever seen him, how can anyone really know him?" Noni asked.

"You can get to know him if you get to know me." He smiled.

What is that supposed to mean? Noni wondered.

"Well, who exactly are you?" Beehart asked bravely.

"I've been described in many different ways." His face shone in the filtered darkness. "Some say I'm a prince or a king. Some call me a shepherd. Others call me a lamb. And still others say I'm a lion."

"What should *we* call you?" Beehart persisted.

"Just call me Ameno."

"We heard about you from our neighbor and the Purpits. Stories about you seem to follow us *everywhere!*" Noni tried not to chuckle and then suppressed a yawn, thinking neither was appropriate at this time.

"*You* are very tired and can barely keep your eyes open!" Ameno smiled.

"But we want to know more about you." Beehart shot Noni a look. "*I have more questions!*"

"We'll have time tomorrow," Ameno assured. "I'll still be here. Now, you need your rest."

It was hard for them to stop their insistent, questioning thoughts, so Ameno sang softly in a language they'd never heard. His voice, like a lullaby, was soothing, and his glowing heart warmed them. Pulling up their blankets and settling down near him, they drifted into peaceful slumber.

Before he fell asleep, Noni remembered something Grooma had said. *"When he spoke, you felt like you were being bathed in a clear mountain stream, refreshed and clean. His words were like poetry. He made you feel special, because, when he spoke, you felt as if you were the only one he saw or cared about."*

chapter thirteen

Stories in the Stains

Early morning light streamed through the stained-glass windows, and Beehart woke with an all-over warm feeling as he watched countless colors dance across the room. He was fascinated by the changing patterns of red, yellow, purple, and blue, and his *wows* woke Noni, who sat up, mesmerized by a rainbow darting across his chest. He'd never seen such a kaleidoscope of coloration.

Remembering their visitor from the night before, they looked around to see if Ameno was still there. Facing one of the windows, he called out to them.

"I want to show you something," he said.

Feeling surprisingly refreshed, they threw aside their blankets and jumped up to join him. He wasn't wearing his cloak now, and his dark hair shimmered in the windowlight. A multicolored robe hung from his broad shoulders past his knees, belted with a braided rope. Beneath it, his legs shone like bronze. He motioned for them to come closer. As Noni approached, he felt very small. But Ameno put his hand on the boy's shoulder and his warm touch reminded him of when his father would place his hand on him for comfort and assurance, and he shuddered.

Ameno pointed up at the narrow window in front of him. The scene showed a woman holding a baby with a few animals nearby that looked like grats and sapies. She wore a hooded cape like Ameno's, and a bearded man stood beside her and smiled.

"These are my parents." Ameno said. "I had a pretty humble birth."

"I thought you said your father is from another world and is invisible," Beehart broke in.

"Good memory, Beehart!" Ameno laughed. "You're right. My real father lives beyond this world. The man in the picture is my stepfather."

Beehart's forehead crinkled in thought.

"Was it hard to be raised by someone who was not your real father?"

"No, because I could also talk to my real father every day," Ameno answered matter-of-factly.

"What do you mean?" Noni asked. "How could you talk to him if he lives in another world?"

"And if he's invisible, how could he have children?" Beehart's brow furrowed.

"Well, Abba created me inside my mother, and I was born and grew up, just like you," Ameno explained.

"Why did Abba want a child? Wasn't it hard for him to watch someone else raising you?" Beehart persisted.

"So many questions!" Ameno laughed. "I'll start with Noni's. You see, when people were created on the earth, Abba made a way for them to talk to him, even though they couldn't see him. But, the first people decided not to listen to him. They wanted to do things their own way, and then many of their children stopped paying attention to what he wanted for them, which was to live, love, and be happy. They lost the ability to talk to him. Some of them even denied that he ever existed. This made Abba very sad. He wanted so much for people to know him and have the things he desired for them. But as the years went by, more and more children grew up not knowing anything about him.

"This broke Abba's heart, especially as he watched so many people suffering from sickness, disease, and death, because they were separated from him, and he couldn't help them. He wanted to tell them how much he loved them and teach them how to love and be well again, but he couldn't. The only way he could do this was to send someone from his world to tell them."

Ameno glanced up at the window. Tears, like small shiny gems in his eyes, sparkled in the light. He pulled the boys close to his sides. They could feel his sorrow from under the warm robe, and they felt sad for the absence of their own fathers and the love they missed.

"That's why I came. I wanted to tell people that Abba loves them like me, as a son or a daughter."

Ameno moved to the next window and pointed to a picture of a boy wearing a tunic and sandals and sitting on marbled steps surrounded by some serious-looking old men with gray beards and hooded heads. The men gazed down at the boy, whose dark hair curled around his face as he studied a scroll in his hands.

"This is me," Ameno smiled. "When I was twelve, I left my mom and dad, and they couldn't find me. They got pretty upset with me, but, at the time, I was so intent on fulfilling my mission that I forgot to let them know where I was! I realized, when they got upset with me, how important it is to acknowledge and respect your parents."

They walked to a window on the other side of the sharetoo. The stained-glass showed Ameno as a grown man sitting on hilltop holding a basket of fish and bread and looking down at a huge group of people. It reminded Noni of the Purpits and Sir Hatwig's description of days spent in the meadow listening to Ameno teach from a hill.

"Is this hill near Mussford?" he wondered.

"It could've been." Ameno laughed. "I've sat on many hills teaching people about Abba and how he hears them and gives them what they need when they ask."

At another window, Ameno stood in a garden facing soldiers and people carrying torches. They looked angry though he seemed at peace.

"What's happening here?" Beehart asked.

"I'm being arrested," Ameno said sadly.

"Why? Did you do something wrong?" Beehart pursued.

"No," Ameno sighed. "Some people just didn't like the things I said."

"Did you let them arrest you?" Noni asked. "Even though you were innocent?"

"Yes, I did," Ameno said. "I let them take me away."

"*Why?*" Beehart asked. "Why didn't you fight them?"

"Because my father told me to go with them," Ameno answered.

"Ok," Beehart puzzled. "That's sort of strange." He thought about how he always fought against people who tried to do things to him he didn't deserve.

They moved to the next window, where the scene was even more disturbing. Beehart's stomach lurched to see a beat-up man trying to carry a heavy wooden beam on his back. His body was covered with bruises and cuts and blood. Under a thorny crown, his dark hair hung in bloody clumps around his neck and face. It was hard to make out his face, and he was surrounded by angry, yelling, squinty-eyed people. His own swollen eyes gazed out at the hateful people with compassion.

"What's going on *here?*" Beehart rasped.

"The people want to kill him." Ameno sighed.

"*Why?*" Beehart raised his voice in alarm. "*What* did he do to them?"

"Nothing. Some of them were just angry at the things he said, and they wanted to get rid of him. He was a threat to them and what they believed," Ameno explained.

"*Why* did he let them do this to him?" Beehart grimaced. "Couldn't he get away?"

"He could. But he let them because he loved them," Ameno looked over at the boy.

"*Wha-a-at?*" Beehart's face twisted.

"I love *some* people, but *I wouldn't let them hurt me like that!*" Noni huffed.

"You shouldn't!" Ameno touched Noni's shoulder. "But it was the only way he could show them how much he and Abba loved them."

"*I don't understand!*" Beehart groused.

"It doesn't seem to make sense. I know." Ameno turned to Beehart. "Remember how people turned away from Abba and didn't know who he was anymore?"

"Yes," they answered together.

"Well, a person could show love by the things he did," Ameno tried to explain. "But that wouldn't make a way for people to communicate with Abba or really understand him."

"So, how *could* he make a way?" Noni puzzled.

"There was really only one way," Ameno continued then paused. "By dying."

"*Wha-a-at! No way!*" Beehart stepped back. "Are these people really worth it…*worth dying for?* They seem like a bunch of losers to me! Look at them! So hateful and *mean* to him!"

"Abba knew it was the only way to win people back to him." Ameno sighed. "If he let his own son come and show them love, even die for them, maybe they would realize how much he loved them."

"So, this was *you?*" Noni looked at Ameno's face and saw a shadow of pain reflected in his eyes. "Were you *killed? How* are you alive *now?*"

"Yes. It's me." Ameno nodded. "They nailed me to that beam I carried and hung me up." He showed them the scars on his wrists and feet where they hammered in the nails, then he opened his robe to show a red gash-scar on his side, near his heart. "I did this for my father."

"*Wow!*" Beehart gasped. "I'm glad my father never asked me *to be killed for him!*"

"Well, but there's more to the story." Ameno stepped to the next window and pointed to the picture that showed people gazing up as a man rose up into the clouds. Their faces glowed as they reflected light radiating from the man's iridescent robe. His dark hair was shining, and his eyes were flashing light. "This is when I went up to join Abba and he gave me a gift that I can share with others who believe in me."

"What kind of gift?" Noni asked.

"Touch me!" Ameno encouraged.

Noni reached over to touch Ameno's arm, and his hand went right through it! His eyes shot wide open.

"See how my body isn't like yours," Ameno explained. "I have a 'spirit' body now. I can travel through space and walk through walls!"

"*Wha-a-a?*" Beehart's mouth dropped. "*How?*"

"Because my body isn't flesh and blood like yours. When I went to Abba, he gave me a new body made of what he is—spirit. It's kind of like light. I can speed up and travel fast, or slow down and look more like you!"

"So, *this* is the gift?" Beehart wondered. "Do *we* get a body like yours if we believe in you? Can we do what you can?"

"While you're living in this world, you can have this spirit-gift from me inside you, and it helps you do many of the amazing and wonderful things I can do. But you're still flesh and blood. You can still feel pain. And you can't walk through walls yet," Ameno smiled. "But, after you die, your body will be entirely made of spirit, and you can do everyhing I can."

"*Wow!*" Noni's eyes brightened. "I want a body like *yours!*"

"You will someday, if you believe in me and that Abba sent me," Ameno's face shone. "And the spirit part of your body will never die!"

"I *do* believe in you, Ameno!" Beehart exclaimed.

"*I do too!*" Noni sighed as he passed his hand through Ameno's robe to touch the visible scar near his heart.

In that moment, the fullness of morning light pierced through the panes of the large eye above the platform and caused rainbow patterns to dance around them across the floor. But something else delighted them even more. Brilliant red lights glowed from their chests.

Ameno laughed at their surprised faces, and then *he* exclaimed.

"Your new gifts are burning super-bright to let you know they are there!"

chapter fourteen

Power in the Flames

Noni and Beehart warmed their hands over a fire behind the share-too. They sat on a yellow and purple-striped wool rug that Ameno placed there for them. Bundled up in blankets to ward off the morning chill, they watched as Ameno, wrapped in his gray cloak, rotated a defeathered turntoo on a makeshift spit over the flames. The burning wood smelled good, and, for now, they were not concerned about enemies lurking in the shadows. Ameno assured them that no one could harm them while he was near.

When the roasting bird turned a golden brown, Ameno took a knife and cut off chunks of steaming meat and handed them each a piece. They sighed with pleasure at the first taste of the fire-roasted turntoo. As he ate, Noni watched the fire, wondering how the flames never seemed to diminish.

"Do you have power over fire?" he asked.

"Yes. And over other kinds of fire too," Ameno smiled broadly.

"What do you mean?" Beehart asked.

"Well, you saw the flame burning inside you last night." He pointed to their hearts.

They both nodded.

"Your flames grow brighter when you think good thoughts about me, interact with me, or share my words with others," he explained.

"Really?" Noni looked down at his glow.

"Yes, *really*. But you must be careful," he warned.

"Of what?" Beehart asked.

"Of the enemy," Ameno said.

Noni wondered what he meant by "the enemy." *Was he referring to the Surlies or the Zamzummim?*

"There definitely *are* bad people in the world," he said. "We've encountered a few of them. But you sound like there's only *one* enemy."

"I'm talking about the Dragon." Ameno stared straight at Noni. "You can't see him, but he uses fear to try to lessen your glow and take away the power your spirit gives you. He can never steal your spirit, but he'll try to convince you that it can't help you. He really wants to extinguish your flame by suppressing your spirit."

Noni remembered his dreams.

"I've seen a dragon in my dreams," he said. "But how do we recognize him in real life if we can't see him?"

"That's easy," Ameno explained. "When you see people being hateful, offensive, selfish, and evil, you know he is behind it. He's very crafty and devious! He deceives people into thinking that if they do what he tells them, they'll get what they want. But those who follow his lead always end up losing what's most important to them."

"How can we fight against him?" Beehart asked, glancing down at Truelight, lying next to him.

"He mostly tries to make you fearful." Ameno rotated the turntoo on the spit. "Because then you're weaker, and he can lure you into siding with him. When you're afraid, turn your thoughts to me. I'll always make things clear and show you how to deal with any situation. Remember that my powerful spirit is inside you. Listen for my voice in your heart. You'll be able to recognize it. Never allow the enemy to divert your attention away from me. He'll try to get you to focus on other things. He'll try to make you feel bad about yourself by using the unkind and thoughtless words or actions of others. Be wary of his ways. They're meant to block the light you shine to others.

"Don't focus on the darkness, or evil, in others," he continued. "This will only hinder your ability to be strong. If people reject you and what you can do for them, move away from them so their darkness doesn't overwhelm your ability to shine." He handed them each another tasty morsel of meat. "I need warriors like you to help me," he gazed into their eyes. "I need people who understand the fire inside them and how to use the flames of my words to overcome the enemy. You can be strong warriors for me if you rely on my gift to guide you and freely eat my manna."

They silently chewed on his words and the meat. Beehart stared up at the purpit vines that climbed over the peeling sharetoo walls. He thought about the thorny vine-like crown Ameno wore as he carried the beam on his back in the window scene. He frowned and pressed his lips together. Ameno read his thoughts.

"It was so people could know Abba."

"What?" Beehart asked, startled that he knew what he was thinking.

"The crown, the horrible death."

"It may have been, but I still don't understand how Abba could ask you to go through that. He *is* your father."

"You're right. He *is* my father, *and* he knew what the outcome would be." Ameno's eyes glistened. "Not only did he love me, *he loved you!* That's what you must understand. If it hadn't happened, I would not be sitting with you now, in a new body!"

"If he loves us so much, why does he still allow so much evil in the world?" Beehart pressed. "Why do bad people still control so many things?" He looked down at Truelight and fiddled with the sheath.

"Remember what I told you about people walking away from him?" Ameno watched Beehart's hand moving over the sword. "Even after he gave them so much and let them run things as they chose? Yet they decided to exclude him and run things their own way. That's when the evil came.

"He sent me to show them how goodness *can* come out of the evil and to bring as many as I can back to him. He wants them to know about a better way to live. Unfortunately, even after I came and gave my gift, people still get deceived by the Dragon, who wants them to keep doing evil so he can control them. All because he hates Abba.

"Once he was Abba's best friend, but he decided *he* wanted to be in charge," Ameno went on. "Because he turned away from my father and drew others with him, Abba had to throw him out of his world. He landed here. And now his goal is to steal, kill, and destroy the people in this world—the ones Abba created. But my death and new life changed all that, especially for those who believe in me and what I did."

Beehart looked over at Ameno, avoiding his eyes and trying not to get emotional.

"I have a hard time with how he asked you to suffer and die for him," he admitted. "I never really knew *my* father. I wish he hadn't died. I have a lot of questions for him. Did you ever feel like Abba wasn't there for you?"

"I understand how you feel, Beehart. When I hung there dying, I couldn't breathe. And I felt the same way…all alone. I even called out to Abba! But, in the end, I understood that it was up to me to take away the results of people's disregard for my father. I had to bear the evil in myself so good could come again." Ameno paused. "And, I knew how much Abba really loved me…and you.…

"Beehart, your father loved you more than words can say. He could never tell you, but some day he will."

A lump formed in Beehart's throat, choking back words he couldn't say, and Ameno reached over and hugged him. Noni watched and felt sad, thinking about his own father and how much he missed him. Ameno straightened up and looked at Noni, anticipating more questions.

"Is *my* father still alive? Or my mother? Do you know?" Noni's voice cracked.

"I know how much you want to know, Noni. But I can't tell you now." Ameno sighed. "Trust me that you won't be disappointed." He paused then looked at Beehart. "You had another question about the purpit vines."

"I…yes. I wondered about the purpit flowers. Why were so many things named after them?"

"The purpits *are* very important," Ameno explained. "The purple viny flowers have their own unique meaning. Some people call me 'The Very Vine' and say they stand for me."

"Why do they call you a vine?" Noni asked.

"Well, a vine can bear blossoms *and* fruit, if it's rooted in good soil."

"And you're rooted in your father, right?" Noni nodded.

"Absolutely! Since I listen to Abba and do what he tells me, I produce good things, like reaching people who were separated from him. When you're rooted in me, you bear beautiful blossoms too, like the purpits." He pointed at the vines.

"So, if we listen to you, we can help more people," Noni reflected. "Do the purpits stand for anything else?"

"Their purple color means royalty."

"Do you mean that if we believe in you, we're royal, like knights or people related to a king?" Beehart asked.

"Not only related! But real sons and daughters of *the* King!" Ameno's face shone.

"Abba's the king, right?" Noni asked.

"Yes, and *you* are princes like me, but you're also knights or warriors, because you fight against evil!

"So, the people who became Purpits must have been special too." Beehart's brow twisted in thought.

"That must be why the Surlies turned them into purpit flowers," Noni speculated then grew concerned. "Ameno, we have to help them *before they die!*"

"Well, that's why I came to you now. *Look!*" Ameno stood up, and his cloak slipped from his head and shoulders and fell to the ground, revealing a brilliant, fluorescent-blue robe underneath. Beneath the hood, he wore a colorful turban made of blue, purple, and red cloth. A gold plate in front read, *"Holy to the Lord."* Over the robe hung a golden breastplate attached to a vest with 12 colored stones in four rows of three. Like a rainbow, they represented every color, and they shone so brightly that their eyes had to adjust when they tried to look at them.

"Each of the gems has a specific meaning," Ameno pointed out. "They represent 12 tribes of people that were very special to Abba because their fathers loved and served him. Together, the gems show the characteristics of a perfect person. In ancient times, priests wore this breastplate as a reminder that one day Abba would bring this person to build a new city for them, where they could live together and be free from evil. I was that person. Abba asked me to build this new city with the help of others, who will reign with me as princes and princesses."

"Can we help you?" Noni asked.

"Yes. Absolutely."

"What can we do to help?" Noni persisted.

"Just follow my lead." He pulled two stones from their gold settings on the breastplate. He held one of the perfectly round stones out to Beehart. "This is a sapphire. It represents protection for those who love me. It also reminds you of the strength I give you." He carefully placed the brilliant bluish-purple stone in Beehart's right palm. Beehart stared down at the generous gift in his hand.

Then Ameno held out a sunshine-yellow stone to Noni.

"This is a topaz. It represents my love for you. It will remind you that I am always near." He placed the gem lovingly in Noni's hand. Noni squeezed the precious prize. "These stones will mean more to you later," he explained. "They represent the stones my father and I will use to build our new city."

Noni held the stone up to light that streamed between the tree branches. As he did, it caught a beam and flashed an intense streak of light so powerful that it almost blinded him. He quickly brought it down to eye level.

"You can see the potential power of the stones," Ameno laughed. "Especially when you hold them up to light. It's almost like fire that's latent until it's lit with a match. That's the kind of fire-power you both have inside you. The gems represent your ability."

"Will Ranni get a stone?" Beehart was thinking about his sister and all that she was missing. "Will you help us find her?"

Ameno stooped to pick up his cloak. He pulled it over his blue robe and breastplate before turning to walk back into the sharetoo.

"I will help you find her," he promised.

"Will you go with us?" Beehart wondered.

"No. But I'll lead you to her," Ameno smiled.

"Does she have any idea we're trying to find her?" Noni asked, remembering his vision of her in the fire.

"Yes," Ameno assured. "When I saw her, I told her you were coming. But, like you, she has many questions.

"Where is she?" Beehart asked.

"She's in a jail in Sur," Ameno answered. "But don't worry. I'll make sure you find your way to her. It'll become clearer as you go. Just follow the signs." He motioned to Beehart to come closer. "Reach into your tunic and pull out the chain around your neck."

He did as Ameno said.

"You see the gold key?"

Beehart nodded.

"When you were at the inn, you saw how it opened the chest and gave you what you needed for this journey," Ameno said.

"Yes. I wondered how my mother knew to give it to me," Beehart puzzled.

"Years ago, Bleamer's dad, Oni, handed it to me when I came to visit him, right before his death. He asked me to give it to your mother. She would know what it was for, he said. Later, when I visited her, I presented the key to her. She knew right away what it was. I told her that you would need it one day, Beehart, and to make sure you had it when she felt it was the right time. She knew that moment had come before she left to go on the last trip."

"I remember when she gave it to me." Beehart looked at the key, some emotion welling up in him.

"She's a very wise woman." Ameno beamed. "She knows *you* are becoming a wise man. See, you listened to her and kept it with you. We both knew you would."

"But how did she know it would open the chest at Bleamer's?" Beehart puzzled.

"Someday you'll understand."

They walked back into the sharetoo, where they sat on the platform steps together before leaving.

"You know, you are with each other for a reason," Ameno smiled. "Together, you're strong. But, remember, you must bend a little and give a lot to accomplish what's needed. The enemy will try to divide and separate you. His purpose is to weaken the power you have as a team. Think of the difference between a thread and a rope. A rope is stronger because it has so many strands." He paused. "I am sending you ahead of me to make a way," he glanced at them both. "I'll follow and bring more help. You'll find yourselves in some tricky situations, but don't be afraid. You'll always have what you need and end up where you belong. Trust me in this.

"But, never get distracted from your mission—to find Ranni." He stood up. "And, one more thing, I may not be physically with you all the time, but, because my spirit is inside you, you can pray to Abba in my name, and this brings power to your prayers."

Noni gazed up at his radiant eyes and detected some sadness. He felt that Ameno didn't want to leave them, and he looked down at his boots, trying to hide his own emotion as Beehart sighed.

Ameno extended his right hand to Noni, and the boy could feel his life-giving power, like electricity, rushing through him. Then Ameno did the same to Beehart.

Overcome with emotion, the boys hugged their friend. When they broke away, they could see tear stains on the front of his cloak. But they weren't theirs.

Then Ameno made a promise that they would never forget.

"I will always be near you—in your hearts."

chapter fifteen

Spies at the Spring

After Ameno left, the boys sat for a while behind the sharetoo and appreciated the warmth of the dwindling fire. They'd identified a good route to Sapwood, with Ameno's help. The "Crossing Clearus Creek" map showed a path that led from the sharetoo through a forested area to a hill overlooking the creek. Their only concern was what Bleamer had said—that the creek was heavily guarded by Surlies.

They packed up their food and filled their canteens with water from the rain barrel. Noni carefully placed *Ameno's Manna* in his canvas frontpack, under his tunic, and put the purple and yellow striped rug Ameno gave them in one of his bags, realizing that its colors were the same as their gifted stones. When they set out, Beehart found an eye symbol carved into the bark of a tree beside the wooded path. It was the same symbol as the one used on the maps to mark the best places and paths, and they knew they were on the right track. As they walked, they watched for more signs.

Trekking uphill to the north of the sharetoo, they reached a small clearing. Noni could barely see the small building through the trees below them. As he glanced back, sunlight bounced off the large window above the platform, which faced northeast, and created a beautiful rainbow that arched toward them. But it wasn't the rainbow that grabbed his attention.

"Oh my gosh!" he yelled to Beehart. *"Look!"* He pointed to the window as his friend turned around. Their mouths dropped open as they gazed at the stained-glass face. The eyes shot fiery flames toward them, and they both knew it was Ameno's way of reminding them that he was watching over them.

They stared until the vision faded, then they moved in the direction of a hill on the map. On the other side of it would be Clearus Spring and the creek. They followed an up and downhill path through woods that seemed to go on forever. The trail was well worn, so they thought it was once heavily trafficked, but they didn't see anyone now. The entered an overgrown area and fought against branches that swatted them in the face as they passed by. After a few hours, they found another eye carved in a tree by the path right before they reached a meadow surrounded by trees. A hill rose up on the far side, and they thought this might be the one they pursued, so they pushed through the tall grass until they found a mound of soft moss in the middle of the meadow. Hidden by the grass, they threw down blankets to rest and eat.

Noni's mouth watered as he took out the left-over roasted turntoo meat and some sweet moggies he'd saved. He took off the frontpack and pulled out *Ameno's Manna* so he could read a few verses after eating. He noticed that someone had placed a dried leaf in it, so he flipped to the marked page and saw an underlined message, *"He will guide them to the springs of the waters of life."*[8] He read the passage aloud to Beehart, who listened as he dug through his bags.

"I wonder if it has something to do with the spring?" Beehart looked up when he produced a canteen of water.

After eating, they both dozed off. Lying on sun-warmed blankets, surrounded by the fragrant smell of fresh grass, and absorbing the sun's light, they were oblivious to something moving in the woods. A persistent rustling sound stirred Beehart, who reached for Truelight. He shook Noni, who sat up and rubbed his eyes as Beehart nodded silently toward the trees.

"What is it?" Noni asked, alarmed but irritated by the interruption to his sleep.

"I heard something…over there," Beehart rasped and pointed toward the woods.

Noni listened intently for a few minutes but heard nothing. Fully awake now, he stood up stiffly, stretched his arms, and began throwing everything back in his bag then carefully placing *Ameno's Manna* inside the frontpack. Beehart followed suit, and they made their way through the tall grass to the hill. At the top, they were overwhelmed by the view on the other side.

Colorful orange and red rocks of a canyon stair-stepped down to a crystal-clear creek that sparkled like glittery gold. On the left side of the canyon, a spring shot water from a crevice in the rocks and created a waterfall that cascaded down into the creek. Unfortunately, the breathtaking canyon was surrounded on all sides by treacherous, steep cliffs. On the far side, one cliff bore the scar of a narrow path that wound up from the creek into a patch of trees at the top.

The creek bed at the bottom was covered with lush green moss dotted with white flowers. A wild grat drank from the creek, and its eyes darted up when Noni got too close to the edge and caused some loose rock to crumble under his feet. It sprinkled down the cliff and scared the grat away. Noni grabbed a scrawny tree branch on the ledge to regain his balance. He caught his breath and realized he'd frightened Saron, who broke free from his grip and backed away. Beehart caught hold of her rein before she retraced her steps down the hill.

As the boys enjoyed the view, the waterfall's mist dampened the dust-filled air and moistened their sunburned cheeks. Refreshed at first, they soon felt chilled as the sun ducked behind the cliffs. They pulled cloaks from their bags and scanned the rocks for a suitable path to the creek bed below. Pacing the ledge, they spotted a narrow, winding trail on this side of the canyon, and they quickly decided to try it when they heard voices reverberating from the woods on the other side of the meadow. Leading the grats, they slid down the path and were absorbed by the camouflaging rock layers.

The voices soon echoed down from the top of the hill above them, and they huddled with the grats under a rock outcropping. The animals sensed danger and stood very still. Beehart gripped Truelight at his side.

"I know I saw 'em," a voice bellowed down. "They were goin' 'cross the field."

Beehart gritted his teeth.

"It sounds like Ol' Belial," he whispered. This was the nickname he gave the sinister Surli at Bleamer's inn, because it meant "evil personified."

"I'd like to get my hands on 'em!" the voice continued, and the boys cringed.

"Yea, me too. I wanna squach 'em like a bug!" Another chuckled with a throaty grunt.

"I saw 'em at the inn," Belial said, confirming their fears.

The voices faded as the three Surlies moved away from the hilltop. But Noni and Beehart stayed put under the rock ledge, wondering if the men might go to the other side of the canyon. Noni's legs started to cramp from squatting so long, and he decided to move closer to the edge and look around. He thought he heard the voices again but saw no sign of them along the clifftops. He decided to look over at the creekbed, and he hung onto a tree that clung to the cliffside to avoid slipping again. There, at the bottom of the canyon, he spotted the three Surlies gathering sticks. Their black hair hung in strands around their faces, and two wore tunics made of grat hair. Belial's face was partly covered by a hooded cape. It was hard to make out their words but not their sinister laughter as they pulled bruni ale jugs from their bags.

As twilight colors streaked across the cliffs, the boys made the most of their crude accommodation, realizing they were stuck under the ledge for the night. They moved as far back as they could and tried to stay warm as a harsh wind whipped around the canyon in ear-splitting echoes and sprayed water toward them from the nearby waterfall. Lying on the cold, flat rocks under blankets, they could still feel the damp cold creeping into their bones. The raucous Surlies grew louder and more vulgar throughout the night and kept them constantly on edge. Noni tossed and turned, trying to get comfortable, while Beehart nervously clutched Truelight. Only the glowing moon, now brighter and waning gibbous, reminded them that they were safe, because it made them think of Ameno's eye always watching over them.

A gleam of sunlight finally peeked over the clifftops and painted the canyon walls with brilliant swatches of orange, yellow, and red. When Noni looked out from under his blanket, the colorful display cheered him, and he forgot for a moment how tired and sore he felt. His good mood was interrupted when he crawled out from under the ledge and looked down to see the Surlies snoring around a burned-out campfire. He knew the grats wouldn't last long without food or water, and their bleating would wake the Surlies, so he acted fast and woke Beehart.

"We're about thirty feet above the Surlies," he said, "and if we go now, while they're sleeping, we could make it to the waterfall. The trail goes under a rock ledge behind it, and we could hide there for a while, rest, and get fresh water, at least until they leave."

Beehart nodded and rubbed his bristly face. He was too tired to think, so he rose stiffly, crouching beneath the roof of the ledge, and loaded his gear onto Smithi. Noni mouthed a prayer to Ameno and led Saron as quietly as he could down the narrow path that led to the waterfall. Beehart and Saron followed, and the closer they got, the more their steps were muffled by the shooting water. But, as they approached, the gravel and rocks grew slippery from the spray, and Beehart slid on some rocks toward the outer edge of the slanting trail. He grabbed onto a nearby branch so he wouldn't fall down the cliff, but he accidentally jerked Smithi's head toward him as he slipped. The grat let out a desperate bleat that echoed down the canyon as Beehart groped his way back onto the middle of the trail. Then they both heard the Surlies stirring below, and they cringed.

"Wha's that!" Belial sat up and looked around through his squinty eye.

"Dunno!" another growled and groggily wiped his mouth off with his hand.

The boys froze in place as the Surlies scanned the cliffs. Smithi bleated again, and Belial pointed.

"Over there!" he yelled.

Two of the Surlies jumped up and thundered toward a trail that led up the side of the cliff. The boys watched as they raced toward them. Moving as fast as they could, they skidded over wet, loose stones to get to the waterfall, still a ways from them.

"Ameno, *please* help us!" they both breathed.

Belial bounded over rocks to get to them. Noni gasped as Beehart turned to face the approaching man. Bravely, the boy thrust out his sword as sweat poured down his forehead and he gritted his teeth. Belial cursed and lunged at him, trying to knock Truelight out of his hand. Just as he did, his foot slipped on the slimy rocks and, in seconds, he was screaming and falling down the cliffside. The other pursuing Surli watched open-mouthed as Belial landed in a bush near the bottom of the canyon. But he foolishly pressed on, and, following Belial's lead, ended up slipping and sliding and bumping down the cliffside, thudding to the bottom near his misleader. The two stalkers both lay there groaning.

The boys redoubled their efforts when the third Surli, ignoring the plight of his co-conspirators, decided to extend the pursuit and tore up the trail toward them. When he approached the slippery stones closer to them, he slowed down, and the boys took advantage of his momentary hesitation, quickly closing the distance to the waterfall. Noni could feel its powerful spray as he drew closer, and he pulled his hood over his head. As he dove through the spray and under the ledge behind the waterfall, he spotted a large opening at the back of an unexpected alcove, and he noticed an eye carved into the rock beside it.

He made a split-second decision, and, as Beehart entered with Smithi, he pointed to the eye. His friend nodded, and, almost soaked by the spray, they both entered the dark hole.

chapter sixteen

Cries in the Cave

The hole led into a cavernous cave. They hustled as fast as they could through dark passageways, stumbling over uneven ground. The farther they went, the darker it grew. They groped the slimy walls to find their way, ignoring their disgust. Their main concern was getting away from the Surli, whose voice echoed behind them. So, they rushed down the dank corridors, not knowing where they were going.

Besides the Surli's voice and footsteps, they could hear frightening sounds—the scurrying of tiny feet—around the walls, like thousands of creepy, crawly things scampering along beside them. The scuttling made the grats grow skittish, and they bleated shrilly. The boys tried to calm them, concerned about the Surli just a short distance behind them.

"I can hear ya! And I'll get ya both!" he yelled.

Noni and Saron came to a fork in the passage and veered right. Not hearing Smithi and Beehart behind them, Noni stopped and figured they'd gone the other way and would soon realize it. Not able to yell, he stood silently in the dark for it seemed like forever. Creeped out by what might be lurking around him, he felt Saron's soft muzzle and was comforted by her warm breath. Just then, Beehart stepped up behind him, and he almost jumped out of his skin.

"I'm sure glad you found us," he whispered after catching his breath.

They tiptoed forward as the Surli's voice boomed behind them. But Noni stopped suddenly, frozen by a bloodcurdling, deep-throated howl from farther down the corridor.

"Wha-a-a-t was *that*?" Beehart rasped hoarsely.

"I don't know." Noni's knees shook.

The grats whimpered.

"Sho-o-o-uld we ke-e-e-ep going?" Beehart stuttered.

"My gawd, *wha' was that*?" The Surli yelled behind them, and his stomping steps stopped suddenly then thudded away, echoing down the tunnel behind them.

The horrible howl came again, and the boys stood still, not knowing what to do.

"We have to keep moving," Noni finally said. "We can't stay here, and we can't go back. You know the Surli will be waiting for us at the entrance."

Groping the walls, they came to another fork, and Noni bore right again with Beehart close behind him. Then Saron let out a high-pitched bleat, and it alerted whatever lurked ahead.

"*Who's there?*" the creature roared.

Realizing it was a person, Noni bravely yelled back.

"Ju-u-ust two Gomies," his wavering voice echoed through the dark passageway.

"What kind of Gomies?" the person shouted.

"Inodian Gomies," Noni ventured.

"Where in Inod?" he boomed back.

"Gratville," Beehart replied.

"*Come this way!*" he commanded.

Noni clutched Saron's reins and shuffled ahead. As he did, he muttered a plea to Ameno for help. Beehart and Smithi followed, both shaking. Suddenly, a soft red glow reflected from the cave wall directly in front of them, almost like a guiding night-light. Noni was puzzled by it at first then chuckled when he realized it was a reflection of his own heart-glow.

"What's so funny?" Beehart rasped.

"I'll tell you later," Noni whispered.

They entered an alcove dimly-lit by smoldering coals that glimmered from a mound of ashes in the middle of the small "room." A large, burly man sat on a black rug with his back against one wall. Cloaked with rags, he barely resembled a human being. Thickly matted gray hair hung past his shoulders, and a bristly silver beard swirled down to his bare chest. Two rusty metal handcuffs dangled from chains hammered between the rocks behind him, and sticks were piled in another corner. Crude drawings decorated the soot-covered walls. Beehart noticed a picture of what looked like a cabin surrounded by trees.

"*Who are you?*" the man bellowed.

"Our names are Noni and Beehart," Noni answered, startled by his roaring voice. But then he saw the man's heart glowing. "*Why* do you roar like that?" he asked, more bravely now.

"*Why do ya care?*" the man demanded.

"How long have you been here?" Noni realized the man's eyes peered sightlessly in the semi-dark.

"*Why?* he thundered. "Come closer!"

Unafraid, Noni let go of Saron's reins and stepped toward the man.

"*What* are you doing?" Beehart gasped.

"I don't know. I just think it's ok," Noni whispered.

"What're ya saying there?" The man was suspicious.

Beehart was alarmed when Noni extended his hand, and the hideous man grabbed his arm and pulled him closer, making Noni yell out with fear.

"I won't hurt you!" the man growled.

Noni's body stiffened as the man blindly touched his face and hair.

"Where did ya say you were from?"

"Gratville," Beehart spoke up, groping for Truelight.

"I once knew someone from Gratville," the man's voice softened. "His name was Stade."

"Stade was my father!" Noni forgot his fear and relaxed a little.

"Your father, eh? Yeah, sure. Your face does seem similar to his," the man loosened his grip on the boy as his fingers felt his face.

"How did you know him?" Noni asked.

"I don't want to say jus' yet," he answered mysteriously.

"Where are *you* from?" Beehart boldly asked.

"Once lived in Mussford," he said.

"How did you end up here?" Noni ventured.

"Surlies captured me." He let out a big sigh. "They blindfolded and dragged me here. They kept me bound and chained and tried ta kill me. But I outlasted them. Sometimes I still hear 'em outside, so I stay hidden."

"What'd they want from you?" Beehart asked.

"That's a long story. One for another day."

"How'd they get you?" Beehart persisted.

"I was tendin' my graynights in the barn, and they came outta nowhere and grabbed and gagged me. It happened so fast I couldn't even yell for help."

"We met a man on our way here. He had graynights," Beehart spoke up, remembering his meaningful time in Mussford.

"What was his name," the man asked.

"Mosi," Beehart said softly, recalling the time with their new friend and his graynight.

The man paused and sighed.

"That's my son." His vacant voice begged to emit emotion as his sightless eyes teared up and shone in the dim light of the dying fire.

"Mosi is *your son?*" Beehart moved closer.

"You must be *Leopol!*" Noni burst out.

At the mention of his name, the man extended his arms like he was reaching for a long-lost friend. He opened his mouth and let out a disturbing moan. Then he drew his arms back, wrapped them around himself, and rocked back and forth. His blind eyes watered and created cleansing troughs down his cheeks, cutting through layers of dirt. Then suspicion seeped in through his overwhelming grief.

"But how can I be sure you're good guys?" he said with fear in his face. "This could be another trap."

The boys sat quietly and wondered how they could prove to him that Mosi was their friend and their intentions were good. Suddenly, Noni thought of something and he spoke up.

> *"In the night, when the dragon roars,*
> *Protect me, Ameno, with your sword.*
> *Help me trust in you alone,*
> *Here within my little home."*

Leopol's breath hitched. Then, he took a deep breath and finished the poem,

> *"On this side of Adamant's shore,*
> *Visit often, we implore.*
> *Remind us of your presence sure.*
> *Give us your strength to endure."*

He sighed and melted before their eyes.

"Do you know the Purpit Puzzle then?"

"*Yes!*" they said. "*We do!*"

Together, they recited,

"Once I heard tales of a wanderer,
Full of great wisdom and yen,
Marking a passage of distance,
Speaking of this time and then."
Relating a story of meaning,
Telling a tale of truth,
Revealing a new way resembling
A meadow of flowers forsooth."

"*Well done*, my Gomies!" he beamed, his face almost bursting. "*Well done!*" Then, "Please tell me, how is my son? Is he well? How'd ya meet him?"

"It all started when my sister disappeared," Beehart started. "Someone took her away, and we're trying to find her."

Noni then told him about the Purpits and how they met Mosi.

"The shoonums scared the heck out of us," Noni laughed. "But they grew on us. Mosi showed us the cabin and the pictures of you on the wall."

Leopol's eyes clouded.

"I miss him so much! I know he thinks I'm dead. I really wish I could see him again."

Beehart pulled Truelight out of its sheath and held it out to Leopol so he could touch the blade and hilt.

"This was Mosi's gift to me," he sighed.

Leopol took and held it gently like he was cradling a baby. Running his fingers over the blade, he read the inscription, *"The right hand of the Lord does valiantly and achieves strength!*"[4] Then he smiled proudly. "This was my father's sword."

"We heard about his exploits." Noni took off the frontpack and reached inside. "Mosi also gave me this." He handed *Ameno's Manna* to Leopol.

"This brings back so many memories." He breathed in the musty scent of the pages. "My father, Sagius, gave it to me before he died. Ameno's words helped me through the toughest times, 'specially when my wife died."

"Sounds like it means a lot to you," Noni reflected, looking down sadly at the precious book in Leopol's hand. "You should keep it. I didn't know it was a gift from your father."

"No. *No.* I want you to keep it," Leopol insisted. "You'll need it in your quest."

Noni breathed a sigh of relief.

After settling the grats down in a corner with blankets, food, and water, the boys listened to Leopol's stories far into the night. They had no idea what time it was—when the sun set or when the moon emerged, and Noni missed seeing its growing face. They shared their food as he talked about the cave drawings. He'd created them with chalky bits of rock and coal from the fire to pass the lonely hours before he went blind, he said. And, as the boys asked about each picture, he went into detail about the scenes from the Surli War and the colorful history of Inod and Sur as described to him by his father.

Bedding down close to the embers, Beehart begged one more question.

"Why do you think the Surlies captured you?"

"They thought I knew the whereabouts of a woman from my area, someone called Adamantine."

"We heard about her from Mosi," Beehart said.

"I never knew what happened to her," Leopol continued. "When she left Mussford, I lost track of her. So, I couldn't help 'em. But they didn't believe me."

"Looks like they tried real hard to hurt you," Noni gazed at the cuffs and chains on the wall. "Did they torture you while they held you hostage?"

"Yep. They did." Leopol slumped against the wall. "They kept me blindfolded and chained for a long time. Sometimes they'd hit me with clubs 'til I passed out. Their blows to my face made me lose my sight. When they couldn't get what they wanted from me, they just left me here. They took off the cuffs when I went blind. They knew I wouldn't go far. When they stopped bringing me food to keep me alive, so they could get more information from me, I made my way to the entrance. I listened for the waterfall and felt my way there. But I knew there were steep cliffs on the other side. I could hear the sounds echoing from below, and I knew the way down would be treacherous. I wasn't confident enough to make that steep descent without sight, and I did not want to be recaptured and tortured again.

"But, every few days, someone would leave food, and sometimes sticks for a fire, in the alcove behind the waterfall. Once, the person left me this rug." He pointed to the black wool rug he sat on, and Noni wondered about the significance of its color—if it meant something— like the rug Ameno had given them.

"So, you never saw the person who brought you these things?" Beehart asked.

"No. I never saw him, though I've long suspected who he was."

"Hmmm." Noni thought about Ameno. Still wondering about Leopol's captors, he asked, "Why do *you* think they want to find Adamantine?"

"Because of one of her children."

"What do you know about her children?" Beehart stared intently at Leopol.

"They believe one of them will help the Inodians break down the barriers between Inod and Sur once and for all—a savior of sorts—and they want ta prevent this person from destroying the control they have over the lands. Rumor has it they call this person the 'Reignbreaker.'"

"Do you think the stories are true?" Beehart pressed, thinking about what the Purpits had said about a "Reignbreaker."

"Yes. I do," Leopol answered matter-of-factly.

"Do you know if Adamantine had this child—the one they're after?" Noni asked.

"I heard she had two while in Mussford and more in Gratville. I never saw any o' them, but I heard about them from Ailis b'fore she died. She said they had beautiful blue-green eyes, like hers and Adamantine's."

Noni drew in a long breath as he glanced at Beehart, whose teal eyes were fastened on Leopol's face, and he held his breath thinking about Ameno's eyes, the eye in the sky, and all the enigmatic eye symbols they'd seen along the way.

"Hmmm," he finally released his pent-up breath.

chapter seventeen

Ada's Alias

Noni couldn't sleep. Wrapped up like a log in his blanket, he rolled from side to side all night on the cold stone floor and kept inching closer and closer to the smoldering coals. It was difficult for him to shake the shivers. His clothes were still damp from dodging the waterfall, and the cave's clamminess didn't help. Even the now-dying fire couldn't get rid of the moldy smell.

Beehart had no problem with being sleepless. He snored loudly from the other side of the room, and Leopol's head bobbed soundly as he slumped against the wall.

Noni's mind wouldn't shut off as he thought about Leopol's words. *Was Adamantine who he thought she was? And who was this Reignbreaker?* Beehart stirred when he heard Noni muttering, and he sat up.

"For grat's sake, Noni! *What's your problem, dude?*"

"I just keep thinking about Adamantine and this Reignbreaker."

"Yea. I wonder about them too. But, geez! Can we get some sleep and talk about it in the morning?"

Leopol grumbled and yawned.

"What's goin' on, fellas? Somethin' botherin' ya?" He rubbed his eyes and groped toward what was left of the fire. He held his hands over the ashes. They emitted a little warmth, but not much. So, he crawled to the corner and felt around for more sticks, then he tossed them onto the coals. After a few minutes, a small flame emerged. The boys drew closer to it.

"Can you tell us more about this Adamantine person?" Noni asked.

"Sure," Leopol affirmed as he shook his head to come fully awake. "Uh…I knew her from the time she was a baby and into her late teens, when she had long blond hair and Ailis's eyes."

"What else do you remember about her?" Beehart bent over to push at the fire with a stick after adding even more stick-fuel to enlarge the flame.

"Well, she had a dimple on her cheek and a funny sense of humor. She had a contagious laugh, and she loved to sing. One of her favorite songs was one she learned from me." He chuckled.

"What was the song?" Beehart sat up.

"Well, every summer she'd come trottin' over to our cabin with a basket and ask if she could pick moggies from the bushes near our barn. I'd stop workin' long enough to get Mosi, and we'd all go moggie pickin' together. The song went like this…

"Moggie picking is so much fun.
Filling our baskets one by one.
Twiddle dee and twiddle dum.
Twiddle dee and twiddle dum."

The boys looked at each other as he sang the song they'd grown up hearing Ranni sing, and their hearts pounded. In the dim light, Noni thought he saw tears in Beehart's eyes as he poked fiercely at the fire.

"We know who Adamantine is!" Beehart burst out. "We know where she lived and who two of her children are."

"What? How do you know?" Leopol's eyes grew wide.

"I know because *she* was *my mother!*" Beehart's feelings spilled out through his voice.

"Your *mother?*" Leopol's face screwed up.

"Yes. Everyone called her Ada. I think that's short for Adamantine." Beehart stood up and walked over to the sticks in the corner. He kicked them, and they scattered from their neat pile.

"Where is she now, son?" Leopol grimaced.

"Don't know…." Beehart's voice faded.

"We're hoping we can figure out what happened to her and my parents too while we search for Ranni," Noni explained. "They disappeared more than a year ago. They were on a trip to visit friends on northern Inod. We don't know what happened to them. No one does."

"My mother never told me where she was from or anything about her past," Beehart said, emotion in his voice. "I just knew she came from somewhere in Inod and met my dad in Gratville."

"Come here, Beehart." Leopol reached out to the boy. When Beehart approached, he touched his curly hair with his coarse hand.

"What color's your hair, son?" he asked.

"Red."

"Hmmm." Leopol's hand brushed across Beehart's bristly cheeks, and his face flushed a deep red that made the whites of his sightless eyes stand out even more. "Do you have her eyes?"

"Yes," Noni answered. "He *does.*"

"I wonder if *you* are the Reignbreaker, the one they've been looking for!" Leopol held Beehart's forearm. "That would explain a lot!"

"How-w-w would I know?" Beehart stammered, recalling Belial's death stare at the inn. Then his words came fast. "Do you think the Surlies are after *me?*"

"Ranni's capture may be a plot to lure *you* in," Leopol surmised. "That's what I'm thinkin'."

Beehart sighed and sank into the corner near the sticks. Noni thought about Ada's mysterious past, the possible connection with Ranni's disappearance, and why they were being followed. As he lay on the floor, his fears were magnified by shadows on the walls created by the fire, and his eyes darted to the warlike graphics. They suddenly came to life, and he shuddered as he watched men dancing and waving clubs. Graynights pranced and snorted, and their riders let out war whoops. People clashed and died before his eyes. Exhausted by his imaginings, he closed his eyes and curled up on the rug Ameno gave them.

It was still dark when Noni reopened his eyes. He knew it must be morning, because his stomach growled. Leopol came in, carrying a pot of water from the waterfall. He set it down near the dwindling fire and heard Noni rustling.

"Voices echoed up from the creek," he said. "I heard a Surli yelling about you two. He said he followed you into the cave."

"Yeah," Noni murmured, rubbing his eyes. "They almost got us on the way here, but two of them slipped and fell off the cliff. The last one followed us into the cave but got freaked out when he heard your howling!"

"Apparently, they're still hanging around and anxious to get a hold of you! They're talking about searching for you in the cave." While Leopol related the conversation, Beehart sat up and stared at him.

"I knew they'd come back and look for us," he said. "I wonder how much time we have."

"Not much," Leopol said.

As they packed, Leopol told them he knew another way out of the cave—a secret exit. They agreed to follow him as he groped his way down dark tunnels, some of them very narrow and low. Though he was blind, his mind was sharp, and his memory was good. He had spent years exploring these obscure alleyways, so he could easily escape if he needed to. The boys struggled to keep up with him, because he could find his way without light by feeling the walls.

Through multiple tunnels, it seemed like forever before they finally saw some rays of light ahead. They entered a large, cavernous room with an opening at the top, high above the floor. A narrow ledge wound up one side to the opening.

"It's the Dragon's own den!" Noni exclaimed as he looked around at the stalagmites that jutted up from the floor like crystalline nails and the huge, sinister-looking stalactites that hung like thrusting swords from the high ceiling.

They followed Leopol as he felt his way around the sharp obstacles to the ledge. Noni clenched his teeth as he led Saron up the treacherously narrow ledge. It was hard for him not to look down at the large needle-like icicles that pointed up at him. Leopol managed the climb without any fear of falling, in spite of his blindness, and slid easily along the cave walls, using his feet to position himself.

He reminds me of the mountain grats, Noni thought as he watched the man. He remembered his mother's stories about these animals that used their flexible hooves to climb along the rocky slopes of the Initian Mountains that rose prominently across the land of Sur, in the middle of Init Isle, and down into western Inod. They could jump from cliff to cliff, and this fascinated Noni.

"With practice and confidence in your own ability, you can survive and thrive like the mountain grats," she would say.

The boys followed Leopol's lead by placing their feet where he placed his. The biggest challenge was leading the grats, who had to manage with four legs instead of two. About halfway up the ledge, they heard voices reverberating from the hole at the top. Leopol turned toward them and put his finger to his lips. As the voices grew louder, they leaned into the wall.

Suddenly Smithi's hoof slipped, and he bleated. Beehart let out a yelp, and Noni gasped. Their sounds echoed upward. Paralyzed, with their backs against the wall, they held their breath. The outside voices were suddenly silent, and it grew eerily quiet. The cavern felt like a tomb, and they could hear water dripping off the melting stalactites and plopping into a growing pool below.

Then the boys heard a familiar voice.

"Should we go in?" Belial's face peered through the opening. Light streaming behind him created a gigantic looming shadow on one wall. "All I c'n see are sharp things sticking up like huge knives at the bottom, and there doesn' seem to be a way to get down there."

"I ain't goin' down there!" another Surli sneered. "Le's try the other side by the waterfall."

Leopol stood still until he knew they'd gone, then he motioned for the boys to continue. He waited on a ledge at the top, and, when they got closer, he motioned for them to look out and see if the way was clear. Noni hoisted himself onto some rocks. Saron jumped up behind him, and they stepped outside the cave. He saw no sign of the Surlies, but he did see a path from the hill down to the creek and the other leading from the creek to the trees at the top of the cliffs on the other side. He stepped back inside to give them the report.

"Go quickly!" Leopol said, following Noni and Beehart and the grats outside. "While they're wandering around on the other side."

"But we want you to go with us!" Beehart exclaimed.

"*No!* I'd hold you up. We'd all be killed!" Leopol insisted.

"If you stay, you'll get caught. And who knows what'll happen to you!" Beehart grew emotional.

"*No.* I have hiding places in the cave. I can take care of myself. It's important that you find Ranni. Besides, I know you'll come back for me." Leopol's face expressed determination.

"Shouldn't we ask Abba for help before we go?" Noni asked.

"Yes. Good idea." Leopol motioned for them to come closer. He grabbed their hands and bent his head. "Abba, guide and protect Noni and Beehart on their journey."

"And take care of Leopol," Beehart added.

"Call me Leo, *please!*" Leopol said, lifting his gray head with a smile then bowing it again.

"Abba, use Leo as a secret weapon against the enemy," Noni added, "and heal his eyes. In Ameno's name, we ask."

"*Amen!*" they said together.

chapter eighteen

The Curious Crosses

Noni hugged Leo before leading the way down the path to the creek. He was so relieved to be out of the suffocating cave and in the sunlight again that he forgot for a moment the danger of being spotted by the Surlies. He glanced around the empty canyon, sighed with relief, and pressed forward. But he had other feelings when he looked up toward the camouflaged cave entrance, and he saw Leo barely visible behind bushes at the top of the hill.

He knew Leo was listening to hear if they were safe, and his heart ached that they were abandoning him. He was reminded of his father, and he thought about how much he missed Stade. His heart was severely pierced, but not as much as Beehart's, he later realized.

As they walked, his friend contemplated all the unanswered questions this visit stirred up. Many of them swirled around in his mind, like wind that whipped up whatever was in its path until it became a cyclone. *Why hadn't his mother told him about her past or her parents? Did she have other children, and, if so, what happened to them? Was he the Reignbreaker these evil monsters were trying to find? If he was, what would they do to him if they found him?*

Beehart tried to contain his feelings of anger, fear, abandonment, guilt, and rejection, as the emotions exploded like fireworks inside him. Noni pushed ahead, consumed by his own thoughts and oblivious to his friend's delirium. They reached the creek and quickly filled their canteens with fresh water. As Noni bent over the bubbling creek, he glimpsed something carved on a tree by the bank and immediately recognized the carved eye. He motioned to Beehart to come look. Then he saw something else.

Below the familiar symbol were three carved crosses. He ran his finger over them, feeling the scars in the tree. His foot accidentally kicked a rolled-up piece of bark on the ground, and he bent to pick it up. It looked like a scroll, and he unrolled it carefully. Faded words were scrawled on it with a charred stick, and he could barely make them out. "*He will guide them to the springs of the water of life.*"[8] Forgetting their urgency for a moment, Noni showed the scroll to Beehart, and he wondered, *Who wrote it and why?* He wrapped it in a cloth and placed it carefully in one of the bags on Saron's back.

It was oddly quiet. Feeling like the Surlies could reappear at any moment, they hurried to the path leading out of the canyon. A familiar eye reassured them from a tree at the base of the trail, which twisted up the cliff. Though it was not as treacherous as the trail *to* the waterfall, they discovered other obstacles. Overgrown trees, shrubs, and bushes pressed in on either side, making it almost impossible to climb through. They shoved, whacked, kicked, and moaned, but still the branches hit them in the face, on the side, or at the back of their necks.

As they huffed and puffed and pushed their way to the top of the cliff, they realized they were mostly hidden by trees, and they started to feel more protected from the Surlies' view. Noni looked for a flat area, where they could rest and eat. It was quiet all the way up, but eerily so, like the calm before the storm. *Where are the Surlies?* Noni wondered. They were warned that the area was heavily guarded, but, so far, they'd only encountered the three. Their worst enemy all morning had been the overgrown plants. Exhausted and covered with welts on their arms and necks from the snapping branches, they found a large, flat rock near the clifftop, and they spread out blankets. The surrounding trees provided soothing shade and seclusion, and they opened their bags to get out some food, along with their canteens filled with the refreshing creek water. After eating, they dozed off, feeling overcome by the climb and the heat.

Disturbing sounds startled Noni awake. He sat up and poked Beehart, who grabbed Truelight beside him. They peered through the trees and down to the creek to see what was causing the commotion. They were startled to see Leo on his knees, with his wrists tied together in front of him, being smacked by Belial. Beehart's lips twisted, and his exploding emotions resurfaced, as he began to rage, especially when he saw the Surli kick his friend, and he heard Leo cry out. His friend's moans echoed up the canyon and reminded Beehart of the near-death howls of a snared animal.

Another Surli yelled and spit at Leo, whose head hung down as he kneeled before his captors. Belial dragged him across the sharp rocks toward the creek. Though he was a large man, Leo did not defend himself. Beehart clenched a fist, threw down his canteen, and pulled Truelight out if its sheath. He was ready to go.

"Stop!" Noni grabbed his arm. "I want to help him too, but *we can't!*"
Beehart jerked his arm back, still clutching the sword.
"If we don't go down, *they'll kill him!*"
"My heart says *'Don't go!'* And I *have to* listen to the voice in my heart. *That's what Ameno said!*" Noni stepped back when he saw Beehart's hand nervously shaking the sword back and forth.
"Well, *my* heart says *to go*, and *I have to listen to my heart!*" Beehart turned away from his friend and faced the path, while tightly clutching the death-weapon.

"It's *not* your heart talking, it's *your emotions! Can't you tell the dif- ference, dude?"* Noni lunged for Beehart's tunic and grabbed the back of it. He held on as Beehart struggled to move ahead. The tunic tore, and Beehart reared around and swung at Noni with the sword. Danger- ously near the cliff's edge, Noni threw himself at Beehart, avoiding the weapon-bearing arm, and pushed him down. Truelight clattered to the ground. They pitched around in the dirt with their fists swinging and pummeled each other's faces and chests. Noni finally rolled over onto his back and raised his arms up, like he was surrendering. His lip and nose were bleeding, and his eye was swelling up. More of a practiced warrior, Beehart stood up, quite unscathed, and kicked Noni in the side.

"I *know* how you feel," Noni groaned as he turned over and got up stiffly. Undeterred, he was insistent. "But we *have* to keep going."

"What about *saving the life of a friend?*" Beehart spat out angrily as he spun around to pick up his smashed canteen. He hoisted it up, ready to throw it down again, but he stopped mid-swing and cursed.

Noni, trying to ignore his friend's emotional outburst, breathed a prayer and tried to pull himself together. He loaded his grat and moved in slow motion toward the path. After a few steps, he turned to see if Beehart was following him. He wasn't. He was still standing at the site, gazing down at the creek through the trees, his hands hanging limply at his sides. Noni waited as his friend slowly hurled a bag over this grat's back and secured Truelight to his side.

"Ameno will take care of him," Noni said under his breath, assur- ing himself.

Muttering, Beehart lagged behind Noni as disturbing sounds con- tinued from below. They both cringed with each echoed outburst, and Beehart's face and neck burned bright red. In a clearing, they glanced down to see Leo on his knees and Belial standing over him, flailing his arms furiously. Noni's heart hurt for his friend, and he wondered, *Did I turn my back on him? Am I doing the right thing?* Then he recalled

Ameno's words before they left, and he realized this might be the most courageous thing he'd ever done. *"When you're afraid, turn your thoughts to me. I'll always make things clear and show you how to deal with any situation. Remember that my powerful spirit is inside you. Listen for my voice in your heart. You'll be able to recognize it."*

Noni felt sure the voice inside him had told him to keep moving and was reassuring him that Leo would be all right. He thought about how Ameno's suffering and death had somehow brought good. Maybe Leo's suffering would bring some good too. He turned to look at Beehart. As he did, his friend glanced up and met his eyes with his lips were pressed together. He maintained eye contact, which gave Noni some hope, and he remembered Ameno's words about bending a little.

"Sorry for the scuffle," Noni spoke softly but loud enough for Beehart to hear. "I just felt like we needed to keep going and that Leo would want us to. I may be wrong 'cause I'm as unsure as you are about what might happen to him, but I *do* believe what Ameno told us—that he'd take care of us—and I think he'll take care of Leo too." His voice faded as he spoke, and he heard Beehart mumble something behind him.

As they emerged from trees at the summit of the hill, they could hear nothing. The Surlies and Leo were gone now. Noni glanced down at the empty creekbed then shaded his eyes from the setting sun on their left as he turned his head to look out over the other side of the hill. The treetops on the other side of a deep valley shimmered like gold in the sun's lingering rays. A town sat comfortably near the bottom, a few miles away, with houses lining lanes that looped like yarn around the edges of a slope. Smoke rose from stone chimneys, and Noni imagined sitting by Mosi's fire with him again. He wondered if this was Sapwood, and he pulled out the "Friendly Forest Paths" map to see where they were. "Humbert's Home" was marked as a good place to stay in the area. He wondered if they could find the place before dusk and if the owner would welcome them. He spotted an eye mark on a tree next to an adjoining downhill path, and he made his way toward it. Beehart followed.

They felt a sudden chill as they entered woods along the trail. A heavy, stress-induced weariness hung over them like a shadow, but they continued to descend with legs and hearts that ached, wanting to get to Humbert's before dark. Noni felt an unwelcome and growing sense of dread, especially when he heard screeches echoing through the trees. He screamed when a large, winged creature soared toward him, squawking loudly. It lunged and thrust its sword-like beak at him, and he jumped behind a tree as the hideous bird drew its long legs up and flew away. He shuddered when he saw its sharp curled talons. These would have cut him to pieces if the creature's beak hadn't killed him first. He shivered as it dove several times then swooped up to a high tree, where it wrapped its treacherous talons around a branch and peered at him hungrily through beady evil eyes. A plumed black-feather crest rose from its gray head, and a black-feather "cape" extended from the bottom of its long gray neck over its back, partly covering its wings.

Noni had heard whispers in Gratville about wicked birds to the north on Init Isle. They called them *tinshemets*, and they were said to attack and kill people, musses, sapies, and grats, then feed on their dead bodies. Warding them off was nearly impossible, it was said, because they only came out at dusk or nighttime and attacked lone and vulnerable travelers.

Suddenly the bird spread its enormous wings and let out a bone-chilling screech. Beehart responded by growling loudly, like a wild animal, to scare it away. Instead of frightening the bird, who squawked and coolly flew away to look for easier prey, he terrorized the skittish grats, and they both reared up, almost throwing off the bags on their backs. Beehart tried to calm Smithi by holding onto his lead; Noni had a hard time controlling Saron.

They watched warily for more unusual appearances. Noni noticed that the smallets here were different from the harmless little brown ones that scampered around the trees at home. He saw hollows in the trees, where these larger gray creatures, similar with bushy tails and small pointed ears, peered out at them suspiciously. Unlike the smallets at home, they chattered like they were whispering secrets about the boys. This sinister "gossiping" disarmed Noni, who wondered, *Can they understand us?* Despite his sore legs, he moved quickly down the path, not wanting to bed down here for the night, where they'd be surrounded by these quirky creatures.

Beehart suddenly yelled and pointed, and Noni jumped. A faint light glowed through the trees ahead. It came from a cabin window. The path to it crossed a small wooden bridge over a creek and led through a garden of flowers, straight to the cabin's crimson door. Green shutters fanned out from windows on either side, and candlelight flickered from inside the diamond-shaped windowpanes. As they got closer, they saw that the eave above the door was decorated with painted flowers, and they smelled a wonderful woody fragrance from smoke that drifted out of the cabin's chimney.

The place *seemed* inviting, but the boys still approached cautiously. Suddenly, the front door flew open, and a short plump man stepped out. Noni jumped back and Beehart reached for Truelight. The grats bleated loudly.

"*Welcome! Welcome!*" the little man shouted cheerfully. "*I've been expecting you!*"

They stopped, stunned.

"How do you know who we are?" Noni blurted out.

"Oh, I know *all about* you!" The man's balding head, thick beard, and round belly all bounced up and down as he chuckled. His leather-vest buttons looked like they might pop off. They could see a glimmer from under his red plaid shirt. "I knew you were on your way."

"*How* did you know?" Beehart was flabbergasted.

"Wouldn't you like to know!" He chortled and motioned toward the door. *"Come in.* Meet the missus! Have some food! By the way, my name is Humbert, but folks call me Humbi!" He held out his hand and shook their hands vigorously as the boys stepped up and tied the grats to posts near the door.

"We know who *you* are too," Beehart smirked.

"Well, *how* did *you* know?" Humbi grinned through an even row of sparkling white teeth.

"*Maybe* the same way you knew who *we* were!" Noni exclaimed and laughed.

chapter nineteen

Humbling History

Humbi's wife, Honi, stepped forward as the boys entered the cabin. Short and plump herself, she bubbled like Humbi. Wearing a red turtleneck with a plaid vest and denim skirt, she walked about in huge, fluffy purple slippers and balanced rimless spectacles on the tip of her nose. The soft gray curls around her face made her look like a kind grandmother. Her brown eyes crinkled as she smiled at Noni and Beehart, and they felt very much at home with her. She reminded them of Grooma.

After Humbi brought in the boys' bags and watered and fed their grats, he ushered them to a table in the middle of the living room. As soon as they were seated, Honi set out plates of steaming hot griffoons, tatas, bettas, and grilled muss meat. The boys' stomachs growled, but they waited patiently as their hosts bowed their heads to pray.

"Abba, you're so gracious," Humbi began. "You're so kind and generous. *So* loving. Thanks for all you've given us. And for sending us these new friends. In Ameno's name we pray. *Amen.*"

"*Amen,*" the boys added, with eyes wide open and forks poised. Finally, they all dug in. Between bites, Noni and Beehart tried to answer

Honi's questions: "Where do you come from? Why are you here?" After they'd explained as much as they could about their background and adventures, their hosts were silent for a few minutes. This gave the boys time to shovel down enough food and still relish every bite. They were grateful when Honi brought in more platters, since the last real meal they'd had was with Bleamer, and it seemed like an eternity ago. To top off the meal, she served moggie pie with a golden-brown, crunchy crust, covered with sweet grat cream.

After dinner, Humbi ushered them to stuffed chairs near a warm firelit hearth in his tiny den next to the living room. Glancing around, they guessed there were only two other rooms in the cabin besides the den and living room: an attached kitchen and a bedroom. They wondered where they'd sleep, since there was no sofa in the living room or den. Noni saw a ladder leading up to a loft overlooking the den, and he wondered if they'd sleep up there. He decided not to worry about it and sleepily enjoyed the warm fire.

A few pictures of people and places hung on the walls of "Humble Haven," the name they gave to their cabin. They had no children and considered almost everyone part of their family. Noni and Beehart were immediately adopted by them.

Though they were tired, the boys wanted to listen to their hosts' stories, including some they'd never heard about their homeland, Inod. It all started with a question posed by Noni.

"We always heard terrible things about the Sapians—stories about how unfriendly they are to outsiders and how strangers are unwelcome in Sapwood. Gratians call them 'Saps' for short. But, after meeting you, I don't understand. Why do Sapians have such a bad reputation?"

Humbi pulled a pipe from his pocket and knocked its bowl against a tray on the side table to free it of ashes. He then stuffed fragrant dried leaves into the bowl until it was overflowing. With a match, he lit the leaves and put the stem end up to his lips. He puffed a few times and finally blew a large smoke-ring that drifted up. Noni watched and thought of Mosi.

"Don't you wonder how these stories get started?" Humbi's eyes crinkled.

"Sure do." Noni nodded.

"I'll tell you." Humbi took another puff. "After the Surli War, the people of Sur were weak. Their homes and businesses were destroyed. Because they were desperate and had no help from the Inodians, because of the way they'd treated them, they made alliances with the evil leaders from the north. King Zoar of Zamzum took advantage of their weakness and gained total control of Sur. But his real goal has always been to take over Inod. This is a prize to him, because we've been successful in managing what we have.

"Think about how the Mussians are good at raising musses, the Sapians have large herds of sapies, and the Gratians have plenty of grats. The people in each shire, or county, in Inod stick to what they do best, and they willingly trade what they have with people in the other shires, like musses for sapies or grats for musses." Humbi smiled at the boys. "Zoar has been using the Surlies to infiltrate Inod and change the way we live. He gives them land, money, and provisions like food to get them to work for him. So, they move into Inod and promise to improve the schools and make life safer by protecting them from Zoar. This is why Inodians have allowed Surlies into their towns—because they are afraid of the Zamzummim. Most people in Inod don't know what's really going on. They just accept the Surlies' being here and think they're kind of obnoxious and pushy.

"But the truth is that the Surlies have a sinister scheme to take over Inod and bring it under Zoar's rule. So far, they've been successful in spreading their evil tentacles throughout northern Inod, in towns like Mussford and Sapwood. They're just working their way south to Gratville." Humbi tapped his pipe on the tray.

Truelight clattered to the floor, and they all jumped. Beehart had been polishing it as they talked, and his nervous fingers slipped. When he bent to pick it up, he noticed his friend's face growing animated.

"It all makes *so much sense!*" Noni sputtered, recalling stories he'd heard since childhood of evil giant kings and bad people who lived in Init Isle's northern lands. He'd always wondered if these were just fantasies or made-up stories invented to scare children.

"You see," Humbi continued, "the Zamzummim never taught their own citizens how to make use of what they have by raising animals or crops so they have enough food to eat and can trade what they don't need to get what they don't have." Humbi brought the pipe up to his lips and puffed a few times. "All they know is to hoard what little they have out of fear of not having enough. So, of course, no one ever has enough.

"Zoar promises the people who serve him that he'll give them more provisions and land if they do what he says, but he doesn't have that much to offer. So, he just takes what he can from the other lands. At one time, the Surlies resisted his promises, because they knew he'd make them his slaves if they turned to him for help. They'd lose what freedom they had. But, after years of ruthless attacks on their land, most of them gave in to Zoar out of fear.

"The ones who submitted to him are now his most vocal puppets. They try to convince others that living under King Zoar's rule is good, because they themselves benefit from what he gives them. You see more and more of these 'Zoar Zombies' in our towns now."

"We don't see many Surlies in Gratville," Noni said.

"Believe me, you will soon, if nothing changes," Honi warned. "Many Surli spies work for Zoar and hope for more opportunities in his kingdom. They're coming across the border from Sur—more and more every year—-looking for new areas to populate.

"You see," she said, "the real reason we have so much here in Inod is because of Ameno. Years ago, he came and showed us how to prosper.

He taught us how to share what we have. Many Inodians believed him and, as a result, we all prospered.

"The Surlies and Zamzummim never accepted Ameno." Honi frowned. "They always wanted to do things their own way. This hasn't worked very well for them. They never seem to have enough. They're self-centered and jealous of what we have. Instead of learning from what we've done, they choose to take what we have for themselves. You know, years ago, the only inhabitants in Inod were Gomies." Honi glanced over at the boys.

"It's true!" Humbi said. "The first Inodians were Gomies."

"Where did the Krochits come from?" Beehart scratched his head.

"They were the lowest class of the Zamzummim. You see, Zam-zammi people are very tall—taller than Surlies. They stand up to ten feet tall! And, on the other side of Zamzum, in Bashan, the people are even bigger! King Og of Bashan lives in a city called Argob and sleeps in a bed that's fifteen feet long!" Humbi's eyes bulged.

Beehart winced. Noni cringed.

"Krochits were outcasts to the Zamzummim. They're shorter, though still taller than Gomies, with smaller knobs on their temples. Some suppose they're a cross between the Zamzummim and the Surlies, since their height is somewhere in between the two people. Since they were never fully accepted by the Zamzummim, or the Surlies, they were forced out of both lands into Inod," Humbi went on. "Since Gomies like us have always been open and friendly, we welcomed the Krochits to our land. We saw how good they are at teaching and leading, so they ended up running our schools and managing our towns, while Gomies were better with physical work, like farming and raising an-imals, since this is what they've always done. This arrangement has worked well overall."

"My dad also told me the Gomies were here first," Noni reflected. "I never knew why this was important."

"I'll tell you why it's important!" Honi emphasized. "The Surlies who work for the Zamzummim use the Krochits' ability to lead and manage things. They promise them a better life if they'll commit to giving them part of what they make. If they do, they're given more land and money. Many Krochits have gone over to the 'Surli side' because of what they can make if they do. These are the bad Krochits. What they don't realize is that the goal of the Zamzummim is to take over *all* the lands. They want more power over Init Isle. If they can unite Zamzum with Sur and Inod, they can easily overcome the king of Bashan and then control the entire isle."

"There are some good Krochits, mind you!" Honi nodded. "These are the ones who don't work for the Surlies."

"The Krochit woman who lives above us is really nice. She told us about Ameno!" Noni smiled, thinking about Grooma.

"Many Krochits believe in Ameno." Honi agreed. "But you hardly ever hear them talk about him, because so many are afraid of the Surlies. A few have been imprisoned for being outspoken about their beliefs. It's the evil Krochits we must be wary of—the ones manipulated by the Surlies."

"It's too bad that most young Gomies don't know their history or how Ameno's teachings changed our land and made it better. Most don't understand why the Surli and Zamzummim ways are destructive," Humbi added.

"My mom said there were some terrible things going on in Inod, especially closer to Sur." Beehart looked up from his grip of Truelight and laid the sword down beside him. "Before she left, she said she wanted to find out what we could do to keep our land safe."

"She's right! She knows about how the Surlies are gradually moving inland." Humbi set his pipe on the tray. "It's interesting, because, though they encourage the Krochits to run our schools and government, the Surlies themselves are illiterate! Most of them can't read or write. They have no schools in Sur! This is why their land is so poor. They don't know how to manage their own land! They booted out the Krochits, who were smarter and knew how to organize and make things work. This is why the Zamzummim can easily take over Sur. But it's also why the land of Zamzum has gone downhill. After Zoar kicked the Krochits out of his land too, because he decided they were inferior, many of their schools and shops closed, and all the towns suffered. Zoar finally lured back some of the smartest Krochits to keep things running smoothly. But, just like the people in Sur or Zamzum, the Krochits who serve Zoar are forbidden to talk about Ameno, because he wants their loyalty only to him—the king.

"The more Zoar-controlled Surlies and Krochits come into Inod, the more tension there is between them and the Gomies, who want the freedom to share Ameno's teachings. It's worse in Sapwood than in Gratville, because more Surlies live here. This disharmony has caused the rumors that Sapians are mean-spirited." Humbi sighed. "The Surlies encourage this misinformation, because they want to discourage Gomies from coming here. That way, they have more influence over the area. Not knowing what's really going on, most Inodians beyond Sapwood believe the half-truths and stay away."

"Sapians are basically kind and generous folk." Humbi paused to put his pipe to his mouth and draw smoke from it, then he continued. "We can't always speak openly about Ameno, especially if there are Krochits or Surlies around, but many of us meet privately to read *Ameno's Manna* together."

"You'd be surprised how many can squeeze into our little basement!" Honi winked.

"Can we see it?" Noni stifled a yawn and thought this might be a good excuse to head to bed.

Beehart reached for Truelight and jumped up. His face reddened when he realized that his eagerness might appear rude to his hosts.

He smiled sheepishly and waited as they slowly rose from their chairs and shuffled toward the kitchen. He and Noni followed when they motioned for them to come. They watched curiously as Humbi moved his hand over some smooth horizontal logs along the kitchen wall. When he pushed hard against one, it suddenly gave way. They boys gasped. *It was a secret door!* As it opened, a musty smell emerged. Honi lit a candle, and they followed her into a small, shelf-lined pantry filled with jars of preserved vegetables and fruits. At the back, Honi pointed silently to another door that opened when a hidden handle under a shelf was turned.

When they approached and entered the doorway, they stopped when they realized they stood at the precipice of a hollowed-out space. They breathed in more musty air as they looked down a narrow staircase at a rock-walled basement. Following Honi down the rickety stairs, they nervously grabbed hold of a wobbly railing along one side and tested each step as they felt the solid stone wall on the other side. When they arrived safely at the bottom, they sighed and watched Honi's trail of light move to the other side of the dark, dank, underground room. Their eyes lit up when a greater light warmed the space from a lantern she ignited. Humbi came up behind them and gazed around the room with obvious pride. A large striped wool rug covered the floor, and comfortable stuffed chairs huddled around a welcoming fireplace.

"This is where we like to meet!" He sighed.

Honi joined her husband and wrapped her arm around his waist.

"We wanted to make this a place for pilgrims—a special little hideaway. We imagined a time when we'd need a secret retreat," Humbi explained. "Especially when we saw what was happening in Sapwood."

"This room will have more meaning to you both when we tell you who's slept here." Honi winked.

"Tell us now!" Beehart insisted. "*Who?*"

"Well, your parents for one!" Honi smiled, and Noni's sleepy eyes opened wide. "They stayed with us for a couple of nights. We wanted them to stay longer, but they felt they needed to move on. They were preparing for a kind of mission." Honi pursed her lips like she wanted to say more but couldn't.

"What kind of mission?" Beehart's brows furrowed. He'd been gazing at the empty fireplace. Now he looked directly at her.

"How 'bout we talk more about it in the morning?" Humbi sensed the boy's tension. "It's late. And we all need some rest. We'll explain everything tomorrow." He placed logs in the fireplace, lit them and made sure the fire would last a while. He knew the boys would appreciate the warmth, especially after they'd spent the previous night in a cold, damp cave.

When he finished, Humbi turned to help Honi place a thick layer of quilts and blankets on the floor and plump up pillows for them. Then, the couple creaked up the steps to retire to their bed upstairs, leaving the boys to ponder the mysterious ending to the evening's conversation. After blowing out the lantern, the boys lay sleepless in the firelit darkness.

chapter twenty

The Mystifying Fountain

Beehart tiptoed up the steps when his inner clock chimed *"Morning!"* Warm rays greeted him through the red-checkered curtains in the kitchen. He crept back downstairs to wake Noni, and the boys decided to go outside to explore, since their hosts hadn't stirred yet.

A manicured lawn lay lush and green behind the house. They pulled their boots off and bounded onto it with bare feet. Beehart bent to touch the springy grass that felt like grat fur under his toes. They were also fascinated by all the colorful flowers around the yard, and they walked over to look at the purpits that covered a stone wall on one side. Noni thought about the Purpits in the meadow and the purple flowers at the sharetoo, and he went over to examine them. A crack in the wall's stones drew him to peer through and discover what was on the other side. All he could see were trees.

At the back of the yard were standing bird feeders, and a group of smallets hung around them, hungrily chewing on bruni pods as they watched the boys and chattered. One side of the yard was lined with bushes and trees, and Noni spotted a partially hidden, moss-covered fountain. He motioned to Beehart, and they walked behind the bushes to inspect it. The more they looked, the more the fountain mystified them. It was a statue of three people—two women and a man. One of the women was holding a vase with water pouring from its mouth into the stone basin at their feet. Barely visible words on the vase said, *"He will guide them to the springs of the water of life."*[8]—the same words marked in *Ameno's Manna* and on the scroll they'd found by the creek. They looked at each other. Then, as they gazed at the faces of the three people, their eyes bulged, and they both stood gawking for several minutes before dashing back to the house.

They tiptoed back inside so as not to wake their hosts and were greeted by comforting sights, sounds, and smells. Honi hummed as she scrambled turntoo eggs over a stove in the kitchen, while Humbi set out bowls of griffoons, jam, and butter.

"Good morning, my friends!" Humbi motioned for them to sit at the table as Honi entered cheerfully with a large platter of savory bacon. When everyone sat down, they bowed their heads, and Humbi blessed the food. After wolfing down what they could, Noni mentioned the fountain.

"So, you discovered it!" Humbi exclaimed. "We were going to show it to you this morning, but you beat us to it!"

"The faces look just like our parents! Is it supposed to be them?" Beehart asked.

"Yes. As a matter of fact, Honi made the fountain to honor them," Humbi explained, and Honi's eyes grew watery. "Whenever they were in the area, they came to visit us. We became very close to them. We stayed up late the last night they were here, talking and sharing."

"How did you know them?" Noni asked.

"Oni, Bleamer's father, introduced us." Humbi stroked his beard thoughtfully.

"Did his dad know my parents?" Beehart remembered the picture on the wall at Bleamer's inn.

"Oni traveled a lot and made friends wherever he went," Honi explained. "He heard about us from the owner of Prior Place in Sapwood and came here just to meet us. We got to be good friends, and he told Ada and her husband about us. After Beehart's dad died, Ada brought Stade and Lona here to meet us.

"We told them about Ameno, and their hearts changed because of what they learned," Honi reflected.

"I remember something that happened after we met Stade and Lona," Humbi chimed in. "Noni, don't you have a brother named Lelels?"

"Yes," Noni affirmed, his eyes looking down as he thought of his brother alone at home.

"Well, your mom was concerned about him, because he seemed to do things at his own pace, and he didn't have any real interests. Sort of aimless. A 'lost soul,' she said. We prayed with her for him, and the next time she came to visit, she was more peaceful. She said he was doing better. Guess he discovered he really liked to take care of your neighbor's grats. He'd found something he enjoyed doing. And she found peace with that. She stopped worrying and decided to trust that Ameno had a good plan for him." He smiled. "After coming to our house a few times and beginning to understand *Ameno's Manna* and how it gave them peace and joy, they wanted to help others too.

"It took Stade a few visits before he latched onto the notion of prayer and trusting Ameno, but once he was on board with it, well, we watched him become one of our strongest supporters," Humbi continued. "It was during his last visit that we saw him really change. He'd realized how it sets you free to forgive those who've hurt you."

"He did seem happier," Noni recalled. "He and Mom laughed more before they left. I remember asking her why they were both acting so strange. She laughed and said they'd sit down and tell me when they got back. They left that day. We thought it'd be a short trip. But they never came back." He looked down at his empty plate.

"My mom told us something had changed, and she wanted to tell Ranni and me more about it later," Beehart said. "I wasn't sure what she was talking about."

"We'd never seen a copy of *Ameno's Manna* until this journey," Noni remarked. "I guess they must be scarce. I don't know anyone who has it."

"There aren't many copies around," Honi explained. "The Surlies confiscated most of them."

Noni thought about Mosi's rare and precious gift.

"You know, when Ada, Stade, and Lona came here for the last time, they were on their way to a meeting in Sapwood," Honi said, then she stopped suddenly and offered no further explanation.

"What kind of meeting?" Noni noticed her worried look.

"One held by the Purpits." Honi's voice sounded hoarse.

"You mean the flowers?" Beehart choked, almost spitting out his tea.

"No. It's a group of people who call themselves by the flower name. Officially, they're known as the Purpit Planters." Humbi looked over at Beehart. "Before the Surli War, a few Inodians formed a secret society to plot against the Surlies. Since then, they still meet to think of ways to fight against Surli domination."

"In their meetings, they read *Ameno's Manna* and talk about overcoming fear and obstacles. This is important, since the main way the Surlies get control is by making people afraid." Honi waved her spoon for emphasis.

"Ameno told us that Purpits are people set apart for special service," Noni recalled.

"Right." Humbi nodded. "Those who meet take great risks. If they're caught, they just disappear. No one knows what happened to them." He stroked his beard. "We think that's what happened to your parents."

"What do you mean?" Beehart grew restless.

"During their last visit, they said they wanted to go into Sur to rescue some Gomies who were taken captive. They were working undercover and meeting with others near Sapwood to plan a way to free them."

"How did they get involved in this?" Beehart's jaw tightened. "Why didn't they tell us?"

"They were going to tell you," Honi said softly. "But they were caught before they could. After Sapwood, they were returning to Gratville before attempting a rescue mission. They knew it would be dangerous and wanted to warn you." Her eyes grew milky as she glanced at the boys.

"They weren't going into Sur right away," Humbi assured. "They were just making plans while they were here."

"We believe they were captured near Sapwood, but no one really knows," Honi said. "After they left, we never saw them again. Some think Surlies were watching them for a while. We think they're being held in Sur somewhere. Since their capture, it's even harder to get into Sur without being caught though. Spies are everywhere. It's very dangerous to cross the border.

"We talked all night before they left," Honi said quietly. "They shared some things you need to know." She looked into Beehart's eyes. "They said they'd never told you these things, but they planned to when they got home." She looked down then back up. "You see, Beehart, Bleamer is your brother."

"I had a funny feeling about him." Beehart's voice quivered with emotion. "His eyes reminded me of Mom's."

"Well, the story goes that when Ada was eighteen, she married a Surli man against her parents' wishes," Humbi explained. "You can imagine how Ailis and Ret felt. The man was kind to her at first, but he grew cruel after they were married. And Ada discovered that he was a Surli spy who intended to do her harm.

"You see, many people throughout Init Isle have believed for years that someone they call the Reignbreaker will show up one day and free the lands from oppression by the overlords or kings," Humbi continued. "The Zamzummim especially have feared that this person would prevent them from taking over the island. It was rumored that this person would descend from Ailis. Since Ada was her only child, the Zamzummi leaders conspired with the Surlies to kill her, and any children she had, to prevent this Reignbreaker from coming. They bribed her first husband and promised him land and wealth. When Ada became pregnant, she learned about the plot and told her parents, who hid her and the baby as long as they could. They knew this wouldn't work for long, so they secretly gave the baby to Oni and Milli, who raised Bleamer as their own."

"Who was my mom's first husband?" Beehart clutched the cup in his hand.

"We don't know. She never told us his name. We just assumed the Surlies did away with him when he failed to produce what they wanted most—the bodies of his wife and child." Humbi frowned and shook his head.

"Your mom disguised herself and fled to Gratville," Honi went on. "She had to escape from her husband and the conspiring Surlies. The only way was to disappear. She cut her hair, covered herself with a cape, and took on a new identity as a grat herder for a Krochit family in Gratville. Later, she met Beehart's father, who also was a herder. They married and, before he died, she told him that Bleamer was her son and that, one day, she wanted to see him again. When she left here with Noni's parents, they were going to Mussford, after Sapwood, to tell Bleamer she was his mother."

Beehart grimaced, stood up, pushed his chair back, and charged through the front door without a word. Honi looked at Noni, bewildered.

"Beehart felt abandoned by his father," Noni explained. "His dad died before he got to know him, and he always wanted a brother. He loved his mother, but he suspected that she was hiding something. She never talked much about his father or explained anything about where she came from. He never got to meet Ailis or Ret."

"Many young men are fatherless," Humbi clutched his pipe. "They long for the return of dads who left for one reason or another." His eyes crinkled in thought. "I never knew my own father. He died when I was very young too. But it's amazing how Abba uses these things for good in our lives. My longing for a father is what brought me to Ameno. He helped me understand how to trust him and Abba for what I needed. He became the dad I never had."

Noni and Honi sat silently, pondering Humbi's words. Then the front door creaked open, and Beehart, eyes lowered, returned to his seat. After a few minutes, he looked up at them with swollen eyes.

"I always wondered why my mother was so secretive," he rasped. "I guess she felt like she had to protect us." Then his eyes grew wide. "Leo told us Ada had two children before she went to Gratville. I wonder what he meant. Was there another child we don't know about?"

"I only heard about one child, besides you and Ranni." Humbi paused. "But there's more to the story. You, Noni, also have an unknown relative." He looked up from the pipe in his hand. "Your father told us something he'd never told anyone."

"*What?*" Noni held his breath.

"You said you met Mosi on the way here," Humbi spoke slowly. "And he told you stories about his grandfather, Sagius. He even gave you the man's sword. Then you met Leo in the cave and found out that he's Mosi's father. Such a coincidence, eh? Well, your father told us that Sagius had two sons."

"*Two* sons?" Noni knit his brows.

"Yes. After Leo, another son came along, and, when he was sixteen, he made a life-changing decision. You see, Sagius was a very domineering man—difficult to live with. He and this second son didn't get along at all. One day, after a heated argument, the son decided to leave and never return. At least not until this last trip."

"What do you mean by *this last trip?*" Noni felt his hands sweating.

"The trip he was taking when he came here, before he disappeared," Humbi continued. "He was on his way to visit his brother and see his father again in Mussford."

"*Who* are you talking about?" Noni clutched his wet hands.

"We're talking about your father, Noni." Humbi's next words pierced the boy's heart. "Stade was on his way to see his brother, Leo!"

chapter twenty-one

Alarming Revelations

Noni's brain felt like mush as he tried to make sense of what Humbi said. He remembered how strange his dad had acted when he last saw him. He was giddy to the point that Noni was weirded out by his behavior. Now, it all made sense. Ameno's teachings had changed his heart so he could forgive his father and probably wanted to reconcile with him. He also may have wanted to see his brother Leo again, even though they hadn't spoken in years. Of course, his father didn't know that Sagius was dead or that Leo was forced into hiding. He also couldn't have known that Leo had a son, Mosi. Noni thought about how Mosi never mentioned that his father had a brother, and he wondered if he knew about Stade. *Was he in the dark, like me?* He wondered.

Noni's father never talked about his family. Now he understood why. It also made sense now why Stade had named his first son Lelels. People had often asked his dad why he'd given his son such an odd name. Stade never answered them directly, but Noni remembered hearing him once say it was a nickname for "Leopol." He also recalled his mother sternly calling his brother *"Leopol!"* when he'd done something especially mischievous or naughty. Now he knew why. He just hadn't made the connection when they met Leo. *I wish I could see Leo and Mosi now so I could tell them they're part of my family!* He sighed.

While Honi and Humbi cleaned up the breakfast dishes, and Noni reflected on all the extraordinary connections, Beehart brooded over his kinship with Bleamer. He'd always wanted a brother to play ball, climb trees, or practice swinging swords with him. Sisters were all right, but they weren't the same, he thought. You had to be careful with them and use manners. *Not so with a brother.* He sighed.

"We need to get going." Noni suddenly stood up, trying to bring things back to reality. "We can't afford to waste any time. I'm super concerned about getting to Ranni."

After thanking their hosts, they gathered up their bags and headed outside. As Noni loaded his gear onto Saron, he turned to Humbi and pointed toward the back yard.

"Why's the wall there?"

"It was meant to be a barrier between Inod and Sur," Humbi explained. "Years ago, it was built to keep Surlies out of Inod. Now it keeps Inodians out of Sur."

"Can we get through it into Sur?" Noni asked.

"This isn't a good place to cross over." Humbi held Saron's reins as Noni secured the bags. "You're too far from your destination. The main Surli outposts are directly across the border from Sapwood. These are the most likely places to find Ranni. On the other side of this wall are wild woods and treacherous cliffs."

Noni thought about the terrifying birds he suspected to be tinshemets that confronted them on the way, and he cringed.

"I've heard that the owner of Prior Place knows a secret way into Sur." Humbi nodded. "You might go there first and meet with him."

Noni pulled out the map titled "Secret Passages to Sur," and he showed it to Humbi.

"We found this at Bleamer's. It was one of the maps that helped us find you. We think Oni drew them."

"Amazing!" Humbi gazed at the detailed drawing and marks on the map. "Oni really wanted to help people, even ones he never knew. How could he know that someday these maps would lead you to us?" Humbi's expression suddenly changed. "You know, we've never met the owner of Prior Place. His name is Fendem. I hope he can help you."

After hugs, the boys set out. Though the road to Sapwood was clearly marked, they decided to take a more obscure route, since Humbi warned them about lurking Surlies. It took about an hour to get into town, and they found the main street. They could see Prior Place in the distance, but the street was very crowded, so they approached the inn from the back.

They tied the grats behind the building and tapped on the back door. No one responded, so they knocked louder. Suddenly, a thin, tall young man in an oversized apron peered out at them from the other side of the door's glass. His unusual blue-green eyes stared eerily from a dirt-streaked face framed by matted yellow hair. He cracked the door open and leaned out.

"Whatta ya want?" he confronted.

"We're here to see Fendem," Noni spoke boldly.

"He ain't here," he said and slammed the door in their faces.

Noni pushed the door back open and bravely led the way through a mudroom, where a wall covered with pegs held mud-covered coats, and a row of dirt-encrusted boots stood at attention on the floor. They stealthily passed by an open door to a kitchen, where men stood by stoves, stirring pots and yelling above the din of clanking utensils and sizzling food. They tiptoed through a large dining room filled with tables and chairs to a lobby, where benches lined the walls. Angry voices bellowed through an open front door, and a tall man dressed in black stood just outside, facing a crowd. Gray hair hung to his shoulders, and coattails draped to the back of his legs, almost reaching the tops of his high boots. Someone shouted at him, and he yelled back.

"I haven' seen 'em! They ain't here, I tell ya! So get out o' here and leave me alone! How would I know where they are? And why would I help the likes of 'em anyhow? Ya know I support yer cause. If they turn up here, ya know I'd turn 'em in!"

"Well, ya better let us know if they show up, *Mr. Defendem!*" the crowd retorted. "We don't want no troublemakers in our town! We know yer history and that you're jus' the one to hide 'em! If ya do, ya know what'll happen to ya and yer good-fer-nothin' son!"

The man clenched his fists and turned around, and the boys could see his contorted and mustached dark face as he faced the lobby, trying to gather himself. Beehart, crouching in a dark corner, nervously grabbed Truelight at his side and, as he pulled it from the sheath, his sweaty hand slipped, and the sword clattered to the floor. Noni, slinking behind a bench, looked from Beehart to the man, and his eyes grew wide. The man glanced inside and wondered what had caused the commotion. But, distracted by the frenzied mob, he turned back to address the taunts and jeers one last time. Sighing with relief, Noni spotted a stairway that wound up from the lobby, and he motioned for Beehart to follow. They bounded to the top as fast as they could and lunged down a long hall to a door at the end. Noni yanked it open, let Beehart enter, then shut and locked it behind them.

Beehart breathed a sigh of relief as he plopped down on a black velvet settee against one wall. A window next to him looked down on the street below, so he scooted over to open it. A morbid sense of curiosity, and a concern for his own life, made him want to find out what was transpiring between the crowd and the man. But, when he detected a familiar voice, he started to shake.

"It's him!" he rasped. "It's Belial!"

Noni came over to look. They both recognized the Surli as he ascended the front steps, shoved the supposed innkeeper down them, then stood over the man as he lay sniveling on the ground. He waved a long knife in the man's face before ripping up the front of his black coat.

"We know they're here, Fendem!" Belial shouted. "And your inn's the most likely place for 'em to come! We think you're hidin' 'em!" Other people chimed in to support the Surli with yells of *"Huzzah! Get rid of the buzzard and his kind!"*

Beehart pulled Truelight from its sheath and pointed it toward the window. His reaction alarmed Noni, but he also knew that their lives were in great danger.

"We can't be distracted by darkness," he said out loud. "That's how the enemy tries to trap us. We have to focus on our mission and what Ameno said." He sat beside Beehart, motionless on the settee, and tried to redirect his thoughts as his heart pounded. The screams distracted him, and he muttered a plea. *Ameno,* he whispered, *what should we do?*

The voices subsided, and Beehart watched the crowd drift away down the road. He heard the innkeeper slam the front door and throw something against the wall. He scrunched down as they listened to his frustrated yells.

"Where are ya, Sluggli?" Fendem's voice echoed up the stairs and down the hall. *"Come here,* ya good-fer-nothin,' lazy kid!"

"I'm right here," a despondent voice called back.

"Weren't ya s'posed ta clean up the dining room this afternoon?" Fendem screamed. "Well, how could I 'xpect much from such a worthless kid?" he muttered. "Did ya see anyone while I was outside? *Answer me! Who'd* ya see? Two people? *Where'd they go?* Why don't ya know? *Didn' ya watch 'em? I told ya ta watch everyone!* But, why would I 'xpect ya ta remember that?" His voice bounced between outright rage and mumbling. "Ya just *can't trust* anybody these days! Ya think they might be out back? *Ya don't know? Well, go see!"*

Scuffling sounds followed, and Noni froze. *They'd left the grats tied up in back. And all their belongings were strapped to them. They could sneak out the front door, but they'd be spotted. How could they get away without being noticed?* He got up and peered out the window, looking for a possible way to escape. The shingled roof sloped steeply from the window's edge, and it was too far up to jump. Seeing no way that made sense, he paced back and forth in front of the settee.

Unnerved by Noni's edginess, Beehart went over to a desk on the other side of the room and rattled its drawers to see what was inside. Thinking about their unexpected discovery in the secretary at Bleamer's inn, he lifted a pile of papers from inside one wide drawer and discovered an old copy of *Ameno's Manna* hidden at the bottom. He took it to the settee and sat down to read. Noni joined him, and they held the book between them. As they turned the pages, one verse stood out to them both: *"When my spirit grows faint within me, it is you who watch over my way."*

They both breathed a sigh and enjoyed a moment of peace, but it was interrupted when footsteps and voices suddenly thundered up the stairs. They had no place to hide, so they sat and held their breath.

The steps were followed by loud pounds, yells, kicks, and shoves at the locked door. The boys sat silently, shivering and hoping their worst fears would somehow disappear into thin air. But, the door was forced open and Fendem's form filled the doorway. The thin young man at the back door slunk behind him, his eyes cast down, while the innkeeper's eyes glared at them like red hot coals. Beneath the man's ripped-up black coat, and a white shirt that hung in shreds beneath it, *there was no sign of light.*

chapter twenty-two

The Innkeeper's Nightmare

"We know who y'are!" Fendem spurted angrily as he thrust through the door.

Beehart jumped up and pointed Truelight toward him, but the innkeeper quickly grabbed his arm and twisted it before he could wield the weapon, and it clattered to the floor. He kicked the man with his boot and tried to pull his arm free, but Fendem was much larger and stronger. He yanked Beehart's arm behind his back before pushing him across the room and shoving him into a wooden chair. Pulling rope from his pockets, he tied the boy's wrists behind him, securing them to the back of the chair. Beehart screamed and kicked over the table in front of him. It fell over with a crash, and *Ameno's Manna* slid to the floor. Fendem grabbed a handful of the boy's hair and yanked his head back, making him scream in pain. He pulled a dirty cloth from his pocket and stuffed it into Beehart's mouth. The boy gagged and tried to spit it out as the man tied another cloth around his head and mouth to keep it in. Beehart tossed his head back and forth helplessly, while Fendem tied his ankles and legs together so tightly to the chair that he couldn't stand up or walk.

The innkeeper turned to see his son pointing a butcher's knife at Noni's neck. They forced him to stand and move to another wooden chair in the room. Noni sat stock-still as the two bound his wrists together behind his back and secured them to the chair then wound rope tightly around his ankles. They put a rag in his mouth too, held intact with a cloth tied tightly around his head. Noni's eyes watered from the rancid smell of the rag.

"You'll stay here 'til we know what to do with ya!" Fendem sneered and spat. "Sluggli'll guard ya." His eyes shone as he picked up Truelight and brandished it in front of Beehart's face. He laughed when the boy winced and swung his head back and forth as he held the blade close enough to his cheeks that he could shave the boy's whiskers. Clutching the prize, he stomped proudly out of the room, leaving his nervous son, whose shaking hands grabbed the edges of the settee as he slunk down on it. The young man squinted from under his dirty blond hair, avoiding eye-contact with the prisoners, and he flinched when the front door slammed shut.

At the sound of the door, Noni squirmed and wondered, *Where's he going? What will happen to us? Ameno, help!*

After several grueling hours of mental and physical torture—unable to move around, sitting helplessly bound in the hard chairs, trying to free themselves from the painful ropes, and watching their captor doze off on the settee, they heard Fendem's booming voice at the bottom of the stairs.

"I'm back, Sluggli!" Hearing no response, he yelled louder. *"Get down here, son!"*

Sluggli, startled awake by his father's shrill, irate voice, sat upright and reached for the butcher's knife beside him, which his grip had loosened when he dozed off. He grabbed the handle and looked over to make sure the prisoners were still in their places. Then he jumped up and ran to the top of the steps, carelessly leaving the door open. The boys sat stiffly in their chairs as sharp pains shot through their bound wrists and ankles. Their shoulders, arms, and legs ached, and hunger tore at their stomachs. But, even worse, they could hear the alarming conversation between Sluggli and his father.

"They'll come get 'em tomorrow mornin'!" Fendem yelled up the stairway to his son, who moved down a few steps. "The sheriff's havin' his deputy and some others, who're on their way, take 'em to a special jail in Sur. They'll decide wha' ta do with 'em there."

"Who are these guys and what've they done?" Sluggli grimaced.

"They're spies. They've somethin' ta do with the gal they caught," Fendem answered.

"What do you think they want?" Sluggli wondered.

"Whadda ya mean?" His father's voice raised.

"These guys, the gal…. Did they do something wrong?" Sluggli pursued meekly.

"Oh, ya know, the same ol' stuff. They're tryin' ta get power back for the Gomies. They're all in on the same conspiracy. They think that if they go back to the way things were, things'll be jus' hunky-dory. Well, *it's all fantasy!* Jes wishful thinkin'. I used ta think ev'rything would be better after Ameno came, but it's not. *It's worse!* An' I'm sick of it all! *Sick 'n' tired of it all!*"

"What'll they do to 'em?" Sluggli couldn't hide his concern as he hovered above his father.

"Why da ya care?" Fendem sneered. "Don't worry 'bout them! It'll only get ya in trouble. If ya stick yer neck out, it'll only get *yer head chopped off! Look at me!* I get blamed fer ev'rything these days just 'cause I went to a sharetoo a few years ago! And even though I have nothin' to do with those people nomore, I still get blamed! They's sayin' I was tryin' ta hide 'em. How r'diculous! I jus' reported 'em, so all the whisperin' shou'd stop. They made me lose so much business! Well, that won' happen ag'in. *They can't say I'm a traitor now!*"

"Will they kill 'em?" Sluggli lowered his voice, but the boys could still hear him.

"I told ya, *I don' care!* And *neither should you!* That's the least of our concerns. Now, ge' down here and help me in the dining room. And make sure ya check on them Gomies so they don' escape! *Keep that door locked!*"

After this jarring conversation, Sluggli returned to the room, slammed and locked the door, then bounded down the stairs. Noni and Beehart started hearing people's voices in the front lobby, and they wondered if they were customers. They gazed toward the window and watched the sun go down outside as they struggled to loosen the knots around their wrists and legs. Hours passed, and they heard footsteps creaking up the steps. They both shuddered, wondering who or what might descend on them next.

Sluggli slunk into the room and locked the door behind him. No longer wearing the soiled apron, he lowered his eyes like he was still ashamed. The boys breathed sighs of relief as they watched him remove food from a knapsack and set it on the once-capsized table in front of the settee. They were shocked when he walked over to Beehart and began to carefully untie the cloth around his head. He pulled the rag out of his mouth while holding a finger up to his own lips. Relieved to be freed from the rancid cloth, Beehart exhaled deeply then breathed in a lungful of fresh air. While Sluggli tirelessly worked on the knots that bound his friend, Noni noticed something extraordinary, and his eyes widened. As twilight darkened the room, he caught a glimpse of something under Sluggli's brown tunic as he bent over. Barely visible, but definitely there, he detected a glow. And he caught his breath.

Beehart looked up at Noni then over at Sluggli, and he also spotted the glow, prominent in the semi-darkness. And he let out the last bit of foul air from his mouth.

"You're one of us, aren't you?" he ventured.

Sluggli's face twitched, and he didn't answer. Once he'd freed Beehart, he worked patiently to untie Noni. Then he moved their chairs closer to the table, sat down on the settee and produced three small plates from his knapsack. After heaping food on each one, he pushed the plates toward them. The boys massaged their wrists and ankles, still raw from the ropes, as Sluggli produced forks and handed one to each of them. As they consumed the warm meat and tatas, they watched the young man curiously.

"Why'd you free us?" Beehart asked.

"Dunno," Sluggli said after a few minutes.

"We could escape if we wanted to," Beehart shot him a confident glance.

"But you won't need to," Sluggli looked up from the falling strands of dirty-blond hair.

"What do you mean?" Beehart pursued.

Sluggli didn't answer, and the boys glanced at each other with questioning looks. They chewed silently until the young man broke the silence.

"I wanna go with you."

Beehart choked and almost spit out his food.

"Where do you think we're going?"

"It doesn't matter. I just know I have to get outta this place." He wiped the back of a hand across his mouth.

"Your father's mean, isn't he?" Noni asked.

"He's my stepfather. But I don't care 'bout that." Sluggli. "Now I'm mos'ly afraid o' what's gonna happen here. It's gettin' worse, and I can't live this way no more."

"What's going to happen?" Beehart knit his brows.

"There're a few 'meno followers here, but they can't talk ta each other openly. If anyone knew I believed…. Many've disappeared. Nobody knows what happened to 'em. Can I please go with you?" Sluggli glanced up, his eyes imploring.

"First, you might want to know where we're going and why," Beehart answered. "What we're doing is pretty dangerous, as you know, and we could all get caught again. Then who knows what might happen to all of us?

"See, his sister was kidnapped, we think by Surlies. And we're trying to rescue her. We think she's being held somewhere in Sur, and we're hoping to find her. Some people told us Fendem, your stepfather, knows a secret way into Sur."

"He might know a way, but he won't help you." Sluggli looked down again.

The boys glanced at each other. It made sense, seeing the innkeeper's fearful and angry reaction to them.

"But *I* can help you. *I can show you the way*—the secret passage into Sur." Sluggli looked pleadingly at Noni, who gazed into his teal eyes and felt like he could trust him.

Just then they heard a sound coming from outside the door. Sluggli jumped up and bounded out of the room, shutting the door behind him. Noni turned to Beehart.

"We can trust him," he whispered.

"I don't know," Beehart rasped back.

"You saw the glow, right?" Noni confirmed.

"Sure, but that doesn't prove anything." Beehart grimaced.

"We have no other options," Noni said impatiently.

"You sound desperate," Beehart accused.

"We *are* desperate!" Noni said a little too loudly.

"Don't you believe *Ameno* can help us?" Beehart scowled.

"I think *this is how Ameno will help us!*" Noni tried not to shout.

"Well, I'm not so sure," Beehart retorted under his breath.

Sluggli slinked back into the room and quickly threw his knapsack onto his back.

"If you want to do this, *we need to go now!*"

Noni stood up, but Beehart hesitated when he heard an odd noise coming from a room in the hall. And he realized, at that moment, when he reached for his sword, that he'd be leaving without Truelight. He felt a large lump in his throat, but it seemed like he had no choice.

"It's just my stepdad snoring," Sluggli whispered when they heard the sound again.

Down the steps and through the back door, they found the grats still waiting patiently for them in the dark. As they untied the grateful animals, still bearing their bags, Sluggli motioned to them to move fast, and the boys followed him to a shed, where his grat was tied up behind a bale of hay. They grabbed handfuls of the dried grass, fed their animals quickly, then stuffed more of it into a canvas bag that Sluggli's grat would carry as feed for the animals along the way.

They moved silently down a path that led from the inn through a field toward a dark forest. As he shadowed Sluggli, Noni looked up at the fuller moon that shone down brightly on them, and he was thankful that it would help to lighten their way. They were greeted in the woods by the musty smell of rotting wood and creepy noises that sounded like muffled whispers. Lagging behind the others, Beehart almost jumped out of his skin when he heard a shrill scream, and something dove at his head. Remembering the tinshemets, he reached for Truelight then realized again he no longer had his trusty friend. He felt helpless.

"This is a huge mistake!" he rasped to Noni, when he caught up to him. "How do you know we can trust this guy? He might be leading us into a trap! *What're you thinking, man?*"

"*Look*, Beehart! Just trust me in this," Noni said confidently. But then he stopped suddenly when he saw Sluggli reach for something wrapped up—something large and long—tied to his grat. *It could be some kind of weapon!* His thoughts started whirring. Trying to remain calm, he shot a glance back at Beehart, who'd stopped short behind him, his eyes wide.

Just as Sluggli drew the fearsome object out from under the cloth, Beehart grabbed for a knife hidden under his bags. Holding out his dagger, he thrust the blade toward Sluggli, who also held his menacing object out, but in a nonthreatening way. And, at that moment, Beehart's eyes grew wide, and he gasped. *It was Truelight!*

Sluggli smiled, and Beehart's face turned bright red as he stuffed the knife back under his bag.

"I'm sorry," Beehart muttered.

"For what?" Sluggli looked puzzled.

"For thinking you were evil," Beehart looked down at Truelight in his hand.

"He thought you might turn us in," Noni explained.

"No prob, but why would I do that?" Sluggli cocked his head. "Yer my only passport to freedom." He hesitated then continued. "Plus, aren't we friends now?"

"Yes. Yes, we are…." Beehart's voice trailed off and he looked down, embarrassed.

Sluggli's face changed, and he looked like he might melt.

Attaching the sword to his belt and sighing at the reassuring feeling of having it back at his side, Beehart smiled sheepishly, realizing how badly he'd misjudged this guy.

"Thank you," he whispered, his eyes still lowered.

After that, the three walked along the forest trail single file for a while, listening to mysterious sounds with the boys wondering if the creatures uttering them were friendly…or not. Then Sluggli broke the silence.

"Why do some people's hearts shine?" he shyly ventured.

"You mean this red glow?" Noni pointed at his chest.

"Yea."

"When we met Ameno, he told us we'd burn with the spirit if we believed in him, and we did! Our hearts just started glowing! Like a flame! But, you know…your heart glows too!" Noni said, pointing at Sluggli's chest. "We saw it in the room."

Sluggli looked down at the faint glow coming from under his tunic. It reminded Noni of a star being born.

"I know about him," Sluggli said. "I've just never met him."

"We met him in a sharetoo," Noni said. "He told us he's Abba's son."

"When I heard 'bout him, I wanted ta know more. Sometimes I sneak upstairs and read 'bout 'im in *Ameno's Manna.*" Sluggli stared straight ahead.

"How'd you hear about him?" Beehart was curious.

"My stepdad used ta talk 'bout 'im."

"Fendem?" Beehart's eyebrow shot up.

"Yea. He used to believe…a *long* time ago. He ev'n went to a sharetoo," Sluggli smiled then frowned. "But somethin' happened."

"What? *What* happened?" Beehart's voice raised a notch.

"He got scared after some Surlies told 'im he'd lose everythin' if he didn' stop goin'."

"Did you ever go with him to the sharetoo?" Noni wondered.

"Yea. I went when I was younger. I remember the folks were real nice. But then some of 'em just disappeared, like the town baker. I loved that guy." Sluggli looked down. "He'd bring us griffoons hot out o' th' oven. I was so sad when his shop closed. I never knew wha' happened to 'im.

"When Pa stopped goin' to the sharetoo, he changed. He worried a lot 'bout what folks were sayin'. I made the mistake o' askin' the mayor, who ate at th' inn, whatever happened to the baker. His face got real red and I thought he'd explode. He yelled fer Pa and told 'im what

I asked. Then Pa pulled me aside and told me to never ask questions like 'at again.

"After that Pa got real mean. He start'd callin' me names like 'Slow 'n' ugly.' That's where the name Sluggli came from. I think he's jes 'fraid and kinda angry 'bout the way t'ings've gone."

"You know you're not those things, right?" Noni looked over at Sluggli. "When you believe in Ameno, he makes you into something special. He says we're warriors, and like sons of a king."

"I'd like to know that guy better." Sluggli looked down at the path.

"Want to meet him?" Beehart asked.

"Sure. But he mightn't like me." Sluggli stared at the rocks on the trail. "My pa thinks I'm sorta worthless." His voice and glow faded.

Noni and Beehart looked at each other.

"Ameno wouldn't think that about you," Noni said as he tread over some spree needles that sent up a nose-tinglingly fresh fragrance.

The eerie surrounding sounds subsided while they talked, and the forest seemed way less scary after Sluggli assured them that the creatures they heard were harmless. And, as the morning sun peeked through the trees, Noni stepped out of the woods into a bright meadow. He was immediately dazzled by sunlight that reflected from mounds of sweet-smelling white flowers. A breeze blew over them, and their petalled heads danced in waves, like the surges of white-capped sea breakers. He stood, awestruck, at the edge of the meadow. Beehart stood next to him. And they both thought it was almost as beautiful as the Purpit mound.

After some breath-taking moments, they followed Sluggli dreamily down a flower-lined path through the meadow, almost blinded by the brightness. They wondered if the life-like flowers had been people, like the Purpits. They listened for a voice or a sigh, but all they heard was the wind in the trees behind them and an occasional hoot from the forest.

The path ended on the far side of the meadow, where a tall cliff loomed before them. Sluggli veered right onto a secluded trail beside a bouldered wall. Soon, they were hopelessly entangled in the prickly branches of a thorny patch. Oblivious to the obstructing plants, Sluggli left his grat with them, pushed his way through the bushes, and disappeared into the brush ahead. They waited for a few minutes before calling out to him.

"Sluggli! Sluggli?"

Impatient, Beehart handed his grat's lead to Noni and lunged forward, beating aside the piercing branches with Truelight. Noni waited a bit longer but grew antsy himself and tied the three grats to some trees. He then slid along the cliff to avoid getting scratched. The space was very narrow, and a few sharp thorns scraped across his arms and made them bleed.

As he blotted the blood with a rag from his pocket, he glimpsed what looked like partly-hidden stone steps that led down to an opening beneath the cliff's rock wall. Overgrown with vines, they could be easily missed. He moved closer and stepped carefully down the steps to enter a dark, dank underground cave. His eyes adjusted as he felt his way along the rocky sides until he saw a faint light ahead. Sluggli was holding a candle and inspecting a primitive drawing on one wall. Beehart stood beside him, gazing intently.

Noni recalled the pictures in Leo's cave and stepped closer, his eyes trying to adjust to the dim light. This drawing was not of a battle, he discovered. It portrayed all kinds of people—short, tall, plump, thin, dark-skinned, light-skinned, some with knobs, some without. And they all sat in a circle, holding hands.

Noni gazed at the drawing with curiosity. Scratching his head, he wondered what it could meant.

chapter twenty-three

Predators and Prayers

Loud voices echoing across the meadow from the woods outside interrupted their curious inspection of the cave painting. The boys rushed out and stealthily groped through the testy bushes to bring the grats into the safety of the cave. On his way back inside, Noni narrowly spotted an eye marker near the entrance. It had been obscured by the overgrown vines and bushes. *Without Sluggli, we never would've found this place,* he thought.

Their single candle burned down quickly as they proceeded through the cave, so Sluggli pulled a small lantern from a bag on his grat and lit it.

"I love this cave," he admitted as they passed the painted wall again. "It's my secret hiding place." He ran his hand over the pictures. "I dunno who drew these, but they give me hope."

As they followed Sluggli through the cave's maze, they heard strange scurrying sounds, similar to what they heard in Leo's cavern.

"What you're hearing are *smolies,*" Sluggli explained when he saw how the scampering made the boys nervous. "They won't hurt you. They're harmless little creatures. They live in the holes." He pointed out some small cavities in the rock walls.

They were relieved when they finally saw light ahead and followed Sluggli out into the brightness. As the warmth greeted them, a strange sound shook the calm. They trembled when two hooded Surlies moved toward them, shrieking like vultures attacking their prey.

"It's dem!" they shouted. *"We got 'em! What a prize for Zoar! And for us!"*

Beehart drew Truelight from his side and swung the sword wildly toward one Surli with a hooded cape. He screamed when he glimpsed an eye-patch under the hood. The snake-man hurled his arm violently at the boy and thrust Beehart aside like an annoying bug. He fell sideways and, as he went down, he dropped his prize at the man's feet. Belial growled as he seized the precious sword. Laughing, he pointed it at Beehart's side, as he lay defenseless on the ground. Then he plunged the sword's tip into the boy's hand.

Beehart screamed and thrashed as Belial forcefully grabbed and bound his wrists in front with a rope. After roughly tying another rope around his waist and blindfolding him, the snake-man dragged the boy to his graynight and hooked the end of the rope to the horn of his saddle.

The other Surli snatched Noni's hair and thrust a rusty dagger into his chest as hard as he could, intending to kill the boy. The knife went in but stuck fast. When he saw that Noni remained unharmed, the striker realized the boy's chest was protected by something. He tore at the top of Noni's tunic, ripped it down, and realized that, beneath it, he carried a canvas bag with a book inside. Unable to tear the pack from the front of Noni's chest while the boy stood and struggled against him, he cursed, grabbed his arm, and flung him to the ground. Noni screamed when his side struck a rock. While he writhed in pain, the huge man was able to rip off the pack with *Ameno's Manna* inside. Laughing loudly, he pulled the book out and held it up to show Belial, who smirked with pleasure. But the worst was yet to come.

Tossing the precious book aside, the beast howled and waved his dagger close to Noni's eyes. Then, he pointed the knife's tip at his nose. As the boy turned his face helplessly from side to side to avoid the sharp blade, and feeling naked without the protection of *Ameno's Manna* held close to his heart, he realized his only weapon now was prayer. He silently moved his lips, but in his mind he screamed. *Ameno, please help me!*

"Stop yer antics, Blueheel!" screamed Belial, interrupting the Surli's sordid torture. "We don' have time for tha' garbage, and Zoar wants 'em intact when we bring 'em in!"

The monster put his dagger down, but he was still able to strongarm Noni, tie his wrists together, blindfold him, wrap a rope around the boy's waist, and attach the rope to the horn of his saddle. Noni, feeling overwhelmed and helpless, silently screamed, *Where are you, Ameno?*

Meanwhile, Sluggli was hiding behind a bush, waiting for an opportunity to escape. When he saw the Surli looking around for him, he pulled a knife from his belt. But Belial spotted and went for him. Glaring through his serpent-eye, the snake-man swung Truelight threateningly. Sluggli's eyes were fixed on the sword, so he was shocked when Belial hit him across the chest with his other hand, sending him flying backward. He laughed when Sluggli's knife flew one way, and the young man flew the other way. He landed with a thud but bounded back to face the huge man, who lunged so roughly at him this time that they both crashed into a tree. Crushed by the snake-man's weight, Sluggli sputtered to catch his breath. After a few seconds of wheezing and coughing, he passed out. Belial tossed his limp body over his graynight's back like a sack of grain.

Hearing the commotion, but unable to see, Noni was shaken to think that their new friend might be dead. Beehart yelled and spit from under his blindfold as the Surlies sniggered and dug through the boys' bags before taking off. Then Belial noticed the book thrown up against a tree.

"Look a' dat!" He pointed at *Ameno's Manna.* "I knew they was 'menomaniacs!'"

"Yea! An' here's anudder one!" The other Surli held up Sluggli's copy of *Ameno's Manna,* stashed inside one of his bags. *"What a bunch o' losers!"*

"Here's da *best* prize!" Belial yelled and waved Truelight triumphantly over his head. He hoisted himself onto his graynight and took off down the path. The other Surli scoffed and followed, and the blindfolded boys hobbled along behind them, sometimes stumbling, tripping, and being dragged behind the animals. Sluggli flopped like a dead fish behind Belial's saddle, and the grats trailed behind, following meekly.

"How nice o' da guy at the inn to let us know their whereabouts!" Belial let out a sinister chuckle.

"Yea. All we had ta do was show up here an' get 'em!" the other Surli guffawed.

Noni's head almost exploded when he heard this and thought about Fendem's hateful betrayal. *How could a father, even a stepfather, do this to his own son? Unbelievable!* Then his thoughts turned more ominous. *Maybe something horrible will happen to the guy. Maybe he'll die of some awful disease, or someone will kill him…*

But as he stumbled along, muttering under his breath, he suddenly felt the topaz Ameno had given him bouncing in his pocket. For some reason, the Surlies hadn't noticed it. Feeling the stone made Noni sigh as he remembered Ameno's words: *"Don't focus on the darkness, or evil, in others. This will only hinder your ability to be strong."* He took a deep breath and wondered what Ameno would want him to think about. *How do you want me to react to this?* he asked.

Then he heard Beehart moaning painfully behind him.

"This is *all my fault!*" his friend groaned. "What's *wrong* with me? *Why couldn't I beat 'em?* Even with Truelight? I *don't* understand. What good's a sword like that and what good am I?"

Noni's heart hurt for him.

"*Stop it*, Beehart!" he said, loud enough for him to hear.

"Well, *it's true!*" Beehart blubbered. "All worthless—me, the sword, the prayers—all of it! I thought I could do anything with Truelight. So, what *was* the purpose of the sword, anyway, or our meeting with Ameno?"

"I don't have all the answers." Noni sighed. "But I do know that Truelight could never save us. Only Ameno can do that. And your power's not in that sword. *It's in your spirit!*"

"Then why're we tied up, bleeding, blindfolded, and being dragged to our death? When I prayed, *nothing happened!* We're just like sapies being led to a slaughter!"

Just then, Belial yelled, "*Shud up*, you!" He yanked roughly on Beehart's rope and made the boy stumble and fall to his knees. He tugged on the rope again and forced Beehart to fall forward and scrape his arms badly on the sharp stones. He chortled as the boy struggled to stand back up. Noni heard Beehart moaning, and he groped his way toward him. Both Surlies roared with laughter as he stumbled, trying to find his friend. Just as he reached him, extending his arms, Belial pulled on the rope from his graynight and dragged Beehart across the rocks away from Noni, who also fumbled and fell. The villains continued their torture for a while then decided it was time to move on.

It became more and more difficult for the boys to keep up, especially when the graynights trotted downhill. With so many jagged stones to contend with, they were grateful for their thick leather boots. Noni thought about Sluggli, who was wearing sandals. If he was being dragged, as they were, his feet would be severely injured by now.

Just then, Noni heard a sigh coming from Sluggli, like the whisper of a promise drifting back to him. *At least he's still alive*, he thought. But he was soon distracted by other sounds—trees rustling, the ripples of a stream, and disturbing sounds coming from the Surlies.

As they plodded along, the men drank bottle after bottle of bruni ale. Then, each swigged bottle was tossed onto the path behind them. And the boys had to blindly avoid these landmines as the monster-men grew more demonic.

"How could we torture dese guys before we get to the jail?" Belial jested, loud enough for the boys to hear.

"How 'bout we tie 'em up to one of dese trees an' leave 'em for the grizzlies to get?" laughed the other man.

Noni cringed to think what a grizzly was.

"Yea, we could hang 'em from dis tree and see if dey're still there in the mornin'!" Belial chuckled cruelly.

"No. I got a better idea," the other guffawed. "Let's tie one to a log an' set it floatin' downstream an' see how far he goes before drowning."

"Ah, dey'll get tortured enough when dey go to da king. He's eager to get hold of 'em. We've been tryin' for a lon-n-ng time to nab this bunch, particularly dat one. He's da real prize." Belial's voice took on a more sinister sound.

Noni wondered if Belial meant Beehart, since he was most likely to be the Reignbreaker, based on Leo's descriptions. But what sort of torture did they mean? His legs shook with terror and exhaustion. His arms ached, and his wrists were raw and bloody from the constant tugging. They'd trudged along for hours, up and down rocky hills and through dusty fields and syrupy marshes. Even blindfolded, they could tell it was late in the day and past time for a meal, so their bellies hurt too. The sun's warm rays no longer beat down on their backs, and they felt chilled. Sighing, Noni heard Beehart reciting something from *Ameno's Manna* under his breath, and it gave him hope: *"He has sent me to bind up and heal the brokenhearted, to proclaim liberty to the…captives and the opening of the prison and of the eyes to those who are bound."*[3]

They suddenly stopped, and the boys sank to the ground. The Surlies removed their blindfolds but kept their hands bound. Pulling them to their feet, they pushed and prodded them toward a large mud-plastered building with a grass-thatched roof. Belial poked Beehart with Truelight to goad him like a grat. Noni glanced up just in time to see Belial's graynight being led to another building with Sluggli still slung over the animal's back. Their grats followed, loaded with all their belongings. Noni felt a pang of remorse for his new friend and wondered what would become of him.

Their eyes had to adjust to darkness inside the building, where they were herded like the animals. Inside, a heavy-set Surli guard with a black armband sat cursing behind a desk. Stringy black hair surrounded an ugly scar that ran from his ear to the base of his bulbous nose. He growled angrily at them through rotten teeth.

"Just who does we hab here?" He sneered.

"Oh, these ones 're special," Belial announced proudly.

"What d'ya mean, *special?*" The guard smirked.

"Dese are da ones we've been lookin' for, 'specially this one, *the Reignbreaker hisself?*" Belial's snake-eye narrowed.

Noni glanced up to see Belial nod toward Beehart. Beads of sweat formed on his friend's bright red forehead as the guard stood up and walked over to him. After spitting at him, the man grabbed the boy's bristly chin and jerked his head toward him. Then he stared into his blue-green eyes, searching for something.

"I t'ink you'd be right! It's 'im a'right! I'm sure o' it." His hand fell away, and he lugged his large body back behind his desk to plop into his chair.

Beehart winced at Noni, his eyes full of fear. A jingling sound interrupted their thoughts as another Surli guard came in and grabbed a metal keyring from a peg on the wall. He jangled the keys then thrust a large metal one into a keyhole in a heavy wooden door beside them and shoved it open, knocking over a small bald guard on the other side. The desk-guard motioned for the boys to follow the man with the keys, who also wore a black armband.

"This'll be the last of ya!" Belial growled and laughed loudly.

Carrying a lit lantern, the key-guard led them past the little man on the other side of the door, who stood up, stammered, and brushed himself off. The boys followed through a maze of dark halls to a narrow corridor, where they heard moans echoing through the halls. A sewer smell burned their nostrils as they tried to breathe without inhaling. After winding around more corridors, the guard shoved Beehart into a cell that held a filthy straw mattress, a rusty bucket of brown, rancid liquid, and a barred window. After depositing Beehart, he ushered Noni to his own confine, far down the hall from his friend.

Noni tried to breathe as he looked around at the dismal accommodations while the guard brusquely removed the ropes from his bleeding, raw wrists. He slumped down on the mattress and listened as the guard turned the key to lock the cell door. The sun had set and, when the guard left with his lantern, darkness closed around him. The corridor grew breathlessly still, except for the occasional moan that drifted down from other areas of the prison. Yearning to hear or see something that might bring him a little cheer in this seemingly hopeless place, he stiffly stood and stumbled over to the barred window that hovered a few feet above him on the other side of the tiny enclosure. Looking up, he could see the nearly-full face of the moon streaming light down toward him. He sighed and smiled. Crawling back to the mattress, he curled up and dozed off beneath a crusty blanket.

A few hours later, his reverie was interrupted by someone shoving a plate of mushy, days-old floodle under his cell door, along with a cup of bruni ale. As bad as both tasted, he was so starved and thirsty that he gulped them down. Then he lay back down on the bug-infested bedding and tried to sleep before facing the scary unknowns of tomorrow. But it was hard to ignore the throbbing pain in his side and the continuous ache in his wrists, legs, ankles, and feet. Cold air blew in through the open window, and, each time a chilly draft swept over him, he woke up trembling. When he wasn't shaking, he was scratching his arms and legs from the biting mites and the straw that poked through the mattress. Sighing, he worried about Beehart, Sluggli, and Ranni.

Miserable and awake, his hand landed on his pocket. He reached in and pulled out Ameno's gift, still in its place. Holding the stone up toward the window, he smiled to see how its translucent yellow surface brightly reflected the moon's light. This heartened him. Then he heard a whisper. At first, he thought it was the wind. But, when it grew louder, he sat up and was surprised to see a large smallet peering intently through the window bars. He got up, stepped closer, and jumped back when the creature spoke.

"*It's about time!*" it squeaked. "I've been trying to get your attention *forever!*"

Noni rubbed his eyes.

"I d-d-didn't know smallets could *talk!*" he stuttered then did a double-take when another smallet moved next to the first one and peered down at him.

"My name's Salvo," said the first one, with a white-tipped ear. "He's Malvo." The other smallet eagerly waved his white-streaked tail. "We have a plan to get you out."

"Why do you want to get me-e-e out?" Noni stammered.

"Because we know why you're here!" Salvo exclaimed.

"What do you mean?" Noni questioned. "Why do you think I'm here?"

"Well, we know you came to rescue the girl—the one they brought here—the one we call *the Reignbreaker*," Malvo said.

"You mean Ranni?" Noni's jaw dropped.

"We only know her as the Reignbreaker." Salvo scratched his ear.

"Is she all right?" Noni grimaced.

"Yes, but she's very weak." Malvo face fell. "She's been waiting for you."

"Why do you care about any of us?" Noni was skeptical.

"We've been waiting for a *long time* for the Reignbreaker to come, because she's the only one who can help us! We'll explain more later, but, right now, we need to get her out of here!" Salvo rubbed his front paws together. "Here's our plan...." He told them that several smallets would create a distraction outside. The guards would hear a commotion, desert their posts, and run out to see what was happening. During the ruckus, a smallet named Seemi would sneak into the prison, get the keys, then drag them to Noni, who could free himself and Beehart. Ranni's cell was in a separate corridor; Seemi would lead them there to help her escape.

After the smallets explained the scheme, they scampered away from his window. Noni plopped back onto his mattress, his eyes wide open and awake. He thought about it for a moment, scratched his head, then pinched himself to make sure he wasn't dreaming.

chapter twenty-four

The Remarkable Rescue

Noni's eyes popped open. Crashing sounds and shrill voices echoed down the corridor from the front of the prison. Lying with his back against the wall, his eyes darted around the cell as he tried to remember where he was. Shivering and remembering what transpired earlier that evening, he questioned if it was real. Hoping it was, he crept across the dirt floor to sit next to the cell door and watch in case "Seemi" appeared. He looked up at the window and was still able to see the moon's bright light. *It must be the middle of the night*, he thought.

Just then he heard a dragging sound, and he smiled. *It sounds like freedom,* he trembled. Between the bars he could see a tiny smallet far down the corridor, struggling to lug a ring of keys with his teeth. *This must be Seemi!* he chuckled. The smallet stopped to rest every few steps but persisted onward, getting closer to Noni's cell with each new burst of energy. Like others he'd seen on their trip, the smallet was larger than the ones at home. When he reached his hand under the bars to grab the ring and drag it him, he also saw that the animal had white paws. After grasping the ring, he stood up and extended his arm through the vertical bars next to the lock. He turned his hand around and placed a key into the hole on the other side. He had to try several to find the one that fit. Finally, the lock clicked, and the barred door creaked open.

Excited, Seemi motioned with one paw for Noni to follow him. Like a feather in the wind, Noni floated down the dark hall behind the smallet, carrying the ring and trying not to jangle the keys. At Beehart's cell, he tried one key after another until the lock clicked with the freeing sound.

Beehart, still unconscious, snored soundly on his mat, and Noni had to shake him awake. Beehart caught his breath and peered up from under his thick red bangs at Noni. He sat up, rubbed his swollen eyes, and stared in disbelief at Seemi, who waited by the door. A puzzled look crossed his face as Noni whispered.

"Get up! Follow us! I'll explain later!"

Seemi led them through a maze of corridors to Ranni's cell. They found her cowering in a corner, rocking back and forth with her head down and her arms wrapped around her knees. Her beautiful red cape hung from her shoulders in shreds, and the hood covered her face. Beehart started shaking when he saw her. He gritted his teeth as water filled his eyes.

Hearing a rustling sound outside her cell, she froze and peeked out from under her hood. The first thing she saw was Noni's face peering through the bars, and the pallor of her bruised face turned pinkish red as tears streamed down her cheeks. She stretched her arms out to him, and he felt like his heart was breaking up into tiny pieces. He tried to focus as he inserted key after key until one worked and the lock released. The heavy door swung open, and Beehart rushed inside to wrap his arms around his sister before he started to sob. Noni watched in silence, feeling himself crushed with grief. At that moment, Seemi sat up on his haunches and chattered furiously. *Hurry, hurry, hurry!* he squeaked. *Someone's coming!*

The boys quickly helped Ranni up, and she tried desperately to steady herself on feeble legs that wouldn't cooperate. Through swollen eyes, she looked helplessly from Beehart to Noni. Her brother bent to lift her, and, as he raised her from the floor, he was alarmed by how light she felt. Her torn clothes hung limply beneath her cape, and Beehart turned his face to Noni, whose own tear-swollen eyes reflected his best friend's inconsolable distress.

Seemi led them down several corridors to an empty cell, where he pointed out a window. This was their rendez-vous point. Here, they'd climb out the opening, several feet from the floor, to meet the other smallets. The inventive creatures had spent days de-barring the window in this seldom-used cell by chewing the wood around the bars until they could pull them from the wall. The unused space was far enough away from the prison entrance that no one would notice. The distance would also give them an escape advantage. With the window so high up, though, and Ranni so weak, they weren't sure how they could get her out. They hoped the boys would help.

Seemi sprang effortlessly up the cell wall onto the windowsill and slipped through the debarred hole. They heard him whispering on the other side. He poked his face back through the opening and motioned for them to come closer. Just then, they heard angry voices in another corridor, and they knew they had to hurry.

Noni stood beneath the window and motioned for Beehart to bring Ranni over. Beehart helped her onto Noni's back, and she was able to reach and grasp the ledge. With her remaining strength, she pulled herself up and through the opening. Beehart was next. He stepped into Noni's cupped hands and hoisted himself up. Noni wondered how he could get up by himself, then he saw a stool in the hallway and ran to get it. The smallets chattered as the voices grew louder and closer. Noni's heart raced. He could barely lift the heavy stool, but he knew it would make too much noise if he dragged it into the cell. So, he heaved and gradually pushed it until it sat next to the wall. As he wiped sweat from his eyes, he stepped onto it and stretched to reach the ledge. Just then, he heard an angry voice echoing down the corridor.

"My gawd, Cluno, *what was ya thinkin'?"* It was Belial. "You *no good worthless slime!"* A loud thud and a scream followed. "Why'd ya leave yer guard? Now he'll *have our heads!* How could ya let 'em get away? *Ya brute!* He'll *kill us all* for this! Did ya hear that sound? I think dey're down dere. *Come on!* Hurry up, ya stupid good fer nothin'...."

With everything he had, Noni pulled himself up onto the sill and thrust his shoulders through the opening. Beehart reached under his armpits and pulled as hard as he could. The smallets hopped and chattered around them. Breathing heavily, Ranni scooched closer to try to help. Just as Noni's feet slid through the window, she saw Belial pass by the cell. She gasped at the sight of his face. He heard her, turned back, and stopped at the open door. Then he screamed as loud as he could for the other Surlies to come. But no one made out his words because the ensuing moments became a blur.

Salvo motioned, and they all moved quickly. Beehart carried Ranni, and Noni followed, as they ran far across a field in the moonlit dark toward some nearby woods. Noni turned to see guards with torches running frantically around the outside of the prison.

Then he felt a sudden shock and yelled for the others to stop.

"We forgot Sluggli!" he screamed, but no one seemed to hear him.

chapter twenty-five

The Smallets' Surprise

"We *can't* go back!" Salvo emphasized as they entered the forest. "We barely have enough time to get away before they track us down. We'll go back for him later."

Noni felt his heart tearing apart even more as he thought about how they'd abandoned another loyal friend. He also thought about their grats, and all their belongings, left behind. Distracted by painful realizations, he mindlessly followed Salvo and Malvo down a dark path through the woods, trailing behind Beehart and Ranni. His nerves were raw, and he glanced back nervously when he heard rustling. He was relieved to see Seemi's white paws bounding along with another smallet beside him. He was amazed at how quickly the group could span a distance. When they were what felt like a long way from the prison, Salvo stopped to explain where they were going.

"There's a cottage in the woods where the Surlies are hiding some prisoners. Now's a good time to see if we can free 'em. Breeni (he pointed to the smallet who joined Seemi at the back) says that all the guards except one took off tonight to help out at the jail, 'cause of us. You prob'ly heard the commotion when we left." His sharp little teeth protruded in a wide grin, and his white-tipped ear twitched. "The teesdalls helped us, and we were able to create quite a stir!"

"The guards thought they were under attack," Malvo chuckled, flipping his white-streaked tail. "We beat on trashcan lids with sticks and threw cans and stones from the trees. The teesdalls dropped rocks and nuts with their beaks and claws. It was *brilliant!* They just couldn't figure out what hit 'em!"

"Well, they'd never dream li'l ol' smallets an' teesdalls could create such a ruckus! Creatures like us jus' couldn't be that smart. Right?" Salvo winked and flexed his ear. "I'm sure they think it was organized by Inodians trying to start somethin' to free the Reignbreaker. They're still tryin' to figure it out. And callin' in as much help as they can! So, we can use this time to our advantage. But we don't have a lot o' leeway. They'll be searching high and low to find the Reignbreaker *and* who freed you guys."

After a brief break, Salvo yelled, *"Let's go!"* and bounded down the path with Malvo right behind him, his tail twitching. Noni reached toward Ranni, who snuggled next to Beehart. He wept as he touched her thin arms and felt her emaciated body. He was extremely tired and sore from the grueling trek the day before. Hunger and sleeplessness didn't help. But he understood the urgency of the situation and wanted to help so Beehart didn't have to do all the heavy lifting. He suddenly felt supernatural strength to carry Ranni, and, numbly, he made his way between bushes and branches until he saw a moonlit clearing ahead and stopped beside Salvo.

A thatch-roofed cottage stood alone at the far end of a grassy space. It was dingy gray with a peeling red front door and shutters. Boarded-up windows made it look deserted and uninviting. Just as Salvo stepped into the glade, the cottage door opened, and a Surli guard, wearing the same black armband they'd seen on the prison guards, stepped outside. Salvo dove behind a bush, and the others huddled behind him.

The guard didn't see them, but he sensed something and reached for a dagger strapped to his side. His eyes pierced the clearing as he tried to peer into the woods. Some minutes passed, and he slunk down the steps to squat and lean against the cottage wall. After a while, his head slumped to his chest.

"It's time!" Salvo whispered. He crept cautiously into the clearing. The others moved stealthily behind him. Noni held back with Ranni when he saw that she had difficulty breathing. He took her hand in his and sighed to see her heaving chest.

Salvo crept past the sleeping guard up the steps and motioned for Beehart to open the door. He lifted a latch and pressed against the door's weight with his body to enter a pitch-black room. The smallets followed. Their noses wrinkled when a terrible stench overcame them. Seemi sneezed, and the guard's eyes popped open. He jumped up and looked around. Wondering why the door was open, he grabbed his dagger and darted for the steps. Beehart leapt behind the door with the smallets, and he snarled his most ferocious wild-animal imitation. The guard halted at the top of the steps, and his eyes grew wide. When Beehart's beastly roar grew louder and fiercer, the man yelled, cursed, and turned to high-tail it for the woods. The smallets looked up at Beehart and laughed out loud.

Inside, they found flickering embers emitting an eerie, dying light from a sooty stone fireplace. A food-encrusted pot hung from a metal arm inside the hearth with rusty pots and pans nearby. A long table stood at the side of the room circled by chairs. Half-eaten bowls of stew and mugs of ale cluttered the table, along with dirty utensils. At the far end of the room, an old couch spit out its stuffing.

The smallets branched out, opening doors around the large room. One door led to a small room filled with piles of soiled clothes, linens, blankets, and rags. Another room held a large desk with teetering stacks of mildewed papers.

Still at the edge of the clearing, Ranni asked Noni to help her to the cottage.

"We need to go, Noni," she said, summoning all her strength. "I think we need to see what's going on inside."

He supported her across the glade and up the steps, and he gently placed her on the couch inside. That effort alone sapped all her energy, so he wrapped her in a blanket, while the others searched the rooms. As he comforted her, he heard a strange tapping sound. He held his breath to hear it again. It seemed to come from behind a door on the far side of the room. He went over and tried to open it, but it was locked. He threw himself against it with no success. Beehart came over to help him push against it, but it still wouldn't budge. As the tapping grew louder, Noni ran around the front room, looking for a key to unlock the door. He spotted a glimmer from the table. Pushing chairs aside, he grabbed a small metal object that lay between mugs of stale ale. *It was a key!*

Running back to the door, he tried it in the keyhole. *It fit!* The door swung open! Noni ran ahead of Beehart and Salvo down a dark narrow passageway with a row of doors on the left side and boarded-up windows on the right side. He tried the first door. It wasn't locked, and he shoved it open. His eyes had to adjust to the room's gloom. Moonlight glinted in through cracks between the hall window boards, but not enough to see clearly in the room. He heard muffled moans coming from a bed. As he approached, he sensed it was a woman and was alarmed to see her wrists and ankles tied to posts at the head and foot of the bed. A cloth bound her mouth, and she groaned and shivered. He ran and retrieved a knife from the table in the front room then began to cut through the ropes. While he worked to free her wrists, Beehart came and used another knife to cut the cord that tethered her ankles.

Salvo and Malvo moved to the woman's head and used their sharp teeth to release the cloth around her mouth. As they pulled the strip away, they heard a gasp. Ranni had wandered into the room and had slipped, unnoticed, to the head of the bed. She now covered her mouth with her hands. And her beautiful blue-green eyes grew wide as she gazed down at the woman's face.

"Mother!" she gasped.

"Ranni!" the woman barely rasped.

Beehart stopped cutting and went to his mother's side.

"Beehart!" the bound woman cried out, louder now, and the boy leaned over to put his arms around his mother's neck. They all shook with sobs.

"I can't believe you're here!" Her wrists free, Ada sat up stiffly. "Did you find the others?" She expressed immediate concern.

"What others?" Noni asked.

"In the next room," she said hoarsely. *"Go!* You'll see!"

Noni ran to the next room and found the smallets chattering excitedly around a man and a woman in separate beds, also bound and gagged. The man had been tapping his booted foot against the footboard, and Seemi had followed the sound. Noni was hopeful, but he didn't want to be disappointed. Not able to see the man's face, he released his wrists, while Seemi and Breeni helped the woman. Hands freed, the man tore off his gag and sat up.

"Noni, Noni!" Stade whispered as loud as he could as he weakly reached out to hug his son.

After embracing his father, Noni wiped his eyes and went to free his fettered feet. Then he went over to his mother. She moaned happily when she could sit up, with her husband and son on either side of her. Noni held her hand and cried at how much older she looked now.

Salvo interrupted them to announce that they needed to move quickly. He was concerned that the Surli would be back with more guards. Beehart covered his mother's shivering body with a blanket, while Ranni sat next to her weeping. Noni stood next to his parents as they slowly moved around to get their bearings.

Before leaving, they all surrounded the long table, found a few unused bowls, and hungrily finished off the stew from the pot in the hearth. Out the door, Stade tried to help Lona after she stumbled and almost fell down the steps. Noni rushed over and supported her. Salvo led the way across the glade and down a wooded path. Malvo followed, then Noni, Lona, Stade, Beehart carrying Ranni, Ada, Breeni, and, finally, Seemi.

"Where are we going?" Ada whispered to Beehart after they were a good distance from the cottage.

"Salvo said there's a special place prepared for us," Beehart whispered back, shrugging his shoulders.

"The smallets have been getting ready for quite some time," Ranni explained. "They encouraged me in prison and gave me hope. If it weren't for them, I'd probably be dead. I almost gave up." She sighed.

"I'm so glad you didn't," Beehart said and thought about his own feelings of despair when he couldn't help Leo, Noni, himself, or Sluggli. "The smallets seem to know when we need to be dug out of our ditches!" He half-smiled.

"Yes. They do." Ranni beamed through tears.

"They visited us too," Ada added, "and told us they'd somehow free us. That gave us so much hope!"

Noni thought about Salvo's promise to return for Sluggli, and he wondered if he would.

As they walked, the smallets scurried on and off the path, in and out of bushes, while the rest of them maintained a single line. Sometimes they heard birds buzzing overhead, especially as an early gray light peeked between the trees, and Noni shuddered, thinking about the terrifying "tinshemet" he encountered. Lona noticed his reaction to the birds.

"Those are unusual teesdalls," she explained. "They can't talk like the smallets, but they can carry messages back and forth. They communicate with the other animals and warn them about the whereabouts of the Surlies."

Noni realized that the eerie creature sounds—the whispers they'd heard as they traveled—were most likely coming from the smallets and teesdalls as they conspired to help them.

He looked behind at his family and friends reunited, and he smiled. The only family member missing was Lelels, and his hope was that his brother was safe at home. Despite feeling exhausted and numb with a twinge of regret for Leo and Sluggli, he was mostly happy and thankful.

It was daybreak when Salvo stopped at the top of a high hill. Ada and Lona slumped to the ground. Beehart laid Ranni gently onto a patch of grass and sat down beside her. Stade leaned against a tree, and the smallets bounded off to gaze at the land below the hill.

"We're almost there!" Salvo said, smiling. "The hideout is in the woods down there, on the other side of that road." He pointed at a dirt road that wound down from the hilltop to a wooded area then proceeded further down the hill to more open land. Noni's tired eyes gazed beyond the forest to the distant fields and strained to see the wall along Inod's border. But it wasn't visible. *Gratville is really far away*, he sighed, feeling like it had been ages since he'd left home. He longed for his lookout tree and wondered if he'd ever see his treehome, his bed, the den, or Lelels again. He dreamed of sipping a cup of spree tea at his kitchen table, with his dad and mom and brother by his side.

Beehart came over just then. Leaving Ranni asleep in the grass, he interrupted Noni's daydream.

"We'll get back," he reassured, reading Noni's thoughts. "I miss it all too."

Noni smiled, and they sat, side by side, resting their weary legs, while the smallets kept a lookout. They both watched as the velvety deep blue sky gave way to a thickening orange and gold-lined horizon. Like spectators of an unfolding scroll, they took in the emerging light as it created a canvas of red, orange, and yellow that spread across the grassy fields below like an unfurling fire.

But then a dark purple funnel cloud began to form above them, disrupting the colorful morning calm. Its fervor grew and it stirred up a chilly wind that whipped leaves from the nearby trees. A sudden stinging rain fell and pelted against their skin.

"Let's go!" Salvo yelled and motioned for them to follow quickly.

Noni helped Lona up with his aching arms, Beehart lifted Ranni onto his back, and Stade moved behind Salvo as he led the way down the hill and into the forest, where tall needle-leafed trees shielded them from the wind and rain. As they walked, Noni craned his neck to gaze up at the unusual foliage.

"I've never seen trees like these." Beehart noticed them too.

"They're secrela trees," Malvo explained as he scurried between the boys. "They only grow here in Wiggledown Woods. They give shelter to the animals and birds."

The enormous trees were the biggest they'd ever seen. Noni imagined he could build a mansion in the limbs or under the trunks of these trees. The branches were filled with hundreds of nests.

Suddenly, a group of smallets surrounded them.

"They're here to greet us!" Salvo explained. "They heard you were coming."

Noni wondered if the teesdalls had told them, and he glanced back at Beehart. As if in a dream, they were being led into a hidden world. Protected by a thick canopy, an open area emerged, surrounded by bushes. And a fire glowed invitingly from the middle of a stone circle. The boys and their families drew close to the warmth, still shivering and wet from the rain blast. The smallets chattered and motioned for them to sit on large rocks placed around the fire. Looking up, they saw the teesdalls chirping from the limbs overhead.

"They're called *trusser-true* teesdalls," Salvo explained.

"Why the fancy name?" Beehart asked.

"A truss is something that supports," Salvo said. "That's what truss-er-true teesdalls do. They support and help us. They scout out threats and warn us of danger."

The smallets served up stew from pots over the fire and handed them filled wooden bowls and cups of refreshing spring water. Salvo brought over wool tunics the smallets had made for them, and Noni tore off his wet garment and put on the new one, appreciating its fresh fragrance. He hugged it to his body and enjoyed feeling dry and warm, since he'd felt chilled ever since entering the prison cell.

They gave Ranni a beautiful new red cape to replace the tattered one. Noni wept when he saw them place it around her thin shoulders and her shivering stopped.

"The smallets and teesdalls wanted to do these things for you," Salvo explained. "They wanted you to feel welcome, because they know why you're here and what you can do for them. They've lived with fear for so long, and your being here gives them a lot of hope."

"What do they think we can do for them?" Beehart's forehead crinkled.

"Well, a little history…." Salvo said seriously. "When the Surlies and Zamzummim take over a land, they chop down all the trees and leave the place desolate. They leave the smallets and teesdalls with no place to build nests. Since Wiggledown Woods is hard to reach, being high on a hill, and it sits on unproductive land, they haven't pursued this place. But, some day they will. And we'll have no place to go. This is really our last bastion of hope," Salvo frowned. "That's why we celebrate your coming. We know you'll help protect us, especially since you have the Reignbreaker with you."

How sad if the Surlies decide to destroy these trees, Noni thought, then, realizing what Salvo's words really meant, he grimaced. *No pressure! Geez! Now I know why they were so eager to rescue and welcome us!* He looked over at Beehart, questioning how they could possibly live up to these expectations. Beehart returned the glance with raised eyebrows. Inside, he was saying, *What in the world? Really? Holy smoli!*

The others hunched silently over their steaming bowls of stew, avoiding eye contact and secretly wondering what they would have to do. Then Salvo suddenly sat upright on his haunches, making himself taller, and lowered his head.

"I want to pray," he said boldly. The other smallets gathered around. "Abba, we thank you for our guests and for the hope they bring us. Thanks that, with their help, we can live without fear. Thanks for them being here. In Ameno's name we pray!"

The smallets all shouted *"Amen!"* then cheered and clapped their paws, creating an unusual thumping sound that echoed through the forest.

The rest of the day, the exhausted guests rested by the fire, talked to the smallets, ate more stew, asked some questions, and pondered their limited ability and why they were here. Late in the afternoon, seeing how tired they were, the smallets led the Gomies in groups to the secrela trees and pointed out where they'd be staying for the night. The hosts had built oversized nests—egg-shaped cocoons made of twigs and dried mud—in the upper forks of the large limbs. The openings were big enough for them to crawl through and, inside, they were waterproof, warm, and comfortable, and they could accommodate at least two Gomies.

Stade and Lona would stay with Malvo. Ranni and Ada were Salvo's guests. Breeni showed Noni and Beehart how to climb up a tree trunk, using carved notches for their feet and branches as handles, to get to his nest. They were pleasantly surprised to find feather-stuffed grat-skin pillows and soft wool blankets along the walls. As they got settled, Breeni brought them cups of spree tea and a small basket of griffoons that dripped with butter and honey. They were in heaven.

Beehart's wound was festering since Belial drove the sword-tip into his palm, and Breeni watched the boy painfully trying to climb the tree. Once inside the nest, the smallet carefully daubed Beehart's hand with some healing ointment, similar to Mosi's salve, and wrapped a clean cloth around it. The boy sighed with relief.

Feeling comfortable and satisfied, Noni's mind wandered anxiously to Sluggli, and he felt another twinge of painful regret, wondering what'd happened to his friend. Filled with sadness, he yearned for *Ameno's Manna. That wonderful treasure is probably gone forever,* he muttered, feeling angry at the Surlies, who didn't appreciate it but took it anyway. Beehart also reached for Truelight and groaned, missing his prized gift. They both grumbled at the thought of all that was stolen from them: their special gifts, their grats, and some of their friends and family.

"I guess we *can* be thankful that we're here together now, *and* we're *alive!*" Noni interrupted their dismal thoughts. "Our bellies are full, *and* we have a safe place to rest."

Beehart nodded and, as they curled up in the corner of the cocoon, twilight filtering through the leaves around them, they realized that, even without the sword and the book, they might be able to tap into something even more powerful.

While Beehart fell quickly into a deep sleep, Noni lay awake, listening to the wind as it threatened and blew shrilly above the huge tree, unable to disturb the branches around the nest where they lay. As he gazed through the twig-lined entrance, he thanked Abba for this peaceful abode, where he felt protected from the Dragon and his menacing forces. And when an especially strong breeze suddenly whipped through the branches above, twisting and turning them, without any success in reaching the nest, Noni sighed with relief and thankfulness as he spotted a glowing globe peeking through at him. And he noticed that tonight the moon's face was completely full.

chapter twenty-six

Monstrous Memories

Noni woke to the sound of teesdalls cooing. He slowly unwrapped himself from his blanket and stood up. His head touched the twig ceiling, so he bent and crept to avoid crunching the pitched branches beneath his boots. Beehart and Breeni snored like they were singing the same song, and he chuckled as he faced dawn's light through the door and it flickered faintly through the secrelas' needled canopy. Moving quietly outside onto a limb, he grabbed hold of a branch and tried to remember how he'd climbed up the day before. He found a handle by the highest carved foothold and placed his foot into the notch. Then he slowly groped for more handles and notches until he'd made his way safely down. On the ground, he sighed with relief and gazed around. A light flickered from the fire circle, and he made his way there, hungrily hoping that earlier risers were preparing something to eat.

Several teesdalls turned toward him from the circle as he approached, and they cooed to greet him. He was immediately mesmerized by their fluorescent teal feathers, that shimmered and reflected the emerging sunlight, and their brilliant-black onyx eyes that gazed hypnotically at him.

"Good morning, sleepyhead!" Salvo bounced over to welcome him. "The teesdalls brought edible flowers and plants for our tea this morning."

Noni nodded a thank-you to the birds. They beckoned with their beaks as they huddled near the fire. Salvo handed Noni a warm cup of the tea sweetened with honey as he sat on a boulder near the fire, enjoying the morning stillness. As he sipped the flavorful tea, he began to feel a sudden surge of energy, and he wondered if the tea might have the same healing features as Breeni's and Mosi's ointments. He asked Salvo about the ingredients, and the smallet confirmed that the flowers and plants in the tea did bring healing. Ameno had taught them about their life-giving properties.

"But plants can't heal everything," Salvo affirmed. "Only Ameno can completely heal us and make us whole."

Noni nodded, looking down at his near-empty cup, then he thought of something and changed the subject.

"What's the plan today?"

"Well, today we'll all rest. I think everyone needs a day of healing. Don't you?" Salvo smiled at Noni. "Tomorrow, we'll head to Daunt-let's Den."

"What's Dauntlet's Den?" Noni looked up from the cup that warmed his hands.

"It's where the dauntlets live," Salvo responded.

"What exactly are dauntlets?" Noni pursued.

"They're very large, wise birds." Salvo said. "They're mostly brown with black and white spots, and they have white chests and heart-shaped faces with brown beaks. Their eyes are large and dark, and they speak to each other by hooting," he continued. "Many of them used to live throughout Init Isle, but, when so many forests were cleared, they had to move to caves in the Secrela Valley. For years, the Zamzummim and Surlies have pursued them, because they hate them."

"*Why* do they hate them?" Noni knit his brows. "They sound like amazing birds!"

"Because of what they stand for," Salvo answered.

"What's that?" Noni stared at the smallet.

"They're Ameno's warriors. They fight for his way of life, which means treating the land and the people with care and respect and living freely without being forced to pay homage to the leaders of Zamzum and Sur. Because they oppose King Zoar's domination, the Zamzummim and Surli kingpins want to kill them. And only a few of them have survived."

"Hmmm," Noni reflected. "Why are we going to their den? It seems dangerous for us to be there…with them."

"Ranni will explain," Salvo assured. "You haven't had a chance to catch up with her. Ameno told her what needs to happen, and she'll fill you in. Today, you can get caught up with each other and find out about your next assignment."

Noni stared down at his cup and silently wondered, *What does he think we're going to do? Can we do what he thinks we can?* As if he could read the boy's mind, Salvo spoke up.

"You see, while Ranni was in prison, we visited her often after Ameno asked us to watch out for her. He told us how she'd help us, and we started bringing her food and encouraging her. If we hadn't, I'm sure she would've died." Salvo confirmed what Ranni had told them. He stopped suddenly, and his ear twitched. "Ranni will fill you in on the rest."

Noni was anxious to hear more, but he pressed his lips together in thought. He sensed that the smallet didn't want to say any more, so he held onto his questions: *What was his role in all of this? What was Ranni's part? And Beehart's?* He sipped the tea and stared into the crackling fire as the others emerged from the nests. One by one, they made their way to the circle and gladly accepted cups of the healing tea along with savory buttered griffoons. Everyone acknowledged how much better they felt after a good night's sleep. Now, they all enjoyed the energizing drink. Ranni and Ada were the last to join them, and Ranni chose a boulder next to Noni by the fire.

After everyone was settled, Noni turned to Ranni.

"They say you're the Reignbreaker," he said, hoping she'd elaborate.

"Yes," she answered between bites of a griffoon.

"Ameno told us he visited you in prison," Noni gazed over at her.

"He did. He was my only comfort, besides the smallets." Her eyes smiled back at him.

"Did he tell you we were trying to find you?" Noni's fingers tightened around his cup.

"Yes. He promised he'd lead you to me." Ranni lowered her eyes and sighed.

"Did he tell you about this mission—what we're supposed to do?" Noni posed hopefully and waited a few minutes, then pressed. "I just wonder how we can do it."

"All I know is that I'm supposed to unlock a gate between Sur and Inod." Ranni took a deep breath.

"Why do *you* have to open the gate?" Noni frowned, wondering how she, in her frail condition, could possibly accomplish this.

"I'm the only one who can, Ameno said," she spoke matter-of-factly. "He told me that Abba had picked me out for this purpose. He even told me a story—how a long time ago, his own city was locked down with fear of attacking enemies. Then, the king found a hidden scroll, and it gave him so much hope that they could overcome their enemies. It was a woman in the city who helped the king unlock the scroll's message. She explained the words and what they meant. Because of her, the people in the city were able to open their gate and be free from their terror," she explained. "Like her, I must unlock the fear-gate that keeps our people imprisoned. That's my mission, Noni. When I open this gate, all the people of Inod and Sur will be free. It will create a connection between the lands. I don't know yet how it'll happen. All I know is that Ameno will lead and help us." She let out her breath.

"Wow!" Noni's eyes grew wide. "I wonder how we'll do it!"

"*I* have to do it, Noni!" Ranni said firmly. "But *you* can help me!"

"How?" He felt a little crushed by her statement, but he also realized that his once-childish friend had changed. She was no longer the flighty girl who liked to pick moggies and spin around like a doll in her cape. She was now *The Reignbreaker*—a determined young woman with a mission. He respected her for this, and he wondered if months of hardship had forged this new strength in her.

"I don't know yet," Ranni answered honestly. "But I believe Ameno will show us." She smiled faintly and her face started to glow. He felt his heart race as he recognized her inner beauty for the first time.

But his mind was still plagued by questions: *How can we do this without being captured and tortured by the Surlies? How can we fight against a bunch of giants and win?* Trying to refocus his thoughts, he felt some comfort when he remembered something Ameno said: *"I am sending you ahead of me to make a way. I'll follow and bring more help. You'll find yourselves in some tricky and scary situations, but don't be afraid. You'll always have what you need and end up where you belong. Trust me in this."*

His thoughts were interrupted by his mother's voice.

"I am *so* thankful for you, Noni," she said, coming over to him. "You were *so* brave to come for us!"

Noni sank into her comforting embrace while the others continued to talk and eat around the circle. After she sat down next to him, he bade the question, "What led to your capture?" Then he, Beehart, and Ranni listened intently as she and the other parents disclosed the events that led to their capture.

"When we were at Humbi and Honi's, they told us about the Very Vine sharetoo, and we decided we wanted to see it before going to Bleamer's inn," Lona recalled. "I felt a little uneasy, especially when I heard that the Surlies would arrest anyone who went inside a sharetoo. But, when we found it, I thought it was so beautiful! We'd never seen one like it before, and we wanted so much to go inside. We were fascinated by the stained-glass windows. Well, we stayed a little too long, enjoying the peacefulness…."

"We were there too!" Beehart looked up and remembered how serene he felt there too, especially when Ameno revealed himself.

"I heard some Mussians at Bleamer's inn talking about how some folks were accosted there," Noni recalled. "I'll bet they were talking about you!"

"We spent the night inside it," Beehart added. "We met Ameno there, and he told us stories about the windows. That's where we first saw our hearts glow!" He opened his tunic to show them his glowing chest.

Everyone in the circle nodded. They too had seen their hearts change after meeting Ameno. They all sat silently reflecting on this for a moment.

"While we were at Bleamer's, I used a key Mother gave me, and it unlocked a chest he had. And we found some maps that led us to Sapwood," Beehart interrupted the quiet. He pulled the chain from his neck and held up the key. He looked over at Ada. "Tell me about when Ameno gave it to you and what he told you."

Ada gazed lovingly at her son and the key in his hand.

"He gave it to me when he came to see me," she recalled. "All he said was that I should give it to you when I felt it was the right time. He said you'd need it. That's all I knew."

"I *did* need it. We *all* needed it. It led us *to you!*" Beehart gripped the key, then he pulled something from his pocket. "He gave me this at the sharetoo." He held up the iridescent bluish-purple sapphire stone. It sparkled in the firelight.

Noni reached into his pocket and help up his own bright yellow topaz. Lona admired it, then she pulled her own prize from a tiny leather pouch hidden inside her clothes. It was a pure white carbuncle, the same size and shape as his stone.

"It's wonderful, and so sparkly, like snow!" Ranni exclaimed. "When did he give it to you?"

"Early one morning, he came to visit us in the garden behind Humbi and Honi's house. He gave us each our special stones and explained what they meant. He wanted to prepare us for what lay ahead." She gazed down at the gift in her hand then said, "Stade's stone is shiny and black." She nodded toward her husband, and he held out his brilliant, round ebony carbuncle. Ranni oohed and ahhed. She'd never seen such anything like it before.

Noni thought about the statue in Humbi and Honi's yard.

"In their garden, they built a fountain in your honor," he said.

"It doesn't surprise me!" Lona's eyes glistened. "I miss them so much! They were so kind to us!"

Noni looked around and realized that almost everyone was holding up a stone except Ranni and Ada, who gave a dimpled smile and pulled a small leather bag like Lona's from her pocket. Before she drew out its contents, she hesitated.

"It's not the coveted 'Adamant' stone my parents found near Clearus Spring. My mother gave that one to me before I left for Gratville and told me to always keep it hidden until it was the right time to reveal it. She reminded me that the Surlies believed the stone relinquished special supernatural powers to whoever held it, and they didn't want anyone who threatened them, especially the renowned Reignbreaker, to get a hold of it. If they found it with me, I would be in great danger of being killed.

"I kept it for years in a secret place. When Ameno came to see me and gave me Beehart's key, I decided to give him something precious too, mostly because I felt that keeping it was putting my whole family in danger. When I handed him the Adamant, I asked if he would make sure to give it to the Reignbreaker, not knowing who that would end up being. I knew he would.

"When I presented the stone to him, he also gave me my special stone—this one…."

From the tiny bag, she drew out a beautiful blue-green emerald, the same size and shape as theirs—that of a large coin—and held it up for them to see.

"Ameno told me it was the perfect prize for me, because it would remind me of Lake Adamant and how my mother had turned it into a beautiful aqua-colored, spring-fed lake."

Now, all eyes fell on Ranni, in anticipation, as she pulled her stone from a secret pocket in her dress. Clutching it, she slowly unfolded her fingers to reveal a perfectly-symmetrical, round-cut diamond. As she held it up for them to see, a glimmer of light reflected from it and produced a multi-colored rainbow that arched majestically over the circle. They all gasped. As Ranni gazed at the metamorphosing gem in her hand, she explained that this *was* the amazing Adamant stone.

"When did he give it to you?" Beehart asked, staring at the stone.

"When I almost drowned," Ranni whispered, and everyone leaned in closer to hear.

"What do you mean by 'when you almost drowned?'" Ada asked, alarmed.

"On the way to the prison, the Surli you call Belial dragged me across the Testus River using a rope around my waist. Of course, my hands were tied together in front. We didn't use the bridge, because he wanted to stay hidden. When he was pulling me against the rushing water, the rope around my waist came undone, and I was swept away.

It was difficult to use my arms to keep my head above the water, since they were bound, so I kicked with my legs and thrust my arms in front of me as I floated downstream. My body grew numb with cold, and my lungs filled with water. I sputtered and tried to breathe. I thought I would die. And I passed out." She sighed.

"The next thing I knew, I was lying on the shore. I looked up and saw Ameno leaning over me. He gently lifted my head and held me while I coughed up water. When I could breathe normally again, he untied my hands and gave me the stone. He said it would always remind me of how he could make me strong. I could endure anything, he said, if I remembered that he was near, watching over me. But I must also remember that my power came, not from the stone, but from his spirit in me. The Adamant is just a symbol of his unbreakable strength.

"He also told me that he'd give me what I needed whenever I reached out to him, and that his father, Abba, can use bad situations to make the good things in us grow stronger.

"After he left, I lay there admiring the gift. I wasn't even thinking about the Surli and, before I knew it, he burst out of the woods and found me. I didn't have the energy to fight him or run. He tied me back up and carried me away. At the prison, I was miserable and sad. I lay on the cell floor, sobbing and wondering what would become of me. I could hear the guards whispering about keeping me there long enough to capture the Reignbreaker. I didn't know what they were talking about. I wondered how long they'd keep me there and how I could survive. I was starving because they didn't always feed me, and, when they did, I could barely eat the food.

"Sometimes I felt angry at Ameno for leaving me at that most vulnerable moment. I wondered if he could've prevented this and why he didn't take me with him. Then I remembered what he said about trusting him, and I realized that the way I thought he'd rescue me and the way he actually would might be different. Maybe I just had to be patient. It's funny." She held out her treasure. "The guards never discovered the stone in my clothes, and it's been a constant source of comfort to me. It reminds me daily of his promises."

"The Surlies never found ours either," Noni reflected "I thought that was strange. Do you think Ameno protects our stones by preventing people from seeing them?"

Everyone puzzled over the uniqueness of their glowing gems and how the enemy had never been able to steal them. Noni especially admired the crystal-clear pureness of Ranni's and how it reflected colorful rays of light whenever she turned it.

"What do your stones stand for?" He glanced around. "When Ameno gave us ours, he said they represent who we are, how he sees us, and what we can do when we partner with him. My stone reminds me of how much he loves me and that I can love others the way he loves me. What about yours?"

"Mine stands for how he protects me and those who trust him." Beehart held out his sapphire.

"He told me mine stands for beauty, life, and all the amazing things Abba and Ameno created for us." Ada admired her emerald. "It also reminds me of how my parents created a beautiful lake using a stream's cleansing flow and how Abba makes us lovely by his living water."

"Our carbuncles remind us of his faithfulness." Lona held Stade's hand fondly. "And how he helps those who are faithful."

Everyone looked at Ranni. Feeling their eyes, she hunched over and stared down at the radiating gem in her hands.

"My diamond reflects peace and purity," she whispered. "He said peace comes when people's hearts are made pure by good thoughts. This can only happen when they turn their thoughts to him. Then, like the spring-fed creek or lake," she glanced at her mother, "they are washed through. I can bring peace to our land by introducing them to Ameno's goodness. Then they can live as they were meant to." Transfixed by the diamond, she scrunched over, like she was bearing an unseen burden.

Lona noticed and spoke up.

"He wouldn't give you this assignment, dear, if he didn't believe you could do it." She smiled. "You're courageous and strong, Ranni. Like the Adamant. You've already proved that. Most people could never survive what you did!"

Ranni sat up then sank down again.

"It's true!" Beehart emphasized. "I've *always* thought you had a special purpose."

"How long have *you* known she was the Reignbreaker?" Noni turned to Ada.

"I didn't know for sure until this trip," Ada admitted. "I imagined one of my children might be the Reignbreaker because of the stories I was told. I just wasn't sure who. I sometimes wondered if it might be Ranni."

Noni was saddened by the weight he sensed on Ranni's shoulders. He remembered her as being playful and childlike—once carefree. Ranni noticed his expression and reached over to put her hand on his arm. As she did, something lifted, her face brightened, and a song honoring Ameno poured from her lips.

"We now see your beauty
With newfound delight,
And we all have to wonder
At your strength and might.
We now see your colors
And your profound light.
Your beautiful hues
Amaze at the sight.
We now see your rainbow

Of various stones.
It reminds us of your love
And gifts you've bestowed.
You offer them to us
From your great ephod,
Gems given daily
From father Abba.
Each one symbolizes
A quest and a treasure.
Each one offers promise
Of life without measure."

The words comforted them all like a warm, soft blanket. After a few quiet moments, Beehart spoke up.

"Can you tell us more about how the Surlies captured you?" He looked over at his mother and she picked up where Lona left off.

"They found us inside the Very Vine sharetoo. The leader was very tall and wore a cloak with a hood that partly hid his face. He had an eye patch."

"We know him well," Beehart grimaced. "We call him Belial."

"Yes. I'm sure it's one and the same, the way you described him," Ada confirmed. "We were caught off guard with no way to escape. He and another Surli tied our hands behind our backs, then blindfolded and loaded us into a horse-drawn cart and carried us to the house where you found us. At the cottage, they gave us a little food and water and sometimes let us go outside, but not very often. Once, when we were outside and the guards weren't too close, Salvo came and told us he'd bring help. This gave us hope. So we hung on and prayed.

"Every night we were tied to the beds." She sighed and looked down. "The rooms weren't heated, so it was unbearable in the winter months. During the day, they would let us sit around the fire sometimes and eat. We wore the same filthy clothes every day. We were bitten by lice, fleas, and bedbugs. Stade suffered the most. He has sores all over his arms, legs, and feet. Lona has a red festering rash all over her body too. I've had a painful toothache for months."

"Did you ever figure out why they captured and kept you so long? I mean, besides being in the wrong place at the wrong time, was there something they wanted from you?" Noni had his suspicions.

"One night, I overheard the guards talking," Stade recalled. "They said something about us being related to 'this reign person,' as they put it. It seemed like we were the bait they needed for this person to come to Sur. I didn't know who they were talking about."

"I heard that conversation too." Lona nodded. "But I didn't know who or what they meant. I had no idea they were referring to Ranni."

Everyone looked at Ranni, and she struggled to speak.

"I am *so* sorry you had to go through all that because of me." Her voice quivered. "I didn't choose this. It was given to me." She hesitated before continuing. "But I see now how it was all part of this mission to help the land and relieve so much unseen suffering.

"I haven't told you everything." She looked down at her hands, still holding the gem. "Whenever the guards came to my cell, they'd hit me with sticks and scream at me about how they'd make me the bloody bait to attract this Reignbreaker." She paused. "I guess they thought it was Beehart. Couldn't possibly be a girl! Right?" She smiled and showed her dimple for the first time since she was rescued. "But I had no idea what they were talking about, so I just cowered in the corner until they left.

"Belial was the worst!" She shuddered. "Every few days he brought food and water and used them to taunt me. He'd dump moldy food on the floor and tell me to *'Lick it up.'* If I didn't, he'd hit me with the butt of his whip again and again until I broke down and cried. Then, he'd turn the whip around and lash me with it until my arms and legs were bleeding and covered with bruises and welts. I wanted to die!" Her eyes welled up with tears. "Only Ameno's visits and the smallets kept me alive." She showed them the marks on her thin arms and legs. Her mother turned away.

Ada and Beehart shook with sobs while the others wept. Noni bent over and covered his face with his hands. Feeling overwhelmed with sadness, his thoughts sped to innocent days spent in Gratville with Ranni, and a heaviness descended over him, pushing aside the lingering peacefulness from Ranni's song. Then he looked down and noticed his heart-flame had dimmed as a sober silence hung over them.

It was close to noon now, and the smallets tiptoed around the somber group, handing out nourishing bowls of hearty muss stew and savory moggie pie. Everyone ate quietly until Lona spoke up.

"On our way to Sur from the sharetoo, they took off our blindfolds," she recalled. "They set up camp in a canyon by Clearus Creek with a waterfall. They led us there and let us wash our faces and hands and eat some food they cooked over a fire. They kept a watchful eye on us, but, while they were drinking and carousing, I found a sharp stick and carved three crosses on a tree as a sign to anyone looking for us."

"*Yes!*" Noni's eyes lit up. "*We saw them!* And we wondered who'd carved them. We also found a piece of bark with something written on it under the tree. It said something about the water of life. I put it in my bag." He sighed and wondered where Saron and his bags were now.

"I wrote that," Ada said. "I hoped you'd see it and know we were all right."

"We found it when we were leaving Leo and the cave." Beehart winced, and Ada noticed.

"What happened there?" she asked. After a few silent moments, Noni responded.

"Three Surlies followed us to the cave. Belial was one of them. He and another one fell when they were pursuing us, but one was able to track us into the cave. Thankfully, he was scared off by Leo's wild howls. We found Leo inside. He was imprisoned there by the Surlies and had lost his sight. He couldn't make his way back home, but someone was bringing him food. He told us he'd been tortured because they wanted *him* to lead them to 'Adamantine' and, I guess, the Reignbreaker. Of course, he couldn't, so they abandoned him there." Noni saw Ranni look down, and he wished he hadn't mentioned that part about them trying to find the Reignbreaker. He reached over and touched her arm. "In the end, we all ended up where we were supposed to," he encouraged. "If it weren't for Leo being in the cave, we would've been found and captured."

"Yeah, but when we were leaving the canyon, we saw Belial tormenting Leo," Beehart interjected angrily. "I wanted to go back and help him, but Noni insisted that we keep moving."

Noni stared at Beehart, and his friend returned the look with a frown.

"Do you know who Leo is?" Stade turned to face Noni. Without waiting for a reply, he said, "He's my brother and your uncle. Mosi is your cousin!"

"Yes." Noni nodded. "I understand that now—that we're all related. Leo told us!"

"You know," Stade said, "Lelels was named for Leo."

Noni nodded and thought about his brother and wished he was there to enjoy this family reunion. *What would he think of all this?* Most things didn't ruffle Lelels' feathers. But hiking up and down mountains through frightening forests, being assaulted by evil Surlies, marching blindfolded to a jail cell, and sleeping in dark caves and tree nests—these things would have really unsettled him. Noni sighed then remembered someone else—Sluggli.

"We left someone behind," he said matter-of-factly, and his face grew skewed. "Someone very important to us…who tried to save our lives."

"Who, Noni?' Lona looked concerned.

"A friend who showed great courage." He sighed.

"You mean Sluggli?" Beehart asked.

"Yes."

Everyone looked at Noni, and he gazed down at the purple-stained moggie piecrust in his bowl.

"We *have* to go back for him!" He frowned at the thought of what might have become of his friend.

Salvo's ears perked up.

"I've already sent Malvo to rescue him." He grinned and moved his head up and down, showing his sharp little teeth. "He left early this morning, and he'll be back with him before we leave."

Everyone sighed thinking about their impending trek to Dauntlets' Den, and they were relieved to have this time to rest, since their legs and feet and bodies still ached.

"Who's Sluggli?" Ada wondered.

"When we were at the Prior Place in Sapwood we met him," Noni began to explain. "Humbi and Honi told us the owner might be able to help us find a secret way into Sur, so we went there. But, when we got there, the owner, named Fendem, was being threatened by an angry mob who thought he was hiding us. Belial had told them that we might be there, I guess. We hid in a room, but Fendem and his stepson, Sluggli, found us."

"Sluggli saw us at the back door," Beehart went on. "We snuck in when he wasn't looking, but they found our grats tied up in back and knew we were inside somewhere. They searched until they found us. Fendem tied us up and went to turn us in. He left Sluggli to watch us, and we were shocked when he let us go and asked if he could go with us. I didn't trust him at first." Beehart looked over at Noni. "But he ended up showing us a secret cave that led to Sur and being a good friend. He wanted to go with us, because his father is really mean to him, and he saw the persecution toward Ameno-followers in his town."

"What did Fendem look like?" Ada's eyes narrowed.

"He was tall with long gray hair and a mustache, and he wore a long black coat and tall boots. He was mostly fearful about his reputation and his inn," Noni answered.

"Can you describe Sluggli?" Ada's voice wavered.

"Dirty-blond hair and piercing blue-green eyes. Kind of tall and thin. Young but older than a teen." Noni pushed his boot back and forth across the dirt in front of him.

"Was he about the same age as Bleamer?" Ada leaned forward.

"Maybe." Noni looked up at her. "But Bleamer's heavier with short blond hair and glasses." He watched Ada as she hunched over and buried her face in her hands.

"What's the matter, dear?" Lona reached over to rub her back.

"Sluggli…Bleamer," she muttered. "They're both my sons."

Everyone gasped.

"What?" everyone said at once.

"Yes. It's true, "Ada looked up. "When I was eighteen, I met a man near Mussford. I'd never seen a man like him before, and he fascinated me. I didn't tell my parents about 'Clement,' but every day I went to the same place to meet him. He was handsome, tall, and had dark hair and eyes and olive-colored skin. He looked right through me, like he knew everything about me.

"After we'd been seeing each other for several weeks, he asked me to go away with him. I didn't know then that he was a Surli. I'd never met a Surli before. I was so naïve. I left my parents and ran off with him. We lived in his house near Clearus Spring.

"When I became pregnant with twins, he started treating me different, and I knew something was wrong," she went on. "He grew meaner and meaner. And I had no idea why. But soon I realized that he was conspiring with the Surlies to kidnap the twins after they were born. He'd heard the stories that the Reignbreaker would come from Ailis's child—me. And the tales were confirmed to him when he overheard my mother tell my father that she believed one of my children would be the Reignbreaker. So, he decided to use me and my children for his own gain. He told some Surlies that I was pregnant, and they promised him greater wealth if he'd give them over to them so they could 'keep them safe' to live under 'their watchful eyes.' Their justification was that, since one of them must be the famed Reignbreaker, they were in danger of being kidnapped.

"Of course, their real intention was to kill the babies so they would never obstruct their evil plans to control Inod. I believe they also intended to kill me, though I don't know if Clement knew this part. After I had the twins, I saw this conspiratorial side of Clement emerging. I overheard him talking to other Surlies about his plan to hand over the babies for 'safekeeping,' and I was shocked. I went to my parents, confided in them, and they made a way for me and the twins to escape.

"One night, when Clement was out late with his Surli friends, I wrapped the twins in blankets and put them in baskets. I walked as fast as I could to my parents' house and got there before he knew I'd gone. They took me by carriage as far as Gratville and arranged for me to stay with a Krochit family. You don't know this, but it was Groomhilda and her husband who kept me safe until I married Ranhart, Ranni and Beehart's father. They placed the boys, who weren't identical, with separate adoptive parents to keep them hidden. If they stayed with me, the possibility of us being discovered was much greater and more dangerous for us all.

"I heard rumors that when the Surlies discovered their plan had failed, they blamed Clement, and they tortured, beat, and imprisoned him. I also heard he disappeared and died.

"For years, I didn't want to know where the boys ended up. It was too painful for me, and I knew I couldn't go back for them, or we'd all be found out by the Surlies. My parents had the same concerns and never told me where they placed the babies. But, a few years ago, Ranhart and I figured out that Bleamer was one of the twins. We happened to be visiting Oni and Milli's inn, and I saw Bleamer. I just knew he was my son. Of course, Oni and Milli didn't know I was his mother since my parents never revealed that to them. At that time, it was still too risky to tell them because of what was going on with the Surlies and Lord Ludifus in Mussford. But, on our last trip, Humbi and Honi encouraged me, and I decided to take a chance and go see him. I was on my way to tell him I was his mother when we were captured.

"I never knew what happened to the other twin—Sluggli, as you call him. Honi said he was Fendem's stepson and shared her suspicions with me. But we weren't sure. Now, I believe he's the other twin." Ada cried as she thought about the sons she never knew. Beehart's eyes welled up too as he reflected on the father he never got to know, who'd died when he was young, and the brothers he'd always yearned for.

Meanwhile, Noni looked at them both and thought with amazement, *Two of the people who helped us on this journey were Ada's sons and Beehart's brothers!*

"Did Bleamer know he had a twin brother?" Noni asked.

"No, he didn't." Ada sighed. "I was going to tell him."

"I saw a picture of what looked like you and dad in the front lobby of Bleamer's inn," Beehart recalled. "I wondered if it was you."

Just then, Malvo thrust himself into the circle. Standing by the fading fire, he twitched his tail nervously.

"*He's gone!*" he said in his high-pitched voice.

"*Who's* gone?" their voices rose together.

"*Sluggli!* He wasn't there at the prison when I got there. *I don't know what happened to him!*"

chapter twenty-seven

The Dauntlets' Den

Clouds hid the remaining sunlight, and ominous shadows loomed over the circle.

"We'll have to get an early start tomorrow," Salvo stood up in their midst as they wrapped up their conversations around the fire's embers. He glanced at Ada. "I'm sorry, but we *have to* go, even without Sluggli. It's a long way to Dauntlets' Den, and the danger increases the longer we wait. The teesdalls say Surli spies are searching everywhere for you all."

The next morning, Noni was the first one up again. Anxiety about what happened to Sluggli made it hard for him to sleep, even as the luminescent full moon streamed light down toward him through the trees to cheer him. But, for some unexplained reason, he also felt nervous about meeting the dauntlets. Again, he missed having *Ameno's Manna* and the peace it brought him when he read it.

Now, he sipped tea by the fire and listened as the teesdalls cooed and the smallets made hot floodle to warm their bellies on this cool morning. They also set out bowls of butter and honey and fresh-squeezed juice from ripe red pompoons that'd fallen from nearby trees. The others gradually joined him and savored the sweet juice, knowing it would give them needed nourishment for the trek. Without grats to carry their provisions, they'd use leather backpacks made by the smallets. Later, they'd discover bruni nuts, griffoons, and moggies packed inside. They wouldn't need to fill canteens, since there were springs and streams all along the way. Before leaving, they thanked the teesdalls and smallets for all their efforts. Now, the challenge would be to keep up with Salvo, Malvo, and Seemi as they scampered down the narrow trails.

Salvo perked his ears as he led the way. Malvo followed, twitching his tail. Stade, Lona, Noni, Beehart, Ranni, Ada, and Seemi took up their positions in line as a few teesdalls flew ahead to scout for lurking Surlies. After a short distance, Salvo paused in a shaded clearing to assess everyone's ability to keep up. He spotted the gap between Malvo and Stade and realized that Lona, Ranni, and Ada were struggling. Despite his sense of urgency, he decided that the most important thing was to get everyone to the destination in one piece.

The path took them through forests of stately secrelas, and the foliage of the enormous trees made it hard to tell the time of day. They meandered up and down shaded hillsides through miles of soft green ferns and lush bushes loaded with moggies. While the smallets waited for the others to catch up, they nibbled on the sweet berries. They also watched the shadows on the path, since they indicated when morning gave way to early afternoon.

The group stopped in a meadow to rest, and, shielded by tall grass from the warm sun, they settled onto cushiony green moss as they pulled goodies from their bags.

"Thanks, Abba," Salvo prayed. "We're grateful to you for all you've done for us. Protect us on this trip, and get us to the den safely! In Ameno's name we pray. Amen."

"*Amen!*" said the rest in a resounding reply.

The food tasted amazingly good after walking so many hours. Not much remained when they were done.

"Well, I *sure* hope the dauntlets have some food for us when we get there!" Salvo teased.

Though they were refreshed by the break, they soon realized that the trail was all uphill from here. Beehart pointed out a mountain ahead. Ada and Lona sighed, slumped, and trudged on.

"Not too much farther now!" Salvo encouraged. But the mountain still loomed ahead.

As the sun set, the exhausted trekkers reached the summit. They were all relieved that they'd made it, after stopping and stalling many times along the narrow path, trying to bypass sharp rocks and thorny bushes all the way to the top. The stronger ones helped the weaker ones, who often tripped on the unstable rocks that served as steps. Ada, Lona, and Ranni collapsed on the ground at the peak, breathing heavily.

The summit, covered with spiny shrubs, had a spectacular view of the surrounding valleys. Noni gazed down to see if he could catch a glimpse of his distant home, still longing for it. His bones begged for his bed, his stomach clamored for familiar food, and his heart yearned for his brother's companionship. Recognizing Noni's melancholy mood, Salvo came over and pointed out familiar spots, and the boy soon forgot his homesickness as he watched the sun set.

Colorful lines streaked across the sky as if a gifted artist had taken a large brush and created a beautiful painting for him. A luminous golden necklace, with a shining orb in the middle, lay along the horizon.

A scream disrupted his reverie, and he turned to see a humongous flying creature swooping down toward him, screeching loudly as it approached. Lona grabbed Ranni and Ada and pulled them with her behind a large rock. The others ran for cover and cowered in the shadow of some shrubs. Beehart remembered the fearsome tinshemet in the forest, and his heart sank. He froze and shook with fear.

Salvo jumped onto a large boulder and waved his paws like a general commanding his forces. He motioned to the swirling apparition, and it descended gracefully onto the summit's gravel-covered ground. Malvo, unafraid, ran up to greet the giant bird, and it held out a wing so he could huddle under its downy crook. Astounded, Noni remembered Salvo's description of the dauntlets and recognized the markings. Still, it was unlike anything he'd ever seen, and he moved cautiously toward it. The bird gazed down at him through large dark eyes that were set in a heart-shaped face covered with white downy feathers. Noni felt an immediate love for the creature, and he wanted to touch it. The others came up stealthily behind him from behind the rock and shrubs.

"This is our friend, Hupsoo," Salvo announced from atop the boulder, his ears upright as he extended his paw toward the giant bird. "He's here to carry us to the den."

Hupsoo nodded and extended both mighty wings and, from head to tail, he was about the size of a ten-foot-tall tree. Ranni courageously approached him. Reaching out to touch his wing, she gently stroked his soft, brown feathers. Later, she told them he felt like the silky down of a baby teesdall or the velvety underbelly of a baby grat. As she stroked, his dark eyes peered through her, and she started to cry. Noni stepped up and put an arm around her. When *he* looked into the bird's eyes, he felt an overwhelming sense of peace. Gently lifting his huge wings, Hupsoo beckoned for them to climb onto his back.

"He wants to carry you," Salvo explained.

Without hesitation, Noni and Ranni climbed onto his back when he lowered his body closer to the ground. Ranni rode in front and clutched his neck feathers. Noni wrapped his arms around her waist, and the bird flapped his wings rhythmically to lift himself into the air. Soon, they were soaring through the air. Ranni caught her breath, and Noni pulled her closer. They leaned into each other and gripped the bird's broad back with their legs.

As Hupsoo ascended, they relaxed and enjoyed the scenery below. They saw patches of secrela, towser, bruni, housit, and spree trees in quilt-like patterns all over the mountainside. A serpentine stream cut a circuitous trail through a valley below, and sandy banks lined its sides, making the rivulet look wider. Chalky cliffs stretched from the stream to the trees that formed a thick leafy belt around the middle of each mountain. Rocky cliffs resumed where the trees thinned near the mountain peaks.

Noni scoped the slopes and wondered where the den lay. The bird dipped playfully, giving them the best possible views of the valley, which was washed in the sunset's glorious colors. The cliffs shimmered in layers of glimmering golds, fluorescent purples, and pearly whites. The spectacular scene made them breathless.

This is even more beautiful than the flowered meadow, Noni sighed, remembering his longings from the tree perch at home. Ranni gasped as Hupsoo lunged toward a jagged cliff, and Noni held her tight. Then the bird dove between some tall trees that lined the cliff and landed on the outstretched arm of a giant secrela tree. He used his strong talons to grip a limb and steady himself. Then he hopped from branch to branch, unfurling his wings slightly for balance. They could see the entrance to a cave, barely visible behind the large tree. Spreading one wing, Hupsoo motioned with his beak for them to get down, using the wing as a slide.

After a thrilling descent, Noni and Ranni stood on a ledge and gazed into the doorway of a den. They were startled when a small, white-pawed creature darted out. *It was Breeni!* Having arrived the day before, he'd made sure the dauntlets knew they were coming. Leading the way, he ushered them into the den and told them how much the dauntlets were looking forward to their coming.

The cave was carved out by natural springs in the mountain, and the dauntlets had decorated the white marbled walls with beautiful tapestries woven from feathers, flowers, and twigs. They'd also lined the sides with fluffy, feather-filled beds and pillows.

"They spent a lot of time getting things ready for you," Breeni emphasized.

"But we won't be here long," Noni said. "I thought we had to get to the gate as soon as possible!"

"You do," Breeni nodded. "But they still wanted your stay to be comfortable, even if it's only for one night."

Noni didn't fully understand all the effort, but he decided to accept the dauntlets' gracious hospitality. Before long, the others arrived on the backs of other dauntlets. He stood at the entrance and watched as they landed on the ledge. Exhilarated by the flight, they climbed off the birds' backs and turned to peer at the canyon as the last vestige of light descended behind the mountains. The sun's dying rays radiated from their faces, and Noni was awed by the sight.

Inside the cave, Breeni introduced the dauntlets and their mates: Nus and Nasa, Egeiro and Epairo, Airo and Natal. Only Hupsoo had no partner. Even though he was the largest and oldest dauntlet, they still marveled at his beauty. His eyes exuded youth, and his body emanated vigor. The bird seemed timeless.

Hupsoo pointed out the accommodations, and, speaking for the first time, he apologized for the cave's coolness. He explained that they couldn't make a fire, because the escaping smoke would draw attention to the hidden den. But, unlike other caves, this one somehow felt cozier and more comfortable. Noni wondered if it was because of the large birds' body heat. Whatever the reason, he was grateful for a safe, warm place to rest.

He breathed in the fresh mountain air as he sat next to Ranni on a marble bench just inside the entrance, where they could look out as the colorful sky gave way to a velvety darkness. He let his eyes drift from the entrance to glance at her, and his thoughts jumped from one emotion to another. He couldn't help but notice that the bruises on her arms had faded, and a pink, healthy fleshiness had returned to her face. She glanced over at him and smiled. He felt mysteriously faint when he saw the dimple on her cheek and the sparkle in her eyes. Then he reflected on the danger they'd both face at the gate, and he felt a strange anxiety. It wasn't a fear for himself. After all, he'd been through a lot already. *I can make it through almost anything,* he reasoned. But what about Ranni? *She is still so fragile.* And a new feeling stirred inside him—he knew he must protect her. *I've failed her before,* he thought, *and I can't stand for that to happen again!*

Ranni sensed something from him and reached over to touch his hand. Noni's pulse sped up, and he began to feel hot all over, like he was burning up. Then it suddenly occurred to him. *His heart was melting!*

chapter twenty-eight

Terrifying Barriers

Noni woke to the sound of nervous chatter. Rubbing his sleepy eyes, he sat up then stumbled to the front of the cave. The smallets were there with the teesdalls, who'd just returned from the gate. Noni was struck by how the full-moon's light shone down toward them from over the mountaintops opposite the cave and created huge shadows right inside the entrance that made them all look like giant creatures! This made his eyes pop open.

"An unusual number of Surlies have gathered at the gate and they think it's not safe to go there now," Salvo spoke up as the now wide-eyed Noni approached. "The Surlies suspect the Reignbreaker might appear and cause some chaos."

"Will we have to wait?" Noni wondered out loud. He looked back at the others still sleeping, and he knew that the longer they waited, the more dangerous their mission would become. And, the longer it would take for them to get back home.

"I don't know yet," Salvo answered. "We'll see what Hupsoo says when the dauntlets return from their nightly flight."

Noni ate some secrela seeds and moggies set out for them, then he wandered out to the ledge. The sun was rising behind the cave, and the emerging light touched the tops of the mountains in front of him and washed the cliffs with swaths of color. Mesmerized, he was startled by a large looming shadow. His foot slipped when he got too close to the edge, and he started to slide on the loose pebbles. He grabbed for a nearby branch with both hands and hung there, dangling, as his fingers gradually slid down the branch. *Am I going to fall off this cliff and die after all I've survived?* He frantically wrestled mentally and physically.

Terrified, he glanced up and saw the underside of a huge wing above him. Hupsoo swooped down and grabbed the back of his tunic with his beak then lifted the boy, setting him beside him on a limb. Noni's uncontrolled shaking was soon replaced by an overwhelming sense of peace. Before he could say anything, the bird spoke.

"The others are still out scouting," he said. "But they'll be back soon to take everyone to the gate. Surlies are everywhere, but it's important that we go now. We're devising a plan to help you."

Noni felt small in Hupsoo's shadow, and he wondered what *he* could do in this situation. Nervously, he changed the subject and pointed toward the colored cliffs.

"It's so beautiful here. How did you find this place?"

"Believe it or not, it used to be even more magnificent," Hupsoo sighed. "It's known as Secrela Valley now because of all the secrela trees here. But it's nothing compared to what it was a few years ago. Many people used to come here to view its beauty and experience its peacefulness. It was once known as Kindred Valley, and a crystal-clear brook called the Brook Cherith ran through it. Now they call what's left of it the Abana Canal, and it's nothing like it was. Most of the year it's dried up. When it does have water, it's brown and muddy.

"Cascading fruit-filled vines once covered the cliffs. As more and more Surlies and Zamzummim came, it all changed. They scared away visitors and travelers by looting and killing them. Peacefulness was exchanged for panic. People were so afraid of being attacked that they used other routes. Evil scandalized the canyon and brought barrenness. The brook dried up, and the vines shriveled up and died.

"But, one day, it'll be beautiful again!"

"How do you know?" Noni gazed into Hupsoo's dark eyes.

"Because of what *Ameno's Manna* says: *'I will open rivers on the bare heights, and fountains in…the valleys; I will make the wilderness a pool of water, and the dry land springs of water.'"*[10] Hupsoo stopped to reflect on the words. Then he turned to face Noni. "Tell the others what I said—that they must go now." He half-closed his eyes like he was hiding something. "I gave Ranni some instructions to prepare her. I can only tell you that her job at the gate will be the hardest." He hesitated. "But I believe she can do it, that all of you working together can overcome the enemy and take the gate."

What is he hiding? Noni wondered, focusing on Hupsoo's half-opened eyes. *What is it he can't tell me?* But he didn't ask. Somehow, he knew the bird couldn't answer his questions. His stomach churned, and his heart raced, but he knew that he must trust Hupsoo.

"What can *I* do…I mean at the gate?" he asked, hoping for some words to lessen his fears.

Hupsoo was silent for a moment, and Noni's hands began to sweat. His face reddened as he waited for a response. The great bird gazed across the valley, and his white face was bathed in a golden glow from the sun's rays reflected off the yellow rocks of the cliffs. He finally turned toward Noni.

"When the time comes, you'll know what to do. Don't worry, Noni. You have hidden courage that you aren't aware of. It'll be more than enough for when you need it. Be assured. I'll be there for you. Now, I must go. My job is to create a diversion so you can accomplish your mission."

Noni was speechless. He wasn't sure what Hupsoo meant. All he knew was he believed in him. He didn't know why. He just did. The bird's words gave him courage, and, for the first time, he felt like he could accomplish whatever feat lay before him.

Hupsoo looked into Noni's eyes and seemed to read his thoughts. He nodded, acknowledging an unspoken trust between them. Then he turned, faced the cliff, and spread his wings. Noni was transfixed as he watched the giant bird dip slightly then rise into the sky. His shadow lengthened as he swerved and turned, until he disappeared over the mountains.

Noni's heart pounded as he entered the cave. He relayed Hupsoo's message, trying to downplay the danger but emphasize the need to leave as soon as possible. But everyone was distracted. Turning around, he watched as the other dauntlets entered the cave, one by one. He sat down to listen as they described what they'd seen at the gate.

"How will we avoid the Surlies?" Lona asked, concerned. "They seem to be everywhere."

"Hupsoo has a plan," Nus assured.

"Do you know what the plan is?" Stade asked.

"No," Nus answered. "I don't. But I trust Hupsoo."

"So do I." Noni placed his hand on his dad's back. "It'll be ok. I believe it will."

"We understand your concerns," Nasa said. "We know what you all have been through, Hupsoo more than any of us."

How does Hupsoo know so much about us? Noni pondered, still enthralled by the bird's trusting stare. Ranni noticed Noni's puzzled look and gave him a knowing look.

Her gaze made him feel warm inside but created more questions in him. *Can she see through me too, into my thoughts?* He blushed when he realized how long he was looking at her.

"All we know now is that we're to fly directly to the gate," Nus interrupted his thoughts. "Noni, why don't you and Beehart ride with me." He nodded toward them.

"Sure." Noni responded numbly, disappointed but not wanting to reveal how much he'd looked forward to another ride with his arms around Ranni.

"You can ride with me," Egeiro said to Ranni, who looked down at her lap, "along with Ada."

Stade and Lona flew with Airo, and Natal trailed behind to watch for any signs of danger. Epairo and Nasa took the smallets to gather support for the effort.

When Nus flapped his wings and lifted slowly to soar over the canyon, Noni had the same whoosh feeling he'd experienced when riding on Hupsoo. It was early, and the valley was still shaded by the cliffs. As they passed over the snowy summits, they felt the warmth of the sun's rays mixed with the coolness of the mountain air. The higher up they went, the more frigid it became. Noni was thankful for his warm tunic, and he sang out words he'd read in *Ameno's Manna* before it was stolen: *"If I take the wings of the morning.... Even there shall Your hand lead me, and Your right hand shall hold me."*[11]

Beehart overheard him and responded with another verse: *"He was seen upon the wings of the wind."*[12]

They laughed as they clung for dear life to Nus's feathers. But, as they approached the gate, their laughter stopped, especially when they saw Surlies posted at intervals all along the dividing wall, and each held a sword, club, or spear.

"I wish I had Truelight," Beehart murmured.

The dauntlets flew to the other side of the trees to avoid being spotted by the guards and looked down at a wide gravel road that ran up to the Surli side of the gate. A narrow dirt road meandered from the Inodian side and gradually disappeared into the woods.

"We're looking for a place to land," Nus explained as they swooped over the wooded area. "It has to be far enough from the gate that we won't be detected."

He finally motioned with a dipped wing for the others to follow as he dropped down past some trees to approach a field. Egeiro followed, with Ranni and Ada aboard, and gently landed on a smooth patch beside Nus. Surrounded by tall grass and trees, they waited as Airo, bearing Stade and Lona, and Natal descended from over the treetops.

Nus spoke softly as they all huddled together.

"We'll need to move fast so we're not spotted," he warned.

They cautiously approached nearby foliage and Nus found some camouflaging underbrush beneath a canopy of trees. He motioned for them to move into it. It wasn't an ideal place to hide, but it was the best available near the gate. As they made their way toward the dense shrubs, Noni had a sinking feeling that he could not shake. The number of guards at the gate worried him, and he wondered how their little group could ever win against such enormous odds. Nus sensed his concerns.

"Don't worry," he whispered to Noni. "Just stay hidden for now. We're summoning more Gomies and Krochits to help us—as many as we can round up. We'll try to hold off until they get here," he assured.

Noni still shook when he thought about facing mindboggling resistance. But Ranni recalled Hupsoo's words to her the day before and repeated them to Noni. *"Remember these words from Ameno's Manna, Ranni,"* he had said. *"'I will not save by bow or by sword.'*[13] *Abba might not be physically present during the battle, but his power will be with you."*

She knew Hupsoo had put Nus in charge of getting them safely to the gate, while he was away on his own quest, and she trusted them both. She wanted to fight now, but she decided to follow Nus's recommendations to wait. Noni sensed her struggle and watched as she turned her inner turmoil into tranquility. As a result, his own heart grew more peaceful. He turned to see the dauntlets fly away, leaving them here to fend for themselves until their return. And he sighed as their wind-lifted wings disappeared over the distant hills. He joined the others as they burrowed beneath the surrounding shrubs and trees.

But they quickly discovered that their camouflage brought more curses than blessings. Breathing became difficult when they realized that the waxy bush leaves gave off a medicinal smell that caused an overwhelming desire for sleep. The aromatic leaves also hid a horrible secret. They concealed rows of sharp thorns on the branches that clawed at their clothing and skin as they crawled under them. Noni sighed as he looked at his gift from the smallets. Squatting under the bushes, he gazed sadly at his torn tunic and, as hours passed, he grew frustrated. *How long do we have to wait here in this dismal place?* he wondered. Then he glanced at Ranni and remembered that, under her new cape, she hid a shredded pinafore and a ripped-up dress. Her boots also hung in shreds and barely clung to her legs. Tears came to his eyes as he thought about how, despite her plight, she was still so serene. His own concerns suddenly seemed insignificant.

The plants' fragrance became so overpowering after a few hours of laying in place and watching the pacing guards near the gate, that they all heaved weary sighs. Restless from fighting the urge to sleep, Stade decided to move closer to the gate so he could hear what the guards were saying. As the sun drew closer to the horizon, he rustled toward a patch of shrubs near the edge of the woods and his leggings accidentally snagged on some sharp thorns. When he tried to release himself, the thistles cut into his arms so deeply that he bled profusely. He tore strips of cloth from his undershirt and used them to bind the wounds, and he gasped in pain as he tried to stop the flow.

A guard standing close to the woods heard him, and Noni watched an unreal situation unfold. As he frantically motioned to get his father's attention, the guard moved closer, while Stade, unaware of the approaching threat, moaned. Noni held his breath and crouched down as the guard focused on the bushes around his father. Ada looked up, recognized the dilemma, and elbowed the two closest to her. Lona froze, and Ranni prayed. They were all petrified with fear when the guard crept up behind the unsuspecting Stade and swung a club at him. Blood gushed from Stade's head as the large man dragged him, unconscious, through the shrubs onto the road. Then the Surli rolled Stade's limp, thorn-lashed body face down on the gravel and bound his bloody arms behind his back. Yelling to the other guards, he twisted Stade's unresponsive face around for them to see and let his head drop back to the ground with a thud. He wrapped his fingers around Stade's neck, let out a sinister chuckle, and pretended to strangle him. Another hooded guard ran over and kicked Stade savagely in the side then grabbed him by the hair and dragged him across the gravelled road. After turning him over, the first Surli lifted Stade's feet, the other grabbed him under the shoulders, and, together, they lugged him to a small hut near the gate and threw him like a sack of grain into a corner. Lona watched and cried.

Another huge guard came over and used his sword to beat back the bushes around Stade's hideout. Fortunately, the other Gomies had already slunk farther back into the obscuring brush. They all sighed with relief when the guard moved away from them to forage through other areas of foliage. He kept that up for a while, then he stopped abruptly when the wooded area darkened with the setting sun and a hoot echoed from deep within it. They could tell he was visibly disturbed by the sound and wondered if it was one of the dauntlets and if the Surlies were afraid of the huge birds.

"What should we do now?" Lona whispered to Noni. She was trembling. She barely breathed during the attack on Stade and the guard's search.

"We'll do *something*. Just not right now," Noni said, his nerves on edge. "The dauntlets will let us know when the time is right."

"Right for what?" she snapped.

"It's ok, Mom," Noni drew from his own strength to reassure her. "Let's just trust Nus and wait."

"It's hard for me to trust after what we've been through, Noni. Do you understand?" Her voice rose dangerously, and the others stared at her anxiously. Noni reached over to touch her arm, and she turned to see Ranni's peaceful smile. Then she collected herself.

"I'm sorry," she whispered.

Noni nodded but did not answer. His heart pounded as he watched the guards clustering around the gate, and he silently prayed for safety, strength, and wisdom—a lot of wisdom.

As twilight descended, and the guards stopped their monotonous pacing long enough to light torches that lined the walls. New guards replaced the old ones, who sprawled out by the hut to consume barrels of ale. But one tall, hooded guard never left the gate.

No sound came from the hut, and they all wondered if Stade had survived the assault. A dim light shining from inside gave some hope. As semi-darkness hovered, Noni heard faint rustlings from behind them. He touched his mother to wake her and placed a forefinger to his lips. Then he pointed toward the field where the dauntlets had left them, and he slithered like a snake toward it.

The meadow's tall grass embraced him as he crawled. It's tips stroked the starlit sky like broom bristles sweeping away diamond dust from its velvety veneer as a near-full moon shone its light to dramatically enliven the scene. And he was enraptured by the beauty of the star-studded blanket above him. He lingered and lay still. The sight made him sigh.

But then, as he gazed up, his heart stopped. A huge white face suddenly blocked his view, peering down at him through the tall grass. And it wasn't the moon.

chapter twenty-nine

The Sword and The Giant

Noni did a doubletake. He looked again at the giant face staring down at him. *It was Nus!* He sighed with relief when he recognized the bird, who cocked his head and motioned to him. He stood and silently followed the silvery visage into an open area, where the other dauntlets formed a solemn circle. He strained to hear Nus explain a change in plans.

"Hupsoo's been delayed," he whispered, "and we're still trying to round up help. But we know Stade's capture has caused the Surlies to be even more suspicious. They think others are nearby, and they plan to start a more thorough search in the morning. So, we must act quickly! We'll use darkness as our cover and dive down at the guards closest to the gate. This will cause enough of a distraction that Ranni can release the lock so you all can go through."

Noni wondered what they would do once they entered the gate. But he realized that it didn't make sense to ask, since they were taking this whole venture one step at a time. *He may not know either,* he thought as he gazed at Nus. He just hoped that heading home was a possibility in the near future.

One thing Nus did know, which he explained to them, was that the Surlies were deathly afraid of the dauntlets. This confirmed Noni's suspicions. Apparently, the Surlies had heard frightening tales about them, but had never actually seen them, since the birds stayed hidden during the day and emerged at night. So, the Surlies weren't sure if they were mythical creatures, and they assumed that, if they did exist, they had the same evil intent as the tinshemets, who worked for King Zoar and the Zamzummim. Because of their unfounded fears, the dauntlets could create chaos just by appearing out of nowhere in the dark of night.

After hushed prayers, the dauntlets spread their wings and let the wind lift them toward the beckoning stars. Guided by moonlight filtering through the foliage, Noni slithered back into the forest's shrub-filled heart to tell the others about the plan. They huddled together as he whispered.

"The dauntlets will target the guards at the gate. Nus hopes the attack will send the Surlies fleeing. Beehart and I can get Stade while Ranni does her magic, and, after we all get through the gate, we'll be home free." Noni sighed thinking about getting home to his familiar lair.

A few hours passed, and the families pressed in together as shrill shrieks emerged from above the gate. They peered through the leaves and glimpsed the dauntlets swooping down and lunging at the Surlies with their beaks. The alarmed guards ran screaming. Even those lounging jumped up and jolted down the road. Noni watched as a Surli dashed out of the hut. He grabbed Beehart, and they ran to rescue Stade. Within minutes they'd untied and were carrying him, still unconscious, into the bushes. They laid him carefully in Lona's arms.

Spotting the boys, the hooded gate-guard stirred up others. They grabbed clubs and daggers and ran toward the bushes. Noni and Beehart looked at each other and headed toward the road to cause a diversion from the women and Stade. They yelled as they dashed ahead of the bolting Surlies, hoping they'd follow them. It worked at first. The huge men growled, cursed, and stomped loudly after them. The boys, being fleeter on their feet, dashed ahead.

But, as they turned a corner, a guard stepped out in front of them and blocked Beehart's path. The boy slugged fiercely at the monster, with no weapon in his hand, as the large man lunged at him with a long knife and slashed his chest. Beehart fell to the ground moaning and bleeding. Another brute approached quickly, tied his wrists together above his head, and dragged him down the road to the hut.

Noni was able to avoid these Surlies until two others emerged from the woods and tackled him. After pounding the boy with their fists, the men tied his wrists and ankles together and dragged him like a sack of grain to the hut to sit outside beside Beehart. His bruised body didn't hurt as much as his beaten pride, which triggered new feelings of powerlessness, disgust, and shame when he looked at his friend, whose glowering eyes said, *What gives? Aren't we supposed to win this battle?* Noni shook his head at Beehart's sullen stares, as if to say, *Don't blame me, bro'! We're both in the same boat! I have no idea what comes next! Just pray!* His own pain was lessened as he watched his buddy double over, trying to lessen the blood flow from his chest wound.

Ranni watched the whole thing unfold and felt utterly helpless. A brief moment came when the gate was unguarded, but her opportunity was quickly lost. The dauntlets continued their assault, but their moves became more defensive. While diving, Egeiro was struck by a huge axe wielded by one of the largest guards. A deep, bloody gash spread across his beautiful white breast. Weakened but undaunted, he continued his courageous attacks. The others endured similar assaults.

Ada comforted Lona, who sobbed and held Stade close enough to feel his breath against her cheek. Ranni darted in and out of the patchy woods, watching for help to come. She peered down the road, though the visibility was darkness obscured beyond the lit-up gate. The dauntlets' attack had scared off some of the Surlies, but the hooded guard didn't budge, making it impossible for her to get close enough to unlock the gate. She wasn't sure what to do, and she kept watching for a sign to determine her next move. She gazed up from the bushes, where she hid most of the time, and was shocked to see something terrifying through the tops of the trees. Unearthly creatures, unlike anything she'd ever observed, flew overhead. She trembled, remembering the tales she'd heard about the tinshemets and how they mercilessly attacked defenseless creatures with their sword-like beaks and treacherous talons. Noni too gazed up from his captivity by the hut, and he cringed in horror at the sight of the dreaded birds. He counted six of them then glanced over at Beehart, whose alarmed eyes looked like they were going to pop out of his head.

"They were probably sent by King Zoar to protect the gate," Ranni whispered hoarsely to herself. She stared as they perched nearby, their plumed crests spiking sharply above their narrow heads. *They have a sadistic gaze!* She shuddered. And she was unnerved by their piercing, sinister eyes that searched out opportunities to maim and kill their enemies. She shook when one of them barnstormed Beehart, poking at his eyes with its sharp beak. He ducked and recoiled to avoid the bird's thrusts but was unable to defend himself. The tinshemet tried to grab his forehead with an enormous claw, but Nus dove down and pulled out its back feathers, leaving a bald, bloody patch on the bird's back. The evil creature flew away, squawking shrilly.

"Thanks, Nus! And Abba!" Ranni whispered to herself.

In retaliation, the other tinshemets hovered and lunged at the dauntlets in a lightning-zapping, dark-cloudy mass. They first attacked Airo and damaged his wing so badly that he was barely able to fly to a tree, where he nursed his wounded wing. After sustaining several such near-lethal attacks, the dauntlets flew away to regroup. They needed more treacherous tactics, and Nus had an idea.

He led the dauntlets to a pile of rocks near the road then swooped down and lifted a large rock in his claws. The others followed suit. One by one, they dropped the stone-bombs on the diving tinshemets. Screeching, the evil birds winged away to nurse their wounds. Seeing how this worked so well, the dauntlets gathered larger rocks and targeted the Surlies. As the bombs hurtled through the air, the guards fled shrieking into the woods for cover. Beehart cheered, and the women silently yelled "*Hurrah!*"

But Noni worried how long they could keep this up. *When will more help come?* he wondered. *And when will Ranni be able to get to the gate so we can end this nightmare?* He half-expected her to magically release the lock and set them all free. *Isn't she the Reignbreaker? Wasn't she commissioned by Ameno himself?* Then more doubts loomed in his mind. *The odds are stacked against us. How can we win this fight?*

During a brief lull, it grew eerily quiet. The women watched from behind the bushes with Stade, while the boys huddled against the hut. Ranni watched the torchlit gate and sighed. *It still isn't the right time to go,* she decided. A few guards lingered by the hut, and the hooded Surli continued his stance by the entrance. She could hear the soft night sounds of the woods—chirping insects and the wind brushing against the leaves. And she looked over at Stade, whose eyes were still closed as his chest heaved with labored breathing. She decided to pray.

Then an unfamiliar sound caught her ear. She gazed down the road as the din grew louder—a sort of thud, thud, thud, like a drum. Her heart pounded in response, and she watched as a band of giants emerged from the dark folds of the forest. She immediately knew who they were. She'd heard tales of the Zamzummim. But she'd never seen them until now.

Six ogres thundered toward them, swinging their steel swords and machetes that flashed like lightning in the moonlight. As soon as the gargantuan clan gathered near the gate, cowering Surlies crept out of their hiding places to join them and, now bolder, began to throw huge rocks at the dauntlets, who sat peacefully watching from the trees. The brave birds spread their wings and flew to escape the assault. When the Zamzummim began to whack at the bushes near the women and Stade with their machetes, the dauntlets flew back to divert their attention by diving at them, but the giants continued their malfeasance unhindered.

Noni watched, alarmed. The odds just seemed to keep piling up against them. *The giants aren't even going to wait until daylight! Can they see in the dark? What will they do to our parents if they find them?* His worries stole away his remaining peace, and his heart pounded until he felt like it would explode inside his chest. He sat there, unable to do a thing. Then he remembered Ameno's words at the sharetoo.

"Never allow the enemy to divert your attention away from me. He'll try to get you to focus on other things. He'll try to make you feel bad about yourself…. Don't focus on the darkness, or evil, in others. This will only hinder your ability to be strong."

"Ameno, come help us!" he screamed out loud.

Beehart heard him and muttered his own inward plea. Then they both heard a bewildering commotion coming from pretty far down the road. The growing sound caused the bush-whacking Zamzummim to stop for a moment and listen. It was hard for them to see through the darkness, and they tried to penetrate it with their squinting, evil eyes.

As the torches behind the giants grew suddenly dim, the lantern in the hut behind the boys shone brighter, and the light beckoned, like a distant star summoning wise men to a promise.

"Hear *that?*" Noni whispered to Beehart.

"Yeah. *What is it?*" Beehart asked, looking puzzled.

"Dunno," Noni rasped. *"I just hope it's help."*

The sound grew louder. It was a combination of chanting, clanging, and banging. Leaning forward, they could just make out the words.

"Fearlessly, we conquer,
fearlessly we save,
with new hearts of courage,
strength that makes us brave.
His we are, his helpers,
come to save the day.
No one can defeat us
when to him we pray."

The Surlies froze and the Zamzummim became like statues as a motley group emerged from the darkness and barreled fearlessly toward them. Noni gasped, and Beehart's eyes grew wide when they saw who marched at the head of the group—a skinny blond man wielding a glistening sword.

"Sluggli!" they screamed together.

Believing this must be the help they'd been hoping for, Ranni ran out and bravely stepped up beside Sluggli to join in the singing. Bleamer, Mosi, Leo, Humbi, Honi, and a squadron of others marched in rhythm. When the giants saw the size of the ragtag group, they chuckled. Some fell over laughing. Ignoring them, Sluggli held Truelight out boldly, and the others linked arms. The enemy's enormity didn't seem to daunt or deter any of them.

Noni and Beehart squirmed to free themselves and Sluggli ran to help them, but a Surli sprang after him. Swinging Truelight, Sluggli turned and struck him broadside on the neck. Gripping his swelling wound, the Surli fell forward, screaming in pain. Sluggli continued his sprint to his friends. Reaching Noni, he lay Truelight down to untie him, but, before he could free him, a huge Zamzummi hovered over him.

He was the largest of the giants, and his name was Ishbi. He wore a helmet and massive coat of mail, and he had six fingers on each hand and six toes on each foot. Grabbing Sluggli by the hair, he threw him aside, like a discarded piece of trash. As the young man lay moaning, the monster's eyes gleamed when he spotted the lustrous sword, and his huge hand moved to lift it. Standing upright, he swung and thrashed Truelight at Sluggli's ribs repeatedly. Then he thrust its point at the young man's heart, but, miraculously, the sword wouldn't penetrate his tunic. The giant growled, cursed, and ran his hand over the blade, thinking it must be dull. While he stalled with the sword, Sluggli rolled out of the way and, hiding his pain, ran for the bushes. Disgusted, the half-wit man-mountain threw the prize down and looked around for better weaponry and easier prey. Still bound, Noni and Beehart grinned at Sluggli's brave and amazing escape.

Mosi fought against several Surlies, using his sword to stave off their onslaughts. Stirred alert by the uproar, Stade watched Mosi for a while. Then, his memory sparked a thought, *Something about that man reminds me of my brother Leo.* Against Lona's pleadings, he struggled to stand. Summoning supernatural strength, he found the jawbone of a grat and emerged from the bushes, flinging it like a madman. His otherworldly screams made the Surlies freeze in terror. And, as Stade swung and shrieked wildly, knocking over several startled Surlies, Mosi stepped in fearlessly to finish them off with his sword. Stade, still was unaware that this was his nephew, high-fived his fighting-friend.

Bleamer and Leo stood side by side, bravely attacking with their knives. They skirted two large, slow-moving Zamzummim and lunged at their arms and legs with quick sharp stabs. Beehart's heart gripped him when he saw that his friend, Leo, had somehow survived the Surli attack at the cave and had also regained his sight. But his heart pounded when one giant lost his cool and swung a metal ball at Leo, who avoided the swing and responded by stabbing the angry monster. Suddenly, the Zamzummi dropped the ball with a thud, and his alarmed eyes popped open when he saw a fountain of blood spurting from an artery his leg. Seeing his cohort teeter, the other brute froze long enough for Bleamer to lunge and stab him too, this time through a vulnerable gap in his chain mail. Both behemoths toppled at the same time like felled trees. One landed on top of the other, and the impact crushed them both..

Small but fierce, Humbi and Honi used long sharp spears to fight. Because the Surlies lacked the Zamzummim armor and heavy weaponry, they were more vulnerable. Humbi took on one after another using his spear like a saber. He danced around the adversaries and overcame them with intimidation, while Honi used her unique skills of swinging and shrieking. When the Surlies tried to grab her and her weapon, they were hoodwinked by her unassuming appearance, and they were soon worn down by her unflinching energy. She bounced around them like a rubber ball, and they finally slunk off to find easier prey.

Ada and Lona watched from the bushes, not confident enough to enter the fight. Ranni also sat on the sidelines, making sure the mothers were safe. The women silently cheered Honi's fearlessness until they decided to join the battle. Hand in hand, they ran between the battling groups to free Beehart and Noni, while the Surlies were distracted. They untied them both, and Ranni ran to help Sluggli, who lay moaning under a bush, still stunned and bruised by the giant's thrashes and thrust. She didn't know that he was her brother. Even Ada hadn't recognized Sluggli or Bleamer yet.

Ranni gently lifted Sluggli's head into her lap and covered him with her cape. Honi came over, and together they moved him to a safer place, farther into the forest. As they lifted and moved him, Ranni spied something shiny on the ground. After making Sluggli comfortable, she and Honi faced the battle. But, this time, Ranni held Truelight.

Noni and Lona found some discarded spears and decided to sneak up on a Zamzummi as he swung a huge sword at Humbi. Seeing he was no match for the giant, Humbi backed quickly into the bushes, and the growling ogre stalked after him. When thorns from the bushes dug into the Zamzummi's legs, he cursed and tried to free himself.

Humbi chuckled but then heard sighs and saw Honi lying close to the giant's feet. Her leg was badly hurt. Freed from the thorns, the Zamzummi turned to face Humbi, who tried to avert his attention from Honi. Suddenly, Noni appeared, threw his spear, and it pierced the giant's huge neck. He clutched the bleeding wound and fell to the ground moaning. Humbi quickly helped Honi to safety in the forest.

Beehart and Ada found some discarded daggers and approached the hooded Surli at the gate. Their goal was to distract him long enough for Ranni to do her job. She was aware of their plan and stood ready with Truelight. But, a more urgent situation unfolded, and the opportunity was lost again.

Mosi and Leo were battling another giant, when Ishbi thundered toward them. The behemoth picked Mosi up with one six-fingered hand and hurled him to the ground. When his son landed on his head and lay there unconscious, Leo cried out, thinking he was dead. His face turned bright red, and his eyes bulged. He spat, whirled to face the growling giant, and held out his knife toward the brute. Saliva dribbled from Ishbi's lower lip as he looked down and laughed at the smaller man. Other Zamzummim and Surlies gathered to join in his laughter and watch as the largest one of them put his huge hand out to smash Leo to the ground and squash him like a bug.

While everyone else focused their attention on Ishbi and Leo, Ranni ran over, clutching Truelight between both hands, her red cape flying behind her. She climbed up onto a huge tree stump that sat conveniently behind the monster, and she lifted the weapon. Swinging the sword as far back as she could, she allowed momentum to whoosh it forward toward the giant's neck. Ishbi's head thudded to the ground, rolled, then thumped up against a nearby tree. Ranni pushed her hood back and looked at the huge face gazing back at her, startled. Clenching Truelight's golden hilt between her small hands and smiling victoriously, she held up the sword, her dimple showing proudly.

The Zamzummim and Surlies stood frozen, not believing what had just happened. Leo's eyes bugged out and his mouth fell open. Then he let out a loud whoop that echoed from the gate. Her action infuriated the enemies. Loudly cursing, they moved toward her. Noni, Beehart, Humbi, Ada, Stade, Bleamer, and Lona ran in to fend them off. Noni used his spear to stab one in the back. Undeterred, the Zamzummi turned to swing a metal ball toward him, but Noni's long weapon pierced his groin. Screaming, he dropped the large ball on his foot and collapsed to the ground. Shrieking and holding his foot, he rocked back and forth, moaning like a baby.

Leo took hold of the chain with unusual strength and twirled the ball like a toy on a string toward some approaching Surlies. Gritting his teeth, he knocked two down and fended off several others while Beehart hurled rocks from a makeshift slingshot. With amazingly accurate aim, he hit one giant's forehead and brought him down just as the behemoth reached for Ranni's neck. Ada, Stade, Humbi, Bleamer, and Lona made a circle around Ranni, facing outward with their weapons drawn to protect her from further assaults.

The fierce fighting ensued into the wee hours and, as the large moon set, and the morning dawned, new light revealed what the night had concealed.

chapter thirty

Incredible Revelations

As sunlight streamed over the tops of the trees and Noni gazed around at the battle fallout, he felt like his heart might fail. The dauntlets had fought courageously, but some endured deep wounds from rocks hurled by the evil tinshemets. Egeiro lay wounded in the woods, his breast heaving. Airo had continued fighting most of the night, despite his wounded wing but now lay motionless on the ground. Natal was hit by soaring rocks and her lovely brown neck feathers were covered with blood. Teesdalls and smallets, who'd arrived during the night, hovered over them crying, not knowing if they would live or die.

After the victory against Ishbi, Noni, Beehart, Leo, Humbi, Stade, Bleamer, and Ranni fought relentlessly against enemy swords, spears, knives, and swinging metal balls—whatever was unleashed against them. Now exhausted, they sat with Sluggli, Honi, and the mothers in the bushes, waiting for the few remaining Zamzummim and Surlies, who huddled near the gate, to regroup for the next attack. Wondering how they could continue when the enemy resumed their effort, Noni whispered a prayer.

"Abba, *please send Ameno!* With *his* help we can have victory," he muttered. "I ask it in Ameno's name." Then he remembered some words from *Ameno's Manna*. "Give *'strength to those [to] turn back the battle at the gate.'*"[14]

Suddenly, a breeze stirred the surrounding trees. At first, it was so insignificant that no one noticed, not even the teesdalls. But it persisted and began to sweep leaves from the trees. Gathering strength, it twirled and spun debris like a dancer demanding attention, pirouetting petulantly. Around and around it went, pushing peevishly at the enemies. The Gomi group hunkered down in the woods and watched through the foliage as even the monstrous men had a hard time standing up against its flurried force.

Daylight increased, and Noni watched the wondrous wind play out its peerless performance. He saw how the sun showed its strength on their behalf—its radiant rays streamed past them to blind the enemies' eyes. Squinting against its intense rays and trying to shield their faces from the whirling leaves and debris, the two remaining giants clambered clumsily as they stood by the gate. They yelled out threats to cut off the Gomies' heads and feed them as tasty morsels to the drooling tinshemets, who squawked and gawked fiendishly from the wall with beady eyes.

One giant, almost as big as Ishbi, screamed out curses, but then let out a roar that shook the earth as an enormous, hovering shadow passed over them and stirred up an even greater whirlwind. Glancing up, he winced and shuddered. With terror in his eyes, he thrashed his huge sword against the powerful wind-gust, then he stomped as fast as he could down the road, away from the gate. Seeing his fear and the ghostly shadow hovering above them, the last Zamzummi and the remaining Surli guards shrieked and dashed down the road to escape for their lives. Also terrified by the huge looming figure, the tinshemets squawked and flew away.

Intrigued by their enemies' sudden exit, Noni and Beehart gazed up to see the cause of the commotion. They caught a glimpse of an enormous bird-like creature moving mysteriously overhead toward the Inodian side of the gate. Because of the swirling leaves, they couldn't tell who or what it was. Before they could determine anything, they were distracted by one remaining Surli, who stood unmoved at the gate. It was the hooded guard.

He'd left his post only once since they'd been there—when he kicked Stade into unconsciousness. He was evil personified. That Noni knew. He'd watched the man and wondered, *Why is he so obsessed with guarding the gate? He seems to be driven by some compulsion.* He had his suspicions about the man's identity, but he wasn't sure, since his face was always hidden by his hood.

Horrified, Noni watched as Ranni suddenly ran toward the mysterious Surli, holding Truelight in her hands. He knew she believed it was her time to open the gate, but was it? All the obstacles but one had been removed, and she was ready. She'd decided that *nothing could stop her now!*

The guard faced the gate, oblivious to her, it seemed. He'd ignored the ruckus and stood apart from it all. He had only one purpose. As Ranni approached him, he turned to face her. Darkened by the hood, she couldn't see his eyes. She swung at him fearlessly with the remarkable sword, believing she could overcome him. But, despite her confidence, the evil man grabbed her wrist with one hand and thrust the sword from her grip with the other. She slunk back, gasping, when she caught a glimpse of his face. His one evil eye glared maliciously at her now as he pointed Truelight toward her heart. Seeing what was happening, the others froze with fear.

Ada screamed. Noni, Beehart, Humbi, Stade, Bleamer, and Leo ran toward Ranni. Before they could reach her, the man swung the sword's tip past her ear and severed one of her beautiful braids. It fell like a swooning bird to the ground. Everyone gasped. As he poised the sword for another swing to cut off the other blond braid, Beehart lunged at his legs, screaming bloody murder. The beast-man stepped back and swept him away with his arm like a pesky gnat. Noni ran in and pointed his spear at the man's neck, but the villain grabbed its tip and broke it off before it could penetrate his vulnerable spot. Then he held the spear at the opposite end and swung Noni to one side. Humbi thrust his spear at him, but the hooded man used the same ploy and swung him handily aside. Leo ran up, swinging Ishbi's metal ball, but he dodged every swing. The others stood to one side, wondering what to do next as Leo persistently swung the ball, not giving up. The enemy teasingly thrust Truelight at the ball as he jumped to avoid it, dancing and howling. Using this entertaining performance to her advantage, Ranni moved closer to the gate, unnoticed. As she approached it, her face changed and she began to shake the heavy metal bars with both fists as she gazed between them to the cryptic bird-creature that had landed on the other side. And she suddenly screamed out at the top of her lungs.

The hooded man was distracted by her high-pitched shriek, and he turned to see what was causing the disturbance. Just as he did, Leo swung the huge ball toward his head, and they all heard a tremendous crunching sound as it knocked him to the ground. Beehart grabbed Truelight from his hand, put one foot on his chest, and held the sword to his neck. Blood oozed from under the man's hood and dripped from his face to the ground. He uttered a final curse then fell silent.

Everyone came and stood over the dreaded dead man. Some smallets and dauntlets crept close enough to see and watched as blood pooled around the man's head. Bravely, Ranni reached down and pulled his hood back so they could see his face. As she did, Noni and Beehart gasped, and Ada screamed, as Belial's evil eye stared lifelessly up at them.

"*It's Clement!*" she cried out. "*I know it's him!*" She reeled backward, and Beehart caught her as she swooned.

After a few ghastly but awe-inspired moments, everyone realized they'd just overcome their last obstacle, and the group moved toward the gate behind Ranni.

"*I saw him!*" she said under her breath. "*I know it's him!*"

"*Who*, dear," Lona asked, trying to understand her excitement.

"*Hupsoo!*" she pointed through the bars. "I *know* it's him!"

But no one else could see him now.

Ranni shook the large lock that hung from a heavy chain wrapped around the bars. After shaking it violently several times, she asked others in the group to help. But no one could release it.

"Would your key work?" she turned to Beehart, and he drew out the chain around his neck, but the key was way too small for the large lock. He held it helplessly.

Noni and Leo tried to pry the lock open with sticks. Humbi, Stade, and Bleamer pushed and shoved with all their might against the gate. But Ranni stood quietly alone thinking and praying. Then, she remembered some words of a song Ameno had taught her when he came to visit her in prison. She whispered the words at first. With each new verse, her voice gained strength, and she began to sing out loud.

> "*Make a joyful noise to the Lord, all you lands!*
> *Serve the Lord with gladness!*
> *Come before His presence with singing!*
> *Enter into His gates with thanksgiving…*
> *And into His courts with praise.*"[15]

Soon, the others joined in to sing along with her. And, each time they repeated the words, their voices grew louder and stronger.

Then, strangely, as if by magic, the large lock fell apart and dropped from the chain, which now hung limply, like an appendage relieved of its burden. The gate swung open of its own accord, and, shouting with joy, the Gomies, followed by the unscathed dauntlets, smallets, and teesdalls, ceremoniously paraded through the gate.

chapter thirty-one

Astonishing Promises

While everyone else gathered to hug and shout in celebration, Ranni went to look for Hupsoo on the Inod side of the gate. She knew he was there somewhere. Seeing a shadow in the woods, she ran to peer around bushes and trees. Calling his name, she was startled when a ghostly figure suddenly appeared from the depths of the forest. As it drew closer, she froze, terrified and too overwhelmed to move.

It appeared to be a man on a graynight, but it was strangely otherworldly, almost transparent. With each step, it became clearer. A mysterious man, wearing a white robe that billowed behind him sat atop a dappled steed on a gold blanket fringed with tinkling silver bells. Two huge blue bags hung behind him tied with a rope across the animal's back. A gust of wind blew his hood back, and she immediately recognized his face.

She laughed and ran to meet him. Pulling her own hood back so he would recognize her, she reached Ameno, who jumped from the graynight and drew her to himself warmly. Ranni wrapped her arms around his flowing robe, which glistened and glowed in the morning light. She gazed up at his smiling face, and his eyes, like lightning, pierced her heart. When she saw how he looked at her, she cried, releasing all the fears, frustrations, and anxieties she'd held for so many months.

"I love you, Ranni." His words were soothing and sounded like lapping waves as he gently touched her dimpled cheek, and the healing warmth of his hand rushed through her.

Looking around and noticing her absence from the group, Noni wondered what had happened to Ranni and ran to search for her. He sighed when he caught a glimpse of her through the trees. Glancing past her, his heart leaped when he recognized Ameno by her side. The first thing he noticed was that his friend no longer wore the headdress, robe, or cape that he wore at the sharetoo. In their place, he donned a golden crown and a white, translucent robe. The green emeralds around the crown were so brilliant that they created a halo around his head. From under the gold-embroidered robe, his legs glowed like fire and his feet shone like burnished bronze. When he moved, a rainbow radiated from his chest.

"Noni, come here, my hero!" His voice rippled as he held out a shining, almost transparent, hand.

Noni's heart swelled, and, when Ameno wrapped him in an embrace, his fears dissipated. He stared at Ameno's legs, curious if they *were* on fire and, when another wind-burst whipped at his robe, he glimpsed words written with fiery light on his leg: *King of Kings and Lord of Lords!*

The others, seeing unusual flickering lights through the trees, approached and shouted when they too recognized Ameno. Nus hurried forward and anxiously told Ameno about the injured dauntlets—Egeiro, Airo, and Natal—on the other side. The smallets ran up and chimed in, chattering noisily as Salvo begged him to come quickly. Ranni told him about the injured Gomies—Sluggli, Honi and Mosi—and gazed at his face, wondering what he would do. Noni especially watched to see if he would lose his cool with all this chaos, especially since *he* felt unnerved by the clamoring.

Not saying a word, Ameno followed the scampering smallets and Nus through the open gate back into dreaded Sur, with the others trailing behind him. Kneeling beside each wounded warrior-bird, he placed a hand on the places that needed repair. Whispering words to Abba, he healed the gaping wounds, opened lifeless eyes, and restored broken limbs. Watching in awe, the others cried and cheered as each incapacitated victim rose to stand beside Ameno.

Then their hero moved into the bushes to heal Honi's bleeding leg and Mosi's injured head, so they both could stand and walk again. Sluggli was last and, by the time he got up, healed and strong again, everyone was giddy with glee.

Reentering their beloved land, back through the gate, Ranni raised her voice, and everyone sang with her:

"We sing to you, dear One,
Because of what you've done.
And we turn again
To seek you as our friend.
Our voices lift in praise
And renewed hopes we raise.
You alone give peace
And from our fears release.
We love you, our dear Lord,
The one we all adore.
Following you, we hail
Our true king to prevail.
We sing of you, our might.
We seek your brilliant light.
You show us how to break

This reign held by a gate!"

Ameno smiled and walked among them, touching each person and creature. Then he beckoned for them to gather around him. As they stood silently in the shadow of the reprehensible gate, the sun beamed down and reflected light from Ameno's fiery eyes as he faced the group. When he opened his mouth, he called Ada to come forward first. He asked her to kneel in front of him and motioned for Beehart to hand him Truelight.

"My effulgent emerald," he said solemnly, "you're my overcomer. Like water, you flow over many obstacles. *You shall be like a watered garden and like a spring of water whose waters fail not.'"*[16]

Taking Truelight in both hands, he lightly touched her shoulders, like he was beknighting her.

"I dub you 'Adamantine,' because you have been a great source of strength," he said. "Your parents named you after the legendary stone, which cannot be easily broken, and you have aptly passed this nature to your children. But, the emerald represents your true character—that of the beauty of God's glorious creation, wisdom, truth, and foresight."

He helped her up and walked to the side of his graynight to draw something out of one of his bags.

"With fire in your belly, you've led others to freedom. I give you this belt of truth to symbolize your courage and wisdom in being a truth-bearer." He held up a beautiful belt woven from gold cords and edged with tiny sparkling emeralds. He gently wrapped it around her waist and tied it in front. Tears flowed down her cheeks as everyone clapped.

Called forward, Stade and Lona came next and knelt together before Ameno.

"My crystalline carbuncles! You've been united in effort, so I'll speak to you as one," he beamed. "You, faithful ones, bring a hopeful message to everyone you see." He touched their shoulders with Tru-elight. "I christen you 'Steadfast' and 'Loved.' *Your righteousness…shall go before you.*"[17]

They stood and hugged Ameno.

"Because of your steadfast service to others," he continued, "your feet will be shod with the good news of peace." From a bag, he drew out two pairs of boots. "These shoes will take you to new places. The carbuncle is a gem of many colors depicting Abba's favor and abundance, and it represents the people of many lands that you and your children will reach."

The supple brown boots fit them perfectly. Showing off their new footwear, Stade and Lona walked back to the group and were greeted with hugs.

Summoned next, Leo approached, seeing eyes lowered, deep in thought. They'd all heard his story. After Noni and Beehart left him by the creek, surrounded by the Surlies, he assumed they'd kill him. But, after they'd beaten him, they left him tied up and assumed he'd be eaten alive or starve to death, since he was blind. As he lay there, he recalled a passage he'd read in *Ameno's Manna* about a blind man who was healed when he called out to Ameno for help, and he asked for his sight to be miraculously restored. Ignoring his pain, he scooched like a caterpillar toward the creek. Then, kneeling, with his ankles tied together, he used his wrist-bound, cupped hands to splash water into his eyes. It didn't work at first, so he kept trying. Believing he'd be healed, his sight gradually returned. At first it was blurred, but, eventually, he could see clearly. And he had to suppress a yell! He was able to untie his wrists and ankles and, hiding in the hills, he slowly made his way back home. Mosi was more than ecstatic to see him again.

Leo knelt now, and everyone clapped and cheered for him.

"Leo, my overcoming onyx, you have a true lion-heart. Healed, you will bring healing to the land. *Then shall your light break forth like* the morning, and your healing...shall spring forth speedily.'"[18] Ameno touched Leo's shoulders with the sword. "I christen you 'Leonine,' which means 'like a lion.' Leonine, you *will roar like a lion...*' and your *'sons shall come...eagerly.'*"[19] After reaching inside his robe to the hidden breastplate and pulling out a glittering black stone, he placed it in Leo's hand. "I present you with this onyx, which stands for strength, beauty, and divine connections, and symbolizes your part in the foundation of my new kingdom."

He walked to his graynight and drew a gold staff with a glittering black ball on top from a bag. Small silver letters around the ball read, *"The scepter shall not depart...nor the ruler's staff."*[20]

"This gift demonstrates your leadership, Leo," Ameno explained. "And how you've led so many to freedom."

As Leo's eyes teared up, and the others embraced him, Ameno motioned, and Mosi came next. He knelt down as Ameno stood over him with the sword.

"My amiable amethyst, I christen you 'Mosaic,' because you bring together many different people for one purpose—spiritual clarity. With the balance of a good heart with good works, you inspire others to clearly do their part in this life. *I will make you ride on the high places of the earth, and I will feed you with the heritage...of...your father.'*"[21]

From the breastplate, he presented Mosi with a brilliant purple amethyst, then he pulled out what looked like a plaque from a bag. Decorated with tiny colored tiles, it reflected a changing image with the faces of people whose lives he'd touched. Turning it, he was over-whelmed by its meaningful beauty. He held it up for everyone to see.

When Ameno's eyes met theirs, Humbi and Honi came up and knelt down.

"My adored agates, you deserve new names: 'Humble' and 'Honored.' Your loving hospitality has provided protection and divine communication and strength to others." He touched their shoulders with the sword and presented them with two light-blue agates that resembled the sky on a clear day. He also pulled out a white marble plaque, which he presented to them. The couple held the gifts in their hands and cried when they saw the plaque.

"This is to hang on your front door," Ameno explained, then, facing the others, he read, "*'As for me and my house, we will serve the Lord.'*[22] It will remind your visitors that your hospitality comes from heart-felt service."

Ameno called Sluggli and Bleamer up next. The fraternal twins stepped forward, and everyone cheered and clapped. They'd all heard how Bleamer found out about Noni and Beehart's imprisonment and bravely made his way to the Surli jail to rescue them. Arriving after their release, he freed Sluggli, along with other prisoners, and retrieved Truelight, which was mounted on a wall in the front of the jail. With the boys' grats and bags in tow, Bleamer and Sluggli escaped unnoticed, since the guards were summoned to the gate. They made their way to Honi and Humbi's house, because Bleamer remembered seeing it on his stepfather's map. When they arrived, they were greeted by Mosi and Leo, who'd heard about *The Battle for the Gate* and were on their way to help. They had also stopped at Honi and Humbi's, after having heard the couple was friendly and might be willing to join them. The twins hooked up with them when Mosi explained that Noni and Beehart were already at the gate. It was during this meeting that they realized they were brothers—a shock to them both.

The applause subsided as Sluggli and Bleamer knelt down, and Ameno said, "Brothers, you are my joyful jacinths, reunited at last. You've always been one in purpose, even though distance separated you. You both withstood hardships and rose above it to help others. Sluggli, you were once known as slow and ugly. From now on you'll be known as 'Sunny' because of what you bring to others—bright hope."

Sluggli shuddered with emotion as Ameno touched his shoulders with the sword to confirm the blessing, then he turned to Bleamer.

"You, sir, will be known as 'Brother,' because of your newfound role and what you are to every person here. The jacinth stands for joy, which brings strength. Because of your inner joy, you are strong. The stone also means wisdom. And, with great wisdom you both will lead, teach, and free many as the 'sunny brothers.'" He handed the purple stones to them then held up two golden helmets with silver words emblazoned on the front: *"That people may know skillful and godly Wisdom."*[23] Solemnly, he placed the helmets on their heads. "These will protect your thoughts from evil and give you wisdom to lead."

Adorned with the helmets, the brothers beamed and faced the others, who cheered.

Ameno asked Beehart to come forward, and the boy knelt down. As he held Truelight above the boy's head, the sword shimmered and reflected the blues and greens of the sky and earth. Beehart shivered when he felt the sword touch his shoulders.

"Beehart, my sapphire soldier, you've obediently served me. Even without your beloved sword, you wisely protected and helped many." He brought out a large, round, glistening object. "I give you this shield, my protection, to guard your heart from discouragement and to enable you as a champion and guardian of my ways. Your name will be 'Bearheart,' because you *'will meet them (your enemies) like a bear that is robbed of her cub.'*[24] He placed the shield's curved handle over Beahart's hand. It fit his grip perfectly. Large enough to cover his torso, the shield's front was decorated with a golden bear, ready to attack an enemy that came near. Beehart gazed with pride at his prize, and, behind the shield, his heart glowed a fiery red.

Ameno motioned for Ranni to step closer and placed his hands on her small shoulders as she stared up at his lovely, rugged face.

"Ranni, you've been brave as The Reignbreaker. This was a role you didn't choose, but, when you saw its importance, you accepted it willingly. You played an extremely significant role in the battle, and it was you who understood what it took to open the gate. With more battles to be fought, I will prepare you, because of the large part you will play in each one. As my delightful diamond, I dub you now officially as the 'Reignbreaker.' *You shall raise up the foundations of…many generations; and you shall be called Repairer of the Breach, Restorer of the Streets.'*"[25]

He handed Truelight to Bearheart and threw back his robe to unveil the glittering breastplate. After untying the ribbons on each side of a multi-colored vest that held the breastplate, he pulled it over his head. Lifting it up by its gold shoulder straps, he showed them the woven silver and gold squares that held rows of gems. He pointed to hundreds of tiny diamonds sewn around the edges of the vest. Then he placed the garment gently over Ranni's head and tied the ribbons at her sides. It fit her perfectly and hid her mangled clothing.

"This breastplate represents all that is just, right, and good," Ameno explained. "The diamonds are clear, but they mysteriously hold all the colors in the universe. They stand for the many people you will touch during your lifetime. I chose the diamond for you, since it represents peace and purity. With your understanding mind and hearing heart, you will establish a haven of serenity. *"Violence shall no longer be heard in your land…nor destruction within your borders; but you shall call your walls Salvation and your gates Praise.'*"[26]

Ameno hugged Ranni, and everyone was too awed by her gift to cheer. They all remained quiet as she gazed tearfully down at the breastplate, and Ameno turned to face them. Even the smallets ceased their chatter.

Noni sat silently behind everyone on a stump. He'd applauded and cheered for each knighted and named person until his voice grew hoarse. But, as each one was called forward, he'd slunk farther and farther to the back, thinking, *Maybe I'm only meant to watch the others get their rewards. Maybe what I did wasn't so great and I don't deserve a gift. Maybe Ameno forgot about me.* He gazed down at the topaz in his hand then up at Ranni standing proudly next to Ameno, and he thought, *She looks so beautiful in her new covering. She deserves to be near Ameno. I don't.*

He kicked a rock and looked sadly at his scuffed boots and ripped-up tunic. Inside he ached, and his heart's glow faded dismally. But then, a familiar sound interrupted his gloomy thoughts.

"Where's Noni?" Ameno's voice rang out.

Everyone looked around, and the smallets spotted him sitting behind them. Salvo's ear twitched, and Malvo jerked his tail.

"Come on! Come on, Noni!" the smallets chattered. *"Ameno wants you!"*

Getting up slowly, head lowered, he fumbled with the stone in his hand and stumbled forward, guiltily trying to hide his shameful feelings. Ameno motioned for him to kneel in front of him, and Noni dropped down.

"I left you for last, Noni, because you're so important to me," Ameno smiled and looked at the boy. "*You* are my truehearted topaz. Because of your love and determination, you brought help and hope to everyone. The bright yellow topaz is meant for you, because it represents hope, love, and light. It also reminds everyone of the things you bring to them—clarity for decision-making, steadfastness, and great brightness. No longer 'Noni,' you'll be known as 'Nonight,' because you replace darkness with light. *'Then shall your light rise in darkness, and your obscurity and gloom become like the noonday.'*[27]

"I had to knight you last," Ameno explained, "because of the special gift I want to give you." He called everyone to gather around. After tapping Noni gently on each shoulder with Truelight, Ameno reached into a bag and pulled out a book. He opened it slowly and recited, *"'I will give you the treasures of darkness and hidden riches of secret places, that you may know that it is I, the Lord…Who calls you by your name.'"*[28] Then he placed the book in Noni's hands.

It wasn't until he held the book that Noni realized what it was. He read out loud the gilded inscribed letters that reflected light from its cover: *"Ameno's Own Manna,"* then he opened the book and read the inscription on the first page: *"'To him who overcomes…I will give to eat of the manna that is hidden.'*[29] *To Nonight, with love forever, Ameno."*

Noni glanced through the pages and saw that each word of the book was handwritten by Ameno! He thought about the special copy of *Ameno's Manna* that Mosi had given him and how he'd felt such emptiness, like a part of him was missing, when it was stolen by the Surlies. He'd grown so accustomed to reading it every night before going to sleep, and in the mornings, to sweep away the cobwebs from his mind. He'd missed it more than he knew.

He held the book to his heart as Ameno knelt and pulled him close, the book between them. The others gathered around and wiped tears from their eyes.

"I never doubted your ability, Nonight," Ameno whispered in his ear. "I've always known and loved you."

Noni gazed up at the light-filled face next to him and saw something shining in the corners of Ameno's crystalline eyes—*tears!*

chapter thirty-two

The Gilgal Gomies

After honoring the Gomies, Ameno called the smallets, teesdalls, and the dauntlets forward. He presented each one with a garland made of strands of gold and colored gems, and he thanked them for their extraordinarily selfless support for the Inodians.

Moving to the walls that separated Inod from Sur, he touched them, and they crumbled under his hands. The barring gate fell over with a thud. With the fallen stones, they all helped to erect a "monument" to commemorate The Battle for the Gate. And they picked up enough wood from discarded weaponry and dead branches from the forest that they could build a big bonfire. Then they sat around the warming flames enjoying turntoos and tatas cooked over broken clubs, spears, and torches.

Sitting close to Ameno on a stump by the fire, Ranni, preferring to use her unassuming nickname, savored the sweetness of his company. As it grew late in the day, and the conversation lulled, many in the group nodded off around the glowing embers. But she sleeplessly sat with Ameno, appreciating the sound of his voice and the compassion in his eyes as he looked around at each person in the circle. When he leaned toward the flames, a feather fell from inside his sleeve, and she had a sudden realization.

"Ameno," she whispered, "are you Hupsoo?"

His eyes met hers and lingered there for a moment.

"Yes. Hupsoo and I are the same." He reached over. She took his hand and gently turned it over to view the vulnerable surface. Her eyes teared up when she saw the barely visible ragged scar on his wrist that jutted out like a landmark.

"Did you know that Abba always turns bad things into good for those who love him?" he whispered, seeing her tears.

Clutching his hand, she shrugged and twisted her toes in the dirt, thinking of all the nights she'd spent in the filthy cell, waiting for someone to rescue her.

"Even that," he looked over at her lovingly. "As Hupsoo, I flew to the land of Bashan," he explained. "And I watched as an enemy enflamed King Og's heart."

Noni and Bearheart, who preferred his new name, stirred from sleep and moved closer to listen. Stade, Lona, and Ada also leaned in as he talked.

"The cities of Bashan are fortified with high walls, and the people are imprisoned by fear," he explained. "The giant kings control the thoughts and beliefs of the people. King Zoar and the Zamzummim worship a silver god they call Tartak. The Bashanies made a golden god named Nibhaz. Each king thinks his god is the right one and that everyone should worship his way. Meanwhile, the real enemy—the Deadly Dragon—uses these differences to create chaos and rivalry. He moves slyly, inciting hatred.

"Right now, he's fanning the flames of war between Bashan and Zamzum by using a small dispute," he sighed. "It all started when a Bashani shopkeeper was offended by a Zamzummi woman, who forgot to pay for her purchases. You see, wars always start over silly things that shouldn't matter in the scheme of things. An incidental moment becomes the death of many.

"This evil distraction—with increased skirmishes between the Bashanies and the Zamzummim—has worked for good in the case of The Battle for the Gate," he went on. "Because the Surlies had no help from the agitated King Zoar, who's caught up in his own affairs, many warrior-giants were unavailable to fight against you. Only a handful showed up, and you were able to overcome them."

"*With your help!*" Bearheart added, and Ameno smiled.

"But this foreign war won't last." Ameno gazed at the distant hills. "And you must use this distraction to unify the Inodians and Surlies, so you are stronger and more prepared for the day when the northern kings turn their gaze once again to focus on your lands and overtaking them. *You* can bring the people of Inod and Sur together into one land. Call it 'Gilgal,' which represents a circle of stones, like the unifying circle we sit in now. It also means 'rolling,' like when you roll away what's bad and replace it with something good. It will remind you how Abba and I helped you *win* this battle." Looking around the circle, he said, "You will all be known as the *Gilgal Gomies*, because you helped to remove the separation between Inod and Sur. And you will unite people and bring them freedom.

"Remember, my warriors, *'You shall not fear them, for the Lord your God shall fight for you.'*[30] The dauntlets will be the guardians of Gilgal and will warn you of danger. They will also ward off the treacherous tinshemets, who are evil scouts for the Bashanies and Zamzummim."

Ameno took a long stick and stirred the fire, making it spike up brightly and light the faces around the circle as the sun's rays sank behind the trees. Noni brought more wood from the forest and threw it onto the fire, making it shoot up even higher.

"I will also restore the Secrela Valley to its original prominence," he promised. "It will be known again as the Kindred Valley, and Abba will *'make the Valley…a door of hope and expectation.'*"[31]

Exhausted, everyone lay as close to Ameno as they could. Spreading blankets retrieved from the hut around the fire, they watched the smoldering embers and the bright glow of his heart. As darkness fell like a shroud, his light hovered over them, even brighter than the moon that night, which was now waxing gibbous, no longer in its fullness.

The next morning, Noni was awake first. He stretched his arms, rubbed his eyes, then looked over at the stump where Ameno was sitting. It was empty now, and he felt a sharp sense of loss and sadness. Then he remembered what Ameno had said. *"Remember, I am always with you."* Even though he couldn't see his friend, he knew he was near.

Ranni saw Noni's downcast demeanor as the others woke and looked around for Ameno. She felt it was important to explain to them what he'd told her the night before.

"Ameno said he'd be back. But, today, the dauntlets will carry us to free the purpits," she said. "The weather will turn colder in a few weeks, and the flowers must be changed back before they die from the frost." Everyone nodded in agreement.

After breakfast, Noni helped Ranni climb aboard Nus, then he moved up behind her. He smiled as he wrapped his arms around her waist and looked back to see the others getting ready to fly on the other dauntlets.

As they approached the Purpits' meadow, Noni and Bearheart were astonished at the number of Gomies and Krochits who'd gathered there. They'd heard from the smallets about The Battle for the Gate and how the Gilgal Gomies were coming to free the Purpits. Now, hundreds of once-hidden Gomies stood around to watch as they flew in on the dauntlets' backs. And, nearby, were the smallets and teesdalls who'd made their way to the meadow.

Looking across the field, Noni reflected on his feelings when this journey began: apprehension, fear, and dread. Little did he know what he'd experience and endure before returning here. Now, standing with Ranni at the same site, he reached for her hand as they stood among the flowers. And he sighed with a sense of calm.

A familiar voice interrupted his peaceful thoughts.

"Ahem! Ahem! May I intrude on this lovey-dovey scene to ask a question?" It was Sir Hatwig. "Are you here to *help us,* or *what?* We wondered if you'd keep your promise and *ever return!* Now, here you are, finally come back! Well, *hallelujah!"*

Noni responded by graciously introducing Ranni as "The Reign-breaker" and the other Gilgal Gomies: Bearheart, Sunny, Brother, Leo, Mosi, Ada, Lona, and Stade.

"Yes, we came back to help you," Noni nodded.

"Well, *get on with it!"* Hatwig chided. "How long *do we have to wait?* Cold weather'll be here soon! Good thing *you finally showed up!"*

Noni motioned with his hand for Brother and Sunny, Bleamer and Sluggli's new chosen names, to come near. He'd asked them to pray for the Purpits, since their jacinth stone's purple color best represented the flowers. They stepped up and, when Brother spoke up, everyone grew quiet.

"Abba, we ask you to help the Purpits. Restore them to their rightful nature and return what was taken from them."

Sunny continued the prayer.

"You're the God of restoration. You alone can restore them. We ask this in the name of Ameno, the Mighty One." When he finished praying, everyone silently waited for something to happen. Seconds became minutes. Salvo's ear twitched. Malvo's tail jerked. Breeni's white paws turned gray as he moved them around nervously in the dirt. Others whispered. Finally, Sir Hatwig cleared his throat, and Ranni let go of Noni's hand.

"Mr. Hatwig, sir!" she spoke boldly.

"Yes?" he replied sulkily.

"Do you *want* to be changed?" She looked down at him sternly.

"Well, *of course* we do! What kind of question is *that?*" he har-rumphed loudly and rolled his eyes.

"Then *you* must change your attitude!" Her eyes sparked a flame.

"What do you *mean?*" The proud Purpit cocked his petal head and squinted up at her.

"What I mean is…. You *don't* believe we can help you! *You* think we're just a bunch of dumb Gomies from Gratville, who have no more power *than you do!*" She crossed her arms.

"No! *Of course* that's not true!" He laughed nervously.

"*Yes, it is!*" She stamped her foot. "And you *won't* get your change until you acknowledge that Ameno gave us the power to do this!"

Everyone moved closer, curious to see what would happen.

"Well, *what* do you want *us* to do!" Hatwig held up his petal arms and looked around at the other flowers for agreement. "We're obviously a bunch of *defenseless* flowers!"

"*You* have a choice!" Ranni wouldn't give in to his pity-plea. "You can *hold onto* your pride and think you deserve *better* than the likes of us! *Or,* you can *get rid* of the bad attitude and *get* what you want more than anything!"

The other Purpits leaned toward Hatwig, their tiny eyes narrowing, and their brown brows knit. Their voices rising all at once, they chanted an angry appeal to their leader.

"*Do what she says! Do what she says!*

"*Ok! Ok!*" He turned a deep purple.

"Do you *believe* we can help you?" Ranni insisted.

Clearing his throat, he glanced up at her face sheepishly, and his eyes met hers.

"Yes." He lowered his voice. "I suppose so."

Sunny and Brother repeated their prayers, but still, nothing happened. Bearheart stepped forward, holding something behind his brilliant gold shield, and everyone gasped when he swung Truelight forward. The sun's light struck its side and created a spectacular rainbow across the flowered field.

"Is *that* what you're going to use to change us?" Hatwig's sarcastic voice cut through Bearheart's concentration, and he looked down at the flower and lowered the sword.

"No," he said.

"What's it for then?" Hatwig said, taunting.

"One day you'll see. *Now,*" Bearheart replied boldly, "do you believe in Ameno's power to free you?"

"Sure. I trust *him.*" Hatwig smirked.

"Do the rest of you believe in Ameno's power to restore you?" Bearheart and Ranni spoke together and looked out across the purple faces.

"*Yes*! We *do* believe!" the Purpits answered in unison.

This time, something changed. A slight wind began to blow. It stirred the farthest flowers and moved slowly across the meadow. As it drew closer, its strength increased, and, one by one, flower petals changed into heads, arms, and legs, and people emerged and popped out from the Purpits.

Sir Hatwig waited and watched, obviously impatient. He looked on dismally as the others cheered their changes, and he wondered if he was cheated because of his chiding. He stretched himself up, trying to be noticed. But no one paid any attention as the others moved away from him and huddled around the Gilgal Gomies, hugging and thanking them for their kindness. Finally, when he decided to humbly participate in the transformation, he felt something stir in his petals, and he watched as his arms and hands began to sprout, then his legs and feet. As his head popped out, his eyes grew larger, and hair grew out from the top of his head. A gray pointed beard protruded from his chin. His familiar clothes returned: a gray jacket, a red bowtie, a tall hat, black knickers, long wool socks, and funny black shoes with gold buckles. He was shorter than all the others, and he grinned up sheepishly as he brushed the dirt from his jacket to remove any trace of his former disgrace.

The surrounding Mussians recognized mothers, fathers, sisters, brothers, relatives, and friends in the morphed Purpits. Hugs, laughter, cheers, and tears followed. Ranni sang, and the Gilgal Gomies joined in, as they all marched into Mussford:

"Spring brought the purpits' debut
In many lavender hues,
Jacinth the gem most resembled,
Royalty and high rank assembled.
By summer, their greatness unknown,
A remarkable group was dethroned.
In purple, re-robed with great splendor,
Forgotten but now remembered.
Their sorrow now turned to delight
By those who were the most unlikely.
They survived through much suffering.
Buffeted, they escape now singing.
Tra la la, tra la la, tra la la
Tra la la, tra la la, tra la la."

chapter thirty-three

Grateful for Gratville

Gratville never felt so much like home as it did now to Noni. He sighed as he looked out at the changing colors of the leaves from Grooma's deck. It was his favorite time of year, and he was here to enjoy it. He'd always thought his hometown was ordinary, even boring. Now, he appreciated the simplicity of life here.

When he returned, a few things changed—some good and some surprising. When Bearheart, Noni, Ranni, their parents, and Sunny came to Gratville, they were heartily welcomed by Mayor Dungtrap, who insisted on holding a grand celebration for them. Although Grooma coordinated the entire event, the mayor proudly patted himself on the back for envisioning it. The townspeople set up tables in a scenic park, and a band played marching music as everyone gathered around, eating homemade pastries, stews, griffoons, bettas, tatas, and fresh scaggons and moggies. The mayor delivered a pompous speech and embarrassed the heroes in front of everyone by exaggerating their exploits. Somehow, he managed to take credit for their successes.

For the grand finale, the band played as fireworks exploded over them and filled the night sky with color. Noni trembled at the explosions. Ranni stood next to him and, sensing his nervousness, reached for his hand as they watched the colorful bursts trickle down in streams like millions of shooting stars against an indigo sky. Noni's eyes met Bearheart's during the display, and they both hid the emotions they felt.

Over the next few months, Noni savored time spent with his parents and brother, Lelels, who'd watched the hills daily for them as he cared for Grooma's grats. Finding everything in order when they returned home made Noni thankful for him, and they all affectionately called him 'L'il Lion,' in honor of his namesake, Leo, though they all laughed that he'd never been really little.

Ameno had visited Lelels while they were away, and he'd given him a special bow with the inscription, *"His bow remained strong and steady and rested in the Strength that does not fail."*[32] He also gave him a shiny purple sapphire, like Bearheart's, to remind him of the strength that comes from Abba.

Grooma graciously gave her grats, including Smithi and Saron, whom the boys had returned safely to her, to Noni's family as a way of showing her gratitude for their safe return. She also wanted to pay Lelels back for the years he'd helped her take care of them. She admitted it was time for her to retire from their care.

Bearheart decided to go to Mussford to live with Mosi and Leo. He loved Lake Adamant and Mosi's graynights and was encouraged by his cousin to come live with them. Bleamer, using his new preferred name—Brother—returned to his inn and promised to visit his mother and friends in Gratville often. He wanted to make the Treatise Tavern and Turret Inn a haven for travelers throughout Gilgal, who could now move freely through the land. He also wanted to share the incredible story of The Battle for the Gate with his visitors.

Ada, Ranni, and Sunny lived happily together in their Gratville tree home, and they savored their sweet family time together. Sunny discovered that Fendem had been jailed in Sapwood when Surli spies informed the mayor that his stepson had helped Noni and Bearheart escape. Alone in a dismal, dirty cell, he'd asked Ameno for help, and Ameno came to him. When Fendem told him his fears and reasons for denying him, Ameno graciously forgave him. Then, his heart glowed a bright red once again.

Hearing this story, and wanting to meet her son's stepfather, Ada decided to go and visit Fendem. Setting out with Sunny, she went first to Mussford to see Brother, who decided to join them. He thought he could convince the Sapwood mayor to free Fendem, since he'd heard the new mayor was more open to Ameno-believers, especially after hearing the stories about The Battle for the Gate and what happened at the "Memory Meadow"—the name given to the Purpit's meadow. After talking to the mayor, he agreed to free Fendem with one condition: that Fendem promise to give him any news about Zamzum and Bashan, which he might hear from visitors to his inn.

Sunny forgave Fendem for his past cruelty, and, after they convinced him to come for a visit, he introduced his stepfather to his friends and family in Gratville, who threw him a welcome party. Fendem felt loved for the first time in his life, and he wept openly at the celebration and thanked them for their unexpected kindness.

Over time, Ada discovered how Clement had turned into the evil Belial. Apparently, after she escaped with the twins, the Surli and Zamzummi leaders viciously blamed and persecuted him, driving him to a bitter and resentful hatred that caused him to assume a new identity that was overwhelmingly evil. To "redeem" his failure, he became so obsessed with making up for it, that he ate, slept, dreamed, and lived for one goal—to capture and kill the Reignbreaker. And, this demented pursuit took its toll on him, even changing the way he looked, so that his whole demeanor exuded evil.

In contrast, Noni, Bearheart, Ada, and Sunny watched, amazed, as Fendem grew to be one of the most respected leaders of the newly-united land of Gilgal. He became known as "Fathom" instead of Fendem because, as he said over and over, "I can't even fathom the love Ameno must have to be able to forgive me for the things I've done!"

The Gilgal Gomies encouraged the community leaders in the Inod section of Gilgal to free the prisoners who were jailed for their beliefs. The freed Mussford Purpits initiated this process and demanded freedom for all Inodian Ameno followers. All the town authorities recognized the miracle at the meadow and willingly complied. New governments were established as Krochits teamed up with Gomies to rebuild schools and sharetoos to accommodate everyone. Grateful Gomi children were now allowed to read books and go to school.

During the months after their return, Noni called together all the Gilgal Gomies, with other volunteers, to lead an effort to free the remaining prisoners in the Sur section of Gilgal. Joined by the dauntlets, teesdalls, and smallets, they met in Memory Meadow and set out for Sur. As they passed by where the gate had once stood, they saw the monument they'd made to commemorate the battle and a new sign by the road into Sur that read, "Peace Passage."

Because many Surli warriors were off fighting for King Zoar against the Bashanies, the remaining Surli guards were fearful and few. Entering the Surli villages, the group demanded freedom for the persecuted victims, and the Surlies complied readily, because they'd all heard the terrifying tales about The Battle for the Gate.

After the battle, the people of Gilgal saw new movement between Inod and Sur, along with greater exchange of goods and ideas. The Secrela Valley was now known as the Kindred Valley, and the Abana River was renamed the Brook Cherith as people freely passed through with no threat of harm from the Surlies or Zamzummim.

Noni was especially pleased with another peaceful outcome between the two lands. Happy Housit Days, once just for Gratians, was now celebrated by everyone in Gilgal. Still held in Gratville, it helped the town to prosper, and it gave people in the land more opportunities to sell their goods. Gratians saw a greater influx of food, clothing, animals, and wares at the annual fall event, which included picnics, parades, booths, music, and entertainment. The people of Gilgal loved it so much that they decided to duplicate the festival in every season. "Celebrate Spring" was held in Mussford; "Summerfest" was in Sapwood; and the "Welcome Winter" festival was held in the Kindred Valley near Dauntlet's Den.

After these changes, most Gratians settled into a sort of calm, at least until some news interrupted their lull. First, Noni and Ranni announced their engagement. Since they were still teens, they would wait a few years to be married. Grooma immediately responded by offering her scenic treetop home to the young couple, even though it would be some time before they tied the knot. It was hard for her to keep up with the large home and too roomy for one person. It was also becoming more difficult for her to get up and down the winding stairway.

Not wanting to wait, she offered it to Noni's family and moved to a smaller place in town. Stade and Lona didn't want to leave their small but comfortable home beneath the tree, so they asked the boys if they'd like to move upstairs. Now, L'il Lion and Noni enjoyed the spacious rooms and the freedom, along with beautiful views.

In the days since his engagement, Noni watched the trees from the deck as they changed with the seasons. He enjoyed seeing the branches sprout buds that blossomed into colorful flowers or opened into green leaves that eventually turned red, gold, and brown. He nicknamed the tree "Ed," which means "witness," because he could see the Inodian valley and parts of Sur from the deck. Sometimes he reminisced about the heart-lifting rides on the dauntlets, and he imagined himself as a great bird flying out across Gilgal. At these times, he felt he had found the dream he sought.

Now, winter approached. Clouds loomed in the distance and threatened to bring storms with wind and snow. He looked forward to a new life with Ranni, but, sometimes, nightmarish thoughts disrupted his daydreams. The war between Kings Og and Zoar would not go on forever. He knew that. One day, they would both cast their eyes on Gilgal. And, whichever king was victorious would drool to think of forcing all the lands together under one controlled "umbrella."

But an even greater concern hovered over Noni's thoughts. After The Battle for the Gate, Stade's health had gone downhill. He was involved for a while in helping make changes in Gilgal. But, since he'd never fully recovered from the hardships of imprisonment or the stress from the battle, his overall strength declined. Noni watched his once-strong father grow weaker and weaker.

One evening, after Noni's engagement, Stade asked him to sit with him. He confessed his concern about failing health, and he asked Noni to carry on for him when he was gone. He wanted to make sure someone took care of Lona and L'il Lion. He brought out his gifts from Ameno: the boots and the stone. And he placed them in Noni's hands.

"These are for you and your children," he sighed. "You'll need to be *my* hands and feet one day and take the good news of what we've done with Ameno's help to others." He sighed as he confided that he knew he wouldn't be around much longer. Noni's heart broke with unspeakable sorrow as he sat with his dad and, together, they read these words from *Ameno's Manna: "Hold fast to love and mercy, to righteousness and justice, and wait (expectantly) for your God continually!"*[33]

Hesitating, he accepted his father's gifts and nodded to his requests, feeling heavy and sad for the great gap Stade would leave among them. This was the greatest cloud over his tree now.

Fall's pleasant days were ending and, as Noni looked out toward Memory Meadow from Grooma's deck, he could see the once-wispy white clouds growing darker and more looming every day. They seemed far away now, but winter would bring harsher weather, and he wondered how he could prepare for the coming storms.

Then he remembered some words he'd seen. Going inside, he gazed up at *Ameno's Own Manna* in its honored place on the mantel above the fireplace. Reaching for it, he touched the golden letters on the cover. Pulling it down, he slowly turned the pages and found his favorite verses. He read them out loud:

"The word is very near you, in your mouth and in your mind and in your heart, so that you can do it.… Be strong, courageous, and firm; fear not nor be in terror before them, for it is the Lord your God Who goes with you; He will not fail you or forsake you."[34]

Glossary

Abana River: A dried up river in the Secrela Valley near Dauntlets' Den.

Abba: Ameno's invisible father who lives beyond our world.

Ada or **Adamantine:** Beehart and Ranni's mother.

Ailis: Ada's mother, who lived with her husband, Ret, on an island in Lake Adamant near Mussford.

Airo: A male dauntlet, whose mate is Natal. Nus and Nasa's son.

Ameno: Abba's son who appears and offers help to those who ask.

Ameno's Manna: A book of Ameno and Abba's desires for the people on earth.

Argob: The largest city in the land of Bashan where King Og lives and rules.

Bashan: The land farthest north on Init Isle.

Bashanies: The citizens of Bashan.

Bay of Bashan: A bay off the northeast coast of Bashan.

Beehart or **Bearheart:** Noni's best friend and Ranni's brother.

Beezi: A bee-like insect known for its honey.

Belial: The name given by Noni and Beehart to the Surli villain who pursues them.

Berles: A shoonum, or type of dog, kept by Mosi at his cabin near Mussford.

Betta: A red round root like a beet.

Bleamer or **Brother**: The innkeeper of the Treatise Tavern and Turret Inn in Mussford.

Border Bay: A bay between Inod and Sur on the west side of Init Isle.

Breeni: A smallet, or type of squirrel, who helps with an escape and accommodations for the Gomies.

Brook Cherith: A once-beautiful, then restored, brook in the Kindred Valley.

Bruni: A tree like a maple.

Bruni ale: A fermented drink made from bruni tree syrup.

Brunine: A sweet, warm drink made with grat milk and bruni syrup.

Clearus Creek: The creek that flows from Clearus Spring into Lake Adamant.

Clearus Spring: A spring discovered by Ailis and Ret in a canyon near Mussford.

Clement: Ada's first husband and Bleamer and Sluggli's father.

Cliffs of Pisgah: Mountains in eastern Bashan.

Dauntlet: A large, owl-like bird that lives in Secrela, or Kindred, Valley.

Dauntlets' Den: The dauntlets' cave home.

Deadly Dragon: A deadly force that tries to deceive and harm Ameno and his followers.

Egeiro: A male dauntlet, whose mate is Epairo; Nus and Nasa's son.

Epairo: A female dauntlet, whose mate is Egeiro.

Fendem or **Fathom**: Sluggli's stepfather and the innkeeper of Prior Place in Sapwood.

Flapcake: A type of pancake made from griffa flour and cooked on a griddle.

Floodle: A hot cooked cereal made from griffa grain.

Gilgal: A unified land formed from two lands: Inod and Sur, after the Battle for the Gate.

Gilgalies: The inhabitants of Gilgal.

Goley: A peg used by Krochits in a game called "Goley Holey."

Gomi: A native of Inod most known for short stature, pink skin, and large eyes.

Grappi: A small round purple fruit like a grape that grows on vines along mountains and hills.

Grat: A goat-like animal that roams among the Gratville hills.

Gratian: Someone who lives in Gratville.

Gratian Bay: A bay in southwest Inod near Gratville.

Gratville: A village in southern Inod.

Graynight: An animal like a horse.

Griffa: A grain similar to wheat or rye that grows on Init Isle.

Griffoon: A sweet biscuit made from griffa flour.

Grizzlies: Similar to bears.

Groomhilda or **Grooma**: A Krochit woman who lives in the tree above Noni and Lelels's home.

Hand Bay: A bay in northeastern Inod.

Head Bay: A bay in eastern Sur.

Holding Bay: A bay in eastern Inod.

Honi or **Honored**: Humbi's wife and co-owner of Humble Haven near Sapwood.

Housit: A large, black-barked tree on Init Isle that can hold at least one tree home.

Humbi or **Humble**: Honi's husband and co-owner of Humble Haven near Sapwood.

Hupsoo: The oldest and wisest dauntlet.

Inod: The southern-most land on Init Isle and home to Gomies and Krochits.

Inod Bay: A bay in southeastern Inod.

Inodian: An inhabitant of Inod.

Inodian Ocean: A large body of water south of Init Isle.

Init Isle: A large island made up of the lands of Inod, Sur, Zamzum, and Bashan.

Initian Ocean: A large body of water on the west side of Init Isle.

Ishbi: The largest of the Zamzummi giants in the Battle for the Gate.

Kindred Valley or **Secrela Valley**: A valley in Sur created by the Brook Cherith.

Krochit: A tall Inodian or Surli with orangish skin, straight black hair, small dark eyes, and knobs on their foreheads.

Lake Adamant: A lake near Mussford that was purified by Clearus Creek.

Lelels or **Li'l Lion**: Noni's older brother who has bushy brown hair and brown eyes.

Leopol, **Leo**, or **Leonine**: Mosi's father, who was imprisoned by Surlies in a cave.

Lona or **Loved**: Noni and Lelels' mother and Stade's wife.

Lord Ludifus: A mayor in Mussford.

Malvo: A smallet who helps the Gomies and is recognized by his tail's white stripe.

Marples: One of Mosi's shoonums, like a dog.

Memory Meadow: A meadow south of Lake Adamant where the Purpits were changed into flowers.

Milli: Oni's wife and Bleamer's stepmother.

Moggie: A small, blue berry that grows on bushes throughout Init Isle.

Mosi or **Mosaic**: A Mussian who helps Noni and Beehart on their journey.

Mouth Bay: A bay in eastern Bashan.

Muss: A short, pink, flat-snouted animal, like a pig.

Mussford: A village in central Inod known for its musses.

Mussian: An inhabitant of Mussford.

Nasa: A female dauntlet, whose mate is Nus; Egeiro and Airo's mother.

Natal: A female dauntlet, whose mate is Airo.

Noni or **Nonight**: Stade and Lona's son and Leles' brother.

Nus: A male dauntlet, whose mate is Nasa; Egeiro and Airo's father.

Og: The giant king of Bashan, who rules from Argob.

Oni: The original innkeeper for the Treatise Tavern and Turret Inn in Mussford. Bleamer's stepfather.

Pompoon: Like an apple.

Prior Place: An inn in Sapwood run by Fendem, Sluggli's stepfather.

Purpit: A purple flower resembling an orchid that grows on a vine-like stem.

Ranhart: Beehart and Ranni's father.

Ranni: Beehart's younger sister and Noni's friend from Gratville.

Reignbreaker: A person rumored to be able to unite the lands and bring freedom to the Inodian people.

Ret: Ailis's husband who lived with her on an island near Mussford.

River Jabbok: A river in Zamzum that runs from Head Bay to King Zoar's castle.

Sagius: Mosi's grandfather and Leo's father, who fought in the Surli War.

Salvo: Head of the smallets in Sur, known for his white-tipped ear.

Sapi: A lamb-like animal that lives in the hills around Sapwood.

Sapian: An inhabitant of Sapwood.

Sapwood: A village in north-central Inod, known for its many sapies.

Saron: Noni's grat, gifted by Groomhilda.

Scaggon: A round red juicy fruit like a plum.

Sea of Araba: A body of water along northeastern Init Isle.

Secrela: A giant tree like a sequoia that grows in Wiggledown Woods in Sur.

Secretary: A rolltop desk with drawers and cubbyholes.

Seemi: A smallet with white paws who helps the Gomies.

Sharetoo: A building like a chapel where Inodians pray and worship.

Shoonum: A small animal like a dog.

Sir Hatwig: A Purpit who was once Lord Ludifus's assistant in Mussford.

Sluggli or **Sunny**: Fendem's stepson and Ada and Clement's son who works at Prior Place.

Smallet: A small animal like a squirrel with pointy ears and a bushy tail.

Smithi: Beehart's grat, given to him by Groomhilda.

Smolies: Small creatures like mice that live in caves.

Snee: A cloud.

Spree: An evergreen tree that grows throughout Init Isle and has edible needles like rosemary.

Stade or **Steadfast**: Noni and Lelels's father, who has bushy brown hair and a beard.

Sur: The land north of Inod and south of Zamzum on Init Isle.

Surli: An inhabitant of Sur.

Surli Sea; A body of water to the east of Sur.

Tail Bay: A bay in eastern Inod above the Tailwind Peninsula.

Tailwind Peninsula: A thin strip of land that juts out from eastern Inod.

Tata: An oblong brown root, similar to a potato.

Teesdall: A small black and red bird that flies throughout Init Isle.

Testus River: A river north of Gratville that runs from Gratian Bay to Inod Bay.

Tinshemet: A large, dark-gray bird, like a heron, that lives in northern Init Isle.

Towser: A tree like an aspen with peeling white bark.

Treatise Tavern and Turret Inn: An inn and tavern run by Bleamer in Mussford.

Truelight: Sagius's sword used in the Surli War and gifted to Beehart by Mosi.

Trulit: Beehart's dagger carved from bruni wood.

Turntoo: A chicken-like bird that lives on Init Isle.

Turret: A small tower attached to a building.

Wiggledown Woods: A forest in the hills of southeastern Sur near the Secrela Valley.

Zamzum: A land north of Sur and south of Bashan on Init Isle.

Zamzummi or **Zamzummim**: Inhabitants of Zamzum.

Zoar: The giant king of Zamzum who rules from a castle near the River Jabbok.

References

All Scripture quotations are taken from The Amplified Bible, copyright ©1954, 1958, 1962, 1964, 1965, 1987 by The Lockman Foundation. All rights reserved. Used by permission.

1. Micah 2:13
2. Zechariah 10:4
3. Isaiah 61:1b
4. Psalm 118:16b
5. John 3:8
6. Luke 6:21a
7. Psalm 18:10b
8. Revelation 7:17b
9. Psalm 142:3a
10. Isaiah 41:18
11. Psalm 139:9,10
12. Isaiah 9:6
13. Hosea 1:7b
14. Isaiah 28:6b
15. Psalm 100: 1,2,4
16. Isaiah 58:11b
17. Isaiah 58:8b
18. Isaiah 58:8a
19. Hosea 11:10
20. Genesis 49:10a
21. Isaiah 58:14b
22. Joshua 24:15b
23. Proverbs 1:2a
24. Hosea 13:8a
25. Isaiah 58:12b
26. Isaiah 60:18
27. Isaiah 58:10b
28. Isaiah 45:3
29. Revelation 2:17
30. Exodus 14:14
31. Hosea 2:15
32. Genesis 49:24
33. Hosea 12:6
34. Deuteronomy 30:14; 31:6

Acknowledgements

Many thanks to the people who were willing to offer their input and suggestions on this book, whose insight and contributions were immeasurably helpful in finalizing the manuscript. Greatest appreciation to Bret Kolman, Kay Klement, and Charity Steele, Miriam Brenaman, and Alex Shannahan for being willing to read and comment on these pages and for their inestimable help. Thanks also to Christina Machado for her wonderful drawing of Init Isle. Her artistic ability is admirable.

About the Author

Lele Beutel spent 15 years studying with a biblical research and teaching ministry and was able to acquire an Associate in Theology degree during that time. She went on to gain a BSJ degree from The University of Kansas and a Masters in Christian Counseling from Faith Bible College, then spent 25 years as a CFP© financial advisor, encouraging many people mentally, spiritually, and financially through her faith-based advice.

Since retirement in 2022, she and her husband, Mike, have enjoyed traveling and have found that, with each new excursion, come opportunities to make a difference in people's lives and have their own lives changed as a result. She considers herself to be a "secret agent" for God because of how He often leads her into unexpected situations where she's able to connect with others. They also spend time with their two dogs, Andey and Barney, with grandkids, and as volunteers at their church. She facilitates a single moms group that has been fulfilling for her and the moms who participate. Besides having a passion for writing inspirational books, she is energized by sharing God's love with life group members and people she meets while walking their dogs.

Other books she has written include: *The Camino Connection, Connecting with Life and Commemorating a Death While Walking on the Camino de Santiago,* about her healing and life-changing journey through Spain; *What God Wants You to Know,* a daily devotional that reveals God's heart relating to passages from Genesis through Revelation; *God Answers,* a daily devotional with questions and answers to and from God; and *Lele's Selah: Prayerful Poems that Inspire Hope.*

To reach her, you can find her on Facebook. Or email her at: *apedersen6@comcast.net.*

She would love to hear from you!

Other Books by Lele

In God Answers: A Daily Devotional for Christians, Lele Beutel shares the remarkable journey of twenty years spent in heartfelt conversations with God after a divorce and the death of her son. Capturing decades of questions and the profound ways God answered, this devotional offers readers a unique look into how God moves and speaks in our everyday lives. Each entry is a testament to His presence, designed to help you see and trust His hand at work in your life.

What God Wants You to Know is a different kind of devotional. Not light reading, it takes you on a quest from Genesis to Revelation for deeper meaning. It is for those who want to understand what God is up to when He inspires people to act, write, speak, or even change the world for Him.

Lele's Selah is a refuge. It's a place of peace and a haven of hope. It's a collection of poems that inspire and birth aspirations when there seem to be none that are reachable. Come and experience what you've been looking for—a cadence of quiet and a rhythm of rest.

Read other books by Lele Beutel, sign up for her newsletter, and follow on social media by scanning the QR code or going to the URL below:

linktr.ee/authorlelebeutel